Secrets in Love

BINDI KENNEDY

Copyeditor by Jenn Lockwood
Cover design by Haya in design
Formatting by Champagne Book Design

Published by Bindi K Publishing.

In the interests of a good tale, the locations in and geographical features of Byron Bay, London, New York City, and State, have been fictionalised.

This novel's story and characters are wholly fictitious creations of my imagination. Certain long-standing institutions, public offices & agencies, celebrities, works of literature, film, T.V. & songs are mentioned.

Secrets in Love can be read as a stand-alone, but I do recommend you start with *Rules in Love*—Book One of the West Village series.
Check out Finn & Scarlett's tale here.
books2read.com/u/mvNq5V

"You pierce my soul. I am half agony, half hope…I have loved none but you."

Jane Austen, *Persuasion*

For all the people who've forgotten who they are. May you find your way home safely.

Secrets in Love

Chapter 1

Evie

EVERYONE CALLED ME EVIE, BUT THAT WASN'T my real name.

It was actually Aoife. Aoife Mary Austen.

Pronounced Ee-fa, it was Irish Gaelic for beautiful and radiant. It had something to do with a badass warrior princess in Irish mythology and was kind of beautiful. But it was also peculiar. Especially when you didn't grow up in Ireland but on a beachside farm in Australia.

Depending on who you asked or what you Googled, Aoife was anglicized into Ava, Eva, Eve, sometimes Alfie, or as my little brother Finn used to say, Evie. Of all the names, little Finn's was my favorite. Like him, it was cute. People smiled when they said Evie. They didn't pause, have a crack, get it wrong, and then ask me to repeat myself fifty-two times. "It's EEEEFFFAAAAAA. EEEEFFFAAAAAA."

Formative years filled with people contorting their faces when saying your name could leave you a little…well, bitter, and may have influenced my some-times-prickly disposition. Hence, when a dance teacher called me Foofa in a packed ballet class, seven-year-old me proudly declared, "I've had enough of this shit! No one is ever going to call me Aoife again!"

Since then, only one idiot has had big enough cojones to call me Aoife—my brother's best friend, Nate.

Little did I know, a lighthearted, innocuous exchange between me and my brother, regarding said idiot, was about to rock my world, proving that the most nonsensical conversations could impact your life in the most unexpected and monumental ways.

New York had been our home for a few months, but Finn still insisted on taking his precious Jeep everywhere instead of walking. Considering no one claimed to drive in this city, the traffic was hideous, and I had been keeping myself entertained by upholding a long-standing Austen tradition—mocking Finn for his overly emotional nature. At 6'4", he was a sweet mound of muscle and tears that I wouldn't change for the world. Mainly because nothing made me happier than teasing him about crying. Nate loved it too and was not shy about applying a notorious Australian nickname for one so fragile—Sooky Sooky La La—to his bestie.

Unsurprisingly, Finn didn't take the reminder well. "Bloody Nate could talk. He was always sooking to me about you, but did I tease him? Nope."

All giggling ceased. "Nate was sooking about me? Why would he be sooking about me?"

"Uhh, because he liked you and was madly in love with you?"

"What?" I snapped and delivered a sharp blow to the side of Finn's head. "Nate liked me? Loved me? Since when?"

"Since we were, like, born." Finn's bulging eyes darted between me and the road, which was more than concerning as he was a shitty driver. "You're honestly telling me you didn't know?"

"No, I didn't know! Why would I know? How did you know? Why would you know and never tell me?"

Condescension, protectiveness, and perhaps a touch of love resulted in an eye roll only my freakishly large brother could muster. "Well, I knew because I was his best friend, my girlfriend was his twin, and he talked about you constantly. We even made a deal when we were fifteen. Neither of us was to go near the other's sister. Obviously, I broke that deal, but Nate didn't." Guilt replaced the disdain on Finn's face. "That's part of the reason he was so upset when Shelby and I got together."

A steady and loud stream of what was undoubtedly crap continued to flow from Finn's mouth, but I could only concentrate on the synchronicity formed between the rain pounding against my window and the fierce beating of my heart.

Nate liked me. Had the hots for me? Me.

Finn pulled into the parking lot, and I hastily jumped from the still-moving Jeep, classically landing with a splash in the largest puddle in the lot. Carrying the weight of a million thoughts, my head was down, my mind focused on the cold water now trickling down the backs of my legs and pooling in my shoes, when another voice added to the chaos.

"Evie, wait! Let me help you!"

Armed with an open umbrella and a sexy twinkle in his eye, Christian Alarie, my potential new boss, and owner of my niece Iris's dance studio, raced to my side, sheltering me for the three paces it took to make it inside. Normally, I'd have thought him a tool and taken great joy in pointing out the uselessness of his actions. Three things stopped me. One, too much Nate on the brain. Two, Christian may be in command of my future earnings. And three, the man's sheer hotness, because damn, he was hummina-hummina hot. The most beautiful man I'd seen since arriving in New York. Hot.

As we did that silly, twisty foot shuffle to dry our shoes, he lowered the umbrella, looked between me and the car, and winced. "That was a bit pointless, wasn't it?"

"Pointless? No. Not at all. I was just thinking how gentlemanly of you it was. Though, you'll look like a drowned rat if you do that for every parent."

The smile, which could only lead to trouble, returned as he loomed over me. "I guess it's good there's only one parent I'm doing it for."

I didn't know if hearing yourself blush was possible, but I could have sworn every capillary in my face exploded, and each snap, crackle, and pop was audible. Christian's voice dropped a good octave or two lower as he continued, and it hit my already-on-alert girly bits hard. "I was hoping you would pick Iris up tonight. I also hope you won't sue me for sexual harassment when I ask you this."

"What? Sue you? Why would I do such a thing?"

"Because, Evie, I want to ask you out. I've enjoyed getting to know you since you began your teaching trial." It had been three days, and I think we had spoken three times. "And I'd like to learn more. It's fine if you want to say no. There is no pressure or obligation. I have officially handed over all my boss-like responsibilities concerning you to my second in charge, Jody, who is fully aware of what I am asking for legal purposes."

Soaked socks squelched as I bounced on the balls of my feet. "Okay… While I'm glad Jody knows, I would also like to 'cause you're kind of freaking me out."

"Oh, God, Evie. Sorry for rambling. I've been doing that lately when I'm nervous. I talk and talk and talk, and people get so annoyed—"

He was right. It was annoying. So, to stop it, I held my hand on his broad chest, trying not to place any meaning to the rapidly pounding heart I could feel beneath my fingers. "You're still rambling."

"Right…okay. See, the thing is, Evie. I was wondering if you would like to go on a date…with me. Just a date, not sexual harassment, o-or any sex of any kind at all, really…unless you…you know." Sweat began to drip from his forehead as his eyes drifted to my boobs, lingered, then rose back to my eyes in time with a cute flush to his cheeks. "Sorry. Oh…I mean, no pressure. There could be sex if you wanted, but I just mean dinner and…fuck. I'm so sorry." He wiped his brow, then slid his hands down, concealing his eyes and flushed cheeks. "If you can't tell, I'm…kind of goofy for you, Evie."

Wait…what?

"You…" I waved my hands around his impressive frame, Vanna White style. "Okay, is this a joke? Are you filming this for TikTok? God, you didn't fall and hit your head doing a jetée, did you?"

Christian chuckled and peeked through his spread fingers. Seeming to relax, he then dropped his hands altogether and sighed.

"No, I didn't hit my head. We're not being filmed—at least I hope not—and yes, I am sure." Perhaps conscious of our locale, he stooped and leaned into my ear, whispering, "I find you incredibly attractive, Evie. I have since the first time you brought Iris in. I wanted to ask you out then, but I felt like it was inappropriate. Seeing you dance, though… Watching your body move and come alive…" Dangerous eyes raked over my body. "Inappropriate or not, I just had to ask. You and your petit ballonné are totally worth the risk."

"Wha…"

That was it. That was my response.

I fancied myself a writer. Had penned umpteen unpublished novels, and the best I could summon was, "Wha…" Luckily, Iris's timely arrival prevented my *death by humiliating blank staring*. "Um, I have to go, Christian. My brother is waiting in the car." I grabbed the poor kid by the shoulders and pushed her out the door. "I will get back to you about that…thing. It sounds like it could be fun—if you don't change your mind first, that is."

Christian flashed his polished stage smile and winked. "Don't you worry your pretty little head, Evie. I won't be changing my mind. That *thing* is yours. Whenever you're ready, just say, "Oui."

Back on the road, Iris faithfully detailed every child's step in her class, and I allowed my mind to wander.

Could it be true? Could I, Evie Austen, have a hot man—no, not man, men, as in plural….as in more than one….as in two—interested in me?

For someone like my style icon and favorite New Yorker, Carrie Bradshaw, this would be just another sexy day in the city. But for me, a stumpy farm girl from Australia, it seemed a greater work of fiction than Miss Bradshaw herself.

Via the passenger side mirror, I watched the dance studio, and my chance to delve into Christian's motives, fade into the distance.

But I still had my brother. And when it came to Nate, Finn was a veritable treasure trove of info.

Dare I dig a little deeper?

"He emails me a few times a week, you know." It was more often than that, but I was dipping my toe into the murky waters to test the temperature. "Texts me sometimes too. He always says it's to check in on his number-one girl, Iris, but do you think he…? No. No, that's silly."

"Evie," sighed Finn, "I've told you before. I don't know what you are talking about when you start mid-sentence. Who emails you?"

"Nate," I whispered.

"What? Nate? Nate emails you a few times a week? I'm lucky if I've gotten one message this month, and you've been getting weekly emails *and* texts for how long?"

"Since we left Byron. And he *has* messaged you. You just bloody ghost everyone all the time."

Sounding remarkably like a dog with a bone stuck in its throat, Finn scoffed and whined, "Jesus, Evie. He's still into you. Fuck. That's rich. That bastard gave me so much shit for chasing Shelby, and he's been doing the same thing behind my back this whole time."

As usual, we fell headfirst into an argument, which came to a screeching halt when Finn proclaimed he was putting his foot down. Nate and I had to stop talking. No ifs, ands, or buts about it. I then made my own proclamation: Finn was an asshole who had no right to do anything of the sort. And Iris laughed at us both and learned several choice new words.

Happy days.

❋

It was the perfect evening for a barbeque and a beer. The clouds had cleared. A pink and tangerine sunset illuminated the sky, and a light, cooling breeze carrying that ever-present hint of NYC garbage swept through my room, taking the edge off the sticky heat. But I was locked away. Trapped in my thoughts. A pathetic, sweaty mess.

Over the last nine-ish years, I'd lived a concurrently dramatic, sheltered, yet extraordinary life. My parents lost their lives in a tragic car accident. Shelby, Nate's twin sister, Finn's girlfriend, and Iris's mom, passed away in childbirth, and I became a stay-at-home aunt-mom type to my adorable niece. Somehow, I pushed past the grief and found enough space and balance in my new life to complete my arts degree, qualify as a ballet teacher, and do the whole wannabe-writer thing. To complicate things further, my family—my Aunt Jocelyn, Finn, Iris, and I—left Byron Bay, our beautiful hometown on Australia's east coast, and moved here to the bright lights and filthy air of New York City.

It was a lot. A whole lot. But none of it could've prepared me for haplessly wandering into a metaphorical late-summer sausage-fest. One where I was the guest of honor, and the sausages in question belonged to two opposite yet equally delicious men.

Christian, HotBoss, was quite possibly one of the most perfect-looking men in the history of men. Think of a ripped Jared Leto before he looked like Jesus. Crystal-blue eyes. The lean but muscular body of a dancer. Thighs that could crush a watermelon—or preferably, me. Cultured and sophisticated, he was a former lead with the New York City Ballet who was forced into early retirement when he ruptured his medial ligament for the third time. Instead of laying low, as many would, Christian opened Village All-Abilities Dance, VAAD. A studio welcoming adults and children of able or not-so-able bodies. Neurotypical or neurodivergent. It was a brave move, and he was kind of my hero. My hot, physically agile hero.

Then there was Nate. My brother's best friend. My *kind of* friend. Nate was part of my life like my appendix was. Without knowing why, he was always there, just hovering quietly in the background, doing whatever it was he did, until he got a bit carried away and turned into a massive, completely disruptive pain in your side, talking incessantly and asking you to pull his finger until he was removed.

The problem was that he was also gorgeous. Sandy, sun-bleached hair. A thick, bulking body crafted by years of surfing and farm work. Deep brown eyes that could inspire a million love songs. And most importantly, a complete slut.

Young Nathaniel could sweet-talk his way into anything and proved that by the number of pants he'd gotten into and by being the only male granted membership to the Byron Bay branch of the CWA—the Country Women's Association. Think old ladies, perms, scones with jam and cream, and knitting. Those old birds took sixteen-year-old Nate under their wings and gave him three and a half thousand years of wise, womanly experience, hints, and tips. Hence his successful sluttery. It was all thanks to those old-time skanks…and his undeniable hotness.

As I conjured images of his long, toned body, it dawned on me just how often my gaze roamed freely over his shirtless form when drifting side by side on our surfboards or studied how the veins in his forearms tensed and flexed when effortlessly carting hay. Ohh, and the power grip his thighs had on his horse when riding bareback.

Fuuuccckkkkk.

Okay, I'd possibly nursed a *teeny-tiny* admiration for Nate for a long time, but honestly, I became emotionally stunted when we lost Mum and Dad, and then Shelby so soon after. I was numb for years. I felt too raw to feel more than the bare minimum necessary to function, and the little excess I did have went into Iris. She became our everything—sun and moon, stars, and sea. So even if I did have a childish crush, my heart was too full of pain and Iris to do anything about it. Plus, there was the whole he's-younger-than-me thing. Also, he's my brother's bestie, and my brother would kill him—and possibly me.

But things were…different. Life was different.

Could Nate really be into me? Could HotBoss Christian? What the fuck is happening?

The harmonious bleep of a WhatsApp notification pulled me from yet another spiral…until I saw the name on the screen.

Shit! It's Nate! Nate, who Finn thinks is into me. Shit! Shit! Shit! How do I play this? What should I do? What should I say? Okay, I'll just read the bloody message. It's probably nothing. I'm sure it's nothing. But what if…

Panic gripped me for several minutes. Hair was pulled at and braided. Nails were bitten, and a disturbing amount of gummy bears were consumed in a frighteningly short time.

The only thing that slowed my descent into crisis was Iris calling for me in her sleep. Finn had gone out on a rare non-date with his co-worker Scarlett, so it was up to me to calm her down and settle her back into bed. Once she was sorted, I swallowed the bile in my throat and read the message.

> **Nate: G'day, Lil Gidget. Nate the Great is bringing you the hottest gossip this side of the equator and checking in on his number-one girl.**

See, completely normal. He's checking on Iris, his number-one girl, and calling me stupid names.

> **Me: Hey, Nate the Average, you massive wanker. Ego much? All is well here in the good old US of A. Your girl is in bed after an eventful day full of cute dogs seen on the way to ballet and some kid called Cole's epic backflip and sick dance moves. Now, cut to the chase. What's the hot gossip? Also, when are we going to lose 'Lil Gidget'? I'm almost 27.**

Gidget. Damn, I loathed it. The whole thing started after we watched a terrible 60's surfer girl movie with his mom one rainy Sunday. I hated him calling me Gidget, but not as much as Aoife.

> **Nate: Uhh, never?? You may be a cougar now, but you'll always be my Lil Gidget.**

The phone almost slipped from my grasp. *My Lil Gidget.* I must have read that line a hundred times before reading on.

Now, to the gossip…Bloody Mum and Dad are going to Fiji for Xmas, and I can't handle being alone while they're jet-setting around and drinking cocktails. They asked me to come with them, but I can't stand the thought of that either. So, I was wondering…. I wanna come to see you for Xmas, Eves.

Oh my God. He wants to spend Christmas with me!

Nate: And by you, I mean the family-you. Not just you, you.

Well, fuck me. There goes that bubble.

Nate: I know it's not even autumn for you guys, but I have to organize things here on the farm. If it's not pushing the boundaries of friendship, I'd like to come in early December and stay through to New Year's Eve. Would that be too much Nate in one go?

Nate: You still there, Eves? You're not vomiting into a bucket at the thought of seeing me again, are you?

Me: No, I'm here. Just thinking. I/we would be stoked to have you for as long as you can stay. You're part of the family, remember?

Nate-We are many things, Gidge. Family isn't one of them.

Nate: Night my Lil Gidget.

Me: Night, not-my-family Nate.

Chapter 2

Nate

FOR ME, CRUSHING ON EVIE AUSTEN WAS LIKE breathing. An automatic bodily function I had no control over.

To this day, I can picture the moment I fell for her. Dates and times are spotty at best, but Evie sporting a fetching yellow sweater and a hat so big she could bathe in it was crystal clear. She lay on her parents' lawn, making daisy chains, her hair shining brighter than the sun. Her eyes were the color of the turquoise water I would soon learn to surf in. But it wasn't her beauty that had me hooked. It was the flames leaping from her mouth, the fire in her belly as she chastised her brother for making his bracelet all wrong. I knew right then and there…Evie Austen would one day be mine.

Complications arose when my twin sister, Shelby, who tragically passed away during my niece's birth, also fell in love with an Austen—Evie's brother and my best friend, Finn. Shelby was much louder and more open with her declarations of undying love than I, and it seemed a bit weird for us both to be fawning over the siblings. So, my feelings for my Lil Gidget, my Evie, remained buried deep inside my useless, rusting, Tin-Man heart while I sat on a smelly old barstool, getting turned on by reading her messages.

Evie: You're part of the family, remember?

Me: We are many things, Gidge. Family isn't one of them.

Fuck, I miss her.

I was very used to dealing with public hard-ons should she say something remotely sexy, but crying in public would do nothing for the reputation I'd crafted.

To aid the suppression of any pesky feelings, I'd chosen to drown myself in a bevy of female companions. One-night stands, maybe two if I felt particularly in need of distraction, were my thing. I tried to make them as respectful as a hit-and-run, with no emotions and no strings, could be. It was just sex, and I was always upfront about that.

Maybe I sounded like a complete douche, but I made no apologies, took no prisoners, and suffered no fools. Relationships were not my thing.

This philosophy, or way of life, had worked amazingly well until the fateful day Evie left. Though it had been hard, almost torturous at times, to have her be so close and not be able to touch her, at least when she lived here in Byron, I could keep an eye on her and make sure she was safe and happy. I could drink in that golden skin and those bouncy, sexy curls I discreetly smelled whenever she was near me. Banana shampoo from The Body Shop is what she used, and I may or may not have bought some the day after she left just to feel her presence.

I thought things might have gotten easier, that my stupid sentiments would dissipate without daily viewings. But if anything, my appetite increased, as did the number of women cycling in and out of my bed. I lied, telling myself and those concerned around me that I was just having fun, that it had nothing to do with some girl I used to live next door to. But on an ironically bright and sunny day last week, a rare, excited message from that very girl crushed my soul and finally made me acknowledge how dark the clouds of grief and loneliness had become.

Evie: Nate, guess what! I got a trial as a teacher at

> **Iris's dance school. Apart from the fact that my boss is smokin, I don't have a lot of details. Will let you know more when I do. I am so excited. (Yes, I know how rare that is.) I start tomorrow. Wish me luck.**
>
> **Evie: Oh, and Nate… It's a secret between you and me, okay? Don't tell Finn, or I'll come home and cut your balls off.**

Skipping over the hot-boss comments tearing my guts to shreds, and the threats of violence, which turned me on for some reason, I focused on three words…

You and me.

Even entirely out of context, reading that phrase, picturing it slipping from her grumpy, pouty little mouth, made me see how much I missed her. How rapid my descent into misery had been. How deep my feelings ran.

Evie was gone, living on the other side of the world, meeting new people, and moving on, and there wasn't a damn thing I could do about it.

Well, almost. I guess…maybe…I *could* use this as motivation. I could be more direct. Find the courage to tell Evie—my favorite girl (the line actually referred to her)—instead of pathetically hoping she may one day realize. 'Cause, duh, take the hint, Nate. Nothing will if the 49,894 messages sent during her flight to NYC didn't.

Instead of doing any of the above, in a dumbass, last-ditch scheme concocted while downing several beers with whiskey chasers, I decided to double down and do the complete opposite.

It was time to move on and cure myself of the Evie addiction.

I'm gonna get me a girlfriend.

How hard could it be? Some of the biggest dickheads I knew were happily married. If I was too, I'd satisfy the itch with regular sex and maybe, just maybe, break the back of this Evie thing for good.

It had the potential to be perfect.

I took a long, slow pull from my beer and pondered. Who to pick?

There are loads of nice girls I wouldn't mind sleeping with again, but which of them wouldn't annoy me after five minutes? Definitely not Angel from last night. God, I would shoot myself if I had to hear her voice again. Not Kara, the hot shearer, or her blonde friend—what's her name? Ingrid? Heidi? Whatever it was, they looked way more into each other than me in that menage a trois.

"Jesus, Nate. Are you out on the prowl again? I swear that schlong of yours will drop off in some blonde hand one day."

I knew who it was without looking. Polly Hart. Bartender. Evie's hotty friend. Off-limits.

"Hey, Pol."

"Hey, you who looks like he just ate a bag of shit and returned for seconds. Did some smart woman shut you down before you could bag her for the night?" My eyes left Evie's messages and traveled slowly over the curves of Polly's body. She really was gorgeous. Sexy and a total firecracker. Just like my Evie. Unlike Evie, Polly was tall with jet-black hair and dark-brown eyes that pierced right through me. "My eyes are up here, Nathaniel."

"I'm aware." I nodded as Polly scoffed and served the old man beside me, who smelled like blue cheese. Watching me as she poured his beer, she took his fiver, threw it in the cash drawer without looking and resumed my interrogation.

"You heard from Finn, or more importantly, Evie? I swear it's impossible to catch that woman. She's always off chasing Iris or helping Jocelyn with something. She's a freaking angel."

"That she is. And yeah, I heard from her just this morning, actually. She's good. She'd just picked up Iris from dance and was home in bed writing."

"Aww, she's still writing her little stories?"

Every hair on my body rose. "They are not little stories, Polly. They're novels. You shouldn't dismiss her work like that. She's really talented. In fact, she has more talent in her cute little finger than anyone in this shithole and will probably be like the next J.K. whatever her name is." *Shit, did I just call her finger cute?*

Polly's raised brow and head tilt told me I did. "Calm the farm, Nate. No one is dismissing your girl—"

"Not my girl!" I inserted.

"Whatever you say. Just know that I love her stories and was probably one of the first to hear them. She used to make some up for me when we had sleepovers." Embarrassed over my defensiveness, I took a long, steady sip from my beer and ignored the intense eye-frowning I was no doubt receiving. "So...she messaged you while she was in bed?"

"Well, she wasn't *in* bed, I don't think. More sitting on the bed while writing." *Am I blushing? Since when do I blush?*

"Huh. Is that what you've been staring at all night? Her messages? What did you talk about? Lemme see." Polly launched herself across the bar and snatched my phone.

"Hey, give that back!"

Her laughter was immediate and brutal.

"Oh my God, Nate. This is worse than I thought. 'G'day, Lil Gidget? Nate the Great... Just checking in on my number-one girl?' Holy shit!" Brutal was the wrong word. It was frightfully acidic, and I felt its lethal sting in every pore in my body. "Have you ever told her?"

"Have I ever told her what? What a complete pain in the ass you are? 'Cause I am pretty sure she knows that."

"No, not that. Have you ever told our Evie how you feel about her?"

"And what exactly is it that I feel, Polly? I'll tell you what, nothing. I don't feel anything. I don't have any damn feelings at all. I'm a slut, remember? Hence why you were just making jokes about my cock falling off."

Sidestepping the empty keg of beer another bartender had just wheeled beside her and carrying a bottle and two shot glasses, Polly sauntered to my side and laid her pointy chin on my shoulder. Her hair felt as soft as it looked brushing over my cheek, and I accidentally inhaled deeply. *Mmm, apple pie.* The extent to which I enjoyed it was disturbing.

"Nate. I'm sorry, but it's obvious. You are one of the happiest guys I know, and you've been moping around town for weeks—coincidentally, the same amount of time Evie Austen has been gone."

"You, PollyWaffle, are a fucking idiot, and I have no idea what you are talking about."

Possibly sensing she'd gone too far, Polly slapped my phone on the bar and poured me two fingers of whiskey, leaving her own glass empty. "No one's called me PollyWaffle in years. I'm surprised you remember that."

"I can remember lots of things. I'm clever like that."

"You should be clever enough to put a password on your phone, then. Anyone could discover your secrets."

Deciding I'd had quite enough of Polly, her sexy-smelling hair, and her wisdom, I kept my eyes down, sipping and watching the liquid amber swirling in my glass with unnecessary intensity. It was a good drop, smelled rich and peaty, and its tart, citric bitterness against my tongue helped me ignore a different kind of burn…unwanted attraction.

A persistent tap, tap, tap on my shoulder tore me from a peaceful, Evie-filled dream. I was face down on the bar. The stench of wet, beer-stained carpet filled my nostrils, a half dozen peanuts were attached to my forehead, and Polly's cleavage was right in my face.

"Time to go home, Sunshine. It's two a.m. We're closing, and you're drunk."

"I'm not drunk. I was drunk two hours ago. Now I'm just… nothing."

"Well, drunk or nothing, we are closed, and you need to leave."

"Yes, ma'am, Polly, ma'am." I gave her a sharp salute, wobbled to my feet, and took out my keys.

"Whoa, Nate, you're not thinking of driving, are you?"

"Yes. I am. I told you I'm not drunk."

Polly shook her head and lunged unsuccessfully at my keys. "Well, I have been serving the alcohol wafting out of your pores, and I am telling you that you are most definitely drunk and are not driving home. Let me call you a cab." Again, she lunged but this time snatched my phone and began dialing.

"What is it with you and my phone, Waffles? Sorry to tell ya, but I have no cash left for a cab, and I left my card at home. Besides, I said I am F.I.E.N." I then proved how fine I was by attempting to snatch my phone from her hand and missing it by about a foot.

"You are not driving, Nate. If for no other reason than letting you leave like this would risk our liquor license. I will take you home, but you have to go take a piss first—and ideally vomit if you think you'll have to. I just got the smell of Kapil Raj's puke out of my backseat last weekend." She grabbed me by the shoulders and spun me toward the restrooms. "Meet me out the back when you're done."

Since I saw three Pollys yelling at me, I decided I was maybe too far gone to drive. So, I did as I was told. I staggered off to the toilets, managing to piss and puke as requested, then weaved my way through the bar, bistro, and kitchen before pushing through the fire exits and hitting the still, cool night air with alarms blazing.

"Miss Polly had a dolly. Where are you?" I called at the top of my lungs, wholly amused with myself.

"Right behind you, tool. Get in the car…and DO NOT PUKE." Again, I did as she ordered, climbing in the front seat, and putting on my seatbelt like a good little boy.

"I'm not sure why, but I quite enjoy being bossed around by you, Polly Hart. Kind of gives me a thrill. Maybe even a little dick twitch."

I knew why. It reminded me of Evie, and though I was drunk, I wasn't drunk enough to make that confession.

"Mm. Lovely." She gagged as she sat beside me and started the car. "I think, for both our sakes, it's best if you do not speak from now on."

"Yes, ma'am."

Leaving the noise and lights of town behind, we headed for the water, for home.

My family was full of farmers. Growing macadamia, chamomile, and sheep, we had been caretakers of our land for three generations, and I say caretakers in respect to the Arakwal people, to whom our land first belonged.

When Dad had a minor stroke just days after Evie left me, it became my job to run the place. I loved it and have never wanted to do anything else, but being responsible for the financial fate of my parents in my early twenties, wasn't what I had planned. Neither was living in the small cabin within spying distance of my childhood home. But Byron Bay was home to rich, famous, and beautiful people. Regular Joes like me couldn't afford to rent a gum tree, let alone a house.

For almost the entire drive, Polly's window was down. I wasn't sure if it was to help sober me up or because I smelled like puke, but either way, she looked gorgeous, like a model with a giant fan blowing her hair back and away from her stunning face. Following the twists and turns of the road altered the direction of the breeze and where her ebony locks would fall. Sometimes it blew into her eyes, tickled her nose, or caught on her plump, wet, and shiny pink lips. Like she'd done it a million times before, like it wasn't sexy as fuck, she pursed those lips together and gently blew, freeing herself of its tangles and hardening my cock that little bit more. Occasionally, her hands would dip into the cool summer night air and glide back and forth like they were riding a wave. It was relaxing to watch, almost soothing…so much so that I drifted off to sleep.

Polly's melodic voice awoke me as we turned off the highway. "The chamomile looks like daisies. It's so pretty." I turned to face her and watched a single brow rise. "Evie always liked daisies, didn't she?"

Evie did love daisies. And I loved looking out at the fields from my bedroom window while I thought of her. That had nothing to do with my decision to farm them, though. No, that was purely commercial. There's good money in medicinal herbs. Even in my inebriated state, I knew to ignore Polly's insightfulness. Fortunately, she moved on to safer subjects—or so I thought.

"You know how lucky you are to have all this land near the beach, right?"

"Lucky is not the right word, Pol. We are blessed."

"Especially to have the Austen's as neighbors, eh? That's gotta be the icing on the cake."

Knife. Heart.

"That *was* the icing, Polly," I corrected, "But now all the sweetness is gone because Evie is gone." *Fuck. I should not have said that.*

Polly released a satisfied hum. "Hmm, what were you saying earlier about not having feelings for her?"

Oops.

Wanting to escape the truth and disappear into the darkness, I glanced out the window, but only my pitiful reflection shone back at me. "Alright, maybe I did have feelings once, but they're gone now. Like Shelby is gone. Like Finn is gone. Iris and Evie are gone. Nate's not gone, though. Nate is still right here," I said, emphasizing my point by stabbing my middle finger into my thigh, "and he's all alone."

We pulled up outside my door, and a warm hand caressed my cheek. I turned to my right and found Polly's beautiful face looking back at me, her eyes awash with what was likely pity, disgust, or both.

"You're not alone, Nate. You're just looking for company in the wrong places."

Perfectly proving the validity of her reply, I then said, "You're pretty, Polly. Would you come inside with me so I'm not lonely?"

Smiling, her lips joined her fingers in brushing against my cheek. "Not tonight, buddy. Maybe we can have another conversation if you remember this tomorrow." She leaned over my body and opened the door with a cute grunt. "Get out of my car, Myers."

Blushing like a nun in a brothel, I rolled from my seat onto my porch and lay down. "I'll remember. Bye, Polly."

As I watched the lights of her 2012 Toyota Corolla drive away, I declared to myself, "Polly Hart is going to be my girlfriend. Polly is going to fix me."

Then I passed out.

Chapter 3

Evie

Me: Hey, Nate. Guess what?

Delete, delete, delete.

Me: Hi, Nate. Wanna know a secret???

Delete, delete, delete.

Me: Yay or nay. Should I go on a date with my boss?

Nope

Me: Brace yourself, Nathaniel... I have some news.

No, that sounds like someone is dying. Gahh, why is this so hard?

Under the guise of hot gossip and genuine advice-seeking, I was texting—or attempting to text—Nate, essentially sniffing out his feelings toward me without actually asking. Killing two birds with one stone. Being a complete wimp. Same, same.

Mature, I know. But I couldn't seem to ask him straight out, which was a surprise. I'd never been backward in coming forward, but this...this was different. This was Nate, and I was desiring advice about Christian, and kind of us, and... well... I was a not-so-ugly, mid-twenties woman. I was attracted to men, surrounded by men, but had zero experience dealing with them. Sure, I'd dabbled a little in school and college, but as for real-life, grown-up men? That was negatory.

Again, it came back to my emotional stunting and non-ro-mance-conducive living situation. It was easier to hide away and deal with my grief in my own way. I lost myself in Iris and Finn and created my own safe worlds in my home and on paper. Worlds with joy and laughter and happily-ever-afters. It was also easier because, in general, people suck.

But change was in the air. I could smell it. And I thought I was ready for it. I just needed to know what to do.

"Auntie Evie. I am weady!" Iris's sweet little voice wafted upstairs.

"Okay, honey. I'll be down in a second."

I threw my phone onto my bed and hurried to get changed—again. Today was my fourth day at the dance studio. I was already nervous enough about the trial, but the added pressure of Christian most likely expecting an answer about our date had inspired me to change outfits 675 times.

Iris tried again. "Auntie Evie! I think we will be late if we don't leave now!"

"I know, honey. And I am trying to hurry." Forced to rush, I settled on the 676th outfit—a light-pink bodysuit under black yoga pants, hoodie, and trainers. It wasn't fashionable, but it was standard dance attire…and my butt looked good. I grabbed my already packed dance bag containing my pointe shoes, some strapping, water, and an apple, then took one last look in the mirror. *Don't fuck this up, Evie.*

Iris was waiting for me at the bottom of the stairs, her arms crossed over her waist and her little foot tapping against the hard-wood floor. My Aunt Jocelyn, who my brother and I had lived with since our parents died, and whose swank multi-million-dollar pad we were staying in, was beside her, pulling the same moves. Fresh off the plane from France and full of wine and gusto, Jocie was riding high on the fumes of a sordid affair with a much younger man. Finn had already left for work. Otherwise, he would probably have been there, adding his two cents too. "According to Iris, you're late, and she's unhappy." Jocie playfully grumbled.

"I'm sorry. I'm just really nervous about—" I looked into Iris's eyes and stopped. She didn't know about the trial, and if I told her, Finn would find out in three seconds flat. "About my hair. I'm getting a haircut today. Go grab your bag, honey, and we can go." Once she was out of earshot, I confessed the real reason for my nerves—well, part of it. "I only have two classes of my trial left, Jocie. What if they decide I'm crap."

"They couldn't possibly think that Evie, because you are a wonderful dancer and are brilliant and patient with the kids. Just go out there and give it all you've got. It's your time to shine, my darling."

Her words and death-grip cuddle remained on my mind as we walked to school. While Iris detailed the beginnings of her Christmas list—it was August—I contemplated.

Many would assume or outright claim that the life of a stay-at-home aunt-parent figure is pretty straightforward and mundane. In my mind, anyone who thinks that can go and get stuffed. Staying at home, working from home, to care for families and children, often at the expense of one's dreams and career, is a noble, hectic, challenging, frustrating and sometimes lonely act. But let's face it, a good portion of society ignorantly places little value on domestic duties. I was recently touted as a lady of luxury by a silly, silly delivery man who decided to chat on my doorstep and was lucky to leave it with intact testicles.

Having said that, if you're in a situation like mine and the kids have started school, you can get a little bored some days. Not for lack of things to do, but rather, a lack of things you want to do. Especially when you've almost forgotten what and who you are outside your role in the family. But Jocelyn granting me permission to shine, as she phrased it, felt like I was stepping, perhaps being pushed, back into the role of Evie for the first time in a long time. It felt good but foreign. Like I was the understudy in my own show.

We arrived at school, and after a quick kiss on the cheek, I was immediately ditched by Iris. "Hi, Bunny," she squealed with glee, and ran off to her gaggle of friends without so much as a wave, leaving me to walk the last remaining block to work. I should have been using the time to run over my lesson notes and prepare for the pre-K cuties, but all I could think of was Nate…and Christian too.

"Evie, wait up. Let me walk with you!" *Speak of the devil.* I stopped and tried not to vomit from nerves as the man of the hour gracefully thundered up behind me.

"Good morning, HotBo—Uhh, Christian." *Wow, so smooth.* "You're late today. Aren't you normally at the studio by seven for the seniors' class?"

He couldn't hide his smirk. "Right you are. You know my schedule well, Miss Evie. But Rachel is taking the class for me. I had to run to Bleecker and get something from a little specialty supermarket."

"Oh, I live on Bleecker. Do you mean the Down Under Deli?"

"Yeah, that's it. Do you know it? Oh, wait, of course you do. I imagine it's a favorite. It's funny that I bumped into you, actually. I thought you might like something from home for morning tea and picked this up." A familiar bag containing an equally familiar-shaped packet was passed to me, and when close enough, he smoothly hooked his little finger around mine and held on. Our eyes locked before his half-hooded gaze drifted to my lips. It was really, really…lovely. Yeah, lovely. I think. He stepped closer and smelled good, like chocolate and red wine mixed into some alluring dancer scent. But for some reason, I thought of Nate and how good and sexy he had always smelled—more earthy and raw, manly maybe. It was a confusing momentary distraction, and when I came to, I thought Christian was about to lean down and kiss me.

So, I yelled in his face.

"Tim Tams! Wow, Christian, that's so nice of you."

He jolted back and nervously laughed while rubbing the back of his neck. "Do you like them? The lady at the store said maybe nine out of ten Aussies did, so I figured it was worth a shot. Oh, and they had dark chocolate and originals. I got the original ones because you're an original, Evie." *Holy shit. Is this guy for real?* Poor

Christian. I think I stood dumbfounded for quite a while as I saw panic drift across his face. "Damn, that was super corny. Sorry. I'm such a dork and really, really embarrassed."

I grabbed his hand and squeezed it gently. "No, no, it's not corny. It's charming. I'm just not used to getting compliments and don't know how to take it. Normally, I would presume you were after something or just an idiot, but I don't get that vibe from you. I find it all very confusing, to be honest."

His confidence returned, as did his smile. "Well, you better get used to being confused because you are pretty amazing. The more people discover you, the more compliments will be thrown your way. Also, not everyone is after something, Evie…or an idiot. Some people are just nice." His free hand left his side and playfully tugged at a stray curl beside my ear. "And some people just like you and want to do nice things for you."

Such a simple act set off a reaction my body had rarely experienced, and truthfully, I wasn't sure if it was good or bad. It must have been an attraction as my heart raced, my hand shook, and I could feel and hear my breath falter. "Hmm, hmm. Yes, well, I'll take your word for it. But only because you gave me chocolate, and you smell nice."

He leaned in again. "You think I smell nice, do you? I must remember to spill hot chocolate on my shirt more often."

He was so close. So flirty. So sexy. And I had no idea what to do—other than my go-to snippiness. I suppressed my glee, rolled my eyes, and surprised both of us by looping my arm inside his and dragging him down the street. "Make yourself useful and open these, will you?" I said, shoving the cookies into his hand.

* * *

Attempting to teach ballet to toddlers was a little like herding feral cats. It could be done, but it took skill, patience, Advil, and a big, soppy heart.

When it came to kids, I possessed these qualities in spades. Adults? Not so much.

This was why I loved the no-parents-in-studio rule we had in place. I got to have all the fun with the kids without hearing little Tammy's mom's query if I was teaching first position correctly or explaining to Jeffrey's dad, Bryce, why we were singing songs in ballet class. And yes, Bryce, we sang songs. Pre-K dance was about laying the framework for future learning, basic skills, coordination, and flexibility. Singing a fun song and learning some movements and positions that go with it taught timing, how to listen for and hold a beat, how to take turns, and it helped improve memory. So, while it may have looked like a series of games or a bunch of kids skipping and jumping, everything was done for a reason.

Except maybe the tantrums. Oh, and the pee-pee accidents, of which there are many.

"Okay, kids. Does anyone need to use the bathroom before we start?"

"No, Miss Evie."

"Excellent. Let's begin, then. Should we sing our welcome song?"

"Yes, Miss Evie." *God, I love that.* The welcome song was a favorite. I'd introduced it, and within the three classes I'd taught, the kids had memorized it and seemed to love it.

"Gracie let's start with you. Let's sing, everyone. 1, 2, 3... Good morning, good morning. How are you today? We're—"

"Jumping!" yelled Gracie. The kids started jumping as we finished the song. "We're jumping with Gracie, having a lovely day." Everyone clapped, and then it was on to the next child, Phillip, who had selected the same action each time and did it again. "Farting!" he screamed, laughing hysterically. All the kids then lost it and began singing and sticking out their bums and making farting noises with their mouths—at least, I hoped it was with their mouths. We were all singing, dancing, hopping, and flopping when I heard a door open and close behind me and felt a heated gaze. I was just about to ask the parent to leave when I looked up from the little faces and saw HotBoss's perfection reflected back in the mirror.

"Good morning, everybody."

"Good morning, Mr. Alarie."

"I was just walking by and heard an awful lot of giggling… lots of farty sounds too. Was that all coming from you kids or Miss Evie?" Mass hysteria broke out. "MISS, EVIE!" they all screamed. Kids were dropping like flies, bodies were rolling in hysterics, and farts were flying left, right, and center. It was brilliant, and I knew I had zero to no chance of accomplishing anything useful for the rest of the class.

"Okay, boys and girls. Since we are lucky enough to have Mr. Christian here today, why don't we ask him if he will do a dance for us?"

A massive, "Yayyyyyyy!" echoed through the room, and the kids quickly all sat on the floor before Christian could say no. "Well, okay, then. But only if Katie will come and dance with me." Katie squealed with delight, as did her mom in the waiting area. Katie was a gorgeous five-year-old, a bit of a star, and a child with Down Syndrome. Many kids with Down Syndrome had issues with lax muscles and walked with their feet wide apart, their knees stiff, and their feet turned out. Dance was excellent for this as it increased muscle tone and flexibility, and it was great for the other kids in the class to experience learning alongside a kid with a disability. Benefits all around.

Christian leaned down and took Katie's hand, and after a quick wave to her mom, Katie was whisked off her feet and into the arms of one of New York's most incredible dancers.

Every woman, and possibly a few of the men, was jealous of that kid as she was twirled and whirled, pranced, and danced across the floor. Squealing with glee the whole time, Katie smiled and waved her hands in a fashion remarkably similar to Elsa in *Frozen*. It gave me a brilliant idea. Several, actually. Most involved

Christian's body lifting and throwing mine around in a similar, yet naked, fashion, but at least one was related to the class.

For the grand finale, Katie was gently placed on her feet before Christian got down on his knees and whispered into her ear. She took his hand and spun beneath his arm with a cute giggle. It was adorable. The duo then took a bow to a standing ovation. I had never seen a kid look so thrilled in all my life.

Despite the thoughts of Nate still swirling in my head, I reminded myself where he was, where I was, and who was before me. Softly, I padded my way over to the then-standing Christian, stood on the tippiest of my toes, and did a little of my own whispering. "If the offer still stands, I would love to go out sometime."

Chapter 4

Nate

I LOVED FARMING. I REALLY DID. BUT *I HATED* shearing. It paid the bills and kept the farm afloat in the years we had poor crops, but it still sucked. I wasn't even on the clippers this year, and I still hated it. It was hot, sweaty, smelly, itchy, and exhausting.

Our farm was a whopper, as in large. We had thousands of heads of sheep and were lucky enough to have a team of gun shearers that came in every year. A gun shearer could tally over two hundred sheep in an eight-hour day. They were incredible, paid well, and could cut our shearing period by days. That was why I was not shearing this year. These guys—and girls this year—could do it much better than I could.

I looked after the wool once it was off the sheep. In layman's terms, I made sure it was thrown onto what we called a wool table, cleaned up to get the quality fleece separated from all the crappy short bits, rolled out and classed into different qualities. It was then placed into the appropriate wool bin press and stored until transported.

Today was a big day, and by the time I'd dragged my sorry ass into my little cabin, showered, and choked down the shepherd's pie Mum left in the fridge for me, I was done. Bed was calling, and I was ready and willing to answer. I switched on *Sex and the City*—something I had started watching when Evie first left for NYC—and pictured my Lil Gidge walking the same streets that Carrie did in her stilettos and her thongs, and poorly painted toenails, and fell asleep.

At one a.m., a series of notifications woke me.

> **Evie: Nate, I had the best class today. It was brilliant.**

> **Evie: Christian, the senior instructor, came into my class and danced with one of the little girls. It was so friggin' cute. He is so amazing. So talented. So hot. Shit! I just realized it's 1 am there! I'm becoming a real New Yorker. I totally forgot the time difference. Sorry, Natey. Message me when you wake up. xo**

Hot? I am becoming a real New Yorker? What the fuck?
Just knife me in the guts, Gidge.

Jealousy induced a head-to-toe sweat, and the phone almost slipped from my grasp. Was my theoretical, one-sided grip on Evie waning too?

> **Me: Who is this Christian guy?**

> **Evie: Hi. You're awake? Did I wake you? God, Nate. Are you not alone?** 😊

> **Me: No one is here. I'm not a complete slut.**

> **Evie: Sure** 🙄

> **Me: Who is Christian???? Has Finn met him?**

> **Evie: I told you; he is the studio's owner and senior teacher, and yes, Finn has met him. He is Iris's dance teacher. He used to be a pro but busted his knee so many times he had to stop. Anyway, he came into class and danced with one of the kids. I legit nearly cried, and after class, we went and had coffee, and he offered me a permanent role. Four classes a week, Nate!**

Of course, because my life was shit, my phone battery died. On an exaggerated groan, I rolled from side to side in bed, searching for the charger, but came up empty-handed. By flashlight, I tore the house and my truck apart and retraced my steps between the two a hundred times, but apart from a still-good bag of Twisties and a Chocolate Big M, I came up empty-handed. "Shit. I must have left it at the sheds." At that time, I couldn't go back and get it. The shearers' quarters were behind the main shed, and they'd kill me if I woke them up, and Mum would have a heart attack if she heard the truck start up.

With a belly full of fake cheese flavoring, warm milk, and rage for this Christian asshole that I wanted to beat to a pulp, I fell back into bed and lay staring at the roof till dawn.

Shearing wasn't due to start till eight-thirty, but I was out the door and parking behind the shed to ensure I was in the shade by six am. The relief that washed over me when I heard that click and beep were utterly stupid but genuine. I just had to wait for enough charge to message Evie—that was the plan, anyway. What happened was, I fell asleep and woke up with the rapidly heating sun burning the side of my face and a gentle tapping on my shoulder. Whoever it was, I wasn't interested. "Fucking leave me be."

"That's not very nice to say to someone who brought you an egg-and-bacon sandwich and a coffee the size of a small car for breakfast."

The delicious scent hit my nostrils simultaneously as my left eye popped open. The sun was shining right behind the blacked-out figure before me, but with one look at the curvaceous shape, my womanizing eyes knew precisely who it was. "Shit, Polly. What are you doing here?" I quickly stood, wiped the drool from my chin and tried not to breathe anywhere near her as I couldn't remember if I'd brushed my teeth.

"I went to your place, but your mum stopped me and said you had left before six. She figured you would be here, so here I am. Sorry it's so early, but I am heading to Sydney and wanted to see if you needed a lift into town to get your car before I left. "She handed me my breakfast and took a sip of her coffee still sitting in the cardboard drinks tray. "Why are you here so early?"

"Uhh, I left something behind and had to come and get it

before we started." Silence descended as we drank from our cups, and I got engrossed in my sandwich." Mm, this is great. Where did you get it?"

"I made it at home." I nearly spat it all over her lovely low-cut shirt.

"You made this for me"—I glanced at my watch—"at seven-thirty in the morning?"

"No, I made it at six twenty-five in the morning. Then I got the coffee and drove to your house, where you weren't, and then I drove here. Hence why everything is kinda cold."

She sounded a little disappointed.

"Cold it may be, but it's bloody amazing. Especially considering what my last meal was. I'm not sure what I did to deserve all this, but I appreciate it. It's very sweet of you."

"Maybe." She smirked. "Or maybe I just have an ulterior motive."

With a hearty dose of side-eye, I took another bite. It really was good.

"Now I'm kinda nervous. What can I do for you, Polly?"

"Oh, it's just Polly now? No PollyWaffle?"

The egg started to turn in my belly. "Shit. I think you've done enough driving around for me already, Pol. Especially since I was *such* a complete asshole. I'm so sorry… Oh, and Mum and Dad already brought my truck home. It's parked out back." Then I remembered.

I asked her to come inside. Asked her to make me not lonely and decided she should be my girl. God, did I think that bit or say it?

Recognizing the embarrassment on my face, Polly spared me the indignity I deserved.

"Not a complete asshole. Maybe just one cute ass cheek. But it is kind of the other reason I'm here. Something you said got me thinking, and I think I can help you, and in turn, you can help me."

"Sounds ominous. What is it we can help each other with? Apart from breakfast and coffee and driving home when drunk. Oh wait, that's all the things you've already done for me," I said sarcastically. "I guess it's time I did something for you."

Polly smiled and nodded. "Okay, then. Take me out on a date."

"Uhh…what?"

"Take me out, Nate. I think we should date. We're both single, both attracted to each other. You told me you were lonely, and I am kinda lonely too. We're friends. We have fun together. Why not?"

"Uhh. Well, I don't really date people. I sleep with people. That's it."

"Yes, that's been your pattern for a long time, but I think you are ready for a change, and I am the one to change it. So, next Saturday night, take a shower, get dressed up, then pick me up at seven. I'll be waiting." As if this whole sentence hadn't stunned me enough, she then leaned down, placed her hand on my shoulder, and kissed my cheek, catching the very edge of my mouth. Her lips were soft and tasted like berries, her skin smelled like honeydew melon, and her hair like coconut. She didn't smell like Evie, but she smelled like a goddamn tropical party, and it took all my willpower not to drag her onto the floor and fuck the living shit out of her right then.

Those berry lips were still pressed to my cheek, and when she finally pulled back, her hand touched my chin and popped my open-hanging jaw closed. "By the way, it's Sunday, Nate. The boys aren't shearing today." Bopping me on the nose, she gave me a wink, then strutted her way back to her Corolla, leaving me a confused, sweating mess with a lukewarm coffee, a soggy sandwich, and a rock-hard boner.

✳

After being propositioned by Polly, I felt gross messaging Evie. I wanted to congratulate her and suss out the asshole male dancer, but I almost felt unfaithful, which I knew was stupid. I'd never had an issue talking to Eves as soon as I left any girl's bed, but this felt different. Maybe because Polly and Evie were friends? They had been inseparable for years, always dancing or playing with their Tamagotchis, having sleepovers most weekends, and even having joint parties because their birthdays were only a day apart.

Things really changed between them when we were teenagers. I'm not sure if anything happened or if they just naturally grew apart. They remained close, but there was a definite cooling off of the relationship.

Mum was sitting on my porch when I arrived home, with a shit-eating grin and a lemon poppyseed cake on her lap. I knew it was lemon cake as it was her lemon-themed tin. She had a matching container for her favorite flavors: chocolate drops on her chocolate tin, tiny carrots for carrot cake, multicolored apples for apple cake, and even one with little cherubs for her famous angel food cake. I had a suspicion about what the grin was for too.

"Janet," I said curtly. She sighed and closed her eyes. She always hated me calling her by her first name. That was why I did it.

"Morning, Nate. Polly Hart was here looking for you. Did she find you at the shed?"

"Yep."

"Was that egg-and-bacon sandwich on the front seat of her car for you?"

"Yep."

"And are you hung over and forgot it was Sunday?"

"Yep."

"Well, thank you for that thrilling conversation, Nathaniel."

"My pleasure."

Mum continued smirking as I approached and picked the tin up from her hands. "Thanks for this and for the shepard's pie last night. Now, if you don't mind taking off, I'd very much like to go back to bed."

"I'll take off when you tell me why you were rooting around outside at one am, and why Miss Polly has been here twice in as many days."

"You don't miss a damn thing around here, do you?"

"No, I do not. Please tell me you didn't sleep with her, or I will knock your block off. She's a beautiful girl, as is her mum, and I will not be embarrassed by your shenanigans. Tourists and hot shearers are one thing. Childhood friends are another altogether."

I ran my hands through my hair and kicked the pole on the veranda. "Jesus, Mum. No, I did not sleep with her… But I might. She asked me out on a date."

I was glad I'd already taken possession of the cake as Mum leapt to her feet at an alarming speed. "She did not! Did she? A date? Like a proper date? Not hooking up, or getting down, or whatever you call it?"

"Shit, Mum. Please never say that again, and yes, a proper date."

Her arms stopped their flailing and instead crossed over her chest. "Huh."

"Huh, what? That's it? No riot acts. No threats of physical violence toward my head?"

"Well, that depends on what your answer was. Did you say yes?"

"No. But I might."

"Nate."

"Mum." It was a good old-fashioned standoff. We stared each other down, and I mirrored her crossed arms and stance to annoy her.

"I haven't got time for this crap, Nate. I have a shit-ton of ironing to do, and I left your dad pantless on the couch, watching bloody home reno shows. God knows what I am going to find when I get home. He could be half naked on the roof, so let me tell you this before I rescue him from himself, or he has another bloody stroke. Polly Hart deserves better than to be messed around with. If you decide to date, let it be because you genuinely like her and are interested in a relationship. I know how you feel about Evie."

"Mum."

"No, let me finish." Her arms unfurled, and I was wrapped in the kind of smothering, do-as-I-say-cause-I-love-you hug only a mother can deliver. "I know you are hung up on Evie, and I know that's why you have never been serious with anyone else. But if you are ready to move on, and if you think you like her, then Polly is a great choice. Just be careful, though, darling. Alright? Just think of your poor mum." She then kissed the top of my head before slapping it and walking away.

Chapter 5

Nate

As I stuffed a good portion of Mum's lemony, poppyseed deliciousness into my mouth, my dilemma pinged off the walls in my thick skull.

Should I go out with Polly?

More importantly, should I bang Polly from behind? Damn.

It was moments like these that I missed Finn. He was the most frightfully organized person I knew. At the drop of a hat, he could and would make a pros and cons comparison and a ten-point plan of action.

The temptation to call him was strong, but there were two major issues.

One, the last time we spoke, he hung up on me, and I absolutely deserved it. Being an insensitive prick wasn't new for me, but giving him shit about him not dating, getting laid, and implying he lived like a monk was a new low. The guy was a single dad who clearly harbored severe guilt and grief over the death of my beautiful sister. He didn't need a smug prick like me judging him.

Issue number two—Evie. This whole thing with Polly started because of Evie, and I couldn't tell Finn about Evie because Evie was his sister. As per usual with me, everything came back to Evie. I felt like freaking Jan Brady. Evie, Evie, Evie!

So no, Finn wasn't going to be the one I reached out to, and obviously, neither would Evie, which really sucked because she was usually the one I wanted to speak to about everything.

I had other friends I could call, but they weren't really the emotional-support kind of friends. More like a collection of tools I could count on to get me drunk, give me a laugh, and who knew the exact moment to piss off when I zoned in on my evening's target. Talking about feelings and shit wasn't going to fly with them.

The way I saw it, I had two options. Take a good hard look in the mirror, man-up, and actually deal with the emotions swirling in my stomach by myself or talk to the one other person I could think of.

"Nathaniel Myers. Two conversations in one day. I am a lucky lady." Warm, smooth honey dripping over my tongue. That was what I envisioned when Polly's voice dropped an octave and rasped into my ear. Katy Perry blasted in the background, mixed with buffering wind. *She must be driving with the windows down.* The image of her hauling me home from the pub hit me. Raven hair floating through the air, sticking on those pretty lips. I didn't bother with small talk. Neither of us had time. Well, she didn't. I was just getting horny.

"Polly…at the sheds, did you…did you mean what you said? Even with all the slut, STD, man-whore jokes you make every time I see you at the pub, you still really want to go out with me?"

There was a slight pause before she answered with a smile in her voice. "What can I say, Myers? I'm a sucker for a broken boy. They're my favorite book boyfriends. You'll see what I mean when you come and pick me up. If you're lucky, I'll invite you inside to finger through my collection…amongst other things."

Gulp.

I cleared my throat. "And what about…about…?"

"Evie?"

"Yeah, what about Evie? You know, I kinda have…issues, let's call it, where she is concerned. Are you sure you can handle that? Because I may sleep around, Pol, but I am always upfront and honest about what I can give a woman. I can't promise you anything.

I can't tell you that I will magically forget all about her if we do this, and I don't want anyone getting hurt.

Patronizing laughter was followed by a heavy sigh. "Geez. I don't expect you to fall madly in love and propose, Nate. I just thought we could be two friends who hang out, keep each other company, and fuck our brains out."

Double gulp.

"I gotta say, Polly, that sounds mighty tempting and too good to be true."

"Trust me, Nate. You'll soon know how true my words are. You know what else is true?"

I scrubbed my hand over my face. "Nope, but I get the feeling you're going to tell me." *And that I'm going to like it.*

"The way I'm going to make you groan when my lips wrap around that massive cock of yours… Every thought, worry, and memory of anyone else will melt away, Naty. See you Saturday."

Without another word, Polly hung up, which was good because my phone had melted into my palm.

※

Submitting timesheets to our accounting software was supposed to be the boring manner in which one of the oddest few days of my life came to a close. Opening my laptop, signing off on the week's wages, and clicking on processes heralded the start of a new week. A fresh start. Flushing the pipes and bringing me a clearer mind to figure out what the fuck to do. But bang, at eleven pm, an email notification from Evie flashed on my screen, and my waters were once again muddied.

> To: Nate
> Subject: ???
>
> What the hell, Nate? You better have fallen, hit your head, and forgotten about our chat, or did I do something wrong and hurt your precious ego? I haven't heard from you since you hung up on me, and there are only two reasons I will accept why you wouldn't message, call, or email me back.
>
> Get on it, tool.

Love,
Pissed-off Evie.

To: Pissed-off Evie
Subject: SHIT!

Shit, of course you did nothing wrong, Lil Gidget. And no, I didn't hit my head either. My phone died. I'd left my charger in the shed, and I had to wait till morning to get it. When I got there, I fell asleep on the floor, and after that, I was just a douche who forgot. I'm really sorry, Eves.

Congratulations on the job offer, by the way. I am really, really sorry, and super-duper proud. Also, kinda worried about this Christian dude. What's his M.O.?

Also, in future, please refer to me as Nate the Great.

Love,

Nate the Great.

To: Nate
Subject: Really?

Okay, that seems like a reasonable excuse. You are hereby forgiven. As for Nate the Great, you're sticking with that?

Also, what is M.O?

Love,
Evie the Agitated

To: Sweet Evie
Subject: Answer the question.

Fine.

I'll drop the name even though I think it suits me.

M.O.= Modus Operandi=What's his deal?

He seems super dodgy.

My Spidey senses tingle whenever you mention his name.

Love,
Nate the Mediocre

To: Nate
Subject: Really really?

So now you're Spider-Man?

You worry about me too much. Christian is a really sweet guy and the most amazing dancer. He came into my class after you ditched my call and did a routine for all the kids.

It was brilliant. He just comes alive when he dances.

It's very inspiring.

And thanks for the congrats. I finally told Finn about the job, and he was thrilled…though maybe that was just because he was getting the house to himself a bit more often. I was so worried he would hate me not being at home for some reason.

It was stupid, just like you being worried about HotBoss.

Oh, yeah. Christian is HotBoss.

I call him HotBoss cause he's. 🔥 🔥 🔥.

Love,
Evie

To: Evie
Subject: Tool

I can't believe you thought Finn would be upset. The guy's a knob, but not that big a knob. I hope you are celebrating. You deserve it.

Also, are you trying to make me jealous, Lil Gidget?

Nate the Slightly Above Average.

To: Nate
Subject: You wish.

Snort. No. Why would I want to make you jealous?

I'm just pointing out the hotness of my HotBoss.

Oh, btw. How are the hot shearer girls?

I just talked to Polly. She said they've been "keeping you company."

Love,
Evie the Curious.

To: Evie
Subject: ???

Did she now???

The girls are okay, I presume. And they did keep me company. They are not continuing to 'keep me company.' It was a one-time thing, Lil Gidget. Don't get your little panties in a twist.

Also, you are the only person I know who types *snort*.

#cutiepatootie.

Also, you seem kind of jealous.

Love,
Nate the Lover.

To: Nate the Try-hard
Subject: Keep dreaming.

One… Jealous? You wish. You're the least jealousy-invoking person I know. How you make me laugh. HA HA

Two… I do not wear "little panties." I wear undies because I'm Australian, and panties is a gross word.

Three… I am 27. I am not a #cutiepatootie.

Four… When you say THEY kept you company once, do you mean, like, together? At the same time? Like a three thingy?

No love,
Evie

To: Evie #cutiepatootie
Subject: Oh

Oh, Polly left that part out, did she?

Shit. Um, yes, both at the same time, and it's called a threesome, or three-way or ménage a tres. Not a three-thingy.

Sorry to shock you, Lil Gidget.

Love,
Still Nate the Lover

To: Nate, the Try-hard
Subject: Stop

Stop calling me that.

You're gross.

Good night.

To: Evie
Subject: Sweet dreams

Night, Lil Patootie.

Love,
Your Nate.

Chapter 6

Evie

I F YOU KNOW THE TAYLOR SWIFT SONG "BETTY," you'll know all about Betty's friend, Inez. She was the school gossip and the one to rat on Betty's naughty boyfriend, James, for cheating. Well, a call from my high school friend, Polly, turned her into my own Inez. Just like the song, Inez/Polly was not always the most reliable source of information, but James, I mean Nate, confirmed her gossip. Nate had a threesome.

Technically, this was none of my concern. Nate was not my James because he was not my boyfriend. He didn't cheat on me, and the fact that he had a three-thingy should have been no surprise because that was an entirely Nate thing to do. But ever since Finn told me about Nate's alleged lifelong crush on me, I couldn't help but see him in an all-new light. Suddenly, he was not Finn's friend Nate, Shelby's brother Nate, or even Iris's uncle. He was…Nate. Sexy, hot-AF, makes-me-feel-all-warm-and-fuzzy Nate.

This morning, before my eyes had even blinked open, I was touching, caressing, and bringing myself undone to visions of him surfing, his arms slicing through the waves as he paddled back to shore. His wetsuit was half off, lifelessly hanging around his waist, as he ran from the water, his board tucked under his bulging biceps. He whipped his wet hair from his eyes and smiled over his shoulder as I ran to catch up to him. When I did, he took hold of my waist, laid me down in the sand, and violated every inch of my body.

No other man had brought me undone by mere thoughts alone. In truth, no other man had made me fall apart full stop.

You see, I had a teeny-tiny secret. I had a few, actually, but the biggest by far was that I, Aoife Evie Mary Austen, was a twenty-seven-year-old virgin.

A life of celibacy was not my intention. I did not dream of being a nun or starring in the female remake of *The 40-Year-Old Virgin* in an alarmingly short time. Opportunities had arisen here and there in high school and college—the most serious of which was with my first and only boyfriend. I was seventeen, and his name was Luke Bailey. He was kind of a dork, but a super-cute and sweet guy who sat next to me on the bus, where we would hold hands and whisper naughty things. Most days, he would get off a stop early just to walk with me, and he bravely withstood the abuse Finn and Nate hurled the entire time. Our relationship ran almost an entire year, and I fully intended on Luke being my first lover. We got close—naked-and-putting-on-a-condom close—but at the last minute, my ready and willing body surrendered to my freaking-the-fuck-out mind, and I ran.

My hesitation was a blessing in disguise.

Turned out that Luke wasn't so sweet. He was quite the cockhead. One who broke up with me the next day, then slept with my once-best friend Polly that same night.

Yes, Polly.

The very one who'd called me out of the blue and squealed like a piggy about Nate's bedroom tricycle act. The timing of her call was suspicious. She was surrounded by people and an undoubtedly hideous pink-and-blue mess at her sister's baby shower. It was odd, but then again, that was Polly… She never did things by the book.

Speaking of books, my friend Polly was the first to hear the origins of my writing and the first to read a completed work. The collection I'd written in my youth became a series starring my niece, Iris, incorporating Aussie tales my mum told us as kids and the real-life moments from our move from Australia to America. The kid was incredible, coping with the challenges better than me, her dad, or her great-aunt. Her bravery, honesty, and pure brilliance took my breath away, and I couldn't have loved her more if she were my own daughter. Which I truly felt she was. Even though her father is my brother. Note to self: never say that in public.

My mind was in chaotic shambles. Nate, Polly, and my joke of a literary career fought for attention, so I did what I always did—distracted myself and got on with what needed to be done. Since it was Friday, and I was a single woman in New York, I was naturally at home doing housework in my pajamas, nibbling on Vegemite toast while listening to Taylor. Clearly, I had it too loud. I thought I was alone in the house. Jocelyn was supposed to be meeting with Finn at his architectural firm—he was designing Jocelyn's dream home upstate—but as I danced past her study, pulling my best moves with the vacuum, I spotted her behind her desk, and by the looks of it, she was mid-plot.

"What are you up to?" I quizzed, popping out my headphones.

She smirked and released a disturbingly evil chuckle. "I don't know what you are talking about, Evie. I'm working hard here."

"Working hard at trouble. I know that face, now spill." Shutting off the vacuum cleaner, I rushed to her side. Luckily, Jocelyn was not holding any national secrets, and she cracked like an egg.

"Well, I was thinking of a girls' trip and may have been looking at houses available this weekend in Tarrytown. You, me, and Iris. Interested?"

"Bloody oath! A nice, relatively quiet weekend sounds like heaven. But I have to ask, what inspired this sudden need to escape the city?"

"Finn has. Well, Finn and his co-worker slash love interest, Scarlett. A concussion and a rather lot of blood."

My eyes crossed. "Umm, you lost me at concussion."

Jocie closed her laptop and rose, dramatically walking toward the window with her arms in an on-brand, theatrical flurry. "As you know, I went to see Finn and Scarlett about the house plans—which, by the way, look fabulous. The three of us were making our way to the conference room, when poor Scarlett tripped, knocking her senseless and cutting her forehead and lip. Finn and I were forced to take her to the emergency room, which is where she and, most importantly, he remains."

"You seem happy about this, and I'm not sure why. Is the poor girl okay?"

"Yes, yes. She will be fine, but I believe Ms. Grant may need some nursing this weekend, and I believe your brother may be the perfect one to provide it. You know what Finn's like, though. He will have major guilt if he leaves Iris too long, so I plan to steal her away before he can even question it."

"You really are an evil genius, aren't you?"

"Of course I am. Without it, you can't get as far in business as I have."

She was right about evilness and getting far in business. Though I would be hesitant to tell her in fear of her head swelling, Jocelyn was a bit of a hero to me. I'd watched in admiration for years as she ran our family farming empire singlehandedly, taking guardianship of my brother and me when we lost our parents. Not only that, but she had also been married three times and lived an enviable intercontinental lifestyle, including romancing many, many more young men than I could even dream of. Most of our family's land in Australia had been sold off as she had none of her own children, and neither Finn nor I were interested in continuing on the Austen/Crane family farming legacy—not on the scale Jocelyn did, anyway.

She continued to reveal her plans as she resumed her seat and showed me the houses she had found on Airbnb. "This one is perfect, and it has a pool. It's hardly swimming weather, but that won't stop Iris. What do you think?"

"I think it's beautiful, but it has seven bedrooms, Jocie. Last time I checked, you don't need a seven-bedroom mansion for a three-person girls' weekend."

"Honestly, Evie. I wonder how we can be related sometimes."

She sighed, clicking away as she looked at me with dismay. "This house has nothing to do with need and everything to do with want. I want to stay there. I want a chef's kitchen despite the fact that I cannot cook. I want a home theater room, and I want a pool-sized bath in my bedroom, so I will have it. Plus, it's on the same road as my land, so we can walk to the plot and maybe even have a picnic."

"But it's excessive—"

"I do not want to hear it. I do not care, and it's too late because it's done. Now, finish what you are doing—which you wouldn't need to do if we had a housekeeper, like I wanted—and pack your things. We can pick Iris up from school and head off from there."

"Fine. I still think it's too much, though," I added as Jocelyn pushed away her MacBook, took my hand, and began stroking it much like you would a sick, fragile, geriatric cat.

"You need to stop thinking so much and start living a little. You're too young and beautiful to worry so much. Now that my meddling in Finn's life is paying off, I need to start on you." She was right—not about the meddling but the fun. I considered telling her about my current two-man-and-a-coffee situation, and I could tell by her face that she knew I had something to share. She was waiting expectantly, almost giddily, rubbing her hands together in glee.

"You have something you want to tell me, darling, don't you?"

The juiciest of juicy news sat on the tip of my tongue, just busting to see the light of day. The thing was, though sharing was caring, it wasn't my scene.

Shrugging, I left without a word, resumed my vacuuming, then when complete, started packing. With an almost sick sense of timing, Nate messaged me as I was folding my underwear.

Nate: What ya doing, Lil Gidge?

Me: What am I doing? It's after midnight there. What are you doing?

Nate: Can't sleep. Entertain me.

Me: Alright. If you must know, Jocie, Iris, and I

are going to Tarrytown for the weekend, and I am currently folding and packing my underwear.

Nate: See, I told you I had Spidey senses. Take a photo. Show me what you're working with.

After a quick Google search, I sent him a pic of Bridget Jones holding up her granny pants.

Nate: HOT. I fucking knew it. Now send me a pic of you in them.

Me: I've said it before, and I'll say it again. You. Are. Disgusting. Goodnight.

Me: So, do you have a reason for this midnight message or not?

Nate: Ha ha. Knew you couldn't stay away. Not. Kinda missed you, to be honest. Lots of things going on. Feel stressed, and for some reason, your grumpiness has an uncanny ability to make me feel calmer.

I clutched my phone to my heart, caught my reflection in the mirror, and stopped.

Me: Shit, Nate. I'm sorry, but I have to go get Iris and then leave for the country. We're taking Jocie's town car, though, so I will message you when I can.

My finger hovered over *send*. I wanted to tell him that I missed him too and that he could make me feel calm yet also incredibly un-calm. That for the last almost two weeks, I thought very little about him, even went out for coffee with another man.

But I didn't.

Instead, I hit *send*, grabbed my bag, and walked down the stairs.

Damn you, Nathaniel.

Me: I miss you too.

Chapter 7

Nate

Evie: I miss you too.

It was entirely possible that from sun-up, I read that and the several other messages that followed a hundred times. Nothing other than absorbing those words was achieved all day.

Evie: I miss you too

Evie missed me.

Evie. Austen. Missed. Me.

Yet, there I was, standing in front of my bathroom mirror, dressing for a date with another woman. Polly.

She'd also messaged me quite a few times, but none hit me directly in the heart like Evie's did. No, Polly's were aimed at another body part that required a lot of blood to function. If you're not good at reading between the lines, I mean my cock. The same one Polly apparently couldn't wait to get her lips around.

Yeah. Those kinds of messages.

The funny thing was the overtly sexual nature of Polly—something that should have been appealing to a guy like me—did nothing but terrify me. It was Evie's witty banter and innocent confessions that had me all kinds of messed up.

I guess it wasn't *just* Polly's blowjob talk

that had me second-guessing. I had never been on a date. Sure, I'd hung out with women, friends that turned to lovers and back again. I had made out with them at parties and taken them home from bars and clubs, but I had successfully avoided the whole pick-me-up-at-seven-for-dinner thing.

Maybe I should cancel.

No. Evie has moved on. I need to do the same.

Eventually, I decided that if I didn't leave, then I wasn't going to.

Twenty-five minutes later, I was ringing Polly's doorbell. It was a surreal moment, and I did consider bolting…but then she opened the door.

Curves a Kardashian would be proud of smashed me right in the balls, and remarkably, my nerves dissolved instantly. "Polly. Holy shit, you look incredible."

Arching her back, she leaned against the door frame, showcasing the body she damn well knew I was into. The dress she must have poured herself into was doing the Lord's work in trying to cover her ample breasts. It barely covered her ass too and looked suspiciously like lingerie. It may well have been, but the head attached to my neck, and the one pumping between my legs, didn't seem to care.

"You came early, Nathaniel. Let's hope it's the only time that happens tonight."

Polly was intelligent, sexy, and naughty. We talked about football and surfing and reminisced about school while purposely excluding Evie's name at all times. She asked me about the farm and how we had gone through the droughts to see better times slowly. I asked about her plans for her future and listened to her dream of one day having her own farm-to-kitchen restaurant…which was something I could fully endorse after tasting her food.

Initially, we planned to go out for dinner, but Polly felt like staying in, and I couldn't blame her. "The last thing I need is the

Byron gossip wagon delivering my mum the news that we're on a date. I'd never hear the end of it."

I sunk into my seat. "Ahh, shit, Pol. I hope you don't mind, but Mum was on my case about Evie after you came out to the farm, and I may have shut her up by telling her about our dinner."

A wry smile broke over what looked like freshly enhanced lips. "You told Janet about me? What did she say?"

"Yeah, sorry. I didn't even think about the old girl spreading the word. Though, this was last weekend. You'd know if your mum had heard by now. As for what she said, she was thrilled. Told me you were a good choice and, quote, 'Polly Hart deserves better than to be messed around with.' So basically, she likes you better than me." Her smile spread.

"Well, she was always a smart woman, always kept your dad in line. Even after his stroke, she was up and running in weeks. And don't worry about telling her. I get the pressure. Mum's Greek, remember? We Greeks invented marital pressure along with everything else good and proper in this world. Just ask my dad. He and Mum were only together for a few weeks when she started putting the squeeze on."

Sipping from my beer, I shook my head nervously. "A few weeks? Shit. You're not going to try that on me, are you, Polly Waffle?"

She sucked an olive between her lips, chewed thoughtfully, and then dropped the fork full of Caprese salad onto her plate. Leaning across the table, she captured the collar of my shirt between her thumb and index fingers and caressed back and forth around my neck, the slight edge of her nail scratching against my skin. "There are many things I want to try with you, Nate." She then fisted my collar and pulled me onto her lips. "Why don't we start right now?"

❧

Sex with Polly was good.

Really good.

Hot.

She was attentive, assertive, and generous. Feisty, fun, and fit. But if I was honest, that was all it was. Good sex. I hoped being with someone I had history with may have been a game changer. That I would wake from my post-coital, no-cuddles nap a new man, ready for commitment.

Cured. Full. Satisfied.

I didn't. The hunger remained.

Having said that, I was not a quitter. Maybe this type of thing took a few goes.

It couldn't be perfect straight off.

Right?

I mean, people had to learn about each other. What they liked and disliked, the little quirks and kinks. I was sure that was all it was. That was why I did something I had never done before.

Wrapped in her arms, her legs, her hair, I spent the night with Polly. Our bodies came together time and time again, and the next day, we slept in till noon... just not in the same bed. Polly snored away in her bed, while I lay on a pile of spare blankets on the floor beside her. Nate the Slut may have been gone but sleeping together and *sleeping* together were two different things.

That morning, we ate the gourmet breakfast in bed that Polly prepared wearing only her sexy knickers. We licked maple syrup off each other's bodies and then had dirty, dirty sex amongst the dirty dishes. I bent her over and took her from behind in the shower, then we went back to bed and watched horror movies. She dozed on and off. I lay still, not wanting to wake or touch her more than necessary.

It was playful and fun, and the sex did get better. It became great, actually.

Maybe I can do this.

Maybe I am a boyfriend guy.

Maybe Polly can fix me.

When I finally vacated her bed around eight Sunday night, I could hardly walk. Every muscle in my body was screaming for relief. My lips—hers too—were raw and swollen, but none of that stopped Miss Hart from laying a mighty fine farewell kiss upon them. "Nate. I work every night this week, but I don't start till eight on Wednesday. Will you come over for dinner again? I'll even feed you your favorite."

"My favorite? When did I tell you my favorite meal?"

Polly pulled me in close and licked the shell of my ear. "You didn't. But after the way you ate me out last night, I'm taking a wild guess that it's now my pussy."

"Fuck, Polly." I rubbed my hand over my rapidly growing stubble. "You are something, aren't you?"

"Oh, Nate," she laughed, giving me a quick kiss, and then pushing me out onto the curb. "You've got no idea."

My phone buzzed in my pocket as I walked to my car. My stomach twisted. *Please don't let it be her.*

> **Evie: Hey, Natey. It's six am, and I'm wide awake. Iris and Jocie are still asleep. I was thinking of taking a walk to the river. Wanna Facetime-walk with me?**

Fuck.

Chapter 8

Evie

WHY DID I ASK HIM TO FACETIME? Waiting for Nate to get home and call me back gave me a good twenty minutes to fill. After pacing myself dizzy, I put on some tunes and hit the shower. Unnecessarily rough exfoliation became a diversionary tactic, leaving me with little time to worry, and the smoothest, albeit red-as-a-lobster skin in town. But once that was done, I was back to shitting myself. Logically, I knew the hubbub was ridiculous. It wasn't like we would be sexting. *Oh…I wonder if he's done that? Hang on, it's Nate. Of course he has.*

After dressing, braiding my hair, pacing some more, and imagining just how dirty Nate's sexting would be, I could wait no more. An immediate change of scenery was required. I jumped up, pulled on my hiking boots, grabbed my AirPods, puffer jacket, and beanie, and was just about to leave my room when my phone rang.

Borderline hysteria followed. *Shit! Shit! Be cool, dickhead. Be cool.*

I was the opposite of cool. Well, not the opposite because that would be hot, and I sure as fuck was *not* hot. I'd be lucky to be considered lukewarm. And it wasn't like this was an unknown scenario. This was Nate. He and Iris had Facetimed often since we'd arrived, but this felt different. Normally, like most times in my life, I was like a stagehand or an extra floating around in the background, not the on-screen leading lady.

You can do this, Evie. It's just the boy from next door with smelly hair and a goofy grin.

"Natey, hang on a sec, everyone is still asleep. I'm just going to head outside." I held the phone to my chest and rushed as quietly as I could downstairs while giggling at his commentary.

"Geez, Lil Gidge. How big is that bloody house? I'm guessing Jocie picked it and not you?"

The door clicked behind me. I faked the best smile I could and faced the music. To say Nate's appearance was a shock to the system would have been a massive understatement. The possibly freshly showered man was shirtless in bed with a white sheet sitting just below the waistband of his briefs, perfectly complementing his tanned, almost dewy-looking abs. Stunning. I hushed my long-dormant libido and bitched out, "It's a frivolous waste of money, Nate. Of course she did. The upstairs has its own zip code. Oh, and hi again."

Pain sliced through his face, and my shy, very un-me greeting was ignored. "Zip code? You mean postcode, right? You forgot the time here the other day, and now this. You sound like a real Yank, little one. I don't like it. I don't like it one bit."

Grateful for the distraction from his gorgeous face and torso, I joined in his outrage. "I know! I asked Iris if she wanted some candy yesterday, then instantly slapped my own face and corrected it to lollies. I was utterly disgusted with myself. But I guess the real test would be if I was underwear shopping and asked for a thong instead of a G-string. I'm a lost cause if that happens."

I could have pole-vaulted over Nate's raised eyebrows. "G-strings, eh? You like to wear those, do you? So, it's not the granny knickers 24/7, then?"

"Okay. I am hanging up now." Again, I dropped the phone to my chest to hide my shame.

"No, no," he laughed, "please, at least answer this very serious question first… Is my face between your boobs right now? 'Cause motorboating is a particular favorite of mine, and I'm beginning to feel a little warm and fuzzy."

"Oh, for fuck's sake, Nate!" Back on camera, I did my best not to laugh. "Good God. What if Iris was beside me?"

"Is she beside you?" He laughed, causing an unfamiliar ache in my chest.

My reply, "No. We're all alone," came out all deep and raspy. Nate's breathing caught, and I couldn't blame him. Hell, even I thought I sounded sexy.

"Well, there's nothing to worry about, then, right?" A throaty chuckle shook his shoulders, and a lock of damp hair that had been swept back off his face roguishly fell into his eyes. It was obscenely hot. "So, leaving the boob question for later, how is my number-one girl doing?"

For several heartbeats, I just stared at the screen. At the rogue curl being all sexy. Unable to think, breathe, or speak. "Gidge, you still there? Has the internet dropped out, or are you that cold you've frozen? I asked how my number-one girl is?"

Shit! What am I doing? Yes. Back to Iris. "She's perfect, Nate. Curled up—I mean, tucked up in bed, sound asleep after watching *Camp Rock* and laughing at their hair." *Stop talking about hair.*

"Evie, I…" He paused, scratched at his rather tasty-looking collarbone, and huffed out an extended, frustrated sigh. "That's good to hear."

There was an aftertaste of disappointment to his tone. One I had selfishly held no desire to delve into because I was too fearful of the answer. Clearly, he was equally hesitant to elaborate.

So, keen to avoid further eye-to-eye contact, I flipped the camera and began scanning my surroundings. First, the gardenia-lined front path, then the immaculately maintained dirt road leading not only to Jocelyn's land but to the Hudson River. There, I began to narrate my trek. "It's stunning here. You'd love it, Natey. The weather is cooler here than in the city. Next week is the first of fall, so the colors are changing. Every leaf on every tree is a different shade of orange, brown, or red, and they fall from the heavens like snow each time the wind blows. It's like walking on a crunchy—whoop!"

Bang! A slippery pile of the very leaves I'd just complimented sent me and my phone dropping onto the gravel. Sheer embarrassment had me bouncing up to my feet in seconds, but the phone's landing position meant Nate would have seen the whole thing.

"Evie! Evie, are you okay? What happened?" His genuine concern was definitely mixed with restrained laughter.

"Shit! Yep, yep, sorry! I skidded on some leaves and fell flat on my ass." As elegantly as possible, I removed the slimy greenery sitting on my cheek and carried on as though nothing had happened. "As I said, it's like walking on a crunchy, sometimes slippery, carpet."

"Gidge…are you limping?" His face may not have been visible, but I could predict his expression. Brows furrowed. Lips skewed to the right.

Yes.

"Nah, I'm all good."

"Evie. I can tell you are by the jolting of the phone. Your steps are all wonky. Just go back home. We can talk while you ice your foot."

"Nope. That's completely unnecessary."

Sure, my ankle was swelling at an alarming rate, and the dull ache of an impending ass bruise was disturbing. Going home *was* the smart thing to do, but then again, little of my recent behavior inferred a Mensa-level IQ.

Even though I was not at my intellectual peak, I knew enough to know that at home, I had no excuse to remain off camera, and I was neither ready nor capable of facing *that* man with *the* foreign feelings bubbling beneath the surface.

So, I did what I did best. I acted like a defensive cow.

"Nathaniel. You seem to think I can't look after myself, but I assure you I can. I'm fine. Now, do you want to talk and look at the prettiness, or do you want to hang up?"

"Prettiness, please… Oh, and Evie, I know you can look after yourself. You're incredible. You can do anything you want once you set your mind to it."

Predictably, this compliment was handled by snorting and stubbornly continuing on my path. Occasionally, I stole a brief glance at the screen and was rewarded with the image of Nate's lovely pink lips. I hated to admit it, but when combined with his words of praise, the sight had a voodoo- morphine-like effect on the pain shooting up my leg. I felt numbed by a warm and fuzzy feeling of contentment…and a smidge of swooning.

By the time I made it to the block of land, I was a sweaty, huffing and puffing mess, ready to jump through the screen and join him in bed—purely for rest, of course.

"City life is making you soft, Eves. You would have been able to run up that hill with a board under your arm in the old days."

"Pfftt, only because you, Shelby, and Finn would have been throwing crap at me. There was never any respect for the elders with you lot."

"You're hardly an elder, Lil Gidge. What is it, like, three and a bit years? Besides, you always looked younger than we did."

"Yeah, because I was the smallest."

Nate waited a beat before replying, "No, not just that. I think it's because you have that soft, glowy, dewy skin that looks like you've just stepped from a photo shoot, even when you've been mucking out the pig pen. You're beautiful, Gidge. "

"And you're full of shit. You've confused me with Shelby, your *real* sister, and not me, your sister-type friend.

"Uhh, number one, you are most definitely not my sister-type anything. And two, I have spent hours watching you throughout my life, Evie Austen, and trust me, my sister was never on my mind."

I was overcome with a sudden burst of confidence. "Oh, really? What was on your mind, then, Nathaniel Myers?"

"Do you really want to know?"

"Yes. I do. Tell me what you think when you look at me. And be nice. I'm tired and possibly injured."

After mumbling under his breath for a while, the deep, sexy tone was back. "Well. Alright then. But I need your eyes on me. C'mon. Spin that camera around and let me see you."

"No, Nate. I'm all red and sweaty. I look disgusting."

"Impossible. You have never looked disgusting once in your life. Even that day you fell off Finn's horse, Bluey, and had a smashed lip and black eye, you were still the prettiest girl I had ever seen."

"Geez, Nate. You sure know how to give a girl head—a head! Shit! A big head!" Nate's laughter bounced off the trees with vigor. I'm surprised they remained standing. "Can we please just forget I said that? Please?"

"Never. But also, maybe. Only if you flip that bloody camera and let me see you."

"Nate."

"EEEEEvie."

The stalemate lasted until I found a comfy log overlooking the river to rest on. There, I breathed deeply, brought myself back to some semblance of calm horniness, and replied, "Fine. I will. But only because you have your shirt off."

"Whoaaaaa! Are you flirting with me, Lil Gidget?"

Yes.

"No, I am trying to distract you by fluffing your massive ego." After one final breath, I said a silent prayer—please, God, let me look okay—and flipped the camera. Nate's slow exhale and dazzling smile melted my heart and undies. I was a puddle. Much like a frisky puppy, he wriggled side to side excitedly, causing the white sheet that covered his junk to slip lower over his hips, exposing the waistband of his underwear. It did nothing for my sweating. "There she is. There's my grumpy one."

"What, no fluffing-massive-things jokes? I'm rather disappointed, Nathaniel."

"Well, I'm rather occupied by your super-cute braids. They're a major kink of mine, by the way. Same with the beanie. It's totally hot, Gidge. You look like a sexy snow bunny."

Again, I resorted to smarminess. "Ugh. You're such a freak."

"Oh, Gidge, you have no idea."

This level of sexy flirting was too much. My body temperature reached an all-time high, and the sweat dripping down my back was enough to replenish the river should there be a drought. I tried to steer us to safer waters and started prattling on about Iris and school, my new job—minus HotBoss teasing. It wasn't a conscious decision to do so. Christian just didn't enter my mind.

Nate asked how the surf off the coast of Long Island was and, of course, what my surroundings here at Tarrytown were like. All of which I was happy to report, especially about Tarrytown.

"There aren't a lot of places we've been since moving here that I could picture myself living permanently, but this town, this river and piece of land, is one of them. There's something so familiar yet so completely foreign about it. I'd never been here before, I don't know its peaks and valleys intimately, but I had already kind of missed it. Know what I mean?"

It took a second, but the look of pure desire on Nate's face, the roughness of his voice, and the meaning behind the words he spoke were worth the wait. "Yeah. Yeah, I do, Gidge. I know exactly what you mean."

I couldn't look away from his hunger.

From his heat.

We were thousands of miles apart. But I could feel flames licking every inch of my quivering flesh.

His best friend's sister.

My brother's best friend.

Eye-fucking.

That was it. I was going to do it.

"Nate."

"Yes, Evie."

"Can I ask you something?"

"You know you can ask me anything, Evie."

"Are you interested in…umm…"

"In what? Ask me, Evie. Am I interested in what?"

"Are you interested in…" A familiar dread settled over me like a weighted blanket, and I paused, just for a moment. Two heavy breaths were enough to remind me who I was, who he was, and what we should never be. "Me…and Iris, baking?

I was certain his sigh and extended mumbling could be heard on the neighboring farm. "Baking?

"Yeah, baking. Iris and I are making a cake when I get back, and maybe we can Facetime then too so you can see your number-one girl."

Nate's gorgeous face was covered by his hand, rubbing it in what appeared to be frustration, so his words were muffled, but I'm pretty sure I heard him say something like, "Fucking jeepers, help me. "Are you sure that's all you wanted to ask me, Gidge?"

"Yep! Positive. One hundred and ten percent sure…why? Did you think I was going to ask you something else?

"Honestly? Yeah, I did for a second, and it made me really happy.

"It did?"

"Yep. Do you want to know what I thought you were going to ask? And even more importantly, do you want to know how I would have answered?"

I did. I really, really did. But I couldn't. Not yet. Not now. So, I lied.

"Oh, Iris is calling me, Nate. I better go. Talk later?"

Graciously, Nate let the fact that Iris was not with me, that she was likely still tucked up in bed, and that I was a terrible liar, all slide. He couldn't conceal his emotion so easily. His face was the love child of crushed, confused, and pissed.

"Of course. Sure thing. Call me when you start baking. Oh, and Aoife… Just so you know, when I call or message and ask about my number-one girl…as much as I adore her, I'm not asking about Iris. I'm asking about you."

Chapter 9

Evie

EVER MET A PANIC CHUCKER? DO YOU EVEN know what a panic chuck is? How about just a chuck?

A chuck is a vomit, a barf, a puke, a spew, a hurl. A panic chuck is when you get yourself so worked up, ridiculously and absolutely riddled with worry, that you chuck. A panic chucker is someone who has chosen or had this lifestyle thrust upon them.

I am the latter. I am a regular panic chucker, not by choice.

See, on the outside, I could come across as a tiny bit grumpy…crabby…maybe even icy. And to be honest, I liked that and worked hard to push that image.

I felt it kept me safe from those clowns I liked to call the general public, and I needed that because, despite the crispy shell, I had a soft, creamy, chocolatey center. I was an absolute nut job who worried excessively over what people did, thought, and said about me.

The grumpiness was just basic math. The fewer people around me, the less I had to worry, and the less I was inclined to chuck.

After ending the call, the one where I learned *I* was the number-one girl Nate religiously checked on, I—at the risk of sounding super

Aussie—fertilized that plot of land more than a year's supply of hand-tossed, nutrient-rich compost ever could.

That's right. Chucked my freaking guts up. I'd like to say I felt better afterward. That it was cleansing or cathartic. But that would have been a damn lie.

I felt worse. Ten times worse.

I smelled worse too. Especially when trudging back to the house with vomit-soaked shoes. You'd think I would have developed better aim after years of this, but no.

Back at our temporary home, I partook in a final little retch beneath the glorious cover of a maple tree, then ventured inside, hoping to God I could make it to the bathroom undetected.

I did not.

Jocelyn sprang out from behind a door, but I didn't slow. "Evie Austen, stop right there."

"Can't stop. Slipped in cow poop. Need a shower."

"Don't lie to me, girl. We may be in the countryside, but there are no cows within cooee of here. You've been vomiting, haven't you?"

My aunt's freaky magic-psychic shit freaked me out. "How in the hell did you—"

"I saw you under the tree."

"Oh."

"Yes, oh. Now. Tell me what's wrong."

I cringed, my nausea rapidly rising again. "I will, Jocie, I promise. But can I take a shower first? I smell like shit." To demonstrate, I sniffed my shirt and screwed my face in disgust.

I really did reek.

"Fine, but as soon as you're dressed, you come back here and tell me what incited the chucky chucks."

We sat on opposite sides of the table. Two cups of coffee—one smelling suspiciously like it may have been Irished up a little— and a plate of local pastries sat between us. It was Aunt Jocelyn's go-to intimidation technique: ply the victim with warm drinks and sweet, empty carbs.

"So, Finn teased you about Nathaniel, and you've *finally* seen what was blatantly obvious for the last ten or so years."

"Blatantly obvious? Could we really call it blatant if I never caught on?"

"Ha!" With a dramatic flair that only a wealthy widower or gay cabaret star could pull off, Jocelyn laughed and swigged her *juice.* "I took Iris to North Belongil Beach once, and a perfect stranger asked me when you two were getting together. I assure you, my dear, it was most definitely clear to probably everyone in Byron."

"Except for—"

Jocelyn bopped me on the nose. "Except for you."

After downing her drink, she nibbled at the chocolate croissant she seemed to enjoy as much as she did my squirming, then stood. "So, what will you do about it?" she asked, making her way to the coffee pot.

I couldn't respond immediately and not only because I feared over-sharing. Her coffee making was quite distracting. She filled her cup, unabashedly reached into an overhead cupboard, felt around, and found her bottle of Laphroaig, then added a good nip or three. Bear in mind it was a little before nine am.

"Nothing," I eventually replied as she took her first sip and sighed. "That's what I'm doing about it. Even if I wanted something to happen—which I don't—and he was stupid enough to like me like everyone says he does, Nate lives on the other side of the world. He's my brother's bestie *and* Iris's uncle. Not to mention, he's far too young for me."

The coffee, and the whiskey that was back in her hand, hit the floor. "Evie Mary Austen! You take that back right now, or I will wash your mouth out with soap for that blasphemy! Nate is three years younger than you, for heaven's sake. The last man I took as a lover in France was close to thirteen years my junior."

"Eww." I winced. "I know, but it's kind of gross, isn't it?"

By the look on her face, you'd have thought I was asking for her best puppy-baking recipes. "No, it's not gross. It's delicious, just like livier—no wait, Luc it was. No one would think anything of it if I were a man. The real problem here is that you like Nate…a lot. You're scared and looking for excuses."

"Pftt." I waved her off, but she kept right on spilling facts.

"Don't, 'Pfftt,' me. The only legitimate concern I can see is the distance, but even that's not insurmountable if you really care for each other. You could go home. Nate could come here. Anything is possible if you want it badly enough. Now, stop your sulking and help this old cougar clean up her whiskey."

When I made my way to her side, picked up and passed her the bottle, she grabbed my hand, pressed it firmly to her cheek, and held it there. "You are such a beauty, Evie, both inside and out, and just like this thing with Nate, you seem to be the only one not to see it. I'm so proud of you for stepping out and taking the job at the dance school. Now you need to take that extra step and do something for yourself in the love department too."

"Shit! The dance school. I left that bit out."

"What bit?"

"Well, you know Christian, the director?"

"The gorgeous one with the thighs? I'm disappointed you'd even ask." She smirked, nudging me with her elbow and sending me sideways to the floor.

"Well, he kind of…likes me, I think. We went out for coffee, and it was…nice. And he smelled amazing and was all flirty and attentive and touched my thigh and kissed my cheek, and then he said he wanted to get to know me better." I took a breath, then kept right on rambling. "I'm supposed to go with him again on Tuesday after class. I was excited, but now all I can think of is Nate, and…oh my God! Is that slutty? Am I being a slut to go out with one guy but think of another?"

Chunks rose in my throat, and I fought desperately to control them and my breathing.

"Excuse my French, but for fuck's sake, Evie! How did you not tell me any of this, and how the hell does it make you slutty? What is a slut anyway? I hate that term."

"I know it's not nice." I puffed out a breath, then skewed my lips. "But can we agree that Nate's a bit of a slut?"

"Hmm, yes, that is true. But still. You're not. In fact, if things with your... experiences..." She made an O with her left index finger and thumb then repeatedly thrust her right finger inside it. Mature. "...remain the unaltered from the last time we spoke of them, you know full well you're not. As far as I'm concerned, you are dating neither of these men, and even if you were, you have made no oaths of allegiance. You can go out for coffee, drinks, dancing, or have full, fabulous sex in Central Park if you want to. It's no one's business but yours. The feelings you have for Nate need to be explored, but there is no harm in spending some time exploring with Christian. You're young and sexy. He's young and sexy. I say go for it."

I eyed my aunt with pride and a touch of suspicion. "How did you get so cool, old lady?"

"Hey, knock it off. I get enough of the old lady stuff from your brother." Jocelyn smiled and attempted to help me off the floor, but instead, she lost her footing in the whiskey puddle, slipped, and rolled around beside me. The almost empty bottle laid between us until she swooped and swigged straight from the neck. "It's five o'clock somewhere. Cheers, darling."

"Hell, it's ten in Byron." I stole the bottle and took a good long drink. "To not being sluts!"

The rest of our mini break passed with a little more day-drinking, a lot more brunching, and an exorbitant amount of shopping on Tarrytown's beautiful Main Street. After squeezing in some hiking, a trip to a day spa, and more shopping on the way home, I was exhausted. But by the time Tuesday rolled around and I was back at work, I'd also come to some kind of solution for my two-man crisis.

As Jocie had said, despite my recent romantic awakening and subsequent piqued interest in Nate, he was not here. I was young, single, and could go out with whomever I chose. Should that be

Christian, or the entire starting lineup of the New York Giants, so be it.

So yes, it was settled. I was heading out for coffee with HotBoss despite the sporadic thoughts of being Nate's favorite girl and fantasizing about him and those abs of his the entire previous night… and morning—alright, constantly.

The time lost didn't mean anything. Fantasies did not equal feelings.

As my students emptied out of my morning class into the waiting arms of their doting parents, Christian was swaggering in, wearing a white tank and gray sweats that gave a detailed outline of EVERYTHING he was packing.

Was "Pony" by Ginuwine playing out loud or just in my head? Taking my hand, he flashed his million-dollar smile and kissed my knuckles. It was a move I would mock senselessly had anyone else tried it—well, almost anyone.

"Wow, Evie. You really are great with those kids. They love you."

"I love them too. It's weird how attached I feel already."

Moving with the masculine grace you would expect from a male dancer, HotBoss slid behind me, placed his free hand on the small of my back, and dipped me till my hair brushed against the floor.

"I know the feeling."

"Oh my God! Are you for real?" I swooned as he returned me to an upright position.

"I sure am. Let's get out of here, Princess."

Again, from anyone else but him, I would have been all over that. But somehow, Christian did make me feel like a real lady. A Princess, even.

❀

"Moder Fucker!"

A collective gasp echoed through the air.

Mothers covered their children's ears.

Old grannies tutted and shook their heads, and a nearby priest stood and began counting his rosaries as he rushed out the door.

All of this transpired as I crouched on the floor of the cute coffee shop Christian had brought me to.

Curious as to why I was on the floor? Easy. I was picking up the shattered remnants of the mug I'd dropped while nursing what felt like a third-degree burn on the roof of my mouth.

Things had gone well to that point. We'd been so busy laughing and chatting that an hour had passed before we ordered. Christian had briefly touched my thigh. Held my hand. Swept his thumb over my knuckles. And it was…lovely. But now, I could barely speak, feared tongue amputation, and Christian was beside me on the floor, trying hard not to laugh and helping clean my mess.

"Why tho hot?"

"Are you trying to ask why the coffee was so hot?"

"Yes! I'm twying to tawlk. Stop lauwfing."

"I'm trying, I promise. You just sound so cute."

I didn't feel cute and was about to express that when a pair of suspiciously expensive Gucci loafers approached and stopped before me. "Excuse me, Miss. We simply cannot tolerate that language in our establishment, and I must ask you to leave."

I stuck my head out from beneath the table and looked Mr. Gucci in the eye. "Awe, you for weal? You dust burned my mowf, and you want me to weave? I should zoo you!"

Gucci screwed up his face like the confused Chihuahua his loafers were probably made from. "You should what? Zoo me?"

"Noo. Not zoo you. Zoo you. You know, in court…Judge Jewdy…zoo you."

"I think she means to sue you." Christian stood and laughed again, but it was awkward and forced, and it pissed me off. "Sorry about the mess. We will just clean it up and leave."

What?

"No way!" I dropped the collection of cup bits from my hand and let it return to the floor. "Dat coffee was too hot. I'm not cweaning anything." After trying to stand and slipping on the foamy latte-covered floor, I decided it was safer to stay low and just crawl to the door. "Wet's go, Cwistian."

After stuttering, he eventually placed the broken shards on

the table and followed. "I am really sorry for the mess, guys." I felt, rather than saw, his embarrassment, and it wasn't surprising. He'd brought me to his favorite coffee shop. One he'd been coming to for years. Heck, it was likely I was still in school when he first found it.

Humble apologies were coming but paused on my lips when he continued. "Here, take this." I watched over my shoulder as he slipped the manager a twenty. "And please, don't be offended. She's from Australia."

She's from Australia? Like it's a disease?

The manager may not have been offended, but I bloody was. He deserved a mouthful. I wanted to give him that mouthful, but my mouth was full of blisters—oh, and he was my boss...my not so HotBoss.

The jingling little brass bell hanging above the door, the one I found so quaint when we arrived, annoyed the shit out of me as I departed. I stormed down Sixth Avenue, and an entire city block passed before anything other than a grunt or tut passed between us. It was Christian who broke the silence, and I really preferred he hadn't.

"Why did you have to make a scene, Evie? We should have cleaned up the mess. You were kind of rude."

"Wude? I was dwying to clean and would have if da guy—"

"Todd," Christian declared. "His name is Todd."

"Well, I would have if Dodd had apowogized. Listen do me, Cwistian! Dis is cuwte on Iwis, but nod on me. Da coffee was doo hawt. Whad? Did dey brew it on da sun?"

Another half block passed in silence. "Anyway, why did you give him money, apowogize, and say I was Austrawiawn, like it's a condition I need to be vwaccinated forw?

"I didn't mean it like that. It's just you may be slightly less cultured than us—no, not cultured. Wrong choice of words. I mean, less sophisticated—shit, no. I mean—"

"Don'd wowwy, Cwistian. I know exactwy what you mean."

I may have been a good foot shorter than Not-So-HotBoss, but I outpaced him for the rest of the way to the studio, and after exchanging grunted farewells, he slammed his way into his office, and I marched my still-soggy, latte-covered ass back into my classroom for what turned out to be a very long forty-five-minute class.

It was my first-time teaching in a foul mood, and it was pretty remarkable how those little faces and voices that had been so cute and sweet last time were now hideous and shrill…at least for the first half, anyway. By the time the teething gel one of the moms gave me kicked in, we'd had some fun with hula hoops, practiced putting on our slippers, and sang "I'm a Little Teapot," and my mood had shifted significantly. So much so that I began to wonder if I owed Christian an apology.

Mum always stressed the importance of never leaving things on a sour note, and here, we were firmly in sour-grape territory. I couldn't leave things the way they were.

As the last song played, I was ready to beg for forgiveness. He was still in class though. So, I ducked into his office, left him a sappy note, and headed off.

Since the lower half of my body reeked of coffee, and I had an hour or two to kill before picking up Iris, I decided a bath was in order…and maybe a sneaky glass of wine. As bubbles percolated around my boobs and my bath bomb dissolved in *interesting* places, I perused the Gram and *accidentally* landed on Christian's profile.

As expected, it was devastatingly beautiful. HotBoss—yes, wine had elevated him back to pre-coffee-drama status—was one of those people that had a motif, a vibe. Whatever the wanky word was for it, he had it. Shot after shot of glamorous people, poses, and parties burned into my retinas as I swiped. Half-dressed former dance partners, with legs longer than me, draped around and, in more cases than I would like to have seen, kissed him.

What the hell did this guy want with me? An uncultured Aussie shortass with as much glamour as Oscar the Grouch, but with less sex appeal. Christian could have his pick of these chicks and, by the looks of it, had.

Before my inferiority complex had me sinking to the bottom of the bath, I decided to scroll a little closer to home.

Finn's profile took all of two seconds to cover. Much like me, the guy was a social media geriatric and hadn't posted anything in months. As I read his Christmas greeting three years ago, a new story popped up on the profile I'd been pretending not to see—Nate's. Since I didn't care for him at all, I clicked immediately, and my eyes nearly popped from my head. Someone had taken his photo as he tossed a freshly shorn fleece onto the sorting table.

His arms were above his head, and his possibly once-white, now murky-brown t-shirt was sitting high, exposing his bare, air-brushed-looking stomach.

Damn, had the water temp spontaneously surged?

"Evie, darling. Are you home?"

Shit! Water splashed onto the floor as I quickly tried to right myself. "In the bath, Jocie!"

The door opened enough for my aunt to stick her nose in—literally and figuratively.

"How was the coffee date?"

"It wasn't a date. And it was awful. Hence the bath and wine. How was your day?"

"Excellent. I'm rich, single, and in New York. How could it not be?"

"Fair point, old lady."

"Okay. Stop insulting me and tell me what happened on your non-date? Did he kiss you? Gasp! Was it bad? Did he smell like fish and have a slimy tongue to match?"

I almost slipped back under the water. "What the hell, Jocie!"

Her nose bobbed up and down with laughter. "So, did he kiss you or not?"

"Not," I snapped.

"You wanted him to kiss you, but he didn't? Ouch."

"Nope, not that either."

"Just bloody tell me what was so awful, then?"

"Ughh."

Without giving her something, I wasn't getting out of that tub in the foreseeable future, so I divulged it all. The lovely walk we had taken to the coffee shop, how he walked so close beside me I almost tripped on his huge feet, and that our fingers had brushed against the other's so deliciously that a little zip of undefinable energy rushed through me each time. "He was charming, sweet, and attentive, and then I ruined it—or Todd and his stupid coffee did."

Jocelyn responded with hmms and uh-huhs as I described my abhorrent, mother-cursing behavior and the subsequent walk of shame back to the studio. According to my aunt, I wasn't so out of line.

"I would have been angry. He should have defended you, not chastised you."

"Right!" I squealed, jumping to my feet and almost falling straight back on my ass." At first, I thought that too, but I've guilted myself into thinking I was the one in the wrong. I know how bristly I can be."

"Nope. I'm Team Evie all the way. I get that he is a regular there, and the swearing may have been jolting, but that should have made him all the more confident in coming to your aid."

Climbing from the bath, I wrapped a towel around myself and opened the door. "You are biased, though, and can I trust your opinion?"

"Of course you can. You know how brutally honest I am. Remember your last haircut?"

A flashback of the epic failure that was my attempt to rock Taylor Swift bangs flashed before my eyes. "How could I forget?" I muttered.

I moved to exit the bathroom, but she blocked me. "Why don't you seek another opinion. Nate's, for example."

"Jeepers, Jocie. Do you think I would trust Nate if I doubted your independence? Besides, I don't want to tell him." Again, I tried to brush past her, and again I was blocked.

"Why not, Evie?"

"Are you going to let me pass, or do I have to knock you down? 'Cause you know I will."

"Answer the question, and then you're free to go."

"No!"

"We may as well sit on the floor and wait it out, then. I am not moving." We both dropped to the floor and stubbornly stared at each other. I'm sad to say this was not the first time we've stooped to this level. It was stupid, but Jocelyn and I had had many sit-in-style arguments over the years. Our hereditary fiery constitutions meant neither wanted to let the other win.

Goosebumps covered my quivering flesh as we entered the fifth minute of silence. The warm serenity of the bath was a mere memory. I was freezing my ass off and beginning to panic. I had to collect Iris from school. My mental calculations told me I had about fifteen minutes to play with. I just had to hold on.

Jocie's eyes danced with mischief. She and the warm, fluffy, woolen sweater she wore could see and were delighted by my shivering. She could read my thoughts, too, just as I could hers. But I remained silent.

Time moved slowly when you were sitting on cold tiles.

"Goddamn you, woman! I don't want to ask Nate because I like him, and I'm his number-one girl, and I don't want him to know I went out with Christian again…or what a fucking—"

"Language, Evie."

"Sorry, what a bloody loser I am. There. Are you happy?" I threw a toddler-like tantrum as I got to my feet while my near seventy-year-old aunt celebrated her childish victory by dancing while still on her bum. Her age and position soon came back to haunt her.

"Shit. Help me the fuck up, darling."

"Hey! Language!"

"Sorry, sorry!" Jocie held up her hand in both apology and for assistance. I grabbed it, pulled her to her feet, and she pulled me into a vise-like hug. "We must find a new way to solve our feuds, Evie. I'm getting too old for this shi—rubbish."

Chapter 10

I'D NOT HEARD A PEEP FROM EVIE SINCE BLABBING that *she* was my number-one girl, not Iris. No single email, text, or phone call had come my way in weeks. I was sure she'd been flirting with me, but clearly, I'd read things wrong. The notion of us together was so sickening, perhaps even horrifying, that she'd been scared off. Maybe I just pushed too hard, too fast. *DO NOT think about Evie and pushing hard and fast.*

Fortunately, I had a shapely, five-foot-seven, brunette distraction.

Polly was hot, smelled like sin, and was insatiable—coming to visit, then coming on my fingers, tongue, or cock almost every night. Yesterday, she took us into daylight hours and popped into the shearing shed for a quickie behind the bailer. Bending her over, taking her hard and fast from behind, I smacked her ass and took pleasure in how her face pressed against the corrugated iron as she screamed my name and begged me to break her. So loud were her cries that we were almost busted by Gus, the cook who ventured away from his beef stew to see what all the fuss was.

Was I embarrassed to say the risk factor made it even hotter? Not nearly as much as I should have been.

My current distraction was her apparent

love of riding me reverse cowgirl. I must say, it was a spectacular view, and she was outstanding in the saddle.

"Pull my hair, baby, pull it hard!"

"Fuck, Polly!"

As she demanded, her long, chocolate ponytail was wrapped around my wrist. With each tug, her back further arched, she screamed to the heavens, and after getting excited and almost tearing the girl's hair out, we came together in a flurry of expletives.

Polly continued to roll her hips over mine as she floated back to earth before dismounting, kindly disposing of the condom, then tucking in beside me.

Cuddling after sex had always been a big no-no for me. Honestly, I had no idea how to hold her or why touching her so intimately suddenly felt so foreign. A twinge of guilt shuddered over me when her cheek caressed my nipple. Seconds earlier, she was riding me into oblivion, and I was more than okay with that. After all, uncomplicated sex that helped me to stop thinking about Evie was at the core of my plan. But the way she clung to me was… felt…like more. Real girlfriend-boyfriend more.

But that's what I wanted, right? At least I thought that's what I wanted… I think… Right?

I was confusing myself. Polly, playing with the three strands of chest hair I proudly sported, then tracing the small tattoo on my left pec, didn't help. "Why a daisy?"

"What?" I tried to sit up, but she beat me, positioning herself so those beautiful tits fell directly in and brushed my face. What can I say? The girl knew how to get my attention. "Your tatt. Why did you choose a little daisy? Seems a bit feminine for a rough and tumble shearer."

"Umm… I, umm… I think I was drunk. Can't really remember. Want a drink?"

She shook then lowered her head, took my right nipple into her mouth and bit down. "Hmm, you taste good, but I smell bullshit. Are you sure that *wee* flower has nothing to do with a *wee* dancing, daisy-loving lass with blonde curls?"

"Pfft. I don't know what you're talking about." Using more force than on my previous attempt, I again tried to rise. But Polly was too quick, swinging her leg over and straddling my hips, then grabbing my hands and holding them above my head. I hated how good it felt to my treacherous body. "Let me up, Polly, I want to go home."

"I know you do. But I don't want you to…and I always get what I want." I turned my head to dodge her incoming kiss, but I was rapidly learning Polly was no quitter. My lips may have been out of play, but my neck was ripe for the picking. She traced over my Adam's apple with her nose, nipped the skin just above my collarbone, then sucked my flesh like a lollipop.

Like her, it was undeniably sexy, but I couldn't give in…again.

I bit my lip, thought of Nanna, and willed my body not to react. When I succeeded, and Polly realized her attempts were falling flat, she changed tactics. Sucking became soft, languid caresses of tongue. Her touch became gentle. She released my hands and nuzzled into the crook of my neck with a sensual hum. "You're so warm, Natey."

Damn. It worked.

I gave in and rested my chin in her mess of hair.

"Do you want to go do something this weekend?" she asked. "I thought we could go to the farmer's market, then see a movie?"

"The market? A movie? The weekend? This weekend? I don't know what you mean."

"For fuck's sake, Nate, am I speaking a different language? Yes. The weekend. Not the singer, but those days that are called Saturday and Sunday? I have them both off and thought it would be fun to see each other with some clothes on." My body stiffened beneath her—and not in the way I was used to. "I can feel you tensing, Nate. Don't you want to spend time with me?"

Well…

"No, it's not that. Not at all. It's just… I didn't think we were there yet."

French-polished nails traced my nipple, inciting a flush of

goosebumps to break out over my body. "And where exactly is *there*, Nate?"

"Umm, well. Here…you know, sleeping over, seeing each other daily, shopping at markets, cooking. You know, couple stuff. "

Neck kisses with tiny traces of tongue resumed, "And that frightens you? Doing couple stuff?

This was not. Whatever she was doing felt really good. Too good. "Yeah, kinda. I've never really done it before."

"Well, I like trying new things, and I want to try lots of things with you. In fact," she whispered, licking the outer lobe of my ear, then sticking her tongue inside, "I have a whole box of new things I'd like to try hidden under my bed."

"Huh, you don't say."

Grinding commenced. "I do say. So how about it? We go to the market, catch a movie, and then…then you can spend the night at my place with your fingers, and whatever else you like, balls deep in my box."

Gulp.

She hovered above me, her dark hair framing her fucking insane breasts. Hips began rolling as she bent down, biting my nipple—something she really seemed to have a thing for—then traveling her tongue down my stomach before sighing my name and sucking the tip of my cock into her mouth.

"New things sound fun, Polly."

"They are, baby." She sighed between sloppy licks. "You'll discover and plunder so much that by the time we're done, you'll talk like a pirate and call me Captain."

This girl and her mouth will be the death of me. I gripped her head like I knew she liked, then pushed her deeper, which I liked. "I've said it before, and I'll say it again. Fuck, Polly!"

I thrust inside her again and again, losing myself in pleasure… until it happened. Just as I hit the back of her throat, as she grunted and gagged, a vision of blonde curls, a cute, freckled nose and gorgeous blue eyes hit me. "Evie."

We both froze. Polly only for a second before taking me deeply again, then popping off to speak. "You can dream of her, Nate, but remember, Evie has moved on. She's gone. And even if she wasn't…she could never make you feel as good as I can."

I felt sick to my stomach saying another woman's name at such a moment, but also getting the best head of my life. It was a right conundrum, and it really shouldn't have been. *What kind of asshole am I?*

Unable to see, think, or lie straight, I wriggled and pulsed beneath her, not wanting it to feel as good as it did—and man, did it feel good. *Fuck, has she taken a class in blow jobs or something?* The woman had me all kinds of messed up and coming in an embarrassingly short time.

Still on her knees between my legs, her lips plump, red, and swollen, she looked up at me through her curtain of hair, all innocence and fire. "You know, I think we should be a couple, Natey. So, you'll come to the market with me and stay the night too. Okay?"

I began to sit up, but she stopped me by pressing one last kiss to my dick, before pushing me onto my back with just her little finger. "Anything, Pol. After that, I'll do and give you anything."

This chick had me by the balls.

I. Was. Fucked.

❦

As dilemmas and personal crises go, mine was a good one. I wasn't facing a life-or-death situation, nor was I at risk of physical injuries, except maybe sex-induced physical exhaustion. No, mine was a purely self-induced, moral predicament.

Evie Austen, the girl I had wanted for most of my life, was calling my phone. Polly Hart, the girl who had fucked me more than any woman had ever fucked me, and had post-coitally talked me into a relationship, stood before me, holding an eggplant, stroking it seductively as she questioned me over lasagna. "Meat or vegetarian?"

Droplets of rain appeared on my screen as I looked at her

and then returned to my phone. "Which one, Nate? It's not a difficult question."

The ringing ceased, and my heart restarted. "Meat. Eggplant lasagna tastes like dirt."

Polly smiled and slid to my side. "I'm quite fond of eggplant. Especially when it's nice and firm." With no regard for the crowded market or the fact that anyone walking by could see what she was doing, she palmed my cock and gave it a firm squeeze. "This one's a great size. Not quite firm enough...but there's definite potential." Giggling, she leaned in for a kiss but was interrupted when my phone rang again.

Damn. I really wished I hadn't changed my ringtone to "Suck it and See" by the Arctic Monkeys.

"Aren't you going to get it?" Polly quizzed with a raised brow. "Seems someone is desperate to talk to you." With a clear view of the screen, she knew exactly who the *someone was.*

"Uhh, yeah." I nodded, then hesitantly walked away. Unfortunately, even with a sky full of clouds, my second shadow followed. "Hi, umm, Gidge. Hey."

This is not uncomfortable at all.

"Nate. Hi. How are you? I haven't heard from you all week and wanted to make sure you were okay."

God, she sounded so happy and—if I wasn't mistaken—like she'd missed me. Had I been on her mind like she was mine? I was desperate to ask, but I couldn't do it with the eggplant queen beside me, so as always, I let the question slide. "Yeah, I'm fine, Eves. I've just been busy finishing the shearing, the last harvest, and getting everything cleaned and packed up. It's my first year without Dad, and the old coot did more work than I realized. How are you? How's my number-one girl?"

"Your number-one girl is pretty good, thank you. But honestly, I've gotten myself into a bit of a pickle and could use some advice."

My heart leapt into my mouth. "You're calling me for advice? Wow. I'm honored, little one. Shoot. The great one is all yours."

She sucked in a deep breath, then released a string of words that broke—no, pulverized—my heart. "Well, it's about a guy." *Yup. I'm dead.* "My boss, Christian. Remember I told you about him. HotBoss?"

I tried to remain chill. Indifferent. "Uhh, the dancer? Vaguely. I mean, it's hard to forget a grown man that wears tights for a living."

"I'm ignoring that last bit, but yes, he is a dancer. A dancer who asked me on a date…and not for coffee this time. A proper one…in a restaurant…in Soho! What should I do? Should I go?"

Right then and there, it became clear…God truly hated me. The heavens opened, sheets of rain pelted into my skin, but I couldn't move. Evie Austen was asking me for guy advice as Polly stood beside me, practically performing fellatio on an eggplant while looking like she could win a wet t-shirt competition.

I had no idea what to do or say, and my delayed reaction gave Polly time to swoop. "Hi, Evie! It's me, Polly. Have fun on your date. I know I am!" Seemingly happy with herself, she trotted off to take shelter and started feeling up some zucchini.

A soft whimper carried Evie's pain across oceans and time zones and drew my focus back to where it belonged. "Nate. Are… are you walking in the rain while on a date with Polly Hart? My Polly?"

"No. God, no, I mean it is raining, and we were walking. But we're just hanging out and shopping for ingredients for dinner. Then later we might go out for a movie and…"

"That sounds an awful lot like a date, Nathaniel. Didn't she drive you home from the pub a couple of weeks ago too? Is this the first time you two have hung out together since?"

A metaphorical neon sign flashed before my eyes: *Lie. Lie. Lie.* But because I was a true moron, I didn't. "No. No, it's not, Gidget. We are, I guess, kind of dating…I think."

"Oh."

"Yeah. It's all very new and not serio—"

"But you never date anyone. You're a slut."

As true as it was, I couldn't help but take offense. "Geez. For some reason, that sounded an awful lot like judgment, Evie.

Ignoring me all week after…well, after what I told you in our last conversation made it pretty clear that you don't give a shit about me or my feelings. So, I'm struggling to see where you get the right to have any opinions about my love life."

"Your love life!" she scoffed. "Nate, you don't have a love life. You have a sex life. A very active one at that. Free and easy one-night stands and three-thingies with hot shearers and no complications. They're more your scene, aren't they?"

"What can I say, Evie? Things change. I have to grow up, and at some point, I sure as hell can't keep Peter Pan-ing around, waiting for—"

"Nate, babe," Polly called, waving at me from the butcher's stall with two giant T-bones in her hands. "Look at these steaks. Should we have these instead of lasagna?"

"Babe? Oh my God, Nate. Did Polly just call you babe?"

"Fuck me! Have you got supersonic hearing or something? I could barely hear that over all these people and the rain, but you heard it in New York?"

Evie gave an ironic laugh. "What can I say? Polly was always quite vocal."

"No kidding. You should have heard her when I fucked her on the tractor yesterday." The minute it left my lips, I wanted to rip the bone from the steak that Polly, for some inexplicable reason, was still waving around and use it to stab myself in the heart. "Evie, I didn't mean—"

"No, you did. You did mean it. And I'm happy for you. I'm happy that fucking my friend on farming machinery is so great, and I hope you enjoy the rest of your date. I'm sure I'll enjoy mine too."

Jealousy surged through me. "What the hell does that mean? Are you going to sleep with him? Is he pressuring you into sex, Gidget? Are you using protection?"

"Ughh, God. You're such a pig. I can't believe I even considered… Ugh. What's the point? Goodbye, *Nathaniel*."

"Evie! Wait! I'm sorry. What did you consider? What—"

The line went dead, and so did my chance with Evie.

Evie

Being a twenty-seven-year-old virgin had its advantages. For example, waxing and birth control expenses were virtually non-existent. Then there was um…and…hmm. That was all I could think of. Just twenty minutes before Christian was due to pick me up, I was in the bathroom, ripping every hair from my body. The blind rage I had characteristically maintained in the weeks since my last call with Nate ensured my waxing was extra brutal. Every inch of my skin was attacked. I felt like one of those hairless cats by the time I was done. Polly calling to make things right between us soured me even further. Her words may have been sweet and apologetic, but I knew Polly. There was poorly disguised glee in her tone. Glee which had probably been pumped into her by my Nate. No, wait. Not my Nate….by stupid Nate.

The final punch to the junk? My brother's gushy delirium over his blooming relationship with Scarlett Grant. I wanted to be happy for him. I really did. But for some reason, I couldn't.

Was it jealousy? No. I didn't think so.

Was I lying to myself? Most likely.

But I was alone. There was no one else to lie to.

Perhaps the sickening stench of love in the air was why I conceded despite lingering apprehension and a month of to-ing and fro-ing. The meal itself wasn't the most daunting prospect. It was what happened next. After all, if things went well with Christian, I would be alone no more. And as for my V card… Well, it would finally be history.

A prospect that was equally exciting and terrifying.

"You look stunning, Evie. That dress is fabulous. Very sexy." Christian's dreamy voice drew my eyes from the one dark and oddly long leg hair my waxing missed and onto his boob-roaming eyes.

"Oh, this old thing? I'm glad you approve." It wasn't old. It was brand new, incredible, and so expensive the tags sat on my bedside table in the hope that I could somehow reattach them and return it to the store. Soft black satin with a cowl neck and low-cut back that exposed the perfect amount of skin made me feel sexy but not slutty. It was a rare feeling for me—so was my being completely overdressed. When Christian mentioned it was the hottest new place, I presumed it would be dark and moody, serving pretentious canapes and bite-size mains, not gourmet Indian street food in a cool, bright, and colorful party zone. Staff buzzed around like busy bees, and Christian seemed to absorb the chaotic energy. We hadn't been seated for twenty minutes, and he'd already disappeared into the restroom three times.

"So, what have you been doing outside of work this week?" he asked as he resumed his seat. "Anything exciting?" He sexily tore off a chuck of hot garlic roti and popped it in his mouth. Nate always liked roti. He dipped it in milk before eating. *Takes the stang out of it, Gidge,* he'd declare.

Stop thinking about Nate.

Christian frantically waved his hands before my face. "Hello, Earth to Evie."

"Oh, sorry, umm… What did you ask?"

"I asked what you've been doing this week. I really hope you pay more attention than this at work, Evie."

"Right, sorry…umm… What have I been doing? Umm. Well, my Aunt Jocelyn is building her dream home on a gorgeous block of land upstate, and my brother, Finn, an architect, and his girl, Scarlett, also an architect, are working on the concept. When we stayed in Tarrytown recently, Jocie was asking my opinion about the design. I gave her some suggestions, just little things I thought would best suit the site and improve its livability. Most of what I suggested will be incorporated into the design. It's all very exciting."

Christian shook his head and condescendingly smiled. "It is exciting. Evie. More for your aunt than for you, though. It's not like it's your house."

"No, you're right. It's not my house. But she is my family, and it means a lot to me that she trusts my opinion."

He scoffed and nodded again. "So, what were these magnificent suggestions? A koala lookout spot? A Vegemite storage room?"

Patronizing son of a… If I had a dollar for every time I'd been called mouthy and loud, I *could have built* a house for myself. "You know what—"

"Here we go, guys. Hope you enjoy." Halting my rant before I could really wind up, our waitress returned with our meals. At first, I was pissed to have missed my chance, but by the time a bright-orange bowl of mango chutney was placed on the table, I'd decided it was probably a good thing. Freely giving opinions seemed to be a turn-off, and learning to keep my temper in check was vital if I was ever to stand a chance with Christian or any other Nate—I mean, man. So, I swallowed the bitter-tasting vitriol and filled my mouth with food instead.

We were at Dhamaka, one of New York's best restaurants. Dropping the smartass routine, Christian was utterly charming for most of the meal. He'd insisted on ordering for me, which I begrudgingly allowed, and had chosen gurda kapoor for me and a Champaran meat dish with something called gucci vegetable pulao. Whatever it was must have been really hot. It was wreaking havoc on his sinuses. He sniffed like a madman.

I eyed my meal with suspicion, but thankfully it tasted better than it looked, which was not great.

"What exactly is gurda kapoor?" I asked the waitress as she cleared our table. "It had an interesting texture I couldn't place."

"Goat kidney, testicles, red onion, and pao."

"Testicles… I just swallowed a goat's balls?"

"You most certainly did. It's probably a good thing we don't include the English translation on the menu. I don't think it would be so popular if people knew."

Together we enjoyed a good chuckle. HotBoss didn't. And as soon as she left, he turned on me. "Could you have said that any louder? You're not out in the fields with the sheep now, Evie. We are in one of the top restaurants in the world. You need to use your inside voice."

Like the turtle sperm potentially lurking in my upcoming desert, I pulled myself back into my shell. I was doing it again, embarrassing Christian in public. He was a seasoned traveler—a well-known and respected member of the Manhattan *it* crowd.

Remember, you should be thankful he is taking you out. He is showing you the better side of life. He wants to make you better too.

Christian's mood quickly shifted. Nostalgia of past glories and reminders of how lucky I was to work beneath him seemed to really pick him up. It didn't do a lot for me, though, and I was down to the last dregs of my already shaky confidence when a young couple passed our table. "I'm so proud of you, babe. You can do anything," crooned the clearly smitten guy, clinging to his girl's hand.

My attention snapped back to my date when he clicked his fingers in my face. "Hey! Evie!" He then took hold of my chin and held my face to his. "Didn't those parents of yours teach you any manners before they died? I bring you to a place like this, and not only do you not listen to me, but you check out other guys."

Tears began to well as Christian tore his hand away and

continued to scold me. But he was right—not about checking guys out, but about listening.

The sweet boy's words reminded me of another…

I know you can look after yourself. You can do anything you want once you set your mind to it.

When I call or message you and ask about my number-one girl, as much as I adore her, I'm not asking about Iris. I'm asking about you.

The scantily clad bodies, drinking and drugging, flaunting their wealth and prestige on Christian's Instagram flashed before my eyes. Sure, he may have had the wealth, but this guy had about as much class as my little finger.

Fuck this.

"Christian, are you always so condescending toward women, or is it just me?"

"I beg your pardon?" He scoffed, almost choking on his ho-ity-toity twenty-dollar water when I threw my napkin on the table and stood.

"Evie, please sit down. This isn't the local McDonald's. You can't just act like a child."

I stepped to Not-HotBoss's side, leaned down, and breathily whispered, "Then stop treating me like one." Without warning, Christian aggressively pushed out from the table, grabbed my wrist, and squeezed—hard. The clang of his chair crashing to the floor caused dropping jaws and drew every set of eyes in the building. "Do you know how lucky you are to be here with me? Can you wrap your feeble mind around how many other little dancing wannabes I could have chosen?"

His grip tightened and sparked further fight in me. If he expected me to cower, he'd picked the wrong girl. "You are hurting me, Christian. Let go," I growled through gritted teeth.

"No. You will not leave me here like a fool. You will sit down and behave. If you do, and you're lucky, I might forgive you, then take you home and show you just how lucky you are." He squeezed harder again, pulled my lips onto his, and began to push me into my chair as he kissed me. God, he tasted awful, bitter, and sweaty.

Vomit rose in my throat. Tears stung my eyes, but there was no way in hell I would let him see them.

No way in hell!

I struggled, eking just enough space to stomp on his foot and pull my body from his grasp. "Let go of me, you asshole, or I will scream this fucking place down in five seconds flat."

Before I could do that, our cute and giggly waitress was joined by a big guy in a chef's jacket. "Excuse me, Mr. Alarie, but is there a problem here?"

Christian flushed red, whisked a twenty from his pocket and tried to shove it in chef-guy's hand. "No, no, not at all. My date is just a little intimidated by her surroundings. It's a little bit out of her class, you see."

"Oh, you're mistaken, Mr. Alarie. I believe you are the problem. Some of the other guests and staff are offended by your manner. We don't condone physical intimidation on our premises, and I would ask, if you don't mind, that you please leave."

"Me? You're kicking me out? What about Bindi Irwin over here? She's the fish out of water."

Chef guy closed in, towering over Christian and looking down on him like the bug he was. "That's quite enough, sir. I have asked politely. Now, please leave before I call the police."

"Fine. This place is a shithole anyway." Turning to me, he scowled and shook his head. "I'm done slumming it for the night. You can find your own way home. And don't bother coming back to the studio. You and that klutz niece of yours aren't welcome."

Adrenaline coursed through me. I was torn between running and hiding or chasing him down and kicking his ass. But before I could do either, two strong hands landed on my shoulders. "We've got you, ma'am. Come with us." It was only then that I realized I was crouching on the floor. The waitress, Pria, took my trembling hand and kindly ushered me out of the whisper-filled main dining space, through the bustling, steam-filled kitchen, and into a staff rest area. For twenty minutes, I sat in silence, regrouping, hiding. Alternating between shame and pride, smelling cumin, star anise, and cloves. Pria kept me dosed up with affection and unlimited desserts, and when I had my fill of almond kulfi, I called Jocelyn. Thankfully, as soon as she heard my voice, she sent a town car with little to no questioning.

Carrying a month's worth of takeout, I was again escorted from the building, bundled into a black Escalade, and whisked away.

I may have been surrounded by bumper-to-bumper traffic in the most densely populated borough of New York City, but I'd never felt more alone. Or stupid. Naive too. The long-held insecurities that plagued and held me back surged. Was Christian right? Had I ruined my chance?

Unable to hold it in a second longer, the tears I'd stubbornly denied burst free. And as always, just when I needed him the most, Nate's name flashed onto the screen of my phone.

"Nate. He grabbed my arm, and forced a kiss, and pushed me, and…and…I am such an idiot."

"What the fuck, Evie! Slow down. Are you safe? Where are you?"

I did not slow down.

"I'm okay. I was in Soho. Jocie sent a car, and I'm on the way home. I can't believe I let this happen. When he first asked me out, he was so sweet, charming, kind, and dorky. Oh, and he bought me Tim Tams too. But as soon as we went for coffee the first time, it was clear that he was a snob. But he is so great with the kids and so handsome and sophisticated…I just couldn't see it. God, I'm so dumb and naive and desperate that I ignored all the warning signs and was completely swayed by a man that bought me chocolate, and now I've lost the first job I've had in years."

"Jesus, Gidge. Stop right there. You are not an idiot, dumb, blind, or stupid. He is a prick. He is at fault here, not you. As for the job, who wants to work for that asshole anyway."

"I didn't say stupid, but thanks for including it."

"Don't joke about this, Evie. He assaulted you. You should press charges, for fuck's sake. Are you sure you're physically okay?"

Wiping the tears with the back of my hand, I checked my wrist and was shocked to see the clearly visible red and swollen finger marks.

"Yes, I'm okay. I think I might get a doozy of a bruise, though."

"Fucking bastard!" Something—maybe glass or a mirror, some poor bastard's bones—bore the brunt of Nate's frustration and smashed in the background. "Fuck. I am so fucking angry at myself. None of this would have happened if I hadn't been such a dick to you on the phone. I should have been there to keep you safe. To protect you."

God, how I wanted that. To feel his arms around my body. To have his scent infusing into every pore. But that wasn't going to happen. Nate wasn't mine, and I needed to look after myself. "I know you're looking out for me, and I'd hate to burst your ego bubble, but I chose to go out with that dick because he was hot and seemed nice, and I wanted to. But even if what you said was true, it's not your job to protect me, Nate. You're not my body-guard, my brother, or anything for that matter. What you are is Polly's boyfriend, and you should be worried about watching over her, not me."

"Damn it, Evie. Why do you have to be so bloody stubborn? Don't you get it by now? I don't… I don't want to be Polly's any-thing. I want to be your everything!"

Every part of me, except my brain, told me to scream, *I want that too!* But I didn't. I just bit my lip to stifle my cry and listened to his breathing.

"Evie? Evie! Dammit, are you still there?"

"Yes! Yes, I'm still bloody here. But Nate, you don't mean that. There's nothing special about me. You're just confusing what we had. I think we both are. Being so far away from each other is throwing us off—"

"Evie, stop. You are special. You're one of a kind. What we have is one of a kind. Being so far away has helped me see what's real. I know you have feelings for me, and I sure as fuck know how I feel about you. I'm going to prove it to you, too."

"What…what do you mean?"

For a beat or twenty, the world kept moving around me, but I remained frozen in time, trapped in the loudest silence of my life. Then, just like that night in the rain with Finn, everything changed.

"I'm coming to New York. I was going to be there for Christmas anyway, but if I can, I'm changing my flight. Hell, I'll bloody swim if I have to, but either way, I'm leaving tomorrow."

"Nate, this is stupid."

"No, it's not. It's quite possibly the smartest thing I've ever done. Take this as your first and only warning, Lil Gidge. When I get off that plane… When I see, touch, and kiss you, you'll see and feel and know exactly how real and rare what we feel for each other is."

Chapter 12

Nate

I**N MY MIND, THREE THINGS WERE SET IN STONE.**

I was going to New York.

I was going to tell Evie I loved her.

I was going to bring her home.

Outside of my mind, in that little place known as reality, that was not the case.

Well, going to New York was, but that was it.

My bags were packed, and I was ready to go…ready to finally do it. The impending confession had been so close so many times it was ridiculous. Letters had been written, playlists created, and poems memorized. Each time I had been sure it was *the* time. Yet each time, I wimped out. Not this time, though. This time would be different.

Maybe.

Practicalities needed to be sorted before anything could happen. For that, I needed to calm down—something I decided running like a madman on the treadmill at the rear of my little cabin would help me do. It sat by a window overlooking green fields filled with row after row of flowering macadamia trees and a flock of sheep and lambs. Some of my best thinking was done in that spot, especially when newborn lambs were prancing and hopping around. I may have been a rugged and manly Aussie farmer who could carry a sheep under one arm and crack open a cold beer with the other, but I would never be too manly to admit there is nothing in this world cuter than a newborn lamb. Their vigor and energy always lifted my spirits. The only other place that offered me such solace and clarity of thought was the ocean. But I'd not set foot on my board since Evie had left. Each wave that crashed against the shore felt like a nail being driven into my heart. It was torture.

Five kilometers in, the chaos of my mind began to settle, and the planning commenced.

Showing just how well they knew their son, my folks had purchased me a round-trip ticket to the States when they booked their own trip to Fiji. Being the downright cheapskates that they were, the flight was a super-duper cheapskate special that required a kidney, liver, or your firstborn child to be surrendered when changing the travel date, and this was no small change. It wasn't a day or two I would be asking. No, I was going from early December to late October. It was doubtful I was flying anywhere on that original ticket. I was more confident with organizing the visa. I only needed one as a tourist if I stayed over ninety days. Still, that kind of shit changed constantly, so checking that was added to the mental list.

Then there was the big one. Dad. After his stroke at just fifty, he retired. The place and the responsibilities that came with it were now mine. How would he feel about retaking the reins so his one and only son could run off and chase some girl across the globe? Mum and I were so scared of something happening that we'd hardly let him lift a finger for months, apart from the odd jobs Mum had to keep inventing for him. How would she feel about it? Would she want me to risk Dad's health again, even when he had a clean bill from his doctors? Knowing their fondness for Evie somewhat eased my mind, but even if he was happy for me to go, was he physically capable of running the farm?

Again? Even if it was only for a few weeks?

My last issue was the tall, curvy, sexy brunette one. Polly had sunk her claws into me, and I had been more than willing to be dragged into her cave. Within a week or two, we had gone from friends to lovers, boyfriend and girlfriend living in each other's pockets. I doubted poor Pol expected me to break up with her by dinner when she had given me a blowjob before breakfast. Then again, very little of what occurred during our time together was expected. What was, however, was the shit hitting the fan when I told her. I could smell it already. Polly—and Mum, for that matter—were going to kill me.

Deciding to take one of the bulls by the horns, I jumped off the treadmill, picked up the phone, and called the airline. Today's connecting flights were long gone, but I could get on one leaving the local airport at six-fifty am tomorrow, fly into Sydney, catch a connecting flight to Dallas, Texas, and then another to JFK. It would be twenty-six hours of waiting at two airports and in a giant flying tin can, but it also meant I would be back with my number-one girl in less than forty-eight hours.

Full of piss and vinegar, I jumped into the shower, dressed, and then shot off a quick text telling Polly not to come back to the farm but that I would meet her at her place. She'd only left fifteen minutes before Evie's call and planned to return after picking up some dinner and feeding her seventeen bloody cats. Those things hated me. Each time I entered their space, they looked and hissed like I was the devil incarnate. Perhaps they were right. Maybe they foresaw what future me would do to their beloved mum.

In a cloud of dust, I passed my parents' house and was flagged down by a less-than-impressed-looking mum.

"What the hell, Nathaniel? You're going like the clappers. Where's the bloody fire?"

"No fire, mum. Just in a hurry to get into town. I have to talk to Pol about something, and it can't wait." She leaned into the window, looked at my face, rolled her eyes, and slapped the back of my head.

"You're going to break up with her, aren't you? I bloody knew it!" Whack! Another slap. "Her mother is going to have my guts for garters. I told you, Nate. I told you not to go there with her, but you couldn't bloody help yourself, could you?" On and on she went. I could not get a word in edgewise and considered just driving off. But she was leaning so far into the car I may have decapitated her in the process. As tempting as that sounded amid her berating, it wasn't a wise choice. "Where did I go wrong? I know your father dropped you on your head when you were three months old, but surely that wouldn't cause this. All of my friends' kids are settling down and having babies, and you can't help sticking your—"

"Mum!" I yelled at the top of my voice. "I love Evie, and I am flying to New York tomorrow to bring her home!"

She froze.

"Say that again?"

"I love Evie. I love her with all my heart, Mum, and I am flying to New York tomorrow to bring her home. I know it will be hard for Dad, but I'll figure it out, I promise. And yes, I know I am doing the wrong thing by Polly, but Evie is—"

"Screw Polly!" Mum shrieked, and her whole body surged through the window till I found myself in the unenviable position of having her pretty much straddling my thighs as she peppered me with kisses—every son's worst nightmare.

"For fuck's sake, mum. Get off me!"

"Ohhhhhhh! Oh, Nate! I am so happy and so proud of you. I always knew you were a good boy, that you would make me proud and give me lots and lots of fat grandbabies. I can see it now. I can look after the bambinos while you and Evie work on the farm. Then you'll come home, and we'll all have dinner and…"

For some perspective, Mum's parents were Italian, and it was at moments like this, where she daydreamed till her heart's content over my future as a fat baby sire, that it showed. Mum continued to ramble while I continued to remove her from my lap. "Mum, please move. This is so wrong."

Dismissively waving and showing impressive maneuverability for a woman her age, she slipped onto the passenger seat. A vomit-inducing thought of what she and my dad may have gotten up to on the bench seat of his old white Holden truck popped into my brain.

"Okay, Mum. I need you to get out…now."

She stopped mid-sentence and smiled at me deliriously while clutching her clenched hands beneath her chin. "Don't you worry your pretty little head about your father. He'll be fine for a few months. The shearing is done, the crops are harvested, and he has me and enough dickhead friends to help him out if needed. This is more important."

"You're sure about Dad and the farm?'

"Yes, darling. I'm positive. Now, would you like me to come with you? For moral support?"

"Would I like my mother to come with me to break up with a girl?"

"Yes. For moral support."

"For moral support? Hmm, let me think…NO!" I leaned across the giddy woman and opened the door. "I love you with all my heart, but you're crazy. Now please get the fuck out of my truck. I'm losing daylight. And sanity."

"Yes, yes, alright." She slid out of the door and slammed it shut. "On your way, son. Good luck. I'll have lasagna ready for you when you get back. Can't send my boy away on an empty stomach. God knows what rubbish they'll feed you on the plane, though Qantas has lovely meals. Are you flying Qantas, Nate?"

Without replying, I dropped the pedal to the metal and left.

※

"Polly, are you home?"

There was no answer when I knocked. The door was unlocked, so I stuck my head in and called out.

"I'm the bedroom, babe. Just setting up lunch."

Two things bothered me. Polly calling me babe again, and why was she setting up lunch in the bedroom? I got my answer almost immediately upon entering her perfectly styled room.

Polly was stark naked on her bed, except for the sushi strategically placed over her body's more…private places.

"Hope you're hungry, babe."

"Fuck me."

"With pleasure. But only after you've eaten. I hear the Aoyagi is exceptionally fresh and delicious today."

DNA was to blame for my reaction. We men had been genetically geared and designed for thousands of years to react in a particular way to such moments. My body did genetics—Charles Darwin himself—proud. Evolution forced my cock to turn to stone and my feet to drift closer. "Which one is the Aoyagi?"

"This one right here." Polly's words slipped from her smirking lips as she pointed to her freshly waxed hoo-ha. "Aoyagi is raw clam. I want you to eat my clam, Nate. No hands allowed."

I think... I'm pretty sure I had a stroke. I couldn't move, and I sure as heck couldn't talk or think. I could definitely see, though, and what I saw had my hard cock jumping like that once wave-riding tuna fish was before it ended up on Polly's tits.

"You look incredible, Polly. I don't think it's very hygienic, though." She began to giggle. I remained glued to the floor.

"Come a little closer. Let your tongue explore the delights. You know you want it. It's one of a kind."

One of a kind.

Blinking my way back to consciousness, I blurted, "We have to break up."

"What!" Polly sat up straight, causing a fish avalanche of epic proportions. "Are you freaking kidding me? I'm lying here naked with fucking crustaceans on my cunt, and you're breaking up with me?"

For fuck's sake, don't laugh.

"Yes. Yes. That's exactly what I'm doing." Polly's fluffy white bathrobe was hanging on a hook next to me, and I grabbed and tossed it to her. "I'll give you a minute to cover up. I'll be in the living room when you're ready to talk."

"Uh-uh. No way." She commando-rolled off the bed and rose like a ninja, somehow landing right before me. "This is about that pip-squeak moron, Evie-fucking-Austen, isn't it?"

"Don't ever talk about her like that, and for Christ's sake, please cover yourself."

"What's wrong? Worried you can't control yourself?" She stepped closer, took my hand, and placed it on her perfect breast while running her fingers along my chin, down my neck, and beneath the collar of my tee.

"No," I squeaked, "I just prefer not to break up with someone when they are in a vulnerable position. I'm trying to be respectful."

It took me a second to realize I was massaging her breast, but I pulled away as soon as I did. For me, that was a small moral victory. There was only one booby I wanted to hold, and it wasn't this lovely, plump one. My eyes kept fucking dropping, though. Nate the Slut was a thing of the past as far as my logical brain was concerned, but my eyes had a little catching up to do.

"Respectful? You? Nate Myers? The biggest himbo in New South Wales is trying to be respectful? That's new."

"Polly, I know you're upset right now, but there's no need to insult me. I have been respectful. I told you I had feelings for Evie. I thought that spending time with someone as fun and beautiful—"

"And sexy. Don't forget sexy."

"And sexy," I added. "I thought it would help me to move on, but it's done the opposite. I know what I want, and I will get it."

"What do you mean you're going to get it? What, are you going to run to New York after her?" She gave a perfunctory cackle but stopped when my expression failed to change. "You're serious? You're going to New York?"

"I fly out in the morning."

Polly picked a piece of sashimi clinging to her left breast and threw it in my face. "Omg, this is pathetic. She doesn't want you, Nate! She left you behind, remember? She moved to the other side of the world to get away from you. Do you really think she would have done that if she was the slightest bit interested in a relationship with you? She knows you better than anyone, and she left. What does that say about you?"

Anxiety and long-held, deep-dwelling insecurities reared their ugly heads. But that was what Polly wanted. She was fucking gas-lighting me big time, and it wasn't going to work.

"Things change, Polly. People and feelings change. Evie may not have known how she felt before, but I'm confident she does now." I hoped this was as true as it felt. "Look, I don't want this to get nasty. I'm really sorry. I've really enjoyed our time together, but it's done. We're done."

She grabbed me, pulled me close by my neck and kissed me. "I don't accept."

"You don't accept? Pol, this isn't a resignation. There are no cross-offers or negotiations. As I said, I'm sorry if I hurt you, but it's time to move on."

With great difficulty, I peeled Polly's vise-like grip from my neck and bolted for the door. "She can't do to you what I can, Nate. She's frigid. Did you know that?"

I wasn't about to dignify that with a response.

"Goodbye, Polly."

"I don't think so." She laughed as she followed me out the door, still naked and hurling fish. "You'll be back, Nathaniel Myers. Trust me, my bed won't even be cold, and you'll be sick of that little ice block."

Chapter 13

Nate

To: Evie
From: Nate

Hey, Gidge. I know you're probably asleep, and
I know you thought I was full of shit. But I'm on my way.
I've cleared customs, and Operation Convince Evie has
officially begun. My flight # QF 4393 is expected to
arrive at JFK around 10 pm, and I'd really, really, really
love to see your face when I walk-collapse through
those gates.

As I wait in Sydney before floating through the air   a t
35,000 feet to be near you, I thought I'd share a
few treasured memories, hoping you would finally
see how much I treasure you.

1: When I was six, I tried to kiss you in the cubby
your dad made for us in the old chicken coop.
You were not impressed and rightly punched
me in the face. When I started crying, you
called me a stupid baby but fetched me an ice
pack and held it to my face. I remember looking
into your eyes and being terrified while also wanting
to marry you when I was big.

2: When I was ten, I attempted to do a mono on my bike
in front of Harvey's milk bar. My audience was a gang of
older kids I was desperate to impress, mainly because it
included you. I failed miserably, falling backward
into the road, and grazing most of the hair
from the back of my head and the skin on
my ass, back, and arms. You were the only
one to come to my aid, wiping the blood
from my neck with your pink-and-white

hanky, then walking me to Polly's house, berating me constantly for being a pain-in-the-ass idiot but waiting and not leaving my side till my mum came to get me. I still have that hanky. It's in my pocket right now.

3: When we were twelve, Finn, Shelby, and I snuck into your room and went through your things. Finn was looking for a diary he was sure he'd seen you writing in, convinced it would hold enough blackmail material to get him through his and, more importantly, your teenage years.

Luckily, I was the one who found it. I admit to reading a couple of pages before feeling so guilty that I stopped. But I swear there was nothing terrible or overly personal, mostly the odd confession of love for Justin Bieber and notes and ideas for your stories. One was about a little girl who grew up by the beach and dreamed of being a ballerina. It was poetry, really.

The phrasing and language seemed so mature. I couldn't understand most of it, but I remember every word....

"Her slumber brings dreams of worlds so different to those of her every day she struggles to comprehend their existence. She wears princess gowns of tulle and sequined satin. She is all beauty and grace, flittering and fluttering like a delicate fairy, twirling on a shimmering, golden string. But her true and mighty heart beats with the ferocity of a medieval knight, and her blood runs red, burning with the fire of the dragons she will one day slay. She yearns for adventure, for independence. For stages and strangers with interesting faces. Of finding her own way. Of making mistakes and occasionally learning from them. Of finding and falling in love, all the while deeply fearing the unknown realities of leaving everyone and everything she knows. She's both feminine and masculine, diminutive and demanding. Fire and ice.

It was you, Evie. I saw it even back then.

To: Evie
From: Nate

Fuck. Just got a coffee and a muffin and it cost me 15 bucks! Also, why does predictive text change fuck to duck all the time?

To: Evie
From: Nate

4: Christmas day. I was thirteen, and you were sixteen. Your mum had given you a hair straightener, and you had just finished frying the shit out of your curls for the first time. You and Finn then rode over to our place after lunch. Finn strutted into the house like king shit, his new body board tucked under his arm and headed straight for Shelby. You swanned in like freaking Beyonce, flipping and waving your hair to and fro and heading for the mirror Mum still has hanging over the side table in the hall.

You knew how hot you looked. I knew how hot you looked. So hot I had the first of many Evie Austen-inspired teenage boners I would have to hide over the years.

To: Evie
From: Nate

I'm the one who told Marc Loritso you collected toenails from dead people at the funeral home, that you never cut your own, and that this was why you wore Doc Martens—they allowed space for your gross, curled nails, you see.

If the toenail thing wasn't enough to make him cancel your date, I may have eluded to the fact that you were thinking of collecting teeth, too, and warned him not to smile too much, as you may try and pull one of his out.

I didn't expect him to tell everyone in Year 12, or to put it in the school yearbook.

My bad.

To: Evie-
From: Nate

I love how you say or type SNORT instead of actually snorting. It's fucking adorable.

To: Evie
From: Nate

Eves- I'm terrified writing this will change everything, but I can no longer hold it all in. I sound like one of your soft book boyfriends, but if I am to be ruined, let it be you that ruins me. I would rather have the tin can with wings that carried me to you crash to the ground and burn than spend another day not knowing.

I need you, Aoife.

They're calling my flight. I'll send more when I can.

Chapter 14

Evie

LUCKILY, I SLEPT WITH MY PHONE ON SILENT AS I woke Monday morning to a moment of heart-exploding potential. I wouldn't have survived on anything less than a full night's sleep.

Nate was coming.

He was on his way, would be here by ten pm, and had sent me thirty-seven emails, inspiring possibly a thousand awws, OMGs, and countless laughs. In typical fashion, there were frequent mentions of various states of arousal due to my clothing, or lack thereof. My bikini was mentioned several times, as well as an odd wetsuit malfunction or two.

It was a lot to absorb. I wanted to hug and kiss him more than I'd ever wanted to kiss anyone, but I also wanted to kill him. That rumor about the toenails took me years to live down, and I didn't even know about the teeth. At least the mystery of why poor, gullible, gorgeous Marc Loritso wouldn't come within a foot of me without clapping his hand over his mouth and what were, granted, beautiful teeth.

A mental picture emerged halfway through the influx of affection—Nate, hunched over his phone, correcting his sitting position now and then because his mum possessed his body briefly to chastise his appalling posture. I could picture him, his tongue poking out as he typed with one finger.

Hours must have been spent recalling and writing each message. I could count the time, of course. Each message had a timestamp, after all. The math could be quickly done, but that would muddy the pristine waters, removing the romance and making what I desperately wanted to remain illogical, logical.

Never had I imagined someone feeling this way toward me.

Nate Myers said he loved me and was coming to claim me. There had been no formal declaration, but the sentiment was conveyed with honest truths and confessions that only a lovesick heart could make.

Nate. Loved. Me.

Or at least, the memory of me.

With that thought, panic struck. *Shit.* What if that was all this was? Nostalgia? Rose-colored brain farts? My fingers began typing, quickly checking the first online thesaurus Google spat at me.

Nostalgia: a sentimental recollection or wistful affection for a period in the past. "See, that's what this is," I told myself. "That sums it up perfectly. He's in love with the memories, not me."

Persuading myself was surprisingly easy. After all, was it truly possible to love someone you had never held in anything but a friendly manner? Someone you hadn't kissed, or…you know, *bow chika wow wow*? Was it possible for Nate to love anyone full stop?

I needed to reply to Nate but couldn't bring myself to do it. What the hell was I supposed to say?

A full-frontal attack from Iris left little time to ponder. She jumped on my chest. Her strawberry-blonde curls covered my eyes as she began pulling at my cheeks like I was a piano accordion.

"Daddy is making pancakes! Get up! Get up!" With the enthusiastic pizzazz only she—and possibly her father—could possess at seven am, she somersaulted from the bed and landed back on her feet. After knocking my phone from my hand, she linked our fingers and pulled me from bed. The rush of blood from my rapid rise, this morning's Nate news, and the emotionally charged prior evening, left me feeling like I drank a keg all by myself. "Awe you okay, Evie? You look all floofy. A bit kind of wed and yellowy."

"I'm fine, bubs. I just got up too quickly. You go wait for me in the kitchen. And tell Daddy not to burn those pancakes. I could eat the ass out of a rag doll."

"Haha, I heawd a sweaw!"

"Shit!"

"That one too! I'm telling Daddy!"

"Double shit."

Knowing I had plenty to do but not being motivated to do any of it, I stood listlessly, smack bang in the middle of my room, staring out the window at the crisp blue sky and rust-colored leaves falling onto the street below. Nate consumed my thoughts. *Where is he right now? What is he thinking? Will he send more messages?*

The temptation to sneak back into bed, hide beneath my quilt, and reread his word again and again was hard to fight, but the responsibilities of daily life had almost the same pull.

"God. Can't I just be me for one day?"

"Evieee! I need you to do my haiw!" Iris called.

"Guess not." As I padded my way to my door, I noticed my sadly neglected laptop sitting on my desk, gathering dust. I hadn't written for weeks. Not since Finn blabbed about Nate. The forbidden feelings whirling deep inside me, which had intensified with each flirty exchange, had frightened me out of it. Who knew what wanton tales and lustful secrets may spill from my brain if I dared touch that keyboard? An ache, a heat, built between my legs. *Fuck, just thinking about it…him… turns me to mush. How am I going to cope with him here?*

"Perhaps…" I said aloud, shaking my hands and pacing circles on my rug like a crazy person. "Perhaps I need to write this down. Purge it all out. A literary version of rubbing one out to take the edge off before a date. People do that…right?"

The thing was, I wanted to be a children's author, telling stories of brave little girls who dreamed big, not wanton virgins fantasizing about being impaled by…umm…big… things.

Staring back and forth between the door and my bed, I chewed my nails, fidgeted my hair into loose braids, and decided.

"Finn!" I croaked in the sickest voice I could manage while still yelling at the top of my lungs. "I'm not feeling so good. Are you able to get Iris to school today?"

Grumpy mumbles and giant clown feet clomped up the stairs before a mop of blonde curls and worried eyes appeared before me. "You okay? Iris said you looked a bit sick."

"Yeah, nah. I think I might be coming down with something. I must just pop back to bed and try to sleep it off if that's alright."

Finn shook his head, stepped closer, and gently placed his hand on my forehead. At times, I could forget what a hulk of a man my brother was—this wasn't one of them. All six-foot-four of him towered over me as he peered down with kind sympathy. "You do feel a bit warm. Come on. Back to bed with you." He then took me by the shoulders and pushed me back to bed.

"Sorry, Finn."

"Fuck it, Evie. How many times do we go through this? You're not my employee and don't need permission to have a sick day. I'm quite capable of getting myself and Iris ready."

"I know you are, but I feel like it's my job, my contribution to the house. God knows I don't add anything else."

Finn patted my head like a dog and sat beside me.

"Hey, that's not true. You are the heart, the lifeblood of us all. What would I do without your whiny, high-pitched squeal nagging me every five minutes? Besides, you'll soon be bringing home the big bucks as a famous dance teacher–slash–writer. Then I shall retire and sponge off you." Laughing at himself, he pulled the blankets over my face and whacked me on top of my head. "Rest, woman. We need you to be healthy and happy."

He was gone when I pulled myself out of my cocoon of shame. I'd just lied to him, lying right to his face and through omission as well. He had no idea what happened last night with Christian. About me losing my job and Iris getting kicked out of dance school. Not to mention his cluelessness over his best friend sending me flirty messages. And who could forget the minor detail that the very same bestie was currently wing-ing his way to see us...to me.

Time is what I needed, time and space to think and plan and panic. Also required was getting the filth out of my head and down on paper before I saw Nate, 'cause God knew what I'd do to that boy if I saw him in the state I was in.

From the safety and innocence of my virtuous bed, I stared at my laptop. Visions of Nate running along the sand with his board tucked under his arm, of him surfing, of the command he held over the disobedient ocean, propelled me from my comfort zone and into the seat at my desk where soul-deep arousal assisted the sentences in forming.

He holds her body in his hands. With all calmness and strength, his desire appears in check while she shakes, trembling with fear and anticipation.

*Though, on the inside, he is open and raw, longing to possess her. Wanting to taste her, waiting to plunge his...his...*FFUUCCKKKK!

If I can't even type it, how can I ride it?

I sat for five minutes with my finger on the letter C. I switched it to D, but that made no difference. Finn hollered from downstairs that he and Iris were leaving, and Jocelyn did the same a little later, and my response to both was, "Yeah, see ya."

Thank fuck. I was alone.

The house was mine, and I needed inspiration.

Sneaking, despite knowing of her absence, I tiptoed into Jocelyn's room, perusing the immaculately organized shelves lined with a rainbow of dog-eared free books until I found what I wanted. My aunt had been reading a series of books that had her gasping, sighing, and displaying other unmissable pearl-clutching traits you saw in a woman only when reading a truly erotic novel. I was not shy of a steamy book myself—Kandi Steiner, Tessa Bailey, and Tate James were some of my favorites. Those ladies knew how to dial up the heat. But I needed something new, something fresh.

"Ahh, there it is." *The Crossfire Series* by Sylvia Day. It was old school, but Jocelyn was no blushing wallflower. If this got her heart pumping, I couldn't imagine what it could do for mine. Inexplicably still sneaking, I made my way to the kitchen, loaded myself with snacks and soda, and then headed back to bed.

I began my research.

She rode that cock like a cowgirl at her first rodeo. All enthusiasm, no skill or style. The pressure, the stretch, and the tightness all led her to fear he may split her right in two, yet she couldn't stop. "More, give me more!" she demanded, clawing at his chest, opening wounds he would have trouble explaining to his wife when he got home."

"His wife?" I said to myself with an evil cackle, "Wow, I'm bad. This is fun."

"Nathan," she cried, "Nathan. Please. Fuck me like you've never fucked any woman before!" Gripping the small of her back, twisting his hands through her hair, he flipped her, threw her legs over his shoulders, and pounded into her. He bent down to her, drew a tight, pink nipple into his mouth and bit down until she screamed his name.

"Oh God, Stevie!" He came then too, filling her... (Shit, can I? Yes, I can.) *...pussy again and again with his hot cum, then collapsing against her breasts. "You're mine, Stevie. Mine. Forever your first, always your last."*

Pushing my chair away from my desk, I sipped my water, wiped the sweat from my brow, and high-fived myself. I wouldn't win any literary awards, but I had typed cock and pussy, and that was a big step toward freeing the prudish beast lurking inside me. Unfortunately, and possibly expectedly, I had not rid myself of desire.

There was only one thing for it.

I ran a bath. Filled it with the most expensive oils I could steal from Jocelyn's bathroom, then soaked, touched, and brought myself undone to thoughts of Nathan and Stevie and with the knowledge that Nate was coming too...just in a slightly different way.

Chapter 15

UNFOLDING MY BODY FROM THE PRETZEL-like form it had taken during my fifteen-or-so-hour flight was not easy. Neither was navigating the shopping center within Dallas airport, though everything else had gone smoothly since landing. Customs and Immigration were done with minimal fuss. I had time to kill before my connecting flight. Hell, I'd even been hit on by a hot couple of Singapore Airlines stewardesses while we all waited for our coffees. They were cute as fuck and flirted with me incessantly, but I was too distracted, checking my phone and stressing over the zero messages from Evie, to give them my full attention.

A vaguely familiar scent hit me as I wandered aimlessly. I was passing L'Occitane, and on taking a second breath, one of Evie's squeals of delight burst into my mind. Finn had given her a luxurious gift pack for her birthday last Christmas, and the way she'd aggressively ripped open the packaging and tantalizingly applied the lotion to her toned, bronzed legs had tortured me on many a long and horny night.

Suddenly, my credit card began burning a hole in my pocket. It was time for its first US workout.

The name of the fragrance slipped my mind, so I smelled each until I found the right one along with a massive headache. "This is it! Neroli and Orchidee." A second long and deep inhale had me imagining the clean, fruity, and floral scent enveloping every inch of her skin and willing away a hard-on. I may have even moaned a little.

Before I could disgrace myself further, I scooped the full range into my hands, paid, and made a hasty exit. Chanel was next door, so after *relaxing* a little, I wandered in and out twenty minutes and a few hundred dollars later.

Next in my—*I have no idea what I'm doing. Why is everything so expensive?*—shopping was Michael Kors. Fate and the sexy, skin-tight dresses displayed in the window lured me inside, and I was barely two steps in the door when I ran into my friendly little airline hotties. They'd clearly paid more attention to our conversation at Starbucks than I had, as they not only remembered my name—which I couldn't even remember supplying—but where I was headed too.

"Who in New York are you shopping for, Nate? You don't have a ring on that finger, so I don't think it's your wife," asked Jada while holding my hand and suggestively stroking my ring finger.

"Pftt, like that's ever stopped you, Jada," inserted Leia.

I freed myself from Jada's grip and answered before they scratched each other's eyes out. "No, you're right. I don't have a wife, but I hope to one day…shit. I've never said that out loud before. I want to marry her. I want to marry Evie Austen!"

I thought my declaration may have put the girls off, but no, Jada and Leia seemed keener than ever. Had I been up for it, I believe my shearing-shed three-way would have been up for some stiff—pardon the pun—competition. But I wasn't even tempted, and that shocked the shit out of me.

I could still put them to good use, though. "I want to take Evie somewhere really fancy…the ballet, maybe. Would you help me pick her a dress? And she never spends money on herself, so it has to be really special."

"OMG! Nate, you are so cute! What size is she?"

"Hmm. I dunno."

"Well, do you know how tall she is?"

"Yeah, nah. 'Bout this height, maybe." I uselessly held my hand up, and the girls looked at each other and smiled. Jada moved first, grabbing my hands, placing them on her shoulders, then running them down the length of her body, stopping as my fingers passed the curve of her ass and then back up again. The return trip only varied by taking my hands closer to her breasts.

"Does she feel about my size?"

"Or more mine?" Leia smiled. She then repeated the horrible, horrible ordeal over her tight little body. Had this happened to me at any other point in adulthood, I would have banged those girls so fucking hard. But again, I didn't.

It was a big deal.

"Uhh, I think she is about your size, Leia. But to be honest, I can't be sure. I've now touched more of your body than I ever have of hers."

"What?" they shrieked in unison.

Poor Jada looked like she might faint and left the questioning to Leia.

"You're telling us you've flown across the world for a woman you've never slept with?"

"Yep. Never kissed her either."

"What the fuck! Are you real?" Their squeals of disbelief and accompanying poking of my body like I was some kind of science experiment caught the attention of Alexa, a tightly coiffed, terrifying-looking assistant. She glanced at my jeans, CONS, and Rip Curl t-shirt with utter contempt and shuddered.

"Is there anything I can *quietly* help you with?"

My new friends then explained my situation to the ice queen, and she defrosted before my eyes.

"So, she's roughly this one's size?" she said, grabbing Leia by the waist and sizing her.

"Yep, looks about right." I nodded.

"And style-wise, what is she into? Who are her fashion influences?"

I scratched the back of my head and winced. "Umm, honestly, I don't think she has any. She likes Taylor Swift a lot. Oh, and she does ballet and likes daisies. But she's a surfer, a bit of a free spirit and wears lots of old hippie sort of stuff…and thongs. She loves a good pair of thongs. She has amazing feet."

"Ballet, orange, and thongs…on her feet?" Alexa's eyes nearly popped from her perfectly groomed head. "Do you mean thongs as in underwear?"

"Oh, no, shit. I don't know what undies she wears. By thongs I mean feet thongs. You know, flip-flops?"

"Oh my God, shut up!" Jada lunged at me again. "You are adorable, and your accent is amazing!"

After taking a few deep breaths, Alexa's slightly frightening persona relaxed, and she set to work. "Right, then. Let's look at some boho styles."

Too many minutes later, Leia had tried on umpteen outfits, and I found the perfect dress featuring the season's hallmark smocked neckline. It was designed in a relaxed silhouette that gracefully flared away from the body while delicate pleats and poet sleeves infused it with a Bohemian sensibility. I didn't know any of that off-hand, by the way. It was on the tag.

One more thing was purchased—a new carry-on bag, big enough to hide all of my loot and the few items I had brought with me. Once that was packed, it was time for my new friends to catch their flight. But not before doling out one final pep talk. "Nate. If she's as stubborn as you say, she may need some convincing that a relationship with you is okay, especially with your shared past. But she sounds like your true soulmate. Don't give up on her, okay?"

"Thanks, girls. And don't worry, I don't think I could even if I tried."

They had only made it a few steps away when Jada came running back up to my side, planting a massive kiss on my cheek and slipping me a piece of paper. "Here's my number. Just in case you do give up."

"Jada! That's not fair. We agreed he was a no-go!" Still arguing over me, the girls disappeared into the crowd of travelers, leaving me and my massive head to get some Texas BBQ, despair over the lack of messages from Evie, and wait for my next damn flight.

The last thing I'd done before leaving home was sneak into Mum and Dad's. My mission: take a photo of a photo. Time was not on my side. If I was going to escape without waking the olds, who I'd said goodbye to the previous night, I had to snap the first one I found. And oh, what a ripper it was, taken amid the chaos of Christmas lunch, when Evie was still at home with little Iris, Finn was commuting back and forth between Sydney and Byron Bay, and I was taking them both for granted. If only I knew then what little time I had left with my most favorite neighbors, I would have done things differently.

Anyway, the photo itself was a classic, one of my mum's super shit specialties. Each of us wore a stupid but traditional Aussie Christmas paper crown, and no warning was given before she snapped away. Everyone captured was either blinking, drinking, had their mouths wide open or, in Evie's case, crammed full of food. We all looked truly hideous, except, of course, for my Gidget. Somehow, despite gorging on what appeared to be several roast potatoes, having a massive blob of gravy on the side of her lip, and appearing to be mid-argument with Finn, her golden skin and shimmering locks took my breath away.

Predictably, sitting right next to the raging Evie was me, looking at her like the sun shone from her ass and I was just hanging around for the tan.

I was on my third rack of sticky ribs in the airport cafeteria when my phone pinged, and that very photo lit up my screen.

"Holy shit." I coughed at the top of my lungs, spraying meat over the table, and drawing the ire of the cowboy sitting next to me. "Sorry 'bout that, mate."

My shaking hands dropped my fork as my phone kept beeping with three consecutive messages, paralyzing my heart and drawing all air from my lungs. I swallowed the last of my watered-down beer, said a silent prayer, and prepared to read the first text. As I did, a nasal voice overhead began announcing the final boarding for my flight. "Shit!" I hadn't even heard the first two. Gathering the dozen or so shopping bags strewn at my feet, I hustled to the gate, reading Evie's words, and reminding myself to breathe.

> **Evie : 5:50 pm : I can't believe you would waste your money coming over here to prove some macho point. What about the farm? What's your dad going to do without you?**

> **Evie : 5:55 pm : Still can't believe you've done this. It's incredibly irresponsible and impulsive and not at all needed. I am a big girl, and I can look after myself.**

> **Hope your flight was okay.**

> **Evie : 5:00 pm : What time will you be here? I can't wait to see you.**

> **Evie : 5:01 pm : Thank you for the messages. I will never forget them. XXOO**

My grumpy girl was softening.

Chapter 16

"**H**OW FAR ALONG ARE YOU?"

"I beg your pardon?"

Glam as always, water was dripping from my Rudolf-red nose, my damp hair clung to my cheeks, and I must have bloody reeked as I stared back at the smiling stranger's reflection in the mirror beside me. I was at JFK, waiting for Nate, and just finished my third round of hurling my absolute guts up.

Yes, the nervous chucks had struck me again, and it was bad. Real bad. The Pad Thai I'd eaten three days ago made another appearance—bad. Of course, a woman violently vomiting gave a complete stranger—the higher-the-hair-the-closer-to-God type—the right to ask me if I was pregnant. Hair lady picked the wrong day.

"I heard you were sick and thought…your baby." She pointed to my belly. "I was wondering how far—"

"Yeah, I know what you're wondering. I just can't believe you're asking." Her meddlesome smile disappeared, and I went in for the kill. "Is hanging around restrooms and accosting ill women a hobby of yours, or did I just get lucky?"

She blushed from her giant boobs up. "There's no need to be—"

"No need to be rude? No, you're right. There is no need. There is no need at all. How do you know I didn't just eat some bad Chinese? Or have the stomach flu? Imagine if I couldn't have children, and you asked me that."

"I'm sorry, I didn't think—"

"No, you didn't." I threw my paper towel in the trash and charged away with my head held high. My feeling of righteousness lasted maybe ten steps before I realized I'd taken my nerves out on a silly but most likely harmless bystander. I saw her slink past me from the corner of my eye, and I moved to apologize. She saw me coming and squealed—actually squealed out loud—and ran. "I'm sorry!" I yelled after her, but she was gone, lost in a sea of nameless faces.

Okay, that was it. I had to get my shit together before Nate's flight landed…if it ever bloody landed. Qantas flight number QF 4393 had been delayed three times. The ten pm arrival was initially pushed back to eleven, then eleven-thirty, and hopefully, finally, twelve forty-five. If you thought my yelling at the lady in the restroom was horrid, you should have seen me lose it at the insanely beautiful woman at the American Airlines desk.

"You cannot be serious! Twelve forty-five! You don't understand. This guy has had the hots for me since I was a child!" She screwed up her face in disgust. "Oh, please. He was a child too. Don't make it weird. So, tell me, what's with the delay? Why are we all waiting around like a bunch of clowns?"

At that point, I was probably the fiftieth asshole to ask this, and the reply I received displayed the type of thinly veiled disdain you would expect if that was the case.

"Look, I'm very sorry one of our cabin crew becoming violently ill and requiring an emergency stop in West Virginia has affected your love life. I can assure you he's not too happy about lying in a hospital bed on the wrong side of the country either. So, why don't you calm down, sit, and wait like all the other adults. Thank you for flying American Airlines."

She then waved me off dismissively and returned to her computer screen.

"Well…well…don't thank me. I'm not the one flying. Am I?" Brilliant comeback.

Lillian completely ignored me as I continued to pointlessly stand at her desk. She was quite possibly the only person to escape telling me to calm down without copping an absolute mouthful. But as hard as it was to take, I deserved it.

That confrontation led me to wander the shops, then make a pit stop at the restroom to chuck. I resumed my seat in the waiting area and died a little on the inside when I realized the preggo-hair lady was cowering beside me.

We sat in uncomfortable silence for quite some time before her fidgeting and belly rubbing drew my eyes to her stomach.

"You're shitting me," I mumbled. Preggo-hair lady was herself pregnant. Free of the always-flattering, garish illumination of the world's oldest working fluorescent lights in the restroom, I could see she was around my age, maybe even younger, and appeared to be in the later stages of pregnancy.

Bursting into tears was the only logical thing to do. "I'm so sorry!" I spat at her. She jumped six feet in the air, almost landing on the arm of her seat. "I am just a complete bundle of nerves. This guy is coming to see me, and he's my brother's best friend, and he likes me, and I don't know what to do. Not to mention I got fired by HotBoss for not taking his shit while he made me eat testicles, and now my niece can't do ballet, and then you said I was faaattttttt!"

Thankfully, I was blinded by the acidic tears pouring from my eyes and missed the looks of horror and second-hand embarrassment that were indeed displayed by those surrounding me. Sobbing into my hands, feeling like the biggest loser to ever wander the earth, I felt a hand touch me on the shoulder.

"I'm nervous too. That may be why I asked if you were pregnant. I get all floofy and weird when stressed and just start rambling to complete strangers. My husband is a sergeant in the Army. He's been gone for six months." She looked down and rubbed her belly. "He didn't even know I was pregnant when he left, and I didn't want to tell him over the phone. So, when he walks through those doors tonight, he will find out he's going to be a daddy. I'm terrified he's not going to be happy and freak out or just run. God,

I'm just babbling now." She leaned forward, slowly rising from her seat. "Sorry, I'll leave you in peace."

"No!" I grabbed her hand and held it on the joint armrest and nodded for her to resume her seat. "Don't go. Maybe we can wait together and talk. We both seem to need it. My name is Evie, by the way. Evie Austen."

She wiped a tear from her eye and smiled, squeezing my hand as she sat. "That would be really nice, Evie. I'm Shannon. Shannon Morales. And you're Australian? I've never met an Australian before." A smirk spread, and she sat up straight like she had a rod up her ass, "Good day, mate. Let's chuck another shrimp on the barbie." Shannon laughed hard. I didn't. "Sorry, I think I'm funny." She cleared her throat and attempted to redeem herself. "Sit with me some more. Tell me all about it."

So, I did just that. I told Shannon all about Byron and Sydney, Nate and Shelby, Finn, Iris, and Jocie, and the conundrum I found myself in. She told me to stress less and go for it, which she enthusiastically reiterated when I showed her Nate's pictures on my phone. "Hell, maybe we can swap. I'll take home Nate, and you take home the sergeant."

At around midnight, we bitched about the same men we sat faithfully waiting for and gorged on Krispy Kreme's and frappes so ridiculously large I could have fit my head in the cup. At twelve-thirty, we consoled each other when we both felt like vomiting. At one am, we started watching *Legends of the Fall* on her phone… big mistake. And at two, we exchanged numbers, both feeling like we may have found a kindred spirit, one we weren't ready to leave behind that night.

Huddled over a shared screen, talking, laughing, and crying, we kept each other company until two seventeen in the morning when the doors finally swung open and weary bodies began shuffling through. Her husband, Ryan, was the second through the gate and found his wife waiting for him with a sign we made with stationery and paper donated by Lillian, the American Airlines lady. It simply read, *Welcome Home, Daddy* and proudly rested on her bump. Watching the progression of relief, shock, joy, and elation on Sergeant Morales' face was priceless, as was witnessing him bending down to kiss his wife's sorely missed lips and then the baby she carried inside her. It also provided a distraction as the flow of people through the gate had ceased, and I still hadn't seen Nate.

After saying farewell to my new friend and promising to stay in touch, I stood alone and panicked. "Where the bloody hell are you, Nathaniel?"

But then, a second, larger crowd of passengers began to roll out. "How many people were on that flight?" I stood on my tippy toes, trying to see over all the giant, big-headed freaks that all seemed to be waiting in front of me…and there he was.

Have you ever swum in the ocean on a cloudy day? Dove deep beneath the waves, then emerged at the very moment the sun popped out from behind the clouds? I have, and it's magic.

One or two shards of light might pierce the surface even before you break through, and when you do, the world is bathed in a glistening glow that illuminates you as much as everything it touches.

Seeing Nate again, watching him purposefully stride toward me, impossibly beautiful, a picture of relief and determination, induced a feeling akin to—but far superior to—that.

Nate was my sun. The joy in his eyes as he saw me. The blinding beauty of his smile broke through hurried masses, singling me out like those rays had done, bursting through millions of layers of atmosphere to find me, a big-toothed, curly-haired drop in the ocean and warming me from within.

I knew the very second his sun-kissed hand touched mine I was saying goodbye to a part of my life I was hesitant to let go of. There was no going back. Whatever happened between us, wherever we ended up, I knew I would never be the same.

Chapter 17

Nate

WHEN I WAS FOURTEEN, I CROSSED TO THE dark side: engaging in my first experience as a bad boy and dragging Finn along with me for the ride. Looking for some adventure, I convinced him to steal some money from his mum's purse while I stole some beer from Dad's fridge in the shed. We used our ill-gotten gains to buy all matter of crap from Harvey's Milk Bar—chips, candy, soda, and of course, chocolate milk. With arms full of contraband, we made our way to the beach to idle the day away surfing, drinking, and eating. That was the plan, anyway.

Ten minutes and three bags of Cheetos into our epic session, Evie and Polly busted us. The girls had a genuine day off school so their teachers could prepare for their upcoming exams—a minor detail our pea-sized brains had forgotten.

Finn freaked out as Evie stormed down the sand, screaming his name like a banshee, threatening violence, and stopping only when the waves lapped at her perfectly painted toes. There she waited, hands on hips and glaring, for an explanation.

Like Finn, I, too, was freaking out for an entirely different reason. You see, Evie was wearing a skimpy bikini. I'd never seen her in one before, and Lord help me, she was smoking! All I remember is dropping my board, floating to her side, and praying to God she planned to dole out some physical punishment. If my feet touched the ground at all, I don't remember 'cause all I saw was the fire in her eyes, her golden, tousled hair wet with fury sweat, and that tight little body rippling with rage as she ripped us both a new one. To this day, I have no clue what she said. All I know is that she was insanely pissed and hot, and I loved every minute of her meltdown.

Deja vu struck when I saw her waiting for me. She wasn't hard to spot, jumping up and down to see over the taller bodies blocking her view, then grunt-pushing her way to the front with her usual force and determination.

The minute she saw me, her tired eyes glistened with excitement, her face—flushed with fatigue and frustration—lifted to a gorgeous smile, and those tiny little curls, still refusing to be controlled, framed her face so perfectly I could have cried. She was stunning…even more so than I remembered. And once again, I was that dumb, love-sick kid, dropping whatever I carried and floating toward her.

Thankfully, her exuberance matched mine. My number-one girl ran toward me, jumped into my arms, and buried her face into my neck. Through her muffled sobs, I heard her softly whisper, "I can't believe you're here."

"I can't believe I let you leave."

Fighting my body's urge to take her right there and then on the airport floor, I focused on the words, not the round ass that was inches from my fingers as they clenched around her tiny waist and settled on the small of her back. The plump, pert breasts pressing into my chest were another item I was not focusing on, along with her short, sharp, shaking breaths. I closed my eyes and took a deep breath, relishing the feeling of her against me for the first time… and it hit me—banana shampoo. "Jesus," I gasped, "I thought that bloody flight would never end. I've missed you so much, Lil One."

"Nate."

Further tightening my claim on her, I made the move I'd waited for and dreamed of for half my life. Sliding my hands up her curves and weaving my fingers through those curls, I gripped the back of her neck, my thumbs deftly brushing her pouty, trembling cherry lips before cradling her jaw and bending down to taste her. "Aoife."

Reaction-wise, it wasn't what I had hoped.

"Noooohhhh, shit." The girl straight-up panicked, squealing like one of her piglets and turning her head just as my lips were about to brush against hers. They landed on her cheek instead, catching the edge of her salty lips. "I'm sorry. I wasn't expecting…I mean, I wasn't—"

"It's okay, Gidge." I smiled, pressing my lips to her forehead, and laughing. "And for now, that's enough. For now."

Cruising down roads—the names of which I'd heard umpteen times on TV and in movies—next to my dream girl was a surreal and, so far, primarily silent experience. Part of this was due to the bruising I saw on Evie's wrist. That asshole dancer had hurt my girl. Not saying anything was killing me. Not demanding she drive me straight to him to kill him was killing me. But she had been through enough. So, I swallowed the anger down. *His time will come.*

The little conversation we had shared was regarding the well-being of the Austen family and Evie's curse-filled explanation of her evening with Christian.

According to her GPS system, we were nearing home, and to say I was relieved would be the understatement of the century. Not only because I was exhausted from my flight but because of the short skirt riding ever higher on Evie's thighs, and the memory of her body in my hands was stinging my palms. I couldn't wait to get her out of the damn car and feel it again.

"Eyes up, buddy," she snapped, slapping my thigh. "Did you fly all this way to sit next to me, ogle my flesh, and say nothing?" Her eyes fixed ahead on the empty lanes of the Grand Central Parkway, but the hint of a smile graced her lips.

"Nope. I flew all this way to kiss you, romance you, and take you home."

"Snort. You're pretty sure of yourself, aren't you?"

Witnessing a real-life verbal snort sealed part of the hole her departure had left in my heart. There was a long way to go before the little guy was fully healed, but that was a strong start. "Not as sure as I was. That head turn of yours was brutal on my ego."

She stifled a giggle by playing with her lips between her teeth, then licked them as she looked me over. My cock jumped like a trained poodle.

"I'd forgotten what an idiot you are. I'm not going home with you, Nate. I may not even kiss you."

"Wanna make a bet?"

"A bet?"

"That's what I said. I bet you fifty bucks that you'll be tongue-lashing me by the end of tomorrow and have me tied up in your bed by the end of the week."

"Nate!" Tires squealed when she slammed on the brakes after almost running us off the road.

"Sorry, you're right…I'll have you tied up."

Even in the dim, orangey street-light-lit car, I could see her furious blush. "You're an idiot."

"Yes. You made that point already. I'm gonna start a counter. I think we could get you in the *Guinness Book of Records* for idiot hurling."

"Idiot."

"See, three times in seconds. That record is as sure a thing as you falling wildly in love with me is."

Further inaudible mumbling—where I'm pretty sure I heard "idiot" several times—was followed by another chunk of muteness. For my part, it was due to the image of Evie calling me an idiot while being bound to her bed by her red lace underwear, killing off any other thoughts that dared enter my brain. As for Evie, who knew?

"We must be getting close to home by now?" I asked, attempting to kickstart the chin-wagging.

"You're right. We are close, but we're not going home."

"We're not?"

"Nope. We are going here." The car pulled to the left and stopped in front of a multi-story red brick building with a substantial black awning hanging over the door and a top-hat-and-red-vest-wearing doorman standing guard over the double French doors.

"The Bowery?" It was a question as much as a statement. "Evie, I am shocked!" I laughed, elbowing her in the side. "I knew you had it in you."

"It's not for us, idiot."

"Idiot again? That's five already, Gidge. Keep it up, champ." She rolled her eyes and pretended to smile while rushing from the car. My appalling man-packing meant that only the suitcase and my new carry-on needed to be taken from the trunk, and Evie had them out before I'd even shut my door. After dropping them onto the sidewalk with a thud, she began nervously shuffling her feet and pulling her cardigan sleeves down over her hands.

I had her on edge, and I stalked my prey. "Gidge, I know things are different over here, but this is a hotel, not a house."

"Well done, Naty. This is a hotel. Would you like a smiley sticker?"

"Don't be a smart ass."

"Well, don't be a dipshit."

I stepped closer, enjoying the rush of adrenaline surging through me as she released a moany little gasp. "Why are we at a hotel, Evie?"

"Umm. Well, what do people usually do at a hotel, Nathaniel?"

"They fu—"

"Fucking sleep!" she interrupted. "They sleep, Nathaniel. I booked you a room. You, singular, will stay here until Friday night. That's when I'll bring you over to surprise Finn."

Taking another step closer drew another audible moan. "So,

what I'm hearing is that you're locking me up for three days? Are you gonna tie me to the bed, or will I have to wear your pink, fluffy cuffs?"

Blushing profusely, she crossed her arms over her chest and remained defiant as ever. Fuck me if I didn't love it.

"No. There will be no tying up, and there are no pink fluffy things. But yes, you are being locked up."

"Why?"

"Time."

"Time?"

"Yes. Time."

"What do you need time for?"

"Stuff."

"Evie."

"Yes."

"Can you please give me more than that?"

"No."

"Please, tell me what's going on. I won't judge, I promise. You have nothing to be worried about, Evie. Tell me."

She sighed heavily, then looked up through her lashes. Fuck, she was beautiful. "I need time with you…alone." I couldn't help the twitch in my brows. "Not that kind of alone. I mean, I…uhh… umm…"

"Have some compassion for a man's jet-lagged constitution and spit it out, Little One. It feels like I was on that plane for weeks."

Clenching her fists, she looked to the heavens, muttered something under her breath, then floored me.

"I want us to get to know each other without Finn and his giant head butting in, okay? I need it, Nate. I want to understand how you and I fit when it's just us. I've booked a table at a bar on Friday night, and I thought we could surprise Finn then. That leaves us three days to just hang out, and talk, and…"

"And? Evie Austen. Am I your dirty little secret?" I asked, shimmying my hips suggestively and playing with the heart-shaped buttons on her cardigan. At first, her body seemed to collapse as she looked up at me from beneath her lashes. Her cheeks pinkened, and she went all floppy, kind of like she was melting. A tiny little sigh escaped her lips, the sight and sound of which damn near killed me and seemed to snap her out of her daze. She pulled her eyes from mine, went as rigid as my cock was beginning to feel, and quickly stepped away.

"Shop. And shop. You'll need it by the looks of your luggage. You haven't brought enough for a week, let alone a few months. I suppose you thought I'd do your laundry for you, like your mum. You got another thing coming, buddy."

Her faux anger was endearing, and I could see she felt conflicted, and for some reason, I felt the need to make her even more so. Being the asshole I am, I mimicked her pouty, crossed arms pose and stood there awkwardly, staring in awkward silence. And yes, I was making it uncomfortable, but the whole thing was kind of fucking amazing and full of the type of raw, ball-busting sexual tension they write about in novels.

"Well, good night, then," Evie suddenly yelled. "I'll pop in and see you after I take Iris to school in the morning. Oh, and I've already paid for the room, so you don't have to worry about anything. Just have a good rest. Okay. Bye, Nate."

"Wait!" My arm shot out, grabbed her by the elbow, and pulled her against me. "Aren't you going to come in? Check out the room? See where that hard-earned cash has gone?"

"No…not tonight. I don't think that's a good idea…" Her voice trailed off. My eyes followed hers as they moved away from my face to study my thumb as it swept back and forth over her skin. She was flushed with goosebumps after each stroke. It felt so fucking good to touch her. So soft and warm and right.

"Please, Evie. I just want to talk. It's been such a long time. I'll be on my best behavior, I swear." A playful barb sat on my lips. It was clear as day. She began to speak, "I…I want to…" but faltered, then looked at me, at my lips, with wide, innocent eyes that instantaneously destroyed me for any other woman.

"Tomorrow." She smiled, shaking her head as though clearing a fog. "I promise. We can take a tour of the city, or I could drive you out to Montauk to surf if you like."

I tightened my grip. "We could spend the day in a dumpster, and I would be fine with it. As long as I'm with you, Gidge, I don't care what we do."

Evie's eyes closed slowly as she sighed deeply, nervously giggled, and bounced on her toes like she was bursting to go to the toilet. The sighing and eye closing were clear signs of swooning I had seen many times on many girls—the chuckling and the jiggling not so much.

"Oh, okay, weirdo. That's weird…but…I suppose it's also nice." Years of ballet training then came on display as she unconsciously took a perfect ballerina pose, placed her hand on my shoulder, and kissed my cheek. Her lips lingered. The feel of her breath on my skin was hypnotic. She slipped away a fraction but remained achingly close, her eyes hungrily fixed on my lips. "Goodnight, Nathaniel."

I smiled and traced my hand along her modestly exposed collarbone. Christ, she was sexy. "Goodnight, Lil One."

She took a deep breath and kissed my cheek again, gasping slightly as my thumb caressed her neck. Then, she ran.

Chapter 18

Evie

"**I**'M PRETTY SURE I JUST GASSED THE DOORMAN." A trail of burnt rubber and a cloud of sour, toxic smoke heralded my three am-ish escape from Nate. "Holy shit! What the hell was that?"

Now, I have read almost every rom-com, contemporary, dark, wizard-warlock, fairy porn, and romance on Kindle. I thought I'd experienced attraction. But that was the first time I had ever felt that stomach-twisting, knee-faltering, heart-stopping, panty-soaking want that they all write about. And because I was me, instead of confessing my all-consuming feelings to Nate, kissing him as he deserved to be kissed and following my vagina's clear urgings to go up to his room, I acted like a stone-cold, mute bitch, jumping side to side like a toddler bursting to pee. I was trying to control the unfamiliar, hot-as-fuck ache building between my legs, but I was sure he just saw a frigid loser with bladder control issues.

Frigid. I shuddered even thinking about that word. I hated that word.

The last-minute, cherry-popping shutdown of my high-school sweetheart, Luke, had resulted in a flurry of Frigid Evie slurs by him, his friends, and half the town. At first, it was hurtful and so bloody embarrassing that I pretended to be sick for days. But in time, I began to see that I wasn't ready, and Luke wasn't worthy. Had he handled the aftermath in a more gentlemanlike manner—thanks for the words, Lizzy Bennet—I may have tried again, and he may have become my first.

But two things ensured that would never happen. One, his pure assholery in telling his friends all but ensured that he and his creepy little hands would never be touching me again.

And two, something was missing with him, and I knew it even then. My body didn't react to Luke's. It didn't want him. Had I felt half of what I had just felt fully clothed on a New York sidewalk with Nate—melting into his touch, quivering from his words—as I did lying half naked on a bed with Luke, things would've ended differently. But I didn't. I didn't feel what I wanted to feel for the person who would be taking what I could never get back.

Hindsight told me, though, my do-it-myself cock blocking was a blessing in disguise. Maybe, just maybe, I had discovered someone worthy.

Caught in the wilds between horniness and regret while slapping myself on the leg and wondering if it was too skanky to change my mind and turn around, I traveled the remaining distance home and almost hit the roof when my phone rang.

"Evie. Are you alright? Where are you? I just got back from Scarlett's and saw Jocelyn's car was gone. Everything alright?"

"Yep, I'm fine, Finn. I just, um…couldn't sleep. It was too cold to walk, so I took the car. I'm just pulling into the garage now." Yes, a garage. It was a rarity in New York and one we were thrilled to discover when we first arrived. It sat at the back of the house and was accessed by a small, private alley kept ridiculously clean by our neighbor Mr. Yashito. There was no internal access to the place, which meant in the coming winter, our first with snow, we would still have to make a dash between it and the house. But that was a small price to pay for the convenience of off-street parking and storage for our surfboards and Finn's ridiculously expensive bike.

He met me outside, casting a suspicious eye over me as I guiltily shuffled beside him with my head down.

"You're up to something, sis. I can smell it a mile away. Oh my God, I can smell cologne too. Evie, have you gone and got yourself a fella?"

"Don't be stupid," I snapped, punching his arm. "You're the only one slutting around at all hours of the night. I told you I couldn't sleep and went for a drive."

"That doesn't explain the smell. You smell all manly, Evie, and last time I checked, you were not a man."

"No shit, Sherlock." We entered the house, and Finn followed me closely up the stairs, sniffing me like a hound. "Would you piss off? I stopped and got fuel, alright? The attendant smelled like he'd taken a bath in Obsession, and it must have latched onto me. Now fuck off to bed and leave me the hell alone." All this was said in a whisper to not wake Iris or Jocelyn, so Finn didn't hear a word. My glare was enough to either scare him off or satisfy him, and smiling like a freshly laid idiot, he took himself to bed for the same measly few hours of sleep I was about to try and have.

***

Giggles and a sloppy kiss ripped me from a sexy Nate dream at an ungodly hour.

"You were making funny noises like this, Aunty." Iris then again made a series of moans, sighs, and whimpers that I never ever wanted to hear from her again. "You sounded like Daddy when he eats a Caramello Koala."

"What time is it, bubs?" I asked sleepily, ignoring the inappropriate sounds.

"I dunno. Can't read the clock yet, but Jocie said it was time to wake you up. So, WAKE UP!" That last part was screamed right on my face with full kid morning breath.

"Why are we up so early?" I asked as I stumbled into the kitchen. I knew why. My aunt was on a health kick. The long, uphill walks we took on our weekend in Tarrytown had shaken the old thing to her core.

"I'm getting soft, literally and figuratively," she yelled to me over blending her smoothie. "Would you like some? This one is pineapple, banana, chia, almond butter, and milk. Some yogurt, baby spinach, and a dash of maple syrup…and maybe some vodka for a little sweetness."

"Jocie! It's six am!"

"I'm just joking, darling," she muttered, calling me a party pooper as she pushed the sizable Absolut bottle out of view. "Hair of the dog, Evie. I may have overindulged on the rosé while speaking to Olivier last night. Besides, I don't have to go anywhere today."

"Ahh, you're talking with Olivier again?" Olivier was Jocelyn's twenty-something-year-old boy toy in France. The poor kid had gone and gotten feelings for her on her last vacation, and she'd fled in the middle of the night, claiming it was for his own good and that she had no desire to be tied down at her age. But I knew better. She liked Olivier a lot more than she was willing to admit. The sparkle in her eye and wistfulness in her voice whenever she spoke told me so.

"Are you planning on seeing him when you go back? Are you gonna kiss him?" sang Finn, pressing a kiss on his daughter's cheeks as he entered the room. We both regarded each other's disheveled appearance but said nothing.

"Don't you two have anything better to do but interfere in my life? Besides, who says I'm going back?"

"Uhh… Pot. Kettle. Black. Please. Keeping you out of our lives or away from the French wine region and the hot men that call it home is like trying to keep Finn away from chocolate. It's not going to happen."

"Okay, then, let's make a deal. I'll tell you all about my time and non-existent feelings about Lu— France, and you tell me about yours for—"

"La la la." Finn and I jumped to our feet.

Chapter 19

Nate

AT THE BEGINNING OF MY ADVENTURES AS A ladies' man, I carried my reputation like a coat of honor. Women in town knew what I was and what they would get from me, and I loved it. I was THE guy. The guy to turn to after a breakup. The guy to go out with when you needed a fun, no-strings pick-me-up. The weapon to make her real guy jealous. I had been many different guys.

There was a look that women always gave me, too. At first, I mistook it for lust, knowing, and hunger. And sure, there was an element of that mixed in, often a bit of alcohol too. But an overriding component of that particular look was judgment. They all judged me. I was Nate the Slut. Nate, the goodtime guy that could give them a dirty little thrill and a quick O. There was no curiosity, no yearning to know me better, only for what they'd heard—correctly—that I could do with my tongue.

That look got old fast.

It felt like Polly was the first to try and see me, to even attempt a glimpse beyond my hard candy coating, but Evie…yeah, she was different, a whole other level. Conflicted, annoyed, angry, more than a little turned on and scared, but definitely curious. Evie looked at me like I was a puzzle she was desperate to solve, and I was more than willing to let her solve me. Or I was willing to let her slide me into place. No woman had ever looked at me the way Evie did. Not one.

And it wasn't a new thing. Evie had always watched me in a way that heightened my senses.

For instance, the way her eyes just drank me in as I climbed from the hotel pool, then gathered my towel from the seat beside her, deliberately brushing my wet hand against her hip as I did. Every jet-lagged muscle, fiber, cell, and neuron in my body felt her gaze—and my dick...my dick felt it too. It was how I wanted to be looked at for the rest of my life. She could deny it all she liked, but Evie liked me...wanted me...was curious about me. I just had to get her to admit it.

"Why are you swanning around in your swimsuit when I told you to be ready at nine?"

"Why are you stripping me naked as you watch me?"

She rolled her eyes. "Snort. I am doing no such thing." She was. She totally was. I had worn my tiniest, tightest swim shorts to ensure she did.

"Why are your eyes suggestively roaming my body, then?" I saw the bruises again, poking out from the cuff of her shirt, and again said nothing as I began drying my stomach with the towel, enjoying her eyes almost hanging from her head.

"Ach... What? Wh...I...because you're stupid, that's why. I am going to wait in the abs—uhhh...in the cafe, the absolute cafe, the cafe is called the absolute café, and I'll be there. Hurry the hell up and get ready. Oh, and please be dressed the next time you message me to meet you somewhere." She marched off and was totally checking me out in the reflection of the floor-to-ceiling windows as she did.

It was all going to plan—a plan that contained five steps, each devised last night after my third consecutive dream where Evie pulled off the freeway on our drive home, slipped out of her seat, and rode on my lap. If the cards fell as I suspected they would, Evie would be mine by the end of the week. If not, the day and that front-seat action wouldn't be just a dream.

That pool move was step one: get Evie to see as much of my body as she could. Yes, I wanted her to see me in a way other women never did, but she was still a woman at the end of the day. And I was still a wet, naked, muscly man. I had to use what I had.

Step two: be super charming and irresistible…to other women. That would commence as soon as I was showered and dressed to impress.

Luckily, I'd watched enough TV and movies with Evie over the years to learn how she liked a man to dress. Miss Austen was an absolute sucker for a crisp white tee—preferably tight—with my dark aviators tucked into the neck, exposing my collar bone and a tease of my pecs, dark denim jeans and brown leather boots. Oh, and the hair—tousled and twisted, the perfect I-just-climbed-out-of-bed, this-is-how-sexy-I-am-when-I-wake do.

Standing before the mirror, I gave myself a quick pep talk, breath, and pit sniff, and one final hair flick. I had to admit it. I looked good. I was having a hard time keeping my hands off myself. Miss Austen didn't stand a chance.

As promised, Evie was waiting for me in the cafe—surprise, surprise, it was NOT called the absolute cafe—and she looked incredible. I was too busy holding in my gut and flexing to notice her outfit at the pool, but she was wearing a cute, frilly white shirt, an orangey-tan skirt with white tights I wanted to rip off her with my teeth, and a hat. A cute floppy hat the same color as her skirt, covering her curls. She could easily have just arrived in a time machine from the 70s, and it was hot.

Watching me approach the mirror, she clearly mouthed, "OH MY GOD," to herself before frowning as she turned to face me. The girl really needed to become more aware of reflective surfaces.

"About time. I thought Christmas would get here before you. I only have a few hours before I have to get Iris. Let's go."

"Wait," I said, gripping her elbow. "I didn't get a chance to tell you before. You look really pretty today, Little Gidge." Her eyes flicked to mine as I gave her my best Flynn Rider smolder.

She considered me, and a tiny hint of that beautiful smile flashed across her pouty little mouth before it disappeared.

"Move it, Romeo."

This was going to be tough.

I followed behind her like the puppy I was. "Where are we going? Shopping? Sightseeing? Surfing?"

"Do you only know words that start with S?" She laughed at her joke and kept walking. "And yes, we are going shopping. Like I said yesterday, I can't believe you only brought two bags with you. You're here for, like, three months. Like J-Lo said, I ain't your mama, and I am not doing your laundry. You need clothes... socks...and underwear."

"Right. I get it now. This is all an elaborate scheme to see me in some tighty-whities. You do know we don't need to go anywhere to do that. We could just go back to my room."

"Uhh, hard pass. I've already seen you in your swimmers, remember? I think that's more than enough Nate skin for one day."

"Well, why don't we get you into your undies, then? Make it even?"

That didn't even get a response.

Blinding sunlight hit me as we stepped outside. I had expected New York to be blanketed in a constant haze of pollution, but the sky was as blue as Evie's eyes, and the air was surprisingly fresh. It came as quite a relief. Asthma is not a sexy affliction, but it's one I'd had all my life. I was concerned the pollution would wreak havoc on my lungs, but so far, so good.

Sliding my sunglasses out of my shirt and popping them on, I was just about to mention this to Evie, who was furiously striding ahead of me, when she suddenly stopped.

I slammed straight into her back and made a weird *oomph* sound as her head whacked into my chest. My hands protectively fell to her waist, anchoring her to my body to stop us from tumbling.

"Oh my God, Nate! Get off me!" She squirmed in my grip before holding still. "Wait...what is that? Is that your...? Can I feel your…mini-Nate pressing into my back?! Geez, it is always that…firm?"

"My what?" Fuck! Did I have a massive boner I wasn't aware of? I glanced down in horror, for some reason, my hands patting myself down like a prison guard before shielding my crotch…my perfectly non-erect crotch. She was right, though. Something hard was digging into her back.

Laughter rolled through me as I returned my hands to her waist and pulled her firmly against me, adding a tiny little roll of my left hip as I leaned down to whisper in her ear. "Trust me, Evie. If that was mini-Nate pressing into your back, you would know exactly what it was." I pulled my inhaler from my pocket, held it in front of her face between my thumb and index finger, and swung it back and forth.

She spun to face me, her hands flying up to my shoulders, her cute little face full of worry. "You brought your inhaler? Are you alright? Is your asthma acting up? Do you need me to take you back to your room?"

Not going to lie. The temptation to say, "Yes, Evie. I am terribly unwell. Take me back to my room and nurse me in bed," was strong.

"Hey, Lil Gidge, relax. I'm fine. It's just a precaution. Don't you remember how I used to cough all the time when we went to Sydney? I wasn't sure what the air would be like here, and I didn't want to ruin our day looking for a pharmacy—or, you know, dying." Evie laughed and slapped my shoulder…the shoulder her hand was still resting on. My hands were still on her waist. For all intents and purposes, we were in an eighth-grade slow dance position in the middle of a New York sidewalk.

I gripped her tighter, pulled her onto me until she was standing on my feet, and then began to step from side to side. With all the might she contained in her five-foot-nothing frame, she fought the urge to smile…but failed. Ever so slowly, the edges of her lips began to curl. I slipped my right hand from her waist, grabbed her right hand, and spun her beneath my arm. An irrepressible giggle burst from her mouth, and a smile lingered.

"Nate, we can't dance in the middle of the street. People are looking at us."

"They're not looking at us, Evie. They're looking at you…at the ballerina. Even swaying side to side with a clumsy sod like me, the way you move is breathtaking."

There's a moment in the 90's movie, *The Wedding Singer*, where Drew Barrymore and Adam Sandler do a practice kiss for her up-coming wedding to demonstrate the appropriate amount of tongue to be used—"church tongue," as Drew calls it. Anyway, the kiss is amazing, and Drew stands there, looking up at Adam like a giddy, love-drunk idiot, like he hung a crescent moon and she's just a believer, looking up and hanging from its pointy end with all her might. It's an adorable scene, and it's also how Evie was looking at me, proving again she saw me in a way no one else ever had and leaving me feeling numb from the neck down.

"When did Nathaniel Myers, super hoochie, become such a romantic?"

"When he woke up…when he thought he'd lost you."

I stopped swaying, and Evie continued to gaze at me in wonder. I took her hand and spun her beneath my arm again, but this time, I didn't pull her back against me. I let her go, watched her spin away, and caught the hand of a cute brunette who happened to be checking me out as she walked by.

"G'day. May I have this dance?" I gave her my best smolder and thickest accent, which always worked with the tourists at home.

"Well, Good day to you too, handsome. Sure thing." She smiled lazily.

As I gave her a spin, I stole a sideways glance at Evie and almost burst out laughing. She was watching—no, drilling holes into us, with her mouth hanging open, catching flies, and her cute little foot tapping the pavement so hard she could crack it.

I dropped my new touchy-feely friend—who had taken a siz-able chunk of my ass into her hands—into a low dip, the bleached ends of her hair brushing the concrete before I pulled her back into my arms. "I finish work at five," she swooned. "Are you free for a drink?"

Before I could reply, a hand, arm, then shoulder forced its way between our bodies, ripping us apart like the jaws of life would do to a wrecked car door. "No, he is not free. Now fuck off, desperado!" Evie stood before me like a bodyguard, her arms out horizontally at the sides, acting as a curly-mop, human barrier.

"Okay, okay, calm down, lady. Geez, you Aussies are freaking weird." Even after calling me weird, the cute brunette still gave me a wink as she trotted off, keeping an eye on Evie as she left.

"If I didn't know better, I'd swear you were jealous, Lil Gidge," I said, standing dangerously close behind her, taking a deep inhale and smelling her curls. She turned to me but refused to look at my face. Instead, her eyes hovered anywhere between my neck and feet.

"Snort. You wish. I was trying to stop that poor woman from making a fool of herself."

Capturing her jaw, I tilted her chin to meet my eyes.

"I dunno. You shooed her away pretty fast. I swear I see a bit of monster green in those baby-blue eyes of yours."

"Nope. Just trying to get rid of her. I don't have all day to watch you pick up randoms. You need to get new clothes…especially since Desperado has ruined your tee with all her drool."

"Sure, Gidget. Whatever you say." Her cute, freckled little face flushed, she spun on her heels and was off…but not before I gave her a nice little slap on the bum. "Lead the way, Boss."

Chapter 20

Evie

NATHANIEL MYERS AND HIS HEATED GAZE crawling across my thighs had been the first things I thought of when I woke this morning. He'd haunted my dreams that night, too. His stupid smug grin and strong hands gripping me at the airport had me waking up drenched in sweat, my fingers left to finish what dream Nate had started.

That intensity, the cauldron of heat and curiosity those eyes stirred, then accompanied me in the shower. When dressing, they were incredibly helpful, borderline demanding in ordering what I was to wear. The white, thigh-high stockings that my short skirt barely covered and belonged in a K-pop video were their first suggestion. The lacy yellow bra and thong were the second. These random sexy dreams and desires to become a human thirst trap were coincidences. The thoughts I kept having about Nate being mine, about what that would look and feel like…romantic folly. I was just lonely…adjusting…maybe a bit confused, and definitely still reeling from the glut of emosh feelings all the messages he'd sent evoked. Seeing him so soon after reading them was a lot too.

I kept telling myself that was all it was, finding countless excuses, anything other than what I refused to admit—until I watched him get out of that pool. Till I saw him push off the concrete edge, his hard, lean body rising like a god from Atlantis. I saw each individual droplet slide down his body, pooling in the nooks and crevices of his abs and belly button. Till I saw the outline of HIM in those tiny shorts.

Even as I sat waiting for him in the cafe, my freshly lacquered nails digging into the arms of the chair, my legs pressing together to stop the throbbing I was sure must have been audible to passersby, I lied to myself. Sure, he was hot, and maybe I wanted him physically. But it was just the reaction of a sexually frustrated, immature virgin. And Nate was acting like a typical boof-headed bloke, lifting himself out of the water the hard way, the look-how-ripped-I-am way, when the ladder was right beside him. He knew what he was doing. It was all part of his game. Well, I wasn't playing.

None of the thirsty, horny nonsense was acknowledged as genuine, honest-to-goodness feelings by the rational, mum-type part of my brain until I saw him hold that beautiful, elegant, probably experienced, feminine woman in his arms and dip her like in a movie.

Something tore inside me. Snapped. I wanted to scratch her eyes out, discard her, then pull him to the ground and ride him on the street, screaming, "Mine, mine, mine! GET OFF HIM, YOU SKANK. NATE IS MINE. NATHANIEL MYERS IS MINE."

Of course, I did nothing of the sort. I swallowed the wave of like—'cause god knew it couldn't be love—and let it reemerge as snark. "Do you even want to be with me today, or do you want to just drink in some bar and find a woman to plunder in an alley?"

Hurt flashed across his face. "I was just fooling around. Of course I want to be with you. I don't even want to look at another woman. You're it for me, Eves. I'm sorry."

I didn't believe a word he said. Nate Myers not looking at another woman…please. But I couldn't say the same for his expression. He looked pained and worried, and it hurt like a blunt knife twisting in my heart. "Fine. Just stop being so charming and Nate-ish, then."

The smirk was back, but it looked a little forced. "Sooo, you think I'm charming?"

"Oh my God." I couldn't help but smile as I grabbed his hand and dragged him down the street.

Fifteen minutes into our first store, I realized I'd made several mistakes. The first was the store I took Nate to, Rag and Bone on Mercer. It was one of Finn's favorite brands, and I thought the fact that my idiot brother wore their clothes would add enough of an ick factor to render them unappealing on Nate. I was wrong.

My second mistake was sitting outside the changing room while he tried things on. The hot blonde sales assistant, the second woman that morning I had wanted to physically hurt for checking out Nate, had just dumped the pile of clothes and slid the curtain across. But she didn't close it all the way, and Nate didn't either. I could have told him, but for some reason, I forgot to.

Honestly, I hadn't set out to watch him undress. It just kind of happened. There I was, innocently biting my nails, staring at my feet, and wondering where to take him next, when a voice inside told me to look up. I did and was met with the vision of Nate pulling his tee over his head. As always, he wore a white undershirt, and I continued to ogle helplessly as, in slow motion, that, too, was discarded. All that remained were jeans that sat dangerously low on his hips despite the presence of a belt that seemed to be doing absolutely nothing. God bless it.

Sans shirt, he ran his hands through his hair, roughing it up all sexy-like and looking at the shirts I'd selected while allowing him zero input. A wry smile spread to his lips when he picked up the first, a gray Henley with the word DOOFUS written across the chest. He chuckled, his hand scratching at his belly before he slipped it over his head. I mourned the loss of his skin as the soft cotton hid it from view, but even clothed, he was irresistible. After a quick look and approving nod in the mirror, he ripped it off and moved on to the next. This pattern continued for maybe five or six shirts. A teeny part of me was annoyed as he hadn't come out to show me any of them like I'd instructed, but I was too ab-struck to mention it. Then everything changed. He removed his shirt, but the next item he picked up was a pair of pants.

He dropped them back onto the chair beside him, allowing his fingers to slip over his belt, unfastening and sliding the leather through the loops and then the buckle. They dropped lower on his hips, and I watched with mouth agape as his thumbs hooked inside the waist, and he began to pull them down. The swell of a very peachy-looking ass emerged. *Is he wearing any underwear?* I gasped, and his head shot up and sideways, instantly spotting me through my pervert gap.

Time stood still. We watched each other, our chests rising and falling in silent sequence. A smirk spread over his lips. He said nothing but winked, turned his back, faced the mirror, and continued to lower his pants.

My heart stopped. He saw me… He knew I was watching… He was still undressing… He liked that I was watching… Oh, he wore cruelly low boxers. I had just seen him in his swimwear but seeing him there with that thin scrap of material—the only thing protecting him from complete exposure—was so hot and, oh my god, unfucking believable. The man was cut like stone. Hard lines balanced perfectly and were softened by bulging muscle, golden flesh, and a light sprinkling of sandy hair. I licked my lips as he stepped out of his jeans one leg at a time, neatly folded them, and laid them on a chair. His thick, muscular thighs, quads, and calves—the ones I only then realized I thought of so often at the most random times of the day—clenched and tightened as he stepped into the army-green chinos and slid them up over his butt. After another glance in the mirror, he slipped the tee back over his head. His eyes never left mine as he let it fall from his fingers and settle on the top of the pile. It was only then that I noticed the small daisy tattoo positioned right over his heart. *When did he get that tattoo? And why a daisy?* The foolish, romantic quadrant of my mind instantly sprang to a laughable conclusion… *It's for you, Aoife. He knows daisies are your favorite and has it over his heart for you. He loves you.*

"What do you think, Gidge? You like what you see?" I jumped off my seat as he pushed aside the curtain and stood before me.

"I didn't look—see." *WHAT?*

His eyes were full of laughter, but he held it together. "Do you think I need to try on more pants?"

"Yes…well, I mean, these look nice….good…great, if…if you wanted to maybe just get another color. I think they have a few."

He nodded, sucking his bottom lip into his mouth. "Whatever you say, boss." He then strode back into the changeroom, waving slowly as he disappeared from view. "Show's over, lady."

I was lost for words, so wet I feared dehydration, and caught between ignorance and acknowledgment. Do I pretend that didn't happen, or do I roll with it?

"When did you get the tattoo?" And down the hill I rolled.

"Thought you didn't look—see?"

Shit.

"I didn't. I saw it at the pool."

"Nice save, Gidge." He chuckled and stuck his head back through the curtain. "I got it maybe a day or two after you left. You like it?"

"Your man boobs were blinding me, so I didn't get a good look. I just saw a green blob."

"Is this your way of asking me to come out shirtless again?"

Damn the bastard if I didn't laugh.

"No, Nathaniel," I said, raising a brow. "This may come as a shock, but believe it or not, not every thought or suggestion I make relating to you is related to seeing your body."

"Hmm, I say…not."

"What? Not what?"

"Not. You said…believe it or not, not every thought or suggestion I make relating to you is related to seeing your body, and I don't believe it. So, I said…"

"Yeah, yeah, I get the point." I rolled my eyes with all my might and waved him off. "Just hurry the hell up."

The shopping tour rolled onto three more shops before we had a break for lunch at Rubirosa on Mulberry St. "Please tell me you haven't gone vegan since you've been here. I need meat, and I need it now."

"Vegan? Me? As if." I passed the menu to Nate.

"Don't you want to have a look first?" he asked.

"Nope, I come here all the time with Finn and Iris. I know what I'm having."

"Okay, then." He smiled, throwing the menu down and crossing his arms across his chest as our waitress approached. "Hey, Candice."

Young Candice was a super-cute redhead I knew not only from here but from the dance school. Her nephew, Cole, was one of Iris's buddies there—the back flipper. My choice in bringing Nate here was made not only because they have the best pizza in the neighborhood but also as a test. That guy had the biggest perv eyes of any man I've known, and Candice was hot. If his claims about wanting me were genuine, his eyes wouldn't follow that perky ass. If they did, I would know it was the same old Nate.

"Hey, Evie. What can I get my favorite Aussie ballerina today?"

"I'll have the usual but make it a large since I have a big person with me today instead of Iris, and a small cheese too. I want Nate to try both."

"Coming right up." Candice returned to the kitchen, popping her notepad in the back pocket of her denim cutoffs like I hoped she would. I watched and waited.

Nothing.

He. Did. Not. Flinch.

His eyes stayed on mine, and he smiled. "Wow, first-name basis with the staff. You're a real local, aren't you?"

I swallowed the lump in my throat and acted as nonplussed as possible. "You sound disappointed by that."

"I am. It makes it harder for me to take you back home if you've become attached to the place."

"I'm not coming home with you, Nate. My life is here now."

"We'll see about that. I still haven't kissed you yet. I'm pretty confident once I do, you'll pack your bags faster than you can say, 'Lay another one on me, big boy.'"

"God, I would kill to have an eighth of your delusional confidence." I laughed. "Let's see how much you want to kiss me after a few slices of the Rubirosa Supreme—tomato, mozzarella, pepperoni, mini meatballs, and enough roasted garlic to take out the Cullen's."

"I bet it would taste even better on your lips."

"Omg. You're such an idiot." I broke off a piece of my complimentary bread stick and threw it at his face. Of course he caught it and chewed it all sexy, then licked the non-existent crumbs from his bottom lip. *OMG, he is so hot.* "Drinks!" I yelled. "Candice, can we get some drinks over here?"

"Coming right up, Evie."

"Idiot, huh?" Nate sucked his tongue into his cheek and pulled a notepad out of his pocket. "That's the first for the day and number seven overall." I flashed my fakest smile to try and hide my rapid slide into a personal crisis slash hell.

"What, you're keeping a paper tally, now?"

"I told you last night. You have *Guinness Book of Records* potential, kid, and I'm not letting it go to waste." I ignored the cuteness and gulped down the Pepsi Candice had just placed in front of me.

"Oh, Candice," I said, liquid spilling from my mouth as I lunged at her wrist. I was determined for him to check her out. Was it weird? Yes. But I needed him to look at her ass like I needed air. "I didn't introduce you before. This is Nate, Iris's uncle. He's come to stay and annoy us for a while."

"G'day, Candice." Nate smiled and held out his hand to shake Candice's, but his eyes did NOT shift from my face.

"Candice is studying Theater at NYU. Isn't she beautiful? She's going to be a big star on Broadway someday."

"Is that so?" Finally, Nate glanced at Candice. "I should ask for your autograph now. Might be worth a lot of money when you make it big." He gave her his standard, gorgeous, cheeky smile. Not so much as an eyelash on the man's face fluttered.

This was Nate. The biggest flirt I had ever met. The man who picked up a girl and took her home at a FUNERAL was sitting before a 5'10" red-haired glamourpuss with full lips, killer hips, and her giant rack pushed under her chin, and he gave her NOTHING. He then had the audacity to return those shimmering baby blues to me and WINK. HE WINKED.

A giant pit of fire opened in my gut.

HOLY SHIT. THIS IS FOR REAL. NATE REALLY LOVES ME.

Chapter 21

Evie

"W HO EVEN ARE YOU?"
I studied the pale, terri-
fied-looking woman in the mirror
and answered as her weary body collapsed. "I'm you, idiot.
The one Nathaniel Myers flew from Australia to America
for because Nathaniel Myers is legitimately into *you…
me…us."*

It was illogical, yet it was the only explanation. Yes,
I'd read the man's messages, and yes, I'd heard his flirta-
tious words. But until that very minute, until that man
paid little to no attention to one of the hottest young
women I'd ever seen because he refused to take his
eyes off me, I honestly didn't believe it.

I could feel the chunks rising. A panic chuck
that could take down the Titanic was surging and
about to crest when there was a knock on the
door. "Evie, it's Candice. Nate asked me to check on
you. He said you looked as crook as a dog and ran off. I
think he meant you didn't look well."

"Not gonna lie, Candice. I think I could be dying." I
heard her laugh. "Yep, that's right. Laugh it up, lady. This
could be it for Evie Austen. I could drop dead right
here in your bathroom, and you're laughing
like it's the best joke you've heard all day."

"I'm sorry, Evie. I promise I won't laugh
any more. But could you please just let me

in? At least then I will know if we need paramedics or if there's no hope." Candice was a damn liar. I could still hear her laughing as I crawled to the door, reached, and unlocked it. She lasted two seconds without laughing.

"Why are you on the floor? Evie. Oh gosh. You have to get up, sweetheart. My brother was on cleaning duty last night, and I can guarantee he did not mop this floor." That did it. I was up in a flash. "Would this sudden drama episode have anything to do with that gorgeous man sitting out there, waiting for you like a lost little puppy?"

I shrugged. "Possibly. No one can say for sure. Maybe I over-ate…or it's food poisoning from the pizza?"

"You haven't eaten yet."

"Yeah, but still."

"What's going on, Evie? This is the first time I have seen you here with anyone but your family in all the weeks you've been coming here, and it's also the first time I've seen you smile the way you were at Nate. Did he say something horrible?"

"No! Not at all. He's being really sweet. Too sweet. Suspiciously sweet, and it's grossing me the hell out." Laughy Laugh-A-Lot giggled again.

"Ahh, I get it. You like him, and you're not grossed out. You're freaked out." I nodded, grabbed her hand, and clutched it to my stomach.

"What do I do, Candice? I've known him my whole life. He's Finn's best friend…Iris's uncle…and I brought him here as a test. I used you like a fucking honey trap. I thought he would be all over you. I thought he would be hitting on you faster than I could say, 'I knew it.'"

"But he didn't."

"No! He didn't. He looked at you and smiled as a normal person would. He didn't look at your boobs or stare at your perfect ass and make that *whoa* face he always does when a hot chick walks by. You know what he did? He went right back to looking at me, and then he *winked* and…and…what do I do?"

Candice used her free hand to brace my shoulder, then bobbed to my eye level. "First, you will breathe *and* let go of my hand."

"Shit, sorry." I released the poor girl's fingers and took a deep, shaky breath.

"Nate saying hello to me was the first time he took his eyes off you since you came in. You should have seen his face when you ran in here. He was so cute and worried sick. Who cares about Finn and your history? If anything, that makes it even more special. Look at me and my boyfriend, Anthony. I've known him my whole life too. Our dads are best buds. He always hangs out with my brothers, and it's amazing. I know him. I know I am safe. He wouldn't do anything to hurt me. And they would all kick his ass if he did."

"But it's different for me."

"Why, Evie? Why is it different for you?"

"Because…I'm…me. I'm nothing and no one, and *he*…he is everything. Look at him! He's like *gah*, and I'm like *blah*." That was it. The waterworks started. "And he was sleeping with my friend Polly, and he is, like, super experienced, and I am a fucking…" I paused, looked around the bathroom I knew full well no one else was in, and then whispered, "I'm a virgin, Candice. A virgin."

"So what? So am I."

She said what now?

"You! But you're so…so… And you have Anthony, and… I'm ooooolllllddddd." I lost it. I completely and utterly lost it. Poor Candice was supporting my body weight as I leaned limply against her.

"It's okay, Evie. Shh. Don't cry over this. I promise it will be okay. Come on. Come with me." Candice took me by the hand and led me from the bathroom into a small staff room. The fact that this was the second time in a week I was escorted into the staff quarters, a blubbering mess, was not lost on me. "Here, sit down and let me fix you up." I was then popped on a chair and cuddled until the weeping subsided. My face was then washed and dried, I applied a fresh coat of lip gloss, and my hair was smoothed and

tied into a cute bun. "There, fresh as a daisy and twice as pretty."
My savior smiled. "I'm waiting for marriage, and I refuse to get
married until I'm done with school. Trust me, we fool around a
lot…*a lot*. But if you're not ready like me or just not sure, Nate
will have to wait. And judging by the puppy eyes, I'd say he would
wait forever. You're beautiful, Evie. And you're smart and funny
and such an amazing dancer. Cole has been dancing since he could
walk, and you are his favorite teacher ever."

"Was his favorite," I mumbled.

"What, you're not teaching his class anymore?"

"I'm not teaching any classes. Christian fired me."

"Say again?"

I shared my tale of woe. Candice was livid and had her own
to tell…on the phone…to Jody…Christian's business partner, *not*
his second in charge. "She wants to talk to you, Evie." The phone
was thrust into my hand, and Jody's booming voice nearly blew
my head off.

"Evie. You have to believe me. I had no idea what had happened. He told me you had quit when you didn't show up for your
class today. Please, please come to see me tomorrow. You are one
of our most promising teachers, and I am not losing you."

"But what about—"

"You let me worry about dance-boy. He is out of control at
the moment, and I have had enough. Just be here tomorrow at
twelve. Oh, and I expect to see Iris front and center on Thursday."

Still crying, I made my way back to the table. Nate sat nervously, drumming a parmesan grinder against the table, a hesitant
smile on his face and two piping hot pizzas sitting before him.
"Eves! Babe, what is it? Please tell me. Whatever it is, I can fix it."

"It's not you, Nate." *This time.* "I just spoke to Jody from the
dance studio. She didn't want to lose me and asked me to come
and see her tomorrow. I think she is going to give me my job back.
Oh, and Iris can—"

Nate's hand slammed down on the table.

"No way! I won't allow it."

"You won't *allow* it?"

"That's right." He shoved a slice in his mouth and took an exaggerated bite. "You *could* say I forbid it."

"You forbid it?"

"Why do you keep repeating everything I say? Yes. I forbid it, and I'm positive that Finn will agree. He may congratulate me on my stance."

"Oh my God! Who the hell do you think you are?" Before I could stop myself, I picked a meatball off the pizza and threw it in his face. Candice, who was carrying two beers to our table, whistled, spun on her heels, and returned to the bar.

Nate sat with mouth agape…for two seconds till he threw a slice of pepperoni onto my cheek. "I don't *think* I'm anyone. I *know* I am someone who is supposed to look out for you. To protect you. And if you think, for one minute, I will let you back around that goon, you've got another thing coming."

"Nathaniel Myers. I am not a child, and I do not need protection."

"Seemed like you did when you called me in tears in the back of that town car. Look," he snapped, then, in a stunning contradiction, gently lifted my hand from the table and held it in his. "I can still see the bruise on your arm. You think I missed that, did you?" I pulled my hand away.

"If you came all the way here to be my bodyguard, you can fuck right off." I pushed out from the table, stacked four slices of pizza on top of each other in my left hand 'cause there was no way I was not eating it, flipped Nate the bird with the right, and left.

"Come back here, Evie. We need to talk about this."

"No, we don't. You have no idea how the studio works. Jody is an equal partner in the business. I could go through her for everything. It may even be possible to schedule my classes, so I don't see Christian at all. Shit, Nate. Don't you get how important this is to me? And not just because it's dancing, which I love, but because it's mine. I got this job because I can dance and because I have talent. No one else did this but me, and it's the only thing in my whole life, apart from writing, that is truly mine."

Nate stood before me, hands white-knuckled, puffing like he had run a marathon, his cheeks dappled red. He looked so angry, so frustrated, and so fucking hot. I knew we would have a massive fight, and I wanted to. I longed for it. I wanted to yell and scream and let out all the fucking throbbing, aching, grab-him-by-the-hair-and-kiss-the-shit-out-of-him energy trapped in my tiny body.

"You're right, Gidget. You're totally right. I'm sorry."

"Don't you dare tell me—what?"

"You're right. You deserve this because you're talented, and someone like Christian shouldn't have the power to stop you from doing what you love. I will back you one hundred and ten percent. But…"

"But…" He stood menacingly close, and I was overcome with a desire to bite the pulsing vein in his neck.

"If he so much as lays one finger…one breath on you, I won't be held responsible for what I do."

Never before had I experienced the urge to climb a man like a monkey would a tree and wrap my thighs around his face. I was furious. He was being a total boofhead man, and I FUCKING LOVED IT.

With no idea how to deal with ninety-nine percent of the chaos happening within me, I shoved a slice in my mouth and started walking.

"We need to talk about this, Evie."

"No, no, we don't," I huffed around the garlicky deliciousness. "You've known me long enough to know when to quit."

"Well, unlike you, I will never quit on you or us."

"What the hell are you talking about? I didn't quit anything. There is no us, and there has never been."

"Yeah. Keep telling yourself that, Gidget."

Sauce, cheese, and meat dripped from my fingers as I squished my remaining lunch into a ball, pivoted, and threw. Landing right on his nose, he wiped it with the back of his hand, said nothing, and kept going.

"Oh, now you choose to shut up. I should've thrown food in your face the second you got off the plane, and we could have avoided this whole nightmare." I heard a string of obscenities mumble under his breath and saw his shoulders tense, but he didn't stop or even slow. I followed him back to the hotel but was determined to be the one in front and have my way before he walked through the doors.

My legs were half the length of his, so I started running to pass him, then turned and began walking backward.

"You flew all the way here to tell me this? To tell me nothing? Well, that's good because I didn't want to hear what you had to say anyway—whoooa!"

That was when I slipped and began stumbling in that awkward, half-running, half-falling, can't-stop-yourself-from-going-over thing, but backward. Nate was on me in a flash, lunging forward, wrapping his arms around my waist, and plucking me off my feet the very second a cab horn blasted. The sudden whoosh of air as it passed behind me blew my skirt up Marilyn Monroe style, exposing my bottom to the world *and* his strong, calloused palms.

For once in my life, I looked down on someone physically, not just because they were a dickhead.

Nate held me in his arms. His hands protectively covered my ass cheeks before he realized what he was doing. But did he move them? No. He gripped tighter.

And I liked it. Damn, how I liked it.

"Put me down, Nate. Half the street can see my bum." I began to wriggle and protest, but the bastard smiled and threw me in the air. When his hand gripped me again, I was higher against his body, and his palms came to rest on the swell of my thighs, his thumbs brushing my ass. In his eyes, I saw the moment he felt the lace edge of my stockings. I felt his body's reaction on my shin.

"Why did you wear those tights, Evie? Why?" he groaned, dropping his head against my shoulder.

Because I wanted to tease you. Because I wanted to make you hard as you walked beside me on the street. Because I wanted you to tear them off me.

Embarrassed by my traitorous thoughts and with all my fight drained, I resorted to begging. "Please let me go, Nate. Please." I whimpered, my eyes falling closed as my body skated over his on its return to Earth. When I blinked them open, he stood before me, pressing his thumb into his eye like he was trying to poke it or his brain out. "It's been a long day… I'm going home now… I have to get Iris…. It's late…. I'm tired… I have to get Iris."

"You said that already." His poor eye was left alone, and he looked at me like he would devour me. "Don't go, Eves. Stay."

"But Iris!"

"Can't Jocie or Finn get her? Just this once, can't you ask and accept help and do something for yourself?"

"Buhh…I do things for myself," I protested. "Look, I did my nails last night." Nate pulled my signature move, rolling his eyes and crossing his arms. "I promised Iris, I would pick her up, and I am. That's my role in the family. I am the caregiver. God knows I have nothing else to offer."

"Evie, you don't believe that, do you?"

"It's okay, Nate. It's the truth. I'm disgustingly close to twenty-eight, and I've done nothing with my life. I submitted a manuscript to one agent and gave up when I didn't hear anything. I can't even keep a job for more than a week without being fired. I'm emotionally stunted. For fuck's sake, I'm a v—" I just caught myself before I let it slip. "*Very* different person from who I thought I would be at this point in my life." *Fuck, now I'm crying like a moron.* Further sweet consolations offered by a pained-looking Nate were rebuked as I retreated. "I have to go. See you tomorrow. I'll be here at nine, and you can come to the dance studio with me. Don't be late, and for god's sake, have pants on."

Run away, Evie. Run as fast as you can.

Chapter 22

Nate

MY BRILLIANT FIVE-STEP PLAN TO EVOKE Evie's jealousy turned to dust in that changing room. The minute I saw her wide eyes drinking me in, I was toast. Then there was the whole saving-her-from-sure-death thing. The bounce of her boobs before they were squashed into my chest, the smell of her hair… The way she fit so perfectly in my arms… The lace. I could still feel it flush against her skin. Skin that was softer than I could ever have imagined. *I bet those little garters looked bloody spectacular too.*

That asshole, Christian, should have been my priority. I should have been formulating a plan for him—one that would involve kicking his damn ass. But instead, I'd been in bed with a photo of Evie in one hand and my throbbing cock in the other.

My day was destined to end that way the minute I saw her in that fucking skirt, but still, the length and intensity of my orgasm came as a surprise. It took me fifteen minutes, two cold showers and three shots of vodka to be anywhere near settled. Even then, the thoughts continued. *What is she doing right now? Is she in bed? Thinking of me as she touches and brings herself undone?* My cock swelled beneath my towel. *No… Not again. Down, boy, down.*

This had to stop. It was eight pm. I was starving, probably close to dehydration, and exhausted. *I cannot blow my load again. I need to get out of this room.*

A sobering thought hit me as I threw on some sweats and a tee and hit the road. As much as I wanted to bury myself inside of Evie Austen, I was beginning to wonder if I could survive her.

When I walked into Rubirosa and took a seat by the window, I was happy and relieved to see a familiar, smiling face. Candice, our waitress from earlier, was still hard at work, slicing away. She eyed me suspiciously as she made her way to my side and handed me a menu. Evie had mentioned something about her being an actress, so I thought she would have been off treading the boards on Broadway.

"Nate, you're back. And alone."

"I am—not by choice, mind you."

"Aww." Candice dropped her lip into an exaggerated pout. She was a cute chick. One I would have been on like a rash a few weeks ago. "You picked a good night. We're usually a full house at this time, but Wednesdays are our quietest nights. Not sure why."

"Hump day," I said dryly.

"What?"

"Wednesday is called hump day at home. Maybe everyone's at home getting busy."

"Yeah, we call it hump day too." She laughed, "I never thought about it that way. Huh, kinda makes sense now." Instead of taking my order, Candice sat beside me, popped her elbows on the table, and rested her face in her palms. "So, Nate. Tell me. How long have you been in love with Evie?"

I didn't flinch, didn't bother to deny. "As long as I've been breathing."

"Thought so. She loves you too, you know. She might be scared to admit it, but she does. When she was with you today, there was something different about her. A light or energy surrounded her, beamed from her."

"Even when she was hurling on the bathroom floor?"

"Yep, even then. She glows in your presence." Sighing then clicking her tongue, Candice gazed out the window, and we watched New York pass by in silence. "She comes in here once or twice a week," she said suddenly, almost making me jump. "Sometimes with the family, sometimes alone. She smiles and chats and looks content, but I've always sensed a sadness in her. There is always that little scowl and crease in her nose like she's worried she left something behind at home, like something was missing. When I saw her with you, I understood what it was. She left you behind, Nate. You're what she's missing."

My chest almost collapsed under the weight of her words. "You think so? I mean, I hope so. I want that more than anything. But I don't think she trusts me. My past is always going to be an issue for her. She jokes, teasing me that I'm a slut and a manwhore, but I know it bothers her. If only she knew why I am the way I am…was," I corrected.

Candice nodded like she knew what I was blabbing about, then stood, rested her hand on my shoulder, and leaned in. "Maybe you should tell her." She then grabbed her notepad and began writing. "I know what you need…the vodka. It's a creamy, vodka-to-mato sauce with mozzarella. I think you could use it."

Whoever decided to put vodka on a pizza is a freaking genius. That shit was delicious. I ate a whole large, fought the urge to text Finn and tell him how awesome it was, and ordered a small to-go. When I returned to my room, Candice's words were still in the empty space between my ears. *Maybe you should tell her.*

It sounded so simple. But how would I even start the conversation… *'Uh, hi, Evie. I am a manwhore because you stole my heart before I could walk, and I was too scared to tell you, so I shoved my cock into anything that moved to numb the feelings. Wanna be my girl?'*

Stupid. Or was it?

Despite the roundness of my belly, I flipped the lid on the pizza box and grabbed another slice.

Maybe stupid was exactly what I needed to capture. I had to be myself and be one hundred-percent honest. Evie had the best bullshit detector I knew. If I went in half-cocked, spurting out sweet talk and romantic folly, she'd kick me in the nuts and throw me onto the street.

Hmmm. It was a right conundrum. One, ironically, I would normally talk to Evie about. *Stop thinking and eating and fucking do it.*

Before courage abandoned me, I grabbed my phone and sent Evie a message. I hated doing it over the phone, but I didn't think Evie would give me the time of day in person.

> **Me: Evie. I know you have a lot on your plate right now, but there are some things I need to tell you, and I need to tell you now before I throw up the sixty-seven slices of vodka pizza I ate.**
>
> **I know you don't believe me, but I love you, Evie. I always have. My romantic history is a poor, sick joke, but I chose that path because I didn't have the courage to choose you. Watching Finn drown in sorrow after Shelby died shattered me. She was my sister, and I was devastated and grieving myself, but seeing him fall apart broke something inside me. I knew then, in my heart of hearts... If I had you the way I wanted you, Evie... If I was brave enough to hold and kiss you and make love to you... If you somehow gave me the chance—the honor—to protect, cherish, and worship you the way you deserved, I would have died if it was ever taken away.**
>
> **It was easier to swallow the feelings down and become the flirt, the hoochie, the slut, the fuckboy. I shut off the part of me you consumed and only let it breathe and see the light of day when I was with you.**
>
> **But then you left.**
>
> **And I was alone, stagnant and in the dark.**
>
> **I know you don't trust me because I have done**

nothing to earn or deserve your trust. But if you let me, I will spend every minute of every day making up for my mistakes and showing you who I really am. I am the Nate you know me to be in your heart.

And I am yours.

Forever.

Nate.

Chapter 23

Evie

I am the Nate you know me to be in your heart.

And I am yours.

Forever.

Nate.

I'd read those words on a screen, but I heard them in my heart and felt them in my bones.

I shut off the part of me that you consumed.

Nate was so scared to risk his everything that he sought out women that gave him nothing. Avoiding attachment became a personality trait.

Cynicism told me it was bullshit. An excuse he'd concocted in his room when alone and horny. He was just trying to lure me back. To get me in his bed.

But like the man said, I knew who he truly was in my heart.

So, if you know, why don't you believe him?

"What are you studying so intensely over there?" Jocie was sitting on the sofa opposite me, eyes squinting, her face suspicious. Before I could think of a lie, my phone beeped, and the universe gave me one.

"Just a message from Polly."

"That's nice. I'm glad you're still talking. You were always so close."

Polly– Hi, stranger. How's the Big Apple? Guess who I saw at the shops today…

A second later, another message popped up with a photo.

Polly– Luke Bailey! Doesn't he look amazing? He's back in town to visit his parents for a week and is as hot as ever. He asked me how you were, and I told him you were all living in NYC. I showed him that photo you had sent me of you and Finn in Times Square. He was so shocked and even made a joke that Little Frigid Evie had transformed into Hot Evie. I didn't think it was very funny, but he and the other guys he was with had a good laugh. I still can't believe he told everyone you freaked out on sex and ran. It was so wrong of him. People knowing you were a virgin who didn't like to be touched must have been humiliating. I hope that's still not an issue for you.

Anyway, hope you and Nate are having fun. I know we were before he left—wink, wink.

XXOO

Pol

I thought of my day with Nate, of how I reacted—or failed to react—when I saw his body in the pool and change room, and my epic meltdown at Rubirosa. Judging by that and how my body froze in his arms when he plucked me from the street, hence saving me from that cab, Frigid Evie was alive and kicking. Somehow, Polly knew it.

"Something wrong, darling?" I blinked a few hundred times, recovering from Polly's virtual smackdown, and then glanced at my aunt.

"No, nothing's wrong. Do you remember Luke Bailey?"

"Pam Bailey's boy? The one who's an investment banker in Singapore with two Audis, a yacht, and a house on the water? Thanks to his mother's nauseating pride and oversharing, I may have a slight memory of him. Why? Did he buy the Sydney Opera House?"

I forced a laugh.

"Not quite. He's home visiting his family. Polly saw him at the shops and showed him a photo of me at Times Square. He said I looked hot."

"That's because you do, darling. I wonder if he is still a douche."

I dropped my phone and stared at my aunt as she flicked through her latest issue of *Vogue*.

"How do you know he was a douche?"

"Finn told me. I relayed Luke's mother's Singapore-takeover news to him, and he said, 'Luke Bailey is a cockspank-douche-bag, and if I ever see his face again, I'll flatten him.' He then told me that when you broke up in year twelve, he bad-mouthed you to the whole school. "

"Oh. Did he tell you what Luke told everyone?"

"Nope. He just said it was lucky Luke left town before he got a hold of him." Jocelyn looked up from her magazine and gave me a sympathetic smile. "I can see it still hurts. Do you want to talk about it?"

"No. It's okay. I think some things are best left buried."

"As long as those things aren't rotting away inside you. Some things, though, reek and fester long after we think they've been disposed of, and those stinky buggers need to be dug up and tossed out into the compost. You need to ask yourself if this is one of these things, because by the look on your face, that trash is still on the nose." She then stood, shuffled to me in her pink fluffy slippers, and kissed the top of my head. "I'm here if you need a spare shovel."

Angry that this still hurt so much, I waited till Jocie had left before allowing my tears to trickle onto my cheeks, then pulled the cushion from behind my back and threw it across the room.

"Fucking Polly." I cursed under my breath, picked up my phone, and, through blurred vision, typed the most mature response I could come up with.

> **Me : I am SO happy you saw Luke. I am sure it was quite the reunion. Especially if you fucked him like you did fifty-five seconds after he broke up with me.**

My finger hovered over *send*. Frigid Evie wanted me to press it. She wanted me to go harder, to annihilate that bitch and laugh as I stood over her flaming corpse. But the me I wanted to be, the one working toward her dreams and wanting to let go of the past, deleted it.

> **Me : That's nice. I like your top. Off to bed. Chat later.**

Then, I did as I'd told Polly. I let misery carry me to bed. There I lay in my comfiest pajamas, with my head buried beneath the quilt, and waited for unconsciousness to dull my brain.

Sleep proved elusive. It was, after all, only nine pm, and my evening meal was still digesting loudly in my belly. I read for a bit, listened to the ten-minute version of Taylor's "All Too Well" a few dozen times, and was briefly entertained by Finn and Jocelyn. Him with his I'm-going-to-get-laid whistling as he snuck off to see Scarlett, and her with her calling out, "Don't forget to use protection, Finnley," from the bathroom window. But no matter what I did or what unorthodox position I lay in, my mind kept going back to a shirtless Nate and then to me lying on the floor of a public bathroom.

Frigid Evie, indeed.

Why was this still bothering me after all these years? It was back in high school, for God's sake. I needed and wanted to move on and let go of my past, but to do that, would…should I be letting go of Nate?

A smiling, cheeky—even for him—Nate hovered in my face as we waited for our coffee, but the barista making eyes and wriggling his brows at me was occupying my attention. He'd soon be wearing the latte he was making if he kept it up.

Despite my late-evening nervous breakdown and

early-morning hesitation, I decided to spend another day with Nate. After all, he was stuck in a hotel and not in our family home because of me. I could hardly ditch him. And he might prove useful at the dance studio should Christian turn up and try anything. They were the only reasons, though. It had practically nothing to do with him being sexy and me wanting to rid myself of Frigid Evie.

Vivid dreams in rapid succession throughout the night gave rise to an epiphany. There was no issue with my hormones, drive, or want. This was purely psychological, and psychology was one of my majors in college. I aced it and was sure if I harnessed the power of my mind, I could conquer this with a modified version of immersion therapy.

Bit by bit, day by day, I was going to open myself up and hand myself over to Nate, and by the time he went home, he would be taking my virginity with him.

I had no intention of following. This was a short-term thing while Nate was in town, enabling me to pop the cherry and get whatever this attraction, infatuation, and obsession was out of my system and move on. As for my worries about Finn…well, he was never going to find out.

First and foremost, I had to deal with the knob making hearts in my foam. I'd blown him off so hard, but the guy didn't take the hint.

"Why are you so crotchety today? Your cute little face looks all squashed up like a grumpy pug," Nate said beside me.

"Thank you for the flattery. I'm not a crotchety pug. I just don't like people, and there are too many *people* looking at me." *Take that, coffee boy.*

"You do so like people. I'm a people, and you like me."

"Yes, but you're my person…I mean people. You're my peo-ple…one of…my people in the series of people I know." Nate's smirk had me locked in a wet-my-undies stare, and latte-guy was screwing up his face and crossing out the phone number he'd written in my cup. "Shut up!" I snapped after he said absolutely nothing.

I snatched the cup from the counter as soon as it was placed and stormed off." There better not be any bloody pumpkin spice in this. This whole place reeks of it," I yelled over my shoulder. "Nate let's go. We have things to do and people to see."

"I really love it when you order me about, Gidge. Makes me feel all warm and fuzzy…maybe even horny."

My snarky comment was seconds away from launching, but then I remembered my ditch-the-cold-hearted-bitch routine. Nate was sipping from his cup. Stopping just as we exited, I smiled, ran my hand up his arm, and patted him like a dog. He watched my hand slide back and forth as he swallowed, then swallowed again. I upped the stakes, letting my fingers slide back down over his elbow and wrist till I reached his own and squeezed them lightly. "How's the coffee?"

"It's…uhh…nice. Really, really nice." The cutest smile lit his eyes and warmed my heart. Touching Nate and seeing him light up felt nice. "C'mon," I said, squeezing his hand again and then holding it to pull him behind me. "I want to show you something special." He opened his mouth, but I beat him to it. "And no, it does not involve removing any clothing."

"Damn, Gidge. You read my mind."

❉

"66 Perry St, New York, NY 10014, United States. The world. The universe. For years I've wanted to come here, and now, it is just a few blocks from where I live. I can just see her, looking out over the street, cigarette in hand, exhaling her smoke as she writes." I sighed. "Isn't it beautiful?"

"Sure is. The house isn't bad either." I turned to face Nate. He was looking at me, a rare, serious expression clouding his usual golden retriever-like persona. "I watched it every day while you were gone."

"What? *Sex and the City*? Why?"

He shrugged and looked at his feet. "Just to feel close to you. For some reason, picturing you walking in your flip-flops down

Fifth Avenue, looking at all the fancy shops Carrie shouldn't be able to afford and eating in all the restaurants, helped me be okay with it." He sighed again, but his smile returned. God, he was beautiful. "I should have known you'd find her house. How long after arriving in the city did you come here?"

"The first night."

"Thought so." I stood beside him, reclaimed his hand, and watched the cutest soft blush I'd not seen before blossom across his cheeks. "I like it when you do that," he said, his voice deepening.

"I like it too." I waited for the comeback, for the inevitable, *'If you like touching my hand, you should try touching my…'* but it never came.

"Are you still going to see Jody today?" he asked.

"Yep. Are you still going to come with me?"

His grip on my hand tightened. "Yep."

"And do you promise to be a good boy who obeys, sits quietly, and waits while the grownups talk?"

He began clenching, pulsing his hand in mine. "Call me a good boy again, Evie, and I'll do whatever the fuck you like."

He swallowed hard, and I slipped further into lust, becoming hypnotized by the rise and fall of his Adam's apple. "Promise?"

"Fuck, Evie." Before I could blink, Nate dropped my hand and captured my face, roughly clutching my jaw. His thumb swept back and forth, every brush burning against my flushed skin. When he laid his forehead to mine, we shared a shaking, panting breath. "I'm not sure we're picturing the same scenario here, but yes, yes, I promise. Tell me what to do, and I'll do it."

I stepped back enough to see the dangerous heat in his eyes but not enough to cause his hands to shift. "What scenarios are you picturing?"

I'd have given anything to capture his expression. Dumbstruck. Awe. Lust. Pride. Did I say lust? "Evie Austen, are you flirting with me?" Smiling like the devil, he pulled me closer and caressed the tiny sliver of flesh between my shirt and jeans. I couldn't speak. I could only think of his fingers on my skin, and he knew it. "You like that?" he whispered. "You like my hands on your body?" I nodded. "Tell me what to do, Evie. Tell me where you want me to touch you."

"Everywhere—"

"Excuse me, would you take our photo, please?"

"Are you freaking kidding me?!" I pushed off Nate's body and spun on the balls of my feet. Without even looking, I reached out to the intruder. "Camera. Give me the camera."

"Oh, it's just my phone, not a camera—"

"I don't care what it is. Just give it to me so I can take the bloody thing." Nate's laughter rattled in my ears as I took several shots of the admittedly sweet and possibly terrified group of friends who excitedly shared that they were on vacation from Canada. "There," I said, handing the phone back. "Sorry for snapping."

The phone's cute blonde owner's eyes perused Nate, then looked at me. "No, I'm sorry," she whispered. "Really, really sorry." She gave me a wink and trotted off down the street.

Nate sighed and rubbed the back of his neck. "Canadian cock-blockers strike again."

"Oh, this isn't your first time?"

"Nope, a particularly intrusive bitch from Blow Me Down got me just last week."

I whacked him in the chest as he laughed. "Blow Me Down? There's no such place. You lie, liar."

"No lies. I swear it's real. Dad sold macadamias to a tourist shop at the national park there for years. Come to think of it, Blow Me Down isn't too far from a place you'd love called Dildo."

"You're an idiot." I slid my phone from my pocket, determined to have Google prove him wrong. "I know you're joking. As if there would be a place called Dil—holy shit, there is a place called Dildo!"

"Told ya."

"Who the hell names a place Dildo?"

"I don't know. But it's beautiful. Maybe we can slide up in there for a night on our honeymoon."

"Idiot."

"That's twelve idiots, Gidge," he said, marking it down in the notepad tucked safely away in his jeans. "That record is as good as yours, babe."

Chapter 24

Nate

STILL LAUGHING ABOUT DILDO, WE MADE IT TO VAADS, Village All Abilities Dance Studio. For the few blocks we'd walked, we came dangerously close to handholding. Pinkie finger teased pinkie finger as they twisted and twirled in and out of each other's grip. It was ridiculously hot.

Knowing all too well it would be easier for Evie to leave if it was a shithole, I wanted to hate this place. I wanted nothing but bad vibes and cobwebs hanging from the rafters. I was sadly disappointed. "Damn it," I mumbled under my breath. The place was a goddamn delight. It looked like Mary Poppins and Katy Perry had been hired as the interior designers and was so warm, fuzzy, and sunny that I wanted to throw a bloody tutu on myself. Music and laughter filled the air from the second we walked through the doors, and every kid that saw Evie waved and did a little two-step of excitement. Several even ran and clung to her legs.

I hated it, alright, but not in the way I'd hoped. It was bloody perfect for her.

"It's amazing, eh? Do you see now why I love it?"

"Yes. It is. But we still have that small problem called Christian."

Evie rolled her eyes, began peeling children from her body, and pointed us all to a row of chairs in the foyer. "Thank you, Mother

Superior. Why don't you and the rest of the Von Trapp's wait here while I find Jody."

"Yes, Miss Evie," I sang in chorus with the kids as she pushed me in the chest and into a seat.

"So, ballet, eh?" I nodded to the three kids that sat beside me. Two of them nodded back, looking perplexed. The third picked his nose.

"Why are you so tall?" the nose picker asked.

"I dunno. Why are you so small?"

"'Cause I'm four."

"Good answer, kid." I roughed up his curls, which reminded me of Iris's. I couldn't wait to see her, but to be honest, I'd been wholly preoccupied with seducing her aunt. The questions continued.

"Why do you talk funny?"

"Well, to me, I don't talk funny. You do. And it's because I'm from Australia, like Miss Evie."

"Do you have a pet kangaroo?"

"No, just two wombats and a koala. Evie used to have a kangaroo, though. She rode it to school instead of a pony. You should ask her about it someday."

The kids entertained me for the next few minutes until an alarming-sounding voice called out, "There you are!" and a pair of long legs approached. They, and the body attached, stopped before me, hands on hips and lips pursed. "I've been looking everywhere for you three. I turn my back for one second, and you take off."

"We went to the toiwet."

"Hmm. If you went to the toilet, why are you sitting in the lobby with…"

She looked me up and down with a deserved suspicion. After all, I was a strange man surrounded by kids in a dance studio I'd never set foot in before. "Nate." I jumped to my feet and, for some reason, gave her a scout salute. Not suspicious at all. "I'm Nate. I'm Evie's boyfriend…uhh, well, not boyfriend yet, but I will be soon…possibly…hopefully… I'm not a weirdo."

"No, but you are a bloody idiot," Evie's voice echoed down the hall, and I made a mental note: *Idiot number thirteen*. I could hear her laughing, but she stopped as soon as she saw the kids. "Oops. Ignore Miss Evie's potty mouth. Sorry, Jody."

"I'm sure they've heard worse," Jody said before returning to me. "So, you're the Nate this one hasn't shut up about." A blushing Evie elbowed her in the ribs. "Pleasure to meet you. I'm Jody."

"Pleasure's all mine." I flashed her my most charming smile and got a slight thrill from Evie's squinty-eye reaction. She was so freaking jealous. Remembering my quickly forgotten plan from yesterday, I got my flirt on, sliding closer to Jody and giving her a cheeky wink. "So, Jody, what does your boyfriend think about you working around all these fit young men?"

"My *wife* is fine with it, so you can save your pretty, surfer-boy winks for this one." She nodded to Evie. "C'mon, you kids, let's get back to class before we lose anyone else. Give me five minutes, and I'll be back to talk with you." She disappeared and left us alone.

"What do you think of this place? It's pretty special, isn't it?" Evie asked, sitting beside me. She tapped my leg three times as she looked around and left it sitting mid-thigh.

"It is, Lil Gidget," I replied while staring at her hand on my leg. "I can see why you and Finn chose it for Iris. But that doesn't mean I want you working here with—"

"Christian!" Evie jumped to her feet. The man himself stood before us, and dammit if he wasn't just as she described—HotBoss indeed. I hated him even more than I did seconds before and claimed my spot at her side. My nails dug into the flesh of my clench fists in a vain attempt to stop myself from flattening the clown. Something that would have already happened had we not been where we were.

"Evie. I'm so glad you're here. Jody told me you were coming in, and I wanted to see you." He moved to take her hand, but Evie pulled away and almost hid behind me. It was the first time I'd ever seen her frightened.

"Jody said you wouldn't be here," she said, her voice strong, but after years of knowing her, I could hear the slight nervous shake.

"I wasn't supposed to be. I had a meeting downtown, but I overheard her on the phone with you yesterday and left it early. Honestly, she didn't know I was coming."

"Why did you come?" I snarled, stepping into his face. "Keen to hurt my girl again?"

"Your girl? Evie, who is this bumpkin?"

"This bumpkin is the guy that's gonna kick your ass; that's who he is." I couldn't help myself. I nudged him in the chest hard. I fully expected him to lose his footing. He was a woozy dancer-boy, after all. But he was a dancer-boy built like a brick shithouse and didn't move an inch. My aggression seemed to fire up Evie, and she jumped between us.

"Stop it now, you idiots."

"Fourteen," flew from my mouth, and Evie pirouetted on her feet, giving me the incredulous look I deserved.

"Really? Now?"

"Sorry, Eves. It's a habit."

Christian shook his head and motioned toward Evie. I grabbed his wrist before he got close. "DO NOT touch her again. DO YOU HEAR ME?"

"My office. NOW." Jody was back and seemed a lot less entertained than the little faces pressed against the closest studio's glass wall. "Now!" she repeated when Christian and I failed to move. Like petulant children being dragged by our ears, we flopped into Jody's office. "What the hell are you doing here, Christian?"

"Uhh, last time I looked, it was my business, and I can be here whenever I like."

"Despite what you like to tell yourself, Christian, it's *our* business. It is also one you have placed in jeopardy. I know you have some personal issues, crisis, or whatever the hell you want to call it, but that's no excuse. You cannot speak to our employees, or anyone, the way you did to Evie, and you cannot put your hands on them. She has bruises on her wrist, for heaven's sake. You're lucky she didn't charge you."

"You have bruises? I hurt you?" The guy seemed genuinely shocked. Then he did something neither I nor anyone in the room expected. He cried. Like a-baby-wanting-a-bottle cried. Real-life, big, fat, probably salty tears dropped from his ridiculously long lashes onto his quickly reddening cheeks.

Evie dropped her head into her hand. "Jesus Christ."

Jody looked confused. I got up to leave. "Evie, let's leave these two to sort this out for a bit."

"That's a good idea," agreed Jody. "Why don't you wait outside, and I'll come and speak to you after we have collected ourselves a little."

Before Evie could speak, I had her hand in mine and was pulling her out the door.

Ten minutes later, Jody and Christian made their way into the lobby. Christian with his head down. Jody looking stern. Christian stopped before Evie. "Evie, I can only apologize again. I hope once Jody explains everything, you will consider returning. Iris too. And maybe one day, we can be friends again." Mr. HotBoss-Ballet man then began to cry again as he slunk from the building.

Evie dropped a little, "Snort," under her breath as we returned to the office, then led into what looked like a small break room, the walls of which were painted a cheery coral, the staff lockers lining them colored like a rainbow, and each had a mini chalkboard hanging on the door. *Evie* was painted on the sunshine-yellow locker.

Seeing her name in crisp white chalk was a real gut punch, yet another reminder that she'd left me behind. She was a local now, a real New Yorker with a local pizza place where the staff knew her name and order, where she had a job she loved, and a locker painted in her favorite color. The kids here knew her name, and her voice, and saw her once or twice a week. If things didn't go the way I hoped, if I went home without her, I would be lucky to see her once a year.

Even though she should have been the one being taken care

of, she began puttering around the kitchen, fussing over the filthy state of the sink, and making us all a cup of tea. I watched on in silent pride, drowning in something I rarely felt. Self-doubt.

"Christian is on drugs," Jody almost vomited rather than said the words. "He's on drugs and is out of control. Apparently, he started using recreationally after they gave him painkillers for his knee, but he claims he hit his worst and lowest point last week and can hardly remember anything from your date. That's why he was shocked about the bruising. He has already checked himself into an outpatient rehab here in the Village and will take the next few weeks off. He says he's sorry, and he wants you to come back, Evie. I've known Christian for a long time. I have to stand by him, and I also need you now more than ever. I hope you can find it in your heart to give him and us another chance, but I will understand if you can't."

"Shit." Evie sighed as she sat beside me. "Poor Christian."

"What do you mean, poor Christian?" I snapped. "Maybe he is having a hard time, but that's no excuse to put your hands on a woman—especially not my woman."

Evie's tea splashed over her hand as she dropped her mug on the table. "Oh my God. Not everything is about you. For the last time, I am not your woman!"

"Let's put whether you are or are not Nate's woman aside for the moment," interjected Jody. "Like I said, Christian will be away for a few weeks, and hopefully, when he returns, he will be able to redeem himself. Are you willing to come back to work, Evie?"

She answered without hesitation. "Yes, absolutely."

"Gidge."

"Don't judge me, Nate. I am doing this. I love dancing, and I love the kids, and I think if Christian is seeking help, it's only right that I give it and him another chance. If anything happens, I will be out of here so fast you'll see smoke on my heels. But I have to try. I need this. I need something for myself. At the restaurant, you told me you were behind me a hundred percent. Was that all a lie?"

I was going to argue, but then she took my hand. My whole

body came to life with that one touch, and my resolve crumbled when I looked into her eyes. They were pleading with me and tinged with hope. She needed this as much as I needed her.

"No, it wasn't a lie. It was just before I saw the size of the guy. I'm scared for you, that's all. Just promise me you'll look after yourself and stay on those pretty little toes."

Evie smiled and placed a lingering kiss on my cheek. "I'm a ballet teacher, Nate. I'm always on my toes."

Chapter 25

Nate

OVERFLOWING WITH NERVES AND LUST, I swiped my key card and showed Evie into my room. Bringing a chick home with me was nothing new. But this was no chick. This was Evie. My lifelong friend. My best friend's sister. My heart's one desire.

This was a big deal. "After you, Gidge."

Clearing her throat and marching inside, Evie briefly paused at the foot of my bed, biting her lip as she ran her fingers across the unmade sheets.

"It's very comfy. I slept like a baby last night," I lied as I moved closer while desperately trying to stop my hands from shaking. Her blue eyes widened when I was within arm's reach, and she quickly dropped the sheet, let out a cute little squeak, and then shuffled her way to the window.

"Nice view," she whisper-yelled as she gazed down at the alley it overlooked.

"Yup. That's the real New York, right there. I watched two drug busts and possible sketchy police bribery the first night and had lots of fun counting the rats last night."

"Never a dull moment here." She laughed nervously, letting the curtains slide through her fingers as she turned to face me." I always admired that about you. Somehow, even in the darkest tunnel, you always find the light."

"Aoife, I don't want to alarm you, but that almost sounded like a

compliment. I'm glad you see at least one redeeming feature in me. It gives me some hope."

She looked down and picked at her nails. "You have many excellent features, Nate. You're a great guy."

"I thought I was an idiot."

"You are, but luckily for you, I quite fancy idiots. In fact, I'm very fond of one idiot in particular." After taking a deep breath, she padded my way, sat, and placed her hand on my knee. If I wasn't mistaken, my heart went into tachycardia. "You look exhausted, Natey," she said with a squeeze I felt right between my legs. "Why don't you lie down and take a nap?"

I forced my million-dollar smolder. "I will if you will."

Evie's long lashes blinked rapidly, and her lovely breasts rose in a sharp inhale. "Okay."

It was a barely audible whisper. But I heard it.

"What?!" Utterly ruining the sexiness of the moment, I jolted like I had suffered an electric shock and fell from the bed. Slipped right off the side and landed on my shoulder. Riotous laughter roared above me as I scrambled to rejoin her like nothing had happened. "Shit, I didn't expect you to say yes. Are you for real?"

"I am. All that stuff with Christian has worn me out, and I don't have time to go home and rest before I get Iris. But it's just a nap, no funny business."

Fuck. My stomach twisted. I wasn't sure if it was delight or terror. "No funny business. Scout's honor." I could totally handle this.

We sat in silence for several heartbeats. Neither of us seemed willing to make the first move, watching each other from the corners of our eyes.

I needed to break the ice. She must have thought the same because, in perfect synchronicity, we jumped to our feet.

"Do you know there are no tigers in Africa?" I spoke.

"I'll just need to use the bathroom," she said.

Evie disappeared into the bathroom, and I slapped myself in

the face. "Tigers in Africa? What the fuck?" The lock clicked, and I swung into action. Taking off my jacket, I decided it best not to take off my jeans, then laid my notepad and inhaler on the bedside table before doing a quick pit and breath check. Once satisfied I was stink-free, I jumped beneath the sheets.

What girls get up to in bathrooms was a mystery to me—one I was happy to remain unsolved. But this particular girl was taking forever. I needed to know what she was doing in there. Imagining what naughty things it could be made me increasingly impatient to feel that body against mine—if she would allow that, of course. I stared at the wall, the ceiling, the mini fridge, anything I could to distract and contain my excitement. That became a harder task when she emerged from the bathroom. Damn, she looked cute. Her cheeks were flushed the softest pink, and the wisps of hair decorating her face were damp. *She must have washed her face. Maybe she needed to cool down.*

With her head aimed at her now bare feet and muttering that she was setting the alarm on her phone, she shuffled to the bed, placed it and her bracelets next to my things on the nightstand, and then silently lay beside me.

I'm in bed with Evie Austen.

To be honest, it was much more comical than I'd imagined. Perched on the very edge of the bed, she lay stiff as a board with her hand stretched above her gripping the mattress for balance. It worked for the most part, except for the occasional curse-filled wobble.

She didn't want to touch me, so I rolled as close as I could without making contact, and whispered, "Life's tough as an edge dweller. Why don't you shuffle back a bit? No hands. I promise."

"Promise?"

"Promise, Gidge."

"Okay, then. But one false move, and I'm out of here."

"Hey, after the way you were drinking in my flesh yesterday, I think I have more to worry about than you do."

Silent laughter shook her body as I rolled away, and she slowly eased her tight little body back. I tried with all my might not to look at her ass, but I am only a man—and a weak one at that. It was a true thing of beauty—tight, and toned, and plump, thanks to years of hard work and dance practice. The dip of her waist and the curve of her hips had me biting my lip. I sighed heavily, swallowing down the confessions desperate to escape. This was the closest to paradise I had ever been and may ever get. I couldn't let the screaming ache building in my cock ruin it.

"Are you hot or cold? Want some water?" I asked.

"I am a little cold. Why do they always have the air conditioning on so high?"

"That's my fault. I run a little hot when I'm in bed."

"Tell me about it," she whispered. I think it was meant to be to herself. My ego wanted to scream joyfully, but I decided to leave it alone.

"Let me get you a blanket. Or hop under the sheets with me if you like."

"Okay, then." I wasn't sure what she meant for a second. Presuming she wanted a blanket, I began to move, but then she lifted her body and slipped beneath the sheets. There was no edge-dwelling this time. The ass dreams are made of, pressed right against my thighs. I almost died. Unsurprisingly, my cock didn't. *Go down, go down.*

"That's not the inhaler this time, is it?"

"Nope," I said with a pop. "It's just instinctive, Eves. I'm sorry. I swear—"

"It's okay. I get it."

"You do?"

"Of course I do. Despite the attitude, I'm not made of ice. Besides, I think…I want…" she trailed off.

"What do you want, Evie? Tell me what you want." She was silent, and her breathing changed. *Dammit, she's asleep already.*

"I want you too." Her voice was soft, heavy with sleep. But I heard it. Her hand gripped mine as I wrapped it around her waist, pulling her right against me. I smelled her hair and pressed a kiss into her curls. Despite every hormonal, masculine, depraved urge in my body, I relaxed. The comfort of finally holding her, the rightness of it, was soothing. We both sighed deeply and drifted off.

As per usual, images of Evie Austen followed me into my sleep. However, it was the first time I woke from such a dream to find her in my arms. I watched the rise and fall of her body and heard her cute little sighs and mumbles. She was so still, hardly moving in the almost twenty minutes before her breathing changed. Gasping, she looked down at my hand spread across her toned stomach, my little finger tickling her little outie bellybutton.

"Oh, my God." The cutest giggle I've ever heard escaped her lips before she gently slipped from my grip.

My first instinct was to grab and pull her back into me, but I wanted to see what she'd do. I was pleasantly surprised when she stayed in bed, hovering over me, her lips ghosting mine, her breath tickling my nose. I don't know why I kept pretending to sleep but being so close and lying with her so innocently yet intimately meant something. I loved her so much right then I felt it in my bones.

Again, I could smell her hair and the mint of the gum she'd eaten earlier that day. As hard as it was, I waited again. Perhaps I was scared of what would happen. I'd never been this close to her lips. I wanted to taste them, to taste her and claim her, but I held my breath and waited to feel the connection.

It never came.

Her messy curls brushed my chest as she pulled away. I heard her rustling and grumbling to herself as she slipped on her shoes and jacket, then listened as the door opened and closed. She was gone again.

"Fuck it, Aoife."

❖

"Hey, Mum, how's it going on the farm?"

"Bugger off, Nathaniel. Who cares about the bloody farm? Tell me what's happening with Evie? Am I a step closer to grandchildren? And make it quick. I asked your dad to vacuum for me, and I can't leave him alone for too long. He'll break the thing somehow "

"Sorry, Mum. No babies on the way…yet."

She snickered. "What's wrong, Natey? Lose a bit of the old magic on the flight over, did you? I would have thought you'd have her tagged and bagged by now."

"Mum!"

"What? Isn't that what you boys all say?"

"Maybe some guys do, but I don't…especially about someone like Evie."

"Good. That's exactly what I wanted to hear. Your father keeps telling me this infatuation with her will pass once you've slept with her, but I disagree. I think it's true love. Just like your dad and me. I made him wait three months before I gave him my flower."

"Your flower! Oh, for fuck's sake. I think I'm gonna puke. Is there anything else you wanted to know? You neglected to ask about my well-being, I noticed."

The woman wasn't listening to a word I said, but I could hear her sighing wistfully. "He was quite the stud back in the day, your old man. He used to do this thing with his tongue—"

"Ughh, goodbye, Mum." I threw my phone onto the bed and took a swig from my seventeen-dollar room-service beer, but it failed to remove the gross taste from my mouth. I nearly choked when the damn thing started ringing again. Presuming it would be Mum, I let it ring out. But it started again straight away. Without looking at the screen, I answered.

"Spare me the details. I do *not* want to hear about your sex life."

"Well, that's rather disappointing. I'd like to think you, of all people, would be greatly interested."

"Polly?"

"Hey, stranger. Miss me?"

"Honestly, Pol. No. Sorry if that sounds harsh but—" She didn't let me finish.

"Give it time, Nate. I presume Evie's not putting out, and I know you too well. The bluer those balls get, the more you'll think of me and my tits."

"Geez, you're pretty cocky. And what makes you think Evie and I aren't together? I could be lying next to her right now for all you know."

"I messaged Evie yesterday, and she made no mention of you. It was like you weren't even there. Plus, don't forget that whole Frigid Evie thing. Rumor has it she—"

"I'm gonna stop you right there, Polly. I know what you're playing at, and it's not going to work. My interest in Evie is based on a lot more than sex, so you can take your shit stirring and shove it." Laughter rattled down the phone as I hung up.

"Two hang-ups in a row. Doing well, Natey," I mumbled as I returned to my beer. It was only four, and I had no idea if Evie would return before tomorrow. Truth be told, I had no idea if she was coming tomorrow either. We hadn't discussed it all day. And what a day it was. Evie was opening up to me, emotionally and physically. I could feel that barbed wire she wrapped so tightly around her heart beginning to fall free.

By seven I was bored out of my mind and headed down to the hotel restaurant for dinner. The last few hours had been spent bingeing my secret shame, *Keeping Up with the Kardashians*, fitting in a quick weight-lifting session in the gym, and then a shower. Room service was tempting, but the extrovert in me needed to feed off other people's energy.

Within ten minutes of sitting at the bar, I had attracted the attention of a hot blonde in a tight white dress that I prayed to God she wouldn't spill her pink Cosmo on. "Oh. My. God." She sounded exactly like Janice from *Friends*. Had I had the slightest interest in her, it might have bothered me. "I love your accent. Are you from England?"

"No, Australia."

"Oh. My. God. You're so handsome and Australian! I hit the jackpot. I love Australians. Nicole Kidman is an idol of mine. Do you know her?"

"What, like, personally?" She nodded enthusiastically. "Yeah, nah. Can't say I've had the pleasure of meeting Nicole. She seems lovely, though."

"That's a shame. What about Hugh Jackman?" She roared and imitated the claw scratch of Wolverine an inch from my nose.

"Oh, Hugh, I do know. We go way back. He's a great mate of my dad's. Even taught me to drive." He didn't. I do not—repeat—do not know Hugh Jackman. Wishing it was a Carlton Draught, my favorite Aussie beer, I took a sip and watched the thrill of my fibbing roll over my new friend.

"Really? That's incredible. Wow. I'm so excited by that." She dropped her drink loudly onto the bar—I suspected that drink wasn't her first of the evening—and sat still in a yoga–slash–meditation pose. "Manifesting meeting Hugh one day," she chanted.

Get me the fuck out of here.

Once all manifestations were complete, her attention shifted back to me. "My name is Blossom." *Of course it is.* "What's yours?"

"Anthony Albanese," I said curtly, holding my hand out while slipping from my seat. "Lovely to meet you, Blossom, but I have an early start tomorrow and am going up to my room. Have a good night." She grabbed my elbow and hooked her arm inside.

"Wait. I think you are super handsome, and I am super"—she leaned in—"horny."

"Uh. Okay."

"How about I come up to your room with you?" She bit her lip and seductively ran her index finger between her breasts. I'm ashamed to say, for the splittist of seconds, I followed that finger and considered her proposition. I was kind of horny myself, frustrated as all fuck, in truth, and scared and a little mixed up too. My eyes began to skim her incredible body. It would be so easy to lose myself in her for the next hour or two. To bury my feelings as well as my cock. Old Nate would have picked this bird up, thrown her over his shoulder, and had her naked before she could spell my name. But old Nate was dead, and he was the only thing being buried tonight.

"Sorry, Blossom. You're really beautiful—hot, even. But I'm deeply in love with an incredible woman whom I love more and more every day we're together. I've come here to New York to make her fall in love with me too, and I can't do anything to risk that."

"Oh, okay, then. Thanks for the life story I didn't ask for." She forced a smile, slid from her chair, and disappeared.

"You really have changed, haven't you?"

"Evie?" I turned to find her behind me. Her face was flushed red, her eyes glossed over with tears. "What are you doing here?"

"Ventolin," she replied so softly I could barely hear her over the chatter and clinking of glasses. "When I left your room, I must have picked up your inhaler by accident, and I was worried you might need it." She looked so cute, but also kind of confused, as she held out her hand and placed the inhaler in my palm. "Did you mean what you said to that skank?"

My heart began to race. I took my chance, grabbing her wrist, pulling her into me, and letting my hands slide over and cup the curve of her ass.

Looking up through her long lashes, she bit her lower lip and ran her fingers across my chest.

"Look, I would never call Blossom—"

"Snort. Of course that's her name."

"A skank," I laughed, "but yes, I have changed. And yes, I meant what I said. I love you, Evie. I want you to be mine. There's no one else for me. It's always been you." I leaned in, was seconds from tasting her lips, when suddenly, she gasped and turned away, leaving my kiss to land against her soft, tear-stained cheek.

"Shit! I'm sorry, I just… I mean, yes, I mean I'm sorry. I think I did exactly the same thing at the airport, and I'm pretty confident that I said, 'Shit, sorry,' then too. But I don't want our first kiss to be in a bar at a hotel. God, that sounds so stupid. I'm such a freaking child." I was still close enough to stop her rambling with my lips, but I didn't. Instead, I traced the exposed part of her collar bone with my nose, then kissed the tiny spot thrumming in her neck.

"You're not a child, Gidge. You're a stunning, intelligent, brave woman who is also annoyingly right."

"Stop talking!" she yelled and pressed her index finger against my lips, then dropped it slowly as she spoke. "Say that again."

I knew what she wanted to hear, and it wasn't how fucking brilliant she was. "You"—I kissed her cheek—"are"—I kissed the other—"right." I finished with a lingering kiss to the top of her head. "When we do have our first kiss, it has to be special, and it will be special because you will be ready. In fact, I swear to you right now, I will not try and kiss you again, as long as you promise me that you will kiss the living shit out of me one day."

"Promise." She said it without delay and while hopping excitedly onto her toes. "And I want to. I really, really want to, Nate. Especially since you've admitted that I am right and noble and wise." My whole body shook with laughter, and I pressed her tightly into my chest. "I just have to sort a few things out here first." She tapped against her temple and snuggled deeper into me. "Are you sure you can wait?"

"For you, Evie. I can wait forever."

Chapter 26

Evie

FRIDAY CAME TOO QUICKLY—JUST LIKE I HAD done, while alone in my bed, a remarkable number of times since Nate had arrived in New York. There was a good chance I would develop a repetitive stress injury if I kept rubbing it out at this pace. I might just make it into the *Guinness Book of Stupid Nate Records*, but for female wanking, not just idiot hurling.

Thursday had been another day spent lying to my family—who still had no idea Nate was in town—sight-seeing, eating, and laughing our way around Long Island. I literally drove Nate to the end of the world—Montauk Lighthouse. That was what New Yorkers call Montauk, as it was the most eastern point of the state, just like the lighthouse that stood over Byron Bay was for New South Wales. The similarities between the two were kind of uncanny, and I found myself spending a lot of time here while Iris was at school, hiding from people, and writing with my toes buried in the sand. It was the closest thing to home, and it wasn't until I stood on the rocks of Turtle Hill, with Nate's hand in mine, that I realized how often I thought of him while I was here.

We came achingly close to kissing several times as we gazed out over the rolling waves of the Atlantic, but unfortunately, we possessed the ability to attract cock-blockers to our side.

And it wasn't just Canadian ones. It seemed a representative of each NATO nation stopped by and asked us to take photos of them at exactly the wrong time.

Iris returned to dance class Thursday evening, which meant there was no sneaking out to see Nate later that night. I was keen as mustard and knocked on his room door at six am Friday. I'd ashamedly been up for hours, aiming to make myself look as appealing as I could while seeming to have made no effort at all. After loosely braiding my long locks, I chose army-green overalls over a white crop top that showed just a flash of boob and belly, threw on my favorite cardigan and, of course, my go-to white Converse. I had hoped for casual sexy but realized what I was working with, gave up, and settled with cute.

"It's open, Gidge." Just hearing his voice sent a bolt of energy to my core. "I'm in the shower. Won't be a sec."

I don't know why, but I tiptoed in and waited at the end of his bed. "What sort of idiot leaves their room unlocked when they're showering?"

"This one." Hot breath tickled my neck and set stray little hairs beside my ear to flutter, just like my heart. l turned to find him directly behind me, bare chested, his white towel sitting arrogantly low across his hips. In this light, I could see the dusting of sandy hair trailing from his belly button down, and I had the most urgent need to trace its path with my fingers…or tongue. "Take a photo next time, Gidge." He winked and brushed past me, letting his fingers slide across my stomach as he did.

"Pfft. I was looking at the towel if you must know. I'm curious what brand it is. It looks plush."

"Plush?" Nate giggled so cutely I nearly died. I couldn't help but laugh along with him. "You want me to take it off so you can have a feel?"

"Of the towel or…" I raised my brow.

"Evie Mary Austen. I don't know what's gotten into you, but I like it. Oh, and the answer is both, by the way."

"Let's—" My phone ringing stopped my witty comeback. I

shushed Nate and answered as calmly as I could while he slipped his jeans beneath the towel sans underwear.

"Hi, Jocie... Yes, I'm on the way to the airport...Yes, I'll drive carefully." I turned my body away from Nate, stepped into the bathroom, and whispered, "No, I won't throw myself on him and humiliate myself in arrivals... Yes, I promise to keep my knickers on... What?! Geez, Jocie, give me a bit of credit... Yes! I swear I'll be good. Now leave me alone, you weirdo... Also, thanks for taking Iris for me. Love you."

"A few months off the land hasn't changed Jocie much, by the sounds of it. Do I dare ask about the knickers?"

Part hiding my shame, part pretending to avoid the hopefully still half-naked Nate, I threw my hand over my eyes as I exited the bathroom. "Heard that, did you?"

Damn it, he has pants on.

"You were in a room three steps away with floor-to-ceiling tiles and the door open. Yes, I heard you," he deadpanned. "I'm guessing you told her I was coming today?"

"Yep, your secret holiday is over. In a few hours, you'll be covered in Iris's glorious wet kisses and squishy hugs."

"Hmm, I'm not sure what you mean by wet kisses. I think I need a demonstration to be fully prepared. I also need you to stop hiding your face before you walk into something."

"I'm not hiding. I can see just fine," I snapped as I walked straight into the wall. "Fuck it."

Expecting mockery and laughter, I was instead lifted off my feet like a doll and gently placed on the edge of the bed. Nate dropped to his knees before me and held my face in his hands. I didn't think I'd ever felt so safe. Certainly not since Mum and Dad died.

"Are you okay, baby? Did you hit your head? Do you need an ice pack? Are you concussed? You seem concussed. Talk to me, Gidge."

Ignoring the spasms of my heart from hearing him call me baby, I replied as benignly as I could. "I would if you'd let me get a word in." Relief washed over his face, and he kissed my forehead approximately 765 times. "I'm fine, Nate. I walked into a wall, not a volcano."

"Yes, but I distracted you with man flesh, and I would never forgive myself if you got hurt because of my sexy abs. Neither would Finn."

"Your face is too close to mine to tell me if you're joking or not, but I pray to God you are."

"Of course I am—well, half joking. My abs are pretty sexy." One last kiss was placed against my head, then he stood back and threw on the doofus shirt I picked for him on Tuesday. The loss of visible flesh warranted a twenty-one-gun salute, but I thought I disguised my disappointment well.

From the corner of my eye, I watched him watch me as he put on his shoes, grabbed his wallet, inhaler, stupid notebook pencil, and what I believed was the handkerchief of mine that he'd kept since he was a kid. While my heart seized, he nonchalantly tucked them away into the pockets of his snug jeans. "You sure you're okay?"

Well, I can't breathe, I think I may be having a stroke and heart attack, but I am also wetter than I have ever been. Yeah, I'm fine. Shit, he's looking at me. Answer! "Yes, I'm sure. Just shut up and get ready."

"Fuck, I love it when you boss me around." He hissed though his teeth and ran his hand over his jaw a few dozen times, his face twisting like he was in pain. I was in pain too. Bossing Nate around sounded like fun. An image of me tying him to my headboard, slapping him around a little, then riding him caused a throbbing ache between my legs.

"So, Boss. What are you doing with me today?" That didn't soothe it. "Where are we off to? Wait, let me guess….a museum?

"Nope."

"A candle factory?"

"What? No."

"Lingerie shopping?"

"Bingo!"

"Wait…really?"

I nodded. I enjoyed the shock on his face, then replied sternly, "No. We are going back to Montauk, and we're going surfing. The car is loaded and ready to go. I've got Finn's spare wetsuit and board shorts packed for you—oh, and his best board that he will kill me for taking if he ever finds out."

Watching the waves roll in over Turtle Hill yesterday, Nate confessed he hadn't surfed once since I had left Byron.

"But you love surfing," I'd squawked. *"You've always said when we were laying out there on our boards, just floating, surrounded by nothing but blue was the most you ever felt at home."*

"And it always was, but I couldn't do it anymore. I would get there, walk down the sand in my wetsuit with my board tucked under my arm, and just stand there. It didn't feel right. I didn't feel right. All I wanted was to see you out there, smiling, carving it up and glowing like you always do on a wave, but you never were. It wasn't home anymore, Gidge. Not without you."

When I left Nate at the hotel last night, I couldn't stop thinking about it and cried the whole way home. When Iris was in dance class, I hid in the restroom and cried. When we got home, I cried again while balancing on a stepladder to load the boards onto Finn's Jeep, and then again when I lay in bed re-reading all the text messages he'd sent me in the last few weeks. Especially when I hit the one that said, *It was easier to swallow the feelings down and become the flirt, the hoochie, the slut, the fuckboy. I shut off the part of me that you consumed and only let it breathe and see the light of day when I was with you. But then you left. And I was alone, stagnant and in the dark.*

The tears were a mixture of happiness, grief, and frustration… and guilt. When I decided to have Nate take my V-card, I was using him. He had been nothing but honest and sweet with me since he'd arrived. He was carrying around a fourteen-year-old snot rag, for Christ's sake. I had done nothing but be a bitch, and hide my feelings, and plan to sleep with him with no intent of taking it any further. That all changed yesterday with the Montauk confession—shit, that's a great book title. And today, when we hit that water, when we lie on our backs and stare at the sky, I was going to tell Nate how I felt.

"Nathaniel Myers, I am falling in love with you," is what I would tell him. But before he could react, before he could kiss me like I wanted him to, I would tell him we could do nothing about it. I would break his heart and ruin him, just like he predicted.

Chapter 27

Nate

AFTER CHECKING OUT OF THE HOTEL, WE grabbed a quick bite to eat and hit the road. Almost the entire journey was spent half listening to Evie talking about Iris and the dance school or complaining about Finn while I studied her reflection in the window. That and wondering how quickly I could get that jumpsuit, or romper, or overalls—whatever the hell it was—off, should my luck change. I figured I could do it pretty fast since I couldn't see any buckles or ties. Those straps could just slip right off her silky-smooth shoulders, leaving her in that joke of a top and underwear. At that point, I had to stop thinking about it. I could barely conceal the semi I'd been sporting since she checked me out in that towel.

The timing of my shower exit was no accident. My original plan to make her jealous died after I kept forgetting anyone else existed when in her presence, and when I did remember, I had hit on a lesbian. So, I'd resorted to old trusty—my body. I'd been alternating sitting on the toilet and doing pushups on the cold tiles for twenty minutes, waiting to *surprise* her. The boredom, and muscle spasms, and possible hemorrhoids were totally worth it. The look on her face and the hunger in her eyes was priceless and made it damn near impossible not to pick her up and throw her down on the bed.

Now I had to try and control myself when she slipped into her wetsuit.

The surprise surfing day was no doubt a result of my confession yesterday. I hadn't intended on spilling my guts to her the way I did. But she kept finding ways to touch me, holding my hand, brushing sand off my bum, tucking a yellow daisy behind my ear, and calling me Ariel. Who knew skin-on-skin contact and good, old-fashioned, innocent affections from the woman I loved would leave me a pile of mush and systematically dismantle the labyrinth I had built around my true heart?

In three days, she had changed me.

We stood on the edge of the bluff. Some Soviet-era-looking radar thing and a series of tin sheds stood beside us. "Did you bring me here to toss me off and be done with me?"

"I know it's super cliffy and rocky, but the waves are worth it. This is one of the best spots, and because of the scaling required, it's not as packed with idiots and posers. And look at all the old radars and stuff. It was a spy station or something in the cold war. Everyone calls it radars, but the proper name is Camp Hero."

"Camp Hero, eh? Guess I better man up and show you how it's done."

After much cursing, huffing, and puffing, we made it to the water's edge, and my focus shifted from imminent death to much more pleasant pursuits, like watching Evie's overalls fall to the sand. During her epic Finn rant, I tried to make her happy the best way I knew how…by being a creep. "Can't wait to see your tiny bikini, Gidge. It's been waaaaay too long."

Predictably, she'd rolled her eyes and tutted, but I caught the huge smile before she could hide it. "Hate to disappoint, but I'm wearing a one piece."

Now, technically, it may have indeed been one piece of material, but it was a very small piece, a good portion of which was eaten by her luscious ass as she stood before me with her board tucked under her arm. The white suit made her somehow-still-Aussie-bronzed skin glow even brighter, and her golden-blonde hair waved in the breeze. She turned to face me with a smile that stopped time itself.

"God, I've missed this so much."

"Me too, Lil Gidge. Me too."

My ego took a light beating as I stepped into Finn's wetsuit. "I'd forgotten how frickin' wide your brother is. Jesus, he must cost a fortune to feed."

"He does. I think you eat more, though. That's why you're so full of shit." She chuckled merrily to herself as her swimsuit slid farther up her ass before disappearing. "Zip me up?"

Gulp.

I almost broke my neck rushing to her. "Sure." My hands began to shake. *How do zippers work again?* I held the tag between my thumb and index finger and pulled. Each tooth clicking into line ricocheted through my body as my knuckles brushed against hers. I saw the rise of her back as she inhaled, and I waited for the fall, but it didn't come. She held her breath till the zipper slid into place on the elegant neck I had to stop myself from licking. After brushing her hair away, I traced a finger along her shoulders and leaned in. "All done, Gidge. Wanna do me?" She exhaled loudly, swallowed, and said nothing, just nodded.

The same ritual we had completed a thousand times was repeated on me, though it had never felt like that. Sure, I had always loved being close to her. Exposing and seeing so much bare skin got me hot and bothered. But never had I felt the same heat coming from her. I never felt as though my heart would burst from my chest or that I could die quite happily at that moment because her hands were on me, and I never, ever thought that feeling would be shared.

But it was.

I knew it was.

She knew it was.

Time slipped into insignificance as we stood facing the water, her hands lingering on my back long after the zipper was fastened. Those hands were soon sliding around my waist, meeting, and linking across my stomach, and her head fell between my shoulders. "I'm so glad you're here. You mean so much to me. I'm so sorry I didn't know what I had till it was gone."

"Neither of us did, Lil One." I covered her arms with mine and squeezed, and my vision began to mist with tears. I may have changed a lot, but I was still not going to cry in front of my girl. "Are you ready to hit the water?"

"Yep. Just give me one more minute like this. I don't know what will change after tonight, but I know something will."

"Nothing is going to change. I promise."

"Don't make promises you can't keep, Nate." She sighed, her body tensed, and her arms slipped away. I watched as she picked up her board and ran into the water, obsessed over how it became part of her body as her arms cut through the rolling waves. "Come on slow poke!" she yelled over her shoulder. We only have an hour or so out here, and I want to watch you crash and burn as much as I can."

"Be kind, Eves. I'm a bit rusty," I laughed as I splashed into the water, catching her in a heartbeat.

"A bit rusty," she scoffed. "Typical bloody show-off."

We paddled our boards past the joke of a break and lay on our stomachs, waiting for something worth the effort of catching. I didn't mind the inactivity a bit. Sure, I missed that feeling of the swell building beneath me, the heart-pumping surge of adrenaline and burning muscle as you paddled then sprung to your feet before finding that perfect balance on the crest of the wave. But I'd missed the girl lounging on the board next to me more.

"I start classes again next week." She smiled, turning away from our mutual gaze to stare at the clouds rolling above. "You'll have a few hours a day when you're home alone or with Jocie. You'll be alright with that?"

"I'm a big boy, Gidge. I'll be just fine. Besides, Jocie is the biggest lush I know. She'll be whipping up cocktails and lining up shots before you have your pointes on."

"God, I wish I could argue with that, but I can't. No doubt you'll have more fun with her than me."

I shook my head. "Not possible. I have more fun teasing and being bossed around by you than I do with anyone else. You're my favorite person."

Amusement spread over her face. "Even over Finn?"

"Especially over Finn. Everything turns into a competition with him, and I am so sick of losing." She faced me again, the smile gone.

"He's still struggling with everything, you know. But I think he is on the verge of something special. Hopefully you'll see what I mean tonight. I finally think he is going to be happy."

"What about you, Eves? Are you ready to be happy too?" I reached for her hand, but she pulled away.

"Not everyone gets to be so lucky." Her cryptic response came as she flipped onto her tummy and paddled away. Following the side-to-side sway of her ass was also a treat, but I'd have preferred her hand in mine. She'd barely touched me all day. I thought we had turned a corner, but I suddenly wasn't so sure. An ominous doubt settled in my chest.

Luckily, the hour we had in the water was enough. The surf was dead, and it began to rain, so we called it quits. Naturally, I splashed her and flipped her off her board several times before making it to shore and starting our ascent. "I can't believe we had to rappel down, then risk death climbing this fucking cliff for those pitiful waves."

"Wah-wah-wah. God, I'd forgotten how much of a sooky baby you were." I smacked her on the ass and delighted in the fire roaring to life in her eyes.

"You liked that a bit too much, didn't you?"

"Ugh. As if." I swung and slapped her cheeks again, but she started laughing and began running up the hill. I gave chase and caught her just as we reached the car. Gasping for air, we dropped our boards and continued fooling around until it came time to unzip from our suits. Shit got real, real fast. As they dangled around our waists, we stood face to face. Heaving chest to heaving chest. I struggled to focus on anything but the slow descent of the water droplets hugging the golden curves from her neck down until disappearing between her breasts. She seemed stuck too, staring at my lips like she wanted to devour them, her gaze shifting nervously between them, my eyes, and the car. She didn't know what to do.

Every part of my body was aching to touch her, and my brain spat out what was either the smartest or dumbest thing I'd ever said. "You seem conflicted. Who's going to break first?"

Heavy panting was the only noise between us for what felt like an eternity. I didn't think it was possible for us to be any closer, but I was grateful to be proved wrong. She stepped in, pressing her soft body against mine and backing me against the Jeep door as her fingers brushed over my chest and she chewed on her lip.

"I feel like this is a bad decision."

"Oh, it is, Lil Gidge. It's the worst. But bad decisions make life more fun." Every atom in my universe exploded as she stood on her tiptoes and closed her eyes. I closed mine and felt her lips skim mine before landing on my cheek.

"I can't do this. I care about you too much. Please forgive me."

That was not where I thought this was going.

And then she cried. Tears and sobs, the likes of which I hadn't witnessed since the horrible dark days of death in our past, mixed with rain on her cheeks. I cocooned her in my arms, shielding her with every ounce of love I possessed. "You're going home, Nate, and I'm *not* coming with you. My life is here, and if I give into this, if I let myself fall like I think I could, I will never get over it when you leave. Please, I'm begging you. Please let's stop now. Let's be friends—best friends. Let's go home and see Iris, then go to dinner tonight and have a good time with Finn and enjoy the rest of the time we have."

My world crumbled around me as I clung to her and tried to offer words of comfort and reassurance.

I don't remember a word of what I said. All I remember is kissing her wet hair and holding her right until her tears subsided, then feeling her slip away as she left me to get changed in the privacy of the outdoor shower. How we packed up the car and left remains a mystery too. But the silent drive home in wet jeans that made a fart sound with each movement was the epitome of soul-destroying torture, and our looming dinner could only be even worse. Sitting next to her all night, pretending I was okay when I was anything but, would be the hardest thing I'd done since I lost my sister, but I had to do it for her. I was not going to be the one to make her cry like that ever again.

Chapter 28

REJECTING NATE, WATCHING HIM TAKE IT ON the chin and try his best to make me feel better when I knew I had hurt him, opened a hole in my heart that I hadn't expected. Every second I spent with the giant sandy-haired dork endeared him even more and reinforced my decision to stop anything before it started. If I let this happen, Nate would be the death of me.

But I'd put a stop to it, and the only problem I faced was getting my body to catch up with my brain. Controlling the undeniable lust surging through my veins and settling in my undies would not be easy. He was so sweet and hot, holding Iris. The way his forearms and biceps flexed when he picked her up was damn near fatal. We made it back to the city earlier than expected. Picking Iris up was a welcome distraction.

Her squeals of joy were the exact endorphin boost I, and probably Nate, needed. The glow in her cheeks and joy in her eyes as she spotted her beloved uncle at the school gate was something I'll never forget.

"This is the bestest supwise evew!" she shrieked. "Did you bwing me a pwesant?"

"Maybe," Nate laughed, "but if I did, it would be packed away in my bag and buried in the car trunk. You'll have to wait till we get home, Booba."

"You can't call me Booba anymore. I'm too gwown up."

"Oh really." He looked at me and winked. "Well, if you don't laugh while I tickle you, I will stop calling you Booba. If you laugh, I can call you Booba till you're one hundred."

"That's not faiw! You know I wove tickles." She roared, laughing as Nate held her in one arm and unleashed a tickle onslaught. "It doesn't mattew anyway, 'cause you'll be dead when I'm one hundred!"

"Iris!" I gasped.

"Don't worry, Aunty Evie. I'll take care of this cheeky monkey." He threw Iris over his shoulder—in a fashion I wouldn't mind myself had I not just sworn off him—and picked up her school bag in the other. "Now you're really going to get it!"

The tickling lasted the first three blocks home before Iris either passed out from exhaustion and lack of oxygen or fell asleep. In hindsight, that was something I should have checked. During her out-of-it moment, I received a text from Finn.

> **Finn the Dork: Eves. I'm working late with Scarlett. Don't expect me home for dinner.**

> **Me: Working late? Snort. Yeah right. I wasn't cooking anyway. Takeaway night.**

Nate ducked down and whispered in my ear, "You do know that's the cutest thing ever, don't you?"

"What? Finn lying his ass off about working late?"

"No. You typing *snort*."

I jumped to a halt and stomped my feet. "God, you're such a freak. Why are you reading my messages over my shoulder? And how can you even read it from up there?"

"20/20 vision, Gidge. I don't miss a damn thing. Who's Scarlett?"

"That's for me to know and you to find out. I, umm…" I had nothing. Normally, I would slay him with a witty comeback or vicious barb, but I was shooting blanks, and my mouth was as dry as used sandpaper. This was the most we had spoken since we left the beach. I wanted to do our usual sparring, but the closer we got to the house, the grumpier and more anxious I became. My game was completely off, so I shielded my phone with my hand and continued to hurl abuse at my brother as we walked.

We had one street left. This was it. We were about to enter the danger zone.

Alarm bells were ringing in my head, and I had to fight the urge to hold Nate's hand for support. He was the imminent danger after all.

Next week, apart from the hours I was at work, we would be together twenty-four-seven. It was going to be all lust all the time. No more overnight reprieve for the agonizing want. No chance to cool off. No more "alone time" in bed to relieve the pressure unless I could be super quiet. Something I had failed to achieve since Nate had infiltrated my fantasies.

Our rooms were adjoining. Only a thin layer of plasterboard, blankets, and our pajamas would be between us as we slept and nothing more. *That's if he wears pjs. He does seem like a nude-sleeper kind of guy. God, don't think about him sleeping naked.*

I could only pray I was up to the task.

Seconds after we walked in the door, I decided I was most definitely *not* up to the task.

Seeing him walk down my hall with Iris still asleep on his shoulder, smelling his scent as he bent down to lay her in bed, and sensing him follow as I walked toward my room was...indescribable, overpowering, everything I was afraid of. I entered. He walked in behind me and closed the door.

"Well, this is my room, where I sleep in my pajamas, not naked, like you might, and that's my bookshelf where I put things to read, and that's my desk where I write sometimes, and look, there's my ensuite bathroom. I'm just going to duck in there for a second, and then I'll give you a tour—a tour of the house, not the bathroom. You don't need to go in there after me—not that I need to do anything stinky or nasty, I just...I'm going now."

FUCK!

I ran into the bathroom, slipping on the tiles as I skidded to a halt and almost falling into my precious clawfoot bathtub. Then, realizing I left the door open, and he just witnessed the whole thing, I was forced to watch his stupid smug face laughing as I ran back to shut it.

Chunks began rising in my throat, and I scolded my reflection in the mirror. "Not now, Evie. Not now. But really, if not now, when the guy I may or may not be head over heels for was standing in my bedroom right next to my bed, when?"

I was contemplating escaping through the bathroom window when there was a knock on the door.

"You okay in there, Gidge? I can hear you talking to yourself."

"I'm not talking to myself. You're silly. Stop being silly, silly."

"Uhh, okay, then. Umm, I will just go out to the car and get my things, then."

I waited a few heartbeats before cracking open the door. My room was empty, footsteps could be heard walking down the hall, then there was a squeal of delight as he ran into Jocelyn who was just arriving home. With her fussing over him, I had a good few minutes. Without hesitation, I dove into my bed and hid under the blankets, craving the isolation, darkness, and safety only they could provide.

"Evie… Evie, darling. You need to wake up if you want to meet Finn on time."

"What? What happened?"

"You fell asleep. Nate found you but didn't want to startle you when you woke, so he came and got me."

"Oh. Oh, okay. Where is he now?"

"I banished him to the shower. He had half of Montauk's sand stuck to his feet. Now that's something I don't miss about Byron." She chuckled and sat beside me. "You haven't hidden in your bed for a while. Are you finding it overwhelming to have Nate here?"

"Yes, yes, I am finding it overwhelming. Very much so. I ran into the bathroom so fast I almost knocked myself out on the bathtub."

"Sweetheart," she sighed as she wrapped me into a bear hug. "I had a chat with Mr. Myers while you were sleeping. He's completely besotted with you, Evie. I hope you don't stop yourself from feeling and expressing the same sentiments because of a few minor details."

"Minor details?!" I yelled, then clapped my hand over my mouth, remembering that one detail was in the shower just down the hall. "Jocie, he is Finn's best friend, and he lives on the other side of the world. What about that is insignificant?"

I was dismissed with a wave of her hand. "I didn't say insignificant. I said minor. And yes, I believe if you really have feelings for Nate, the distance is a minor detail in the grand scheme of things." The bedroom door shut next door, and the distinct sounds of man-grunting echoed through the walls. "Sounds like someone is out of the shower. Why don't you take one and get dressed? We can talk about this later." Jocelyn stood and made her way to the door. "Don't think yourself out of love, Evie. Trust me, a lifetime is a long time to harbor a regret of that size."

***

"Right. I've messaged Finn, and he's on his way."

"Are you sure this is a good idea? Finn isn't the most spontaneous of men. You do know this much unscheduled activity could end him." My laughter stopped when Nate pulled me against him. "But enough about your brother. You look unbelievable, Gidge. I knew that dress was perfect for you."

Normally, such attention would be rebuffed, but for once, I felt like I looked amazing and accepted the compliment with nothing but a modest blush.

A night intended to surprise Finn had been hijacked by Nate's thoughtfulness. Earlier, a Michael Kors garment bag laid in waiting on my bed after I showered. At first, I thought it would be a gift from my aunt, who loved a designer boutique as much as Carrie Bradshaw. But when I opened the zipper and cautiously removed the gorgeous black dress, a small card decorated with daisies fell to the ground. My heart stopped as I pictured his tattoo.

For my Irish Warrior Princess.
Love, your idiot.

It fit like a dream. Just as my hand did in Nate's for the brief second I'd indulged him while walking the banks of the Hudson. Our table hadn't been ready when we first arrived at the restaurant, M.I.X., so we grabbed hot chocolates and checked out the views along Pier 45. Things had been awkward since the whole friend-zone spiel at the beach, so I felt the time was helpful to find some kind of normality between us before facing Finn.

Clearly Nate didn't feel the same and decided to send us right back to awkwardness. First with the hand holding and then with…

"So, Gidge. There's been one question I need to ask, just for my own sanity, despite the fact that your answer may kill rather than assure me."

Oh my God. He knows. He knows I am a virgin freak. "I don't like the sound of this, Nate." He ignored me and kept going.

"Have you been serious about anyone since you've been here? Like fuck-face Christian? Were you really into him?"

It wasn't the question I was worried about, but still one I didn't want to answer. "Oh, look at the time!" I said, stupidly star-ing at the spot on my blank wrist. "We should be getting to the restaurant. It'll be freezing soon, and you still don't have a good jacket."

Nate let his cup slip from his hands and braced my shoulders. "Stop fussing over me and avoiding the question. Have you had a boyfriend since you've been here? A fuck-buddy. Friend with nauseating benefits—"

"No. Don't be silly. Of course I haven't."

"Don't be silly? Why would it be silly for you to have a boy- or bed-friend?"

"Because, well, because I'm busy, and a homebody, and grumpy, and…me. Guys don't want or even see girls like me."

Nate jolted back like I'd slapped him. "What do you mean, 'girls like me'?"

"You know, shorter, squattier, homely types. They want Amazonian goddesses like Scarlett."

"What?! Are you crazy?" He ran his hands down his face a few times, shaking his head and laughing. "Look, I still don't know who this Scarlett is, so I can't say anything about her, but Evie, you are *not* squatty and homely. You're pretty. Beautiful, in fact. Cute as all hell and sexy as fuck. Any guy would want you, and I'm pretty sure you know you drive *me* crazy."

"Snort. You have to say that 'cause you're my friend."

Biting his lip, Nate smiled, ducked down to my level, and began playing with my hair. "No, I shouldn't say or think that because I'm your and your brother's friend. But first and foremost, I am a guy, and when I think of you, I definitely don't think of squatty and homely."

Gulp.

"Oh yeah, well, what do you think?"

A cool breeze whipping off the water blew between us, and a lock of my hair swept across my face. Nate caught it between his thumb and index finger, then began to twist. "I think of the softest curls I've ever seen. Bright, beautiful, blue eyes, rose-colored lips I can't help but watch and want to kiss whenever you speak, and to be honest…" I turned to mush as my hair was released, then tucked away behind my ear. His free fingers soon busied themselves, tracing the lines of my neck and across my collarbone, releasing the most intense shiver right down to my toes. "…the most fucking lovely breasts and sexy round ass that looks magnificent in a wetsuit but would look even better between my teeth."

I stared at my feet to hide my incandescent blush. What the hell was I supposed to say to that?

"Oh." *Genius.*

My phone buzzed in my pocket. *Saved by the bell.* "That'll be our table," I said without looking.

Nate crushed me into his body. "Let them wait. Please? We haven't finished talking."

With my head squished into his chest, I inhaled deeply, taking in every drop of his delicious scent before I replied, "No, we have finished. For your sake as well as mine, I think we've said all we have to say." I pushed off his chest like it was a solid brick wall and began to walk away. "C'mon. Let's go see your best friend."

M.I.X. was chock-full of people—something I normally hated and would have been bitching about—but I was so relieved not to be alone with Nate I could have kissed every stuck-up wanker and pretentious socialite one by one. The sound of clinking glasses, alcohol-infused chatter, and laughter was the respite I needed.

I'd never been here before, but Finn had been a few times lately and seemed to really like it. Some bubbly blonde, who was way too friendly to Nate while completely ignoring me, showed us to the table, but as soon as she was gone, we hit the bar.

"What can I get you guys?" the gorgeous bartender asked the minute our butts touched the stools. "I'll take whatever you have on tap. Evie, you want a rosé?"

"Yes, please."

"Coming right up." He smiled and began pouring Nate's beer.

"Shit! I forgot to message Finn. Good one, Evie. Forget to invite the guy you're surprising to the surprise."

A loud gasp rang in my ear. "Bloody hell! UH-UH. NO WAY! Did you say Evie and Finn?" I nodded to the excitable British man sitting beside me. "Are you Evie Austen? Of course you are. Look at that hair and those eyes!" His excitement increased tenfold.

"Sure am." I nodded while edging away. "And you are…?"

"Well, ding dang. If it isn't Finn McHunk's sister, Missy McHunk. I'm Teddy, Teddy Digby. I work with Finn and Scarlett at Wise, Bernstein, and Wright."

"Oh, yes. Hi, Teddy. Finn talks about you all the time. You're the guy he went to the pub with who hit on everything that moved."

Teddy's face went from delight to fright, and my gaze shifted from him to the hot bartender placing himself and our drinks before us. "What's this I hear about hitting on people?" he asked.

Teddy lunged across the bar, grabbed him by the shirt, and pulled his ear to his lips. After animatedly whispering, the barkeep smiled and nodded. "Hi, Evie. I'm Asher. This one's boyfriend."

"Shit." I turned to Teddy on my right and smiled through gritted teeth.

"Don't worry, you haven't gotten Ted in trouble." Asher laughed. "Trust me, he can manage that all by himself."

Within ten minutes, Asher had ditched the bar, and he and Teddy were sitting with us at the table, laughing their asses off as Nate and I gave them all the dirt on Finn. Nate had just launched into his favorite—the time the ass of Finn's wetsuit ripped in front of half of Byron Bay—when the man himself strolled through the door, lipstick on his neck and draped all over a dizzy, sex-drunk-looking Scarlett. "Nate, quick, hide. Finn's here." He ducked beneath the table, smashing his head as he did.

"You behave yourself under there, Nate." Teddy smiled. "Or not. Up to you."

I stood to greet the loved-up pair, but their eyes went straight past me and set on Teddy and Asher. Scarlett's confusion showed on her face, twisting from afterglow bliss back to stark reality. "What's going on? How did you and Evie meet?" she asked Teddy.

"Well, I was here at the bar with Asher—fill you in later— and I overheard Evie talking about you two. We got to chatting, and here we are. She's quite the firecracker, Finn. I love her. But us being here together is not your surprise. Is it, Evie?"

"Nope, not even close." I smiled.

"So, where's the surprise, then?" Finn snapped quickly, losing patience with being out of the loop.

"Right behind you." Finn froze, and I quickly captured the moment of recognition on my phone.

"Nate?"

"G'day, bro." Nate threw himself into the back of Finn and wrapped his arms around his chest. Finn twisted his body to face him, and both man-babies looked like they were about to cry. This was nothing new for Finn—he cried all the time—but Nate rarely had the whole time I'd known him.

"Nate! What the hell! You're not supposed to be here till December!" Finn chuckled.

"I know, but things changed. Evie helped me switch flights, and here I am." He was still slapping Finn's back when his eyes settled on and ran over the enviable figure of Scarlett. "And who's this beautiful creature you've come in draped around? You've outdone yourself. It looks like I'm not the only one keeping a few secrets."

Finn and I slapped him on the back of his head before Finn replied, "Nate, this is, um, Scarlett Grant. A work colleague."

Teddy, Asher, and I all exchanged glances. Scarlett was way more than a work colleague to my idiot brother, but I had a suspicion as to why he'd unkindly referred to her as such. "Nice to meet you, Scarlett," Nate said, shaking her hand and grinning like a fool. "Keeping the big fella in line at the office, are ya?"

Poor Scar said nothing, just lost all color in her face and laughed awkwardly as she was guided into a chair by Teddy like we used to do with my drunk nanna at Christmas.

Things then went from bad to worse. Finn decided to ditch his date and sit next to me, but Nate made a sprint and claimed the seat first. Their childish fight and daggers over his victory would have been comical if not so hurtful to Scarlett. Finn did end up next to her but continued to act as though they had just met for most of the evening. Teddy and I did our best to encourage him to open up, but he was acting like a complete dick, pulling away from her touch and borderline ignoring her sometimes. It took all my strength not to beat the shit out of him. Scarlett was an absolute sweetheart and deserved better.

Not that it excused his behavior, but Finn was equally, if not more so, emotionally screwed than me. He wore his guilt and grief over the death of Shelby—Nate's sister, Iris's mum, and his first love—like armor, shielding himself from the world and hiding behind it whenever things were too hard. Shelby had died during childbirth. Finn had never forgiven himself and lived a half-life since. It was something I was painfully aware of and understood completely.

Our night ended with Scarlett losing her shit over something to do with their plans for my aunt's house and storming into the restroom in tears. Emerging a few minutes later with her head held high and toilet paper stuck to her shoe, she marched straight past the table and out the door with Finn running after her, apologizing before he, too, disappeared into the night.

"Well, fuck me," I said, slamming down the last of my cocktail and collapsing face-first onto the table. "That did *not* go to plan."

Chapter 29

Nate

OUR TABLE PRETENDED NOTHING HAD happened for at least forty minutes after the dramatic exit. It was awkward to begin with, but my under-the-table flirting with Evie and Teddy's natural extroversion broke that shit down quickly. He was funny, cheeky, and couldn't *not* flirt to save himself, but the guy clearly loved Finn and was borderline obsessed with Scarlett and her son, Ben, who he had helped raise. No detail was overlooked in the animated retellings of his and Scarlett's meeting at college, their shot-gun co-dependent living arrangements, and their ultimate dual migration from England to the States.

Asher was much harder to read. While far from a closed book, he was much more reserved with his feelings, opinions, and past than his boyfriend, which, for balance, was probably a good thing.

With the passing of time and the consumption of alcohol, the uncomfortableness magically melted away, and conversation flowed. Evie, who was more than a little tipsy, began to relax and show her truly funny and glorious nature. If I was not mistaken, she also engaged me in hard-core eye sex whenever our gazes met. Those baby blues seductively roamed every visible inch of me, even as Asher and I were given the lowdown on Finnlett, Finn and Scarlett's couple name that Teddy had apparently just come up with and promised he would likely forget by morning. "Okay, so let me get this straight." I took a swig of my beer, took a deep breath, and went for it. "Scarlett and Finn are sleeping together and working on Jocelyn's house together, in a workplace where not only is their relationship a secret, but their kids are too? And now Scarlett thinks Finn told Jocie to give her the job so she would sleep with him and had some old creep fired for hitting on her, but he didn't?"

Teddy's eyes and lips shifted to the right as he processed the glut of words. "Hmm, yes, well, he did but didn't."

"Right. Clear as mud. Thanks for rectifying that, Teddy."

"Look, I know Finn," Evie said, emphatically crossing her arms over her chest. "He's a dick and a moron, but he's a moron with morals. He doesn't have a sleazy bone in his body. If he recommended Scarlett to Jocelyn, it was only because he thought she could do better than him. He has worked his ass off on that design for months. He wouldn't hand it over for no reason."

"I dunno," Teddy sighed. "I've watched that boy flitter and float around Scarlett with a dumb grin and a hard-on for weeks. The pressure building up in his balls must have been agonizing, and I'm pretty sure he was thinking about a different kind of bone. A blow job may have sounded like an excellent reason to ignore his moral compass…which, of course, was pointing south…unlike his cock." The sheer amount of cock analogies earned him a high five from me and a roll of the eyes from both Asher and Evie.

"Can you two stop thinking about your dicks for five minutes?" She sighed.

"No," chorused all the men at the table and one waiter who happened by.

"Omg, it's like sitting with a bunch of apes." Evie's look of disgust was quickly replaced with something much more fun and promising as I ran my finger over her knee and squeezed her thigh. She liked it. I could feel her thighs tighten and could see her lip tremble. Her own moral compass was waning.

"Okay, so forget Finn and his either moral or sleazy boner.

What's the reason they both hid the kids?" I asked, still caressing her warm, soft skin.

Teddy took a sip of his margarita, watching us suspiciously as he replied, "Scar's a little traumatized from years of pre- and misconceptions about the age she became a parent. It's understandable. She was only eighteen when she had Ben, and she has been tutted and stared at for years, especially when Ben was a baby."

Evie nodded in agreement. "Finn's the same. They both want to establish themselves without that judgment hanging over their heads. It is totally unnecessary, but I think they're so young and just want a fair go."

"I hope they can sort it out. As hilarious as laughing while they make fools of themselves in front of each other has been, I do love seeing them together. Their chemistry is hot as fuck. Speaking of chemistry, what's the deal here?" Teddy jabbed his finger aggressively at Evie and me.

"There is no deal," Evie answered way too quickly to be believable, and the jolt of shock her body made finally dislodged my hand from her leg. "It's a super un-deal-like situation. Nate is Iris's uncle, Finn's bestie, and one of my best friends too. We grew up together. All of us did—not just me and Nate, obviously. That's it. Nothing else to report." She shifted uncomfortably in her seat and nervously sipped from her rosé. Gossiping with the boys about Finn and Scarlett had delightfully consumed her for the last hour, but the speculation turning to us was clearly far less entertaining. For me, it was much more.

Teddy and Asher looked at each other, then back to us. "I call bullshit," Asher said. "I have watched you two all night, and there have been as many heart eyes and blush-cheeked gazes between you two as there was between the other two."

Teddy agreed. "C'mon, mate," he sang in the worst Australian accent I'd heard to date, "tell us what's going on. I promise we won't tell Captain Koala. Your tawdry affair will be guarded with our lives."

"You know what, Evie? I'd like to hear this too. What is going on between us?" I returned to my seat and smirked. It was unfair of me to put her on the spot. She'd made it clear how she felt, but I couldn't help it. I knew she was lying to herself. She needed a push in the right direction from someone other than me, and Teddy Digby was the perfect man for the job.

Betrayal besieged her face, and she sprung to her feet, knocking her chair over in the process, then tripping over it in her haste to escape. The loud crash as it hit the floor drew every set of eyes in the bar. "Oh! Look at the time. We better go, Nate." She grabbed me by the neck of my shirt, almost choking me as she yanked me to my feet. "We have to be up early tomorrow."

"Do we? What for, Eves?"

"We have that thing, you know…the thing with Iris."

"Nope. Haven't got a clue." I returned her chair to its upright position and tapped the seat. "Sit down, Gidge. Let's talk more about us."

Through gritted teeth, Evie called me an idiot and tried again, "You know, the thing…at the place?"

"Oh, yes. The Iris thing at the place. Now I remember." Over howls of protest and demands of truth, I leaned across the table and shook the boys' hands as firmly as I could while being dragged by the collar and reprimanded by my little firecracker. I enjoyed it way too much.

Evie was so enraged by my outrageous disobedience and Teddy and Asher's speculation that her verbal whipping of me continued the whole way home. The fact that I loved her yelling at me was made evident by my irrepressible smirk, which further fueled her fire. It was a vicious, sexy cycle. The more she yelled, the tighter the clenching of my hand on her thigh became, and the pinkie finger stroking-slash-fucking she began once we were in the back of the Uber was potentially orgasmic.

The touching and tongue-lashing turned to a whisper as we entered the house—or the mansion…the place was massive. Three living areas and a huge open-plan kitchen and formal dining room opened out to a sprawling deck, garden, and garage. Decor and furniture wise, it was all Hamptons style, all Jocelyn, but to the trained eye, there were little hints of Evie, Finn, and Byron scattered throughout. Glass vases filled with shells and sand, ornamental surfboards, coral, and hurricane lamps sat on white credenzas and shelves. Finn's stunning photography, line drawings, and paintings of the coastline, their beautiful family, and their farmhouse lined the wainscot and duck-egg blue walls.

The bedrooms we were heading to were more luxurious than the small hotel room I'd spent the last few days in. They were comparable to expensive suites, containing a private bathroom, enough space for a desk and sitting area, and a king-size bed.

Death was threatened if I dared wake Iris or Jocelyn, even though I hadn't said a word for a good ten minutes. Without letting go of my hand, Evie clomped her way upstairs and down the long hallway. Jocelyn's, Iris's, and Finn's rooms were down one end, while Evie's and mine, separated by a sitting room and bathroom, were down the other. We approached my door but, to my surprise, didn't stop, and the dragging continued until we reached Evie's.

"This is not my room, Gidge," I said, pointing out the bleeding obvious. Evie said nothing but placed her hands on my stomach, just above my belt, and tugged at my shirt till it was free. A tiny squeak escaped her lips as she slowly slipped her fingers beneath the white cotton and made contact with warm flesh. "What are you doing, Evie?"

My heart raced as she ignored me and began to trace the lines of my abs and chest while biting her lip. The upward trajectory of her hands was quickly matched by my cock. By the time she was standing on the tips of her toes in perfect fifth position, sliding her fingers around my neck, I was painfully hard, straining against my zipper, and could hardly breathe. "Shut up and get inside," she whispered.

"I can't believe I'm going to say this, but...no. I can't." The fingers twisting through my smattering of chest hair stalled as she looked up at me. "I want to. Lord knows I do. But you've had a few drinks, and I don't want to do something you might regret tomorrow."

"Well, that's no fun 'cause that's exactly what I wanna do. C'mon, Nate, come to bed and make me regret it."

I slid my palms up her arms, leaving a trail of goosebumps over her skin until I reached behind my neck, wrapped my fingers over hers and released her grip. "I want to go in there and do more to you than you could possibly comprehend, Lil One. I want to lick you, taste you, and fuck you so damn hard you wouldn't be able to walk straight for a week." She sighed and swallowed heavily. "And I will. *If* you wake up tomorrow and still feel the same way, nothing will stop me. Just knock on the wall, and I'll smash straight through the plaster to get to you. But please, please trust me and wait. You mean too much to me to risk our first time being a drunken regret."

She pulled her hands out of mine, and they flew to her hips. On body language alone, you'd take her as furious, but her face showed the fearful sting of rejection. "If I had a hot shearer hiding in there, and we promised you a three-thingy, or...or if I looked like Polly...would you come in then?"

I took a step back and shook my head. "Not only is bullshit like that unfair, but it's also further evidence that you've had too much to drink."

She scoffed, turned, and opened her door, but she stopped a few paces in. "I'm sorry. You're right, and I bloody hate that so much. I don't know what to do with you, Nate. You make me so angry I could punch you right in the junk, but you also make me so happy I want to cry. No one has ever done what you do to me. You look at me, and I quiver. You touch my hand or knee or rest your hand on my back when we walk down the street, and I'm reduced to a simpering mess. I thought I'd been attracted to men before, but you have shown me what attraction and lust really are. It's terrifying and brilliant, and...and terrifying..."

"You already said that." I stepped closer, slipped my hand around her waist, and pulled her against me until her back was flush with my chest. "I know you're scared, and I am too. But you should never, for one second, think that I don't want you. You're beautiful and so fucking hot and smart and furious, and I want you so bad it hurts. I want you in a way I've never wanted any other woman."

"What about…?" I knew what was coming.

"Don't say it."

"Polly. Did you want her like you do me?"

"Evie."

"Did you say those things to her too?"

"Honestly, some of the things, yes. I did say Polly was sexy. Probably hot too. 'Cause she was—or is. She's a beautiful woman, Evie. The world is full of beautiful women, and yes, I have slept with quite a few of them. But none of them compare to you because none of them own my heart like you do. Polly demanded me, Evie. You've possessed me."

Her body went limp in my arms, and I held her, infusing all the love I could muster through my fingertips. I kissed the top of her head, said goodnight, then walked to my room and closed the door.

As I lay awake, still hard as a rock and cursing myself at two am, I heard it. Through the wall, there was a whimper, a sigh.

Evie was crying. I made her cry again.

I turned to my side, unsure if I should go to her. The whimpering became sighing, and the sighing became moaning. I wriggled to the wall and pressed my ear against it.

"Nate. Nate. Yes, please."

Oh my God. Is Evie thinking of me and touching herself?

Without storming in there and joining her—which I did seriously consider—there was no way I could be sure she was even awake. She may have been asleep, just dreaming. She may have been pressed up against the wall, pretending, laughing at me. Or she could have been naked, one hand playing with her nipples, the other with her wet pussy. After a minute or two more of her begging and pleading for my touch, I was matching her, moan for moan, with my throbbing cock, already slick with pre-cum, in my hand, fiercely stroking base to tip, speeding to catch her before my climax. "Evie," I sighed.

"Nate?"

Oh fuck. What the fuck do I do? What do you mean, you cock head? Fucking sex her up!

"Can you hear me, *Gidge*? *Are* you thinking of me? Please tell me you're thinking of me as you touch yourself."

The soft whimpers ceased. *I scared her off.* But then…then… "Think of me, Nate. Think of fucking my mouth instead of your hand."

"Fuck, Evie."

"Nate, I'm, I'm…"

"Wait for me, Evie. Be a good girl and wait for me. Can you do that?"

"Oh my God. Yes. Yes."

I could hear her breathing. Panting. Her sobs catching in her throat. And I could only pray the rooms were separated enough that no one else could hear. I gripped myself so hard and tight it bordered on pain because something told me Evie liked it rough. That she would be just as bossy as she was outside the bedroom, that she would rule and command me with a hard-ass iron fist and that I would love every second of it and beg for it harder. Just thinking of her imposing her will over me had my hips thrusting off the bed and sweat dripping from my body.

"Can you hear what you do to me, Evie? I'm going to come."

"I'm coming too, all over my fingers, wishing they were yours…"

"Fuck, you're so hot, Evie."

"Oh, Nate!"

My body shuddered, and we both cried out. The orgasm was so intense, the pulsing so deep and spilling so hard and long, I swear I went blind. The whole room went black. My lungs were screaming for oxygen as I gasped, sucking in air like I'd been trapped beneath a monster wave and had finally emerged at the surface, and I could hear Evie doing the same. Our breathing slowed until I could no longer hear her.

"I love you, Gidge."

I had no idea if she heard me. With my hand resting against

the wall, I stared at the ceiling till I fell asleep with the biggest smile I had ever had on my face.

◆

Bright and early the following day, I was up, showered, dressed, and making as much noise as I could in the hopes of rousing my wall buddy, but it seemed Miss Austen was out cold. Bored and in search of something to do other than jack off over Evie again, I snuck out into the hall and knocked on Finn's door. I was pretty sure he hadn't come home last night, but just in case, I came up with the excuse of leaving my deodorant at the hotel if I got busted snooping.

As suspected, there was no answer, and I enjoyed looking around. In typical Finn fashion, his room was immaculate, clean, organized, and styled. Nothing seemed out of place. There was nothing scandalous in his drawers or his medicine cabinet. The only thing of interest I found was a sketchpad filled with drawings of Scarlett, some of which were pretty saucy, and a stack of Jane Austen books on his desk. The books were no surprise. Evie had told me he bought them as a gift for Scarlett, had begun reading *Pride and Prejudice*, and had been unable to stop. The poor guy had it bad, but who the hell was I to judge after last night?

There was still no other sign of life coming from the other rooms, so I headed to the kitchen with the dog-eared book, thinking I'd see what the fuss was about over some breakfast. I'd not long sat with a cup of Evie's chai tea and Vegemite toast and been instantly sucked into the world of Longbourn and its inhabitants when I heard the front door creak open.

So loud was Finn's piss-poor effort to sneak back into the house that even the tool's stomach could be heard growling as he tiptoed right past me. The state of his hair and clothing left me to presume he and Scarlett had made up, and I hoped that was the case because Golden-Boy was open for the slaughter, and the carcass I was about to feed from, could provide shelter should he become aware of my own late-night adventures.

"You slut!"

Completely shitting himself, he spun on his toes, saw me, and then froze. Guilt was written all over his face, and hIs eyes were wide as saucers, but only briefly. He soon found his confident, some might of said, arrogant swagger and made an impressive recovery.

"It's called a book, Nate. It has lots of words and tells a story. Some even have pictures."

"Yes, I am familiar with the concept. What I don't get is how a girl that clearly has you so twisted that you've begun collecting and reading Austen is the same girl you treated like shit in my company last night." To emphasise my point, I waved the book in his face.

"I didn't treat her like shit! Well, I did a bit, I guess... But Scarlett will forgive me... I think."

"You think? You doing the walk of shame at dawn implies you already made up."

"We did a bit. But not fully."

Okay. This is getting interesting.

"So, where are you creeping in from?"

After checking the room and ensuring we were alone, he took a swig of the milk he'd just snatched from the fridge, then tilted toward me. "She wouldn't let me in, so I slept on her doorstep."

This is too good.

"Jesus, Finn."

"What?" He cried incredulously, "I thought she'd come back down. Waiting for forgiveness on her doorstep seemed romantic, but then I fell asleep and woke up with a cat licking my face. She did bring me hot cocoa and a blanket, so she can't be too pissed. And I'm sure she'll wake up and see I didn't mean to hurt her. I was just trying to be respectful."

"Respectful? Respectful to who? Pretending you're not in a relationship with someone you apparently love doesn't seem very respectful."

"Isn't it obvious? To you and to Shelby. I didn't want to make you feel awkward by flaunting Scarlett in your face."

"For fuck's sake, Finn. Shelby's been gone over seven years, and while I miss her every day and always will, do you really think I—or she, for that matter—would want you to grieve forever? You deserve to be happy, to have a life of your own outside of the amazing one you've built for Iris. We all do."

"But—"

"But nothing. You made Shelby happy her whole life. Those last few months were precious to us all, but you have to move on. Be young, have fun, have sex. Fall in love!"

The big doofus seemed speechless and took another mouthful of milk. It was poor timing as my beautiful, glowing, rosy-cheeked girl made her grand entrance, promptly punched him in the gut, and snatched the carton from Finn's hand.

I couldn't help but laugh. I had missed watching these clowns fight, but it was momentary as I was quickly distracted by Evie strutting in her sleep shorts and tank top. Her juicy ass swayed side to side, and her braless, free-range boobs jiggled with each step.

"I heard the words fun, sex, and love," she quipped, looking directly at me, and biting her lip to control the smile I could see playing at the edges of her mouth. "Do I want to know what you're talking about?"

Ready to fire back a filthy response, I remembered the 6'4" brother capable of beating me to a pulp standing right beside me. "We were talking about Finn and Scarlett and no one else." I gave her a shake of my head and my best *shut-up* eyes.

"What?" Evie mouthed.

If there was one thing Finn Austen was ever good at, apart from EVERYTHING, it was reading me—my mood, my face, body language, all of it—so I tried as hard as I could to play it cool and not let on that I, his loyal and lifelong best friend, had been engaging in a through-the-wall, joint masturbation session with his sister only hours before. The boiling kettle provided a distraction, and before anyone else could move, I whipped it from the stove and began shuffling around behind Finn. Evie padded to my side, sucking her lip between her teeth as she passed me the milk. Never had the transfer of a dairy product been so sexy.

I could hear her breathing falter as our fingers connected, briefly flirting with entwining. Knowing where those fingers had been and what they'd been doing just hours earlier KILLED ME. She watched me make her tea just how she liked it, flooded with milk and sugar, then took the bread I passed to her without looking and popped four slices in the toaster, all with a luminous pink glow to her freckled cheeks.

Had Finn not been breathing down my neck, she would have been on that counter with my face between her thighs. But he was, so I wasn't.

I dragged my eyes off Evie and caught Finn's gaze in the window. Cogs were turning. His expression was hilarious, reminding me of a cassowary bird I saw on a trip to the Daintree Rainforest as a kid. Just like Dad instructed us to do with the freakishly ugly bird, as long as Evie and I stayed still, the danger would pass.

Danger did not pass. She dropped her spoon, and in unison, we bent down to pick it up and clunked our heads. Giggling nose to nose, eyes locked, I picked up the spoon. I tried not to check her out—I really did—but in her sexy pjs and with the memory of her moans haunting my every thought, it was hard to stay focused.

The shit storm started as a low-frequency rumble, like thunder rolling across a mountain range, and ended as an apocalyptic awakening. "Oh my God. You fucked my sister!!"

Evie squealed, leapt to the counter, and started buttering toast as though nothing had happened. I went into survival mode. I puffed out my chest, huffed out a sigh, and cautiously approached with my hands outstretched, calmly waving Finn down and urging his talons down. "Finn. Mate—"

"Don't fucking mate me. Are you or are you not sleeping with my sister?"

There are two things I knew for sure at that moment. Evie was going to lose it, and I was a dead man. But before I could say-please, Finn. Not the face- my brave girl did as I predicted.

"Yes, he is…" *Uhhh, what now?* "And there is not a damn thing you can do about it. Like Nate said, you deserve to be happy. We all do."

Finn's fists curled at his sides. He may have been tearing up a bit too—it was so Finn. "Eww, this is...is...disgusting. You are practically related. She's my sister, for fuck's sake."

That pissed me right off. Evie and I were not related. I was related to Shelby, though, and Finn seemed to be forgetting the whole, impregnating-my-sister thing. Of course I had to remind him. "Yeah, and Shelby was my sister."

"Pfft, that is completely different."

"Oh really, and how is that different?"

"We were stupid kids who didn't know any better, that's how. You two are fucking adults—well, you're supposed to be."

We were chest to chest now, our bodies jostling for dominance until Evie slid between us. Her face was stained with tears as she pressed her hands into my chest and pleaded with her eyes.

"That's enough. Please, Nate. Let me handle this."

"Handle what, Evie?" Finn snapped. "There is nothing to handle. You two cannot be a thing, and I forbid it, and Nathaniel is going home...today. I want you gone by the time I get back from work...*mate*."

Evie's face distorted, and she spun on her heels to face her brother. "You forbid it?" she snarled, her whole body tight with rage. "Bloody hell, Finn. Who the hell do you think you are? You have absolutely no right to say that to me. I have dedicated my fucking life to you and Iris. I have been happy to do it, too, but I deserve to have something for myself. That something is Nate, so you bloody well better get used to it."

What Evie did next was either a testament to how much she cared for me or an attempt to have me killed. She grabbed me by the scruff of my shirt and planted a massive wet kiss on my lips. I genuinely forgot my name. Before I could register what was happening, or kiss her back, she was dragging me from the room. "The people in your life are not your pens, Finn. You cannot organize, order, and control us to behave in a manner that suits you. This is my life and my house as much as it is yours. Nate stays. If you don't like it, piss off!"

Chapter 30

Evie

THE WHOLE HOUSE SHOOK AS FINN TOOK MY suggestion and pissed off, almost slamming the front door off its hinges on his way out.

That was when reality hit. I, Evie Austen, kissed Nathaniel Myers. Even though it was a thin-lipped, closed-mouthed spite kiss…it was fucking amazing. Day by day, I'd been slowly caving to desire. It was just a matter of time before it happened, but that little performance was not what I had envisioned.

Honestly, though, I couldn't give a flying fuck.

Nate stood facing the door.

"Fuck, Evie. You just kissed me."

"I know. Sorry." I was not the slightest bit sorry.

"I don't want you to be sorry." He turned to face me, his hand burrowing into his hair, his expression hot, dazed, and confused. "I want you to do it again."

My knees buckled beneath me. It was all too much, too soon. My heart couldn't take it.

Trying not to meet his eyes, I paced the length of my bed but couldn't seem to stop my gaze from falling back to him, especially to those soft, pillowy lips. *Fuck,* I wanted to taste them again. To feel them pressed against my own.

A slow and sexy smile spread across his

mouth as he stalked toward me. He knew what I was thinking. What I wanted.

"Let me be perfectly clear, Evie. Apologies will never be required after you kiss me, but I do need to know…why did you kiss me?"

"I…I don't know."

"Don't you? Well, what about the fucking, Evie? Why did you tell Finn we were fucking? I seem to have no memory of burying myself deep inside your sweet little pussy, and I'm pretty sure fucking you till you scream my name and can't remember your own will be something I *won't* forget."

Yep, gonna faint. Maybe die.

Want pooled between my legs as he closed in. I could feel his heat, smell my tea on his breath. *God, why is that so sexy?* Embarrassed by the desire coursing through me, I turned away just as his feet brushed against mine. That same breath tickled against my neck as his fingers played with the hem of my tee. He tugged it lightly, and the crisp morning air kissing my skin was followed by fingers caressing my bare, untouched flesh. Of its own accord, my ass pressed back into him. He was so hard and nestled between my cheeks.

"Tell me why," he whispered. "Is it because of you—"

"I don't want to pretend anymore, Nate."

A low, easy laugh rolled from his chest. "You never had to, Aoife."

"Why do you keep calling me that? No one calls me that." *And why is it so fucking sexy when you do?*

"Because it's your name." He swept the hair off my neck and pressed his lips to my skin. "And it's beautiful." He kissed higher. "Just like you." He spun me to face him, cupped my face with his strong hands, tilted my head back, and crashed his mouth onto mine. My knees buckled. I gripped onto his shirt to stay upright as he softly licked along my bottom lip and moaned. "Aoife, God, yes."

I'd come to accept that Nate really did care for me, and everything he did, the way he held me, the way his hands roamed my body in their desperation to touch and claim every part of me, the words he whispered against my lips as he kissed me deeper and deeper, was further confirmation of that fact.

Trusting his hold on me, I released his shirt, slid my hands up over his shoulders, around his neck, and pulled him down harder against me. I parted my lips and melted even further into him as our tongues swept over each other again and again. Nate turned our twisted bodies and used his weight to back then trap me against the door. He thrust. I gasped and felt his cock thicken. Growing bolder by the second, I ran my fingers through and tugged at his hair, took a little nip of his salty, slightly spiced chai-tea lips, and rolled my hips against his bulge. The hungry growl he released sent a blinding pulse through my body that settled between my legs. I was so wet so fast. It was so new, so sweet and dangerous. He deepened the kiss. I felt myself becoming lost in the wanting, the ache of anticipation. Nothing had ever felt like this, and I knew it was because no one else had ever loved me like this. His love was infused into his every touch and devilish tongue flick.

I broke away, gasping for air, and opened my eyes to find him filled with adoration, lust, and utter confusion, already looking into mine.

"Fuck, Evie, our second kiss is so much better than our first. Not having your brother standing right next to us, looking as though he may punch me in the head, really adds something." I laughed, pulling him closer to my bed, but Nate's face was stern and determined. "Every time I've felt you letting me in, you've pushed me away, but what you don't understand is that it just makes me want you more. That it fuels the fire and makes me even harder. Not this time, though. The games are over, Evie. I want you. I want you right now."

Fuck, he was right. He was so, so right.

"I want you too, Nate, and I know you'll not be mine forever. I know you are going back home and that I am *not* going with you, but for once, I want to have and hold and take something just for me, alright?"

"I'm yours, Eves. I always have been. Take whatever you want because it's always been you."

I jumped into his arms and climbed him like the sexiest fucking tree in the history of trees. Once settled, I wrapped my legs around his chest, feeling his hard dick right below my ass. "But you have to remember, this is just a New York thing to get whatever this is out of our systems, and then we can move on."

"Gidget."

"Yes?"

"Shut up."

"Okay." He pulled my legs free and threw me over his shoulder. "Put me down, you idiot!" It was the last thing I wanted, but I loved the fight, the struggle. Writhing and slapping his broad back in faux anger was just as hot as I imagined it would be. After three giant strides, I was tossed onto my bed and left to watch as he hungrily stalked me. Removing his shirt, he climbed onto the bed, settled between my legs, and trailed kisses up my inner thighs. "Let me show you how good we can be together, Gidge. Let me show you how good I can make you feel." He reached for my pink-plaid-covered pussy and pressed a kiss to the soaked fabric. "So wet for me already. Fuck, you smell amazing."

He continued to kiss, twisting his head side to side, and opening me as his hands slid down my shorts. "Oh God," I moaned, biting my lip, and gripping the sheets, and he tugged the shorts over my hips, thighs, and ankles, then threw them to the floor.

"Evie Austen. Red lace? Were you wearing this for me last night when you came on your fingers?"

"Yes." I sighed. I wasn't at all. But this was hotter.

"I knew it. Such naughty lace for such a good girl."

Oh God, oh God, oh God.

"So fucking beautiful. I can't wait to taste you."

This is happening. This is it. It's now or never. I have to tell him.
Then it hit me.

Frigid Evie.

I tried to push the memory away. Tried to relax into Nate's

heavenly, unholy touch and bask in it like I had been just seconds before. But all I could see was Luke Bailey's face. All I could hear were the taunts and jibes, and all I could feel were the nerves, the fear, the humiliation, and the rejection.

Frigid Evie.

Hot tears began to fall on my cheeks, but Nate was too busy praising, moaning, and devouring me through my underwear, his arm stretching up to cup my breasts—which felt really fucking amazing—to notice my freakout.

Frigid Evie.

It was happening all over again. Before I could stop myself, I pulled my body from his grasp, sending poor Nate face-first into the mattress. I shuffled back against the headboard and held my knees up to my chest. Perhaps he thought it was part of the game as he looked at me with a smile as big as his heart but froze when he saw my face.

"Evie, baby, what's wrong?"

I closed my eyes, willing a black hole or portal to another dimension, one where I was a sexually confident hoochie, to appear before me, but it didn't. I was left facing the most beautiful boy I had ever seen, who had just had his face pressed against my hoo-ha.

"Nate, I'm a virgin!" I spat the words at him, screaming as though he didn't know his head was on fire.

"What?" His expression was everything I'd dreaded for years. Shock, bemusement, horror, pity. "You're a virgin?" I nodded silently, nervously awaiting the arrival of panic chucks, and braided my hair. "A virgin?" he repeated.

"Yes, Nate. A virgin."

"A virgin, as in you've never had sex before?"

"No, as in I'm a non-alcoholic cocktail." I dropped my hair, slapped his head, and rolled from the bed. "For fuck's sake, Nate. Yes, I'm a virgin—as in I've never had sex before."

He sat back on his heels, scratched his belly like I'd asked him what he wanted on his toast, then lazily smiled. "A virgin... I can work with that."

"You can work with that?" His smile broadened, and I saw red. "What an incredibly arrogant, cavalier, asshole of a thing to say to a half-naked, crying woman who just revealed her most embarrassing secret to a man who is also half-naked with a massive boner she can't take her eyes off…and don't you dare laugh at me!"

Completely disregarding my words, he laughed and sprung to his feet. I was in his grip before I could pull away. His hands swept up and down my back before squeezing and settling on my ass cheeks. "I didn't mean to sound insincere or insensitive. I'm surprised and really, really, happy."

"Happy?"

"Yup. I'm stoked. I knew we were made for each other, and this just proves it. You're fucking perfect, and you're mine. It's fate, Gidge. I'm going to be the first and only man you—the first and only girl I've ever loved—will sleep with."

I pushed off his chest in disgust-slash-swoonworthy arousal. "You're pretty cocky, aren't you?"

He smirked smugly and looked down at his still-bulging pants. "You could say that, yeah."

Damn it. Don't look so fucking cute!

My irritation knew no bounds, but so did his adorably playful countenance…and my desire to play. I wanted to be angry, to reject his romanticized claims of fate. But if I was being honest, his words speared my armored heart like a dagger. The idea of having Nate be my one and only felt right. I wasn't going to tell him that, though, and luckily, I didn't have to.

"Nate the gwate! Nate the gwate! Nate the gwate!" Iris banged on his door.

"Bad luck, Stiffy Stifferson." I chortled, reminding myself to stop staring at his erection. "Looks like fate has other plans. You're not going to be my first anything."

"Maybe not now, Evie, but trust me, this"—he pointed to his cock—"will be in that"—he pointed to my lady bits—"before the end of the day."

"Lovely." I rolled my eyes and grabbed and slipped on a fresh pair of basic, ugly, comfy pajama bottoms that no one would find sexy, took my equally unflattering robe off the hook beside my door, turned my back on the sexy, arrogant doofus and stepped from my room.

"Good morning, Bubba." Iris spun to face me, her little face screwed in annoyance. "Evie, Uncle Nate won't answer the door, and I wanna cuddle him."

"I'm sure he wants to cuddle you too, but he had a big trip and is probably sleepy. Big-baby, man-child types like him and your daddy don't cope with jet lag as well as you and I do," I replied loud enough to ensure I was heard. "Why don't you let him rest? You have the whole day for cuddles."

"Okay. Let's make him bwekfast then." Iris grabbed my hand and led me away from danger.

Chapter 31

Evie

IRIS STOOD ON MY FEET, HER ARMS WRAPPED around my waist, and was rambling on about her friend and Scarlett's son, Benny, as we shuffled together into the kitchen. Ben and Iris had no idea their parents were dating. The two cuties attended the same school that sat between the two houses and were thick as thieves within days of meeting. It was all part of the twisted web of fate that brought Scarlett and Finn together. She would have a fit when she learned about it all. Perhaps she'd have a new family too.

It was the first time I'd had that thought. If Scarlett and Finn worked out whatever happened at dinner and stayed together, Iris may end up with a stepmom... and stepbrother too. Where would that leave me?

I gripped Iris tighter, holding onto her as much as she did me. Her affection was grounding, and I *needed* re-grounding. My mind was catastrophizing our collective unknown future while my spirit and libido were off, flying high and horny above Greenwich village and heading for the clouds.

Nate's hypnotic, chaotic sexuality had made me lose myself, and the little one clinging to my body—that, for all intents and purposes, saw me as her mom— needed me, stepmom, or no stepmom. I could NOT fall for a guy who would only be here for a few months. After kissing him and drowning in the crazy, raw, mind-blowing energy between us, I knew if I went through with my plan of letting him take my virginity, he would likely be taking my heart along with it.

Was it—he—worth the risk?

Ten minutes later, he—who should probably *not* be shagged—swaggered into the room, the smell of sausage and bacon and my homemade pancakes a seemingly irresistible lure. My heart leapt into my throat as he brushed behind me, running his little finger along my bum and delivering a discreet slap as I stood at the stove, plating up our food. Leaning on the counter beside me, he annoyingly kicked my foot with his as his eyes burned through the fluffy cotton of my robe.

"Good morning, ladies. How did we sleep?" he asked while popping fresh blueberries into his mouth one at a time.

"Fine, thanks," I replied coolly while Iris ran up to cuddle him, then sat back at the table and began telling him about last Thursday's dance class. Nate watched her, laughing as she spoke, so I seized the opportunity and allowed my eyes to roam his body.

Fuck, he was hot, fresh from the shower, smelling of coconut, some kind of fresh fruit and the briny scent of the ocean. The man was a walking, talking, goddamn tropical island. His wet, slightly-curly-on-the-ends hair fell into his deep, dark-brown eyes, but my own settled on his full, now purplish-stained lips as I recalled the feel of them pressing into my sex. Not only was he drop-dead gorgeous, but he was kind, considerate, loving, and thoughtful. He knew I was a virgin and didn't judge me.

Again, I asked myself the question…*is Nate worth it?*
Yes, he fucking is.

The cheeky bastard caught my gaze, edged closer, winked, and blew me a tiny kiss.

I surprised myself by not gagging, rolling my eyes, or looking away when Nate whispered, "You always smell so nice." Instead, I actively participated in some serious, egg-flipping, blueberry-bingeing, silent eye sex that ended when Jocelyn joined us in the kitchen. Nate and I jumped apart. He and Jocie shared an odd exchange as they met, then simultaneously sat at the table.

"Nathaniel," she said with a suspicious smirk.

"Jocelyn," Nate replied, calling her bluff with an equally distrustful furrowing of the brow.

"How was your night?" they asked with perfect synchronicity.

"Excellent," they again replied in unison before sitting, staring, and sizing each other up while pulling ridiculously dramatic faces like two characters on *The Bold and the Beautiful*.

"Please tell me you two aren't suffering strokes simultaneously." I snorted for real instead of saying it, breaking their odd game.

"What was all that fuss with you two and Finn this morning?" Jocie quizzed. I suspected she'd heard everything because she couldn't stop smiling. *Shit, I hope that's all she heard.*

"Nothing!" Nate and I said in chorus.

"It certainly didn't sound like nothing. It sounded rather a lot like something. An argument over the organization and control of pens, perhaps?" I shrugged nonchalantly. "You know he cares an awful lot about his…" She paused and looked at Iris, then me. "…his pens, and their well-being. I heard him take off, and now he won't answer my calls. Do you know where he went?" Her eyes popped from her head as she popped the end of a thick pork sausage into her mouth and tore the end off like a wild dog.

"Nope." I sighed. "He had his knickers in a twist about this and that, lost his shit, and left."

Nodding in agreement, Nate gazed goofily at me across the table while loading up his and Iris's plates without looking.

"Evie," Iris said, thankfully redirecting everyone's attention, "did you, Daddy, and Nate have a fight last night too? Is that why you wewe cwying?"

"Crying? I wasn't crying, bub."

"Yes, you were. Uncle Nate was too. I got up to go to the bathroom and heawd you both. You wewe like, uhh, uhh, uhhhhh, ooohhhh, like moany, sad ghosts."

I froze. Nate dropped his juice and took on the complexion of the ghost he apparently sounded like. Jocelyn erupted into laughter and started gagging and choking on the sausage she'd just swallowed. Nate jumped to action, leaning over and violently pounding on her back. It did the trick, possibly making him feel better *and* dislodging the troublesome pork piece that flew from her mouth and hit me right in the middle of my forehead.

Entirely unfazed by the chaos around her and not waiting for a reply, Iris picked up her plate, skipped into the living room, and switched on the TV.

Bluey the Dog's voice floated into the kitchen, and Jocelyn seized the day, excitedly grabbing and waving my hand. "I knew it! I knew that's what you were talking about. You two finally got together, didn't you? Didn't you?"

"Jeepers, Jocie. You're going to rip my arm off!" I tore it from her grip and rubbed my red wrist.

"Don't you dare keep secrets from me, Evie," she warned, pointing her finger in my face. "I have waited years for this."

"Pfft, you have," Nate scoffed dryly.

Spinning in her seat, the finger left me and was aimed at Nate. "So, I'm right, then? You kissed Evie?"

"Yep."

"Nate!" I bellowed.

"Though, technically, she kissed me," he added with a grin.

"And I never will again," I lied.

"Oh, yes, you will!" In a remarkable turn of speed, Jocelyn leapt from her seat and squished me into her ample bosom. "Deny it all you like, Missy. But you idiots have been pining for each other for eons. You're like magnets, always finding each other, never able to stay apart when close. I don't think I have a photo of you all where you aren't side by side. Oh, and I will never forget how Nate supported and cared for you after your parents died and how you did the same for him when we lost Shelby." Despite my best efforts, tears fell down my cheeks. "You're both incredible people and deserve to be happy...together." After peppering me with kisses, she moved to Nate and repeated the affections.

"Jocie, you're jumping the gun. We kissed once—"

"Twice," Nate interjected, "and it was a bit more than kissing."

"Nate!" I could have killed him. "And we have some major issues. Finn being one, and a few thousand miles of ocean between us another—"

"Shut up, the both of you," Jocelyn snapped while flashing a disturbing smile. Finn had often compared her evil grin to Cruella de Vil. I never got it till that moment. "I will take Iris out for a few hours and give you some space, but I leave you with a warning." Her finger whipped back out and waved back and forth between us. "Do not fuck this up. Evie, no more pushing people away. No more putting everyone else first. And Nathaniel," she said, spinning to face Nate, "do anything to harm my girl, and Finnley and his fists will be the least of your concerns. Oh, and if you need condoms, I have a box in the top drawer of my bedside table." On that gag-inducing note, she floated from the room.

A frustrating hour or so passed by, and still, no one had heard from Finn.

"I'm not even trying anymore," I snapped, throwing my phone on my bed, and crossing my arms over my chest. "That idiot can get stuffed...oh...maybe I'll try just one more time." I crawled to my bed on my hands and knees and grabbed my phone.

Jocelyn pledged to take Iris out and leave us alone, and Nate and I had been sitting on the floor, trying to call my brother, and killing time without either of us admitting that was what we were doing. We'd ended up in my room in a bid for some kind of privacy. Either Iris, who was understandably excited to see her uncle, or Jocie, who was just plain nosey, had followed us everywhere else we sought solitude. Leaning against walls on opposite sides of the room happened because I was too tempted and refused to sit next to Nate on the bed but felt guilty for making him sit on the floor alone after Iris stole the chair from my room, and I couldn't be bothered retrieving it.

Finn being a big cry-baby—ignoring me, Nate, Jocie, and even Scarlett—and switching his phone off was the icing on the shitty morning cake.

The distraction of it all should have been welcomed. It gave me time, and time felt like my only friend when even my brain had turned on me.

Over the years, I had extensively compartmentalized my life and my brain. For example, there was the house-proud aunty department; the lustful, *Sex and the City* crew; the free-spirited, twenty-something, secretly-yearning-for-adventure gang; Frigid Evie had a little nook; and then there was my personal favorite: the lonely, cranky, moody, virgin-spinster-full-of-fear department—the LCMVSFF—which took up substantial space. But so many of those compartments had now jumped on Team Nate that *I*, being the sensible, rational, logical division, felt like a separate entity. One that was very much ganged up on.

The lusties refused to stop hurling around images of Nate kissing me through my knickers as he squeezed my knockers. The free spirit, traditionally responsible for a lot of my clothing choices, kept suggesting sexy items we could wear while backpacking around Blow Me Down and Dildo in Canada. While the biggest disappointment of them all, the LCMVSFF, had locked Frigid Evie away and was running around naked, twirling my red undies on her finger, and screaming, "Get that boy naked, and let's get this shit done!"

Poor Nate sat on my soft shag rug, reading *Pride and Prejudice* while looking all sexy and shit, with no idea of the lewd, immoral thoughts spinning around in my head or the conflict being waged between myself and my other selves.

A loud knock on my door and Jocie popping her head around the corner scared the crap out of me and snapped me from my impending mental health crisis. "I am so sorry, darlings. I promised you time alone, and I have been unable to deliver." Disappointment crossed Nate's face, and Lizzy and Darcy hit the deck. "Until now!" She chuckled. "Had you going, didn't I, Nate? Don't fear. We are leaving now and will return in a few hours… Oh, and I will send a courtesy warning message when we head home." After a wink and a wave, she was off.

The minute the front door closed, Nate made his move. Crawling toward me on his hands and knees, he resembled a starving, caged lion finally set free to feast on the gazelle that sat stunned, petrified, but equally hungry before it. It was clear by the look on his face that Nate stood with the LCMVSFF, except *he* wanted to be twirling my knickers on *his* finger.

"You're my best friend, Nate. I don't want that to change," I whispered in a tone so sad but sultry I almost didn't recognize it as my own.

He continued crawling. His pace was so slow I began to shake with anticipation. "Things have already changed. It will never be the same between us, Gidge, and I don't want it to be. You're my everything, Evie. I've wanted you for as long as I can remember, but hearing the panic in your voice when Christian hurt you and knowing I could lose you, that I wasn't there to protect you, nearly killed me. But I'm here now, and I'm never letting you go."

His words and the open passion his gorgeous face expressed had that last functional part of my brain—the sensible, rational, logical division—on its last legs. "My heart breaks when you say that because we can't sustain it even if we did want this. I am *not* coming home with you." He stopped at my feet, reached for my hand, and placed a heavenly kiss on the inside of my wrist. My body ignited. Who knew the wrist held such power? "Nate," I sighed with a tremble.

"This is one hundred percent up to you, Eves." He kissed an inch or so higher. "Do you want to keep playing the martyr?" He kissed higher again. "Keep lying to yourself and denying how you feel?" And again. "Will you willingly walk away empty-handed? Or will you be that incredibly fucking brave and brutally honest woman I know you are and forge on, hand-in-hand, with me?" He sensually kissed the inside of my elbow, licking and sucking the soft skin into his mouth in a way that should have felt weird but felt like heaven. "Either way, whatever path you choose, you have to be at least truthful and acknowledge what you want."

I took a series of shallow, shaking breaths as he released my arm and reached out and wiped the tears from my cheek with his thumb. "Please don't be sad, Evie."

"I'm not sad. I'm scared and happy. Anxious to the point of shitting myself, but also…" I paused.

"Also…?" His left eyebrow cocked.

I stood, pulled Nate to his feet, and led him to my bed. "I think…I think I'm ready." Before I could change my mind, I placed his hand on the neatly fastened bow of my robe. A smile of pure joy broke across his face, and he looked at me with such love in his eyes I feared I might explode.

He nodded. "Are you sure?"

I stepped back, the bow fell apart, and my robe slipped open. "Yes. I… I think I've wanted this for a long time. I want you to be my first."

A shudder rolled through his body as he slipped off my robe. It was then I remembered and regretted the ugly, fluffy pajama pants I had put on, but something in the way Nate looked me up and down told me I could have been in a Teletubbies costume, and he wouldn't have cared.

Something slipped into place inside me when I felt the touch of his hands on my face, cradling my cheeks like I was the most precious thing on earth, and he gently pressed his lips to mine. He gripped me tighter, his fingers strong and demanding. His pace was desperate yet timid. The softness of his lips was almost over-whelming, but then again, that was Nate. The boy everyone saw as a badboy, a fuckboy, a bit of a joke was nothing but heart and soft and sweet and fluffy as a marshmallow.

From head to toe, my skin tingled deliciously as he threaded a hand through my hair and behind my neck, the other falling to the small of my back, his fingers brushing the swell of my ass. I hummed, melting in his arms, and felt the cure, the twitch of a smile on his lips.

It was amazing. What I'd always dreamed of being kissed like.

But I sensed he was holding back—I presumed on account of the whole virgin thing, which was brilliant and kind. Still, I was committed and needed to move things along before that frigid bitch in my mind found her way out of the prison the other versions of me had her locked away in. So, when he relaxed his grip and came up for air, I broke away, slid my pants over my hips, slipped my top over my head, then laid on my bed in nothing but my panties.

Nate exhaled loudly, rubbed the back of his neck, and stalked toward me. "Christ. Dammit, Evie. You are so bloody beautiful."

I parted my legs, and he knelt between them, his eyes wider and darker than I'd ever seen them. Any hesitation he may have felt seemed to disappear. He dipped his head to my breasts and made an almost pained cry as he pressed a kiss in the valley between them. "I knew they would be incredible. Can I taste them?"

"Yes, please," I begged. One at a time, he kissed, sucked, and grazed his teeth over my nipples, drawing embarrassingly loud moans and twisting my body. While lavishing one, his hand would caress the other. "Your skin is so soft and sweet, and your nipples are the most gorgeous fucking things I have ever seen." He sighed with his lips still on my body.

My hands fisted his hair, and desperate to kiss him, I pulled him up to my lips. As he rose, the weight of his body against me sent a rush of need to my already wet and throbbing sex, but then his ridiculously hard cock pressed against me, and I squealed in delight and surprise.

"You're so hard, Nate, and we haven't even done anything."

He kissed me harder and deeper than before, and I laughed when he pulled away. "Woman, I'm hard when you walk into the room. Touching you like this has me ready to explode."

"You really think I'm sexy, then?" I asked, one hundred percent wanting to hear something filthy from his mouth.

"Are you kidding me, Evie? I've jacked off while picturing you so many times over my life. My cock is that hard for you. I could spear a hole into the earth's core. Here, feel it for yourself if you don't believe me." He pushed his body off mine, grabbed my hand, and cupped it over his bulge. We both groaned and threw our heads back. "Fuck, Evie. I have to have you, or I'm gonna die. Tell me you feel it too."

"I feel it, Nate. I don't really know what to do, but I'm ready." I dragged him back onto my lips. We kissed and caressed, our hands exploring every untouched part of each other until Nate held me to him, flipped onto his back, gripped my hips, and rolled me over his cock again and again.

"Fuuuccckkk," he moaned. "You're so wet. I can feel it. As for what to do, let your body dictate. Don't think, just feel." I flipped onto my back, and he immediately latched onto my breasts. "Baby, I think you're ready, but I am going to take it slow. We don't even have to do it now. Do you have some toys?" he asked between nips. "Something you're used to that I can start with. Or would you like me to use my tongue or fingers, slowly and gently to—"

My hand shot out, grabbed his jaw, and pulled his face up to meet my eyes.

"Don't treat me like I'm some delicate rose you need to be gentle with. I'm no innocent kid you have to protect. I'm a fucking woman who wants to be railed. Can you do that, Nate? Can you take me and fuck the absolute shit out of me?"

I had stunned him. He froze for the briefest of seconds before shaking his head and smiling down at me. "Yes. Fuck yes."

"Good, 'cause I don't want a finger, and I don't want a toy."

I pushed down his shorts and grabbed his unbelievably hard, somehow silky soft and terrifyingly huge cock in my hands and squeezed. "I want this. I want you to teach me. I want it rough, and I want it now."

"Evie…you got it. But I will not be rough…not to start with, anyway." Nate quickly grabbed a condom from his pocket and discarded his pants to the floor, and I watched in fascination as he quickly rolled it over the glistening crown of his cock. He then took my wrists and placed my hands at the base of his perfect length. With his hands over mine, he pumped them up and down, once, twice, then pulled them off and pinned my arms above my head. He removed one hand and ran his free fingers through my soaked slit. "Okay, being wet enough for me is *not* going to be a problem." He raised his fingers to his mouth and sucked them clean. "But I'm not gonna give you all of me to start with. Too much Nate the Great can be lethal."

"Idiot." I sighed, and he smiled against my lips, shutting me up with a kiss.

"All my favorite memories are of you... I have loved you my whole life. I can remember so many of your firsts—primary school, high school, college. Your first bikini, your license, your first finished book..."

"Nate. Please..."

"And now I—we—have a new first: fucking you senseless as I take your virginity."

"Oh my God, shut up and fuck me before I change my mi—"

I never did finish that sentence. Nate's lips shut me up, and his dick sliding inside my entrance kept me that way...kind of.

"Oh my God. Oh my God. Oh my God."

"Are you alright, baby?"

"Yes, yes."

A sharp stinging and delicious stretch I could have never imagined had me hissing through my teeth. "Jesus, Evie. You're so damn tight. So soft and warm and perfect." He kissed my nose, squeezed my hand, and studied my face in a way no one ever had. "Are you sure you're alright? Please, Evie, you have to tell me if I'm hurting you. I never want to hurt you."

"It does hurt a little, but I like it... Hurt me more, Nate." His eyes rolled to the back of his head, and his chin fell to his chest.

"I'm barely inside, and you and your filthy little mouth and tight cunt have ruined me for anyone else." He pressed in deeper, then stilled, breathing heavily, and allowing me time to adjust and relax before pushing again. I was overcome with the sensation of fullness.

"Yessss," I cried, closing my eyes as the most perfect mixture of pleasure and pain sunk into my bones.

"Open your eyes, Gidge. Let me get lost in them as I lose myself in you." On command, my eyes fluttered open. "Good girl."

He pulled all the way out, grit his teeth, and pumped back in, faster than before but still gentle and cautious. Then he did it again and again, rocking into me a little harder, rougher, each time. I writhed beneath him, still captive by his hand. I wanted to beg for freedom, touch him, and hold him as he bucked into me, but he was fucking the ability to speak right out of me. All I could do was moan, pant, and breathlessly beg with my body.

The pain began to subside, and the feeling of fullness increased with every thrust. "You're so perfect, baby. I know it's new, and you say you don't know what to do, but you've wanted to be fucked for a long time. I can feel it. Can you? Can you feel yourself opening to me? Taking more and more of me?"

I tried to say yes, to tell him how good it felt and how big he was, but it came out sounding like the Swedish chef on *The Muppet Show*. "Yerdy verdy gggoood." Though not able to speak in English, I was beginning to feel more confident and bolder. I released the sheet I was gripping with my right hand and, for some unholy reason, raised it, then slapped Nate's ass—hard. His whole body tensed.

"Jesus, woman. Do it again." I did, again he roared, and I could swear he felt ever bigger inside me.

"Evie, I'm sorry, but I don't think I can last much longer. I want you to come. I want you to feel as good as I do, so I am going to touch you as I press all the way in."

"You're still not all the way in?"

"Not even close, sweetheart." He chuckled proudly, gave me an arrogant wink, and then slipped his finger between us. Like he had done it a hundred times before, he hit the perfect spot on the first go. A hideous memory of Luke Bailey fumbling around in the dark, jabbing me blindly and acting like there was something wrong with me, reared its ugly head. But as Nate whispered sweet praise into my ear and began to push deeper, all memories of Luke and his tiny cock disappeared.

"Oh my God, Nate. I like that… I like that a lot."

"I thought you might." He smiled against my lips. "Me too. No one has ever felt this good."

Every muscle in the lower half of my body began to tremble, quiver, and shake in the most spectacular fashion, and I began to roll my hips to meet Nate's. And the sting…it was sharp and sweet, and I fucking loved it. "Harder. Fuck me harder." My nails clawed into Nate's shoulder as he continued to rub that magic spot.

"Evie. I can feel you clenching around me. I'm going to come, baby."

"Harder, Nate. Harder."

He began to lose control, and the sound of his body slapping against mine, combined with his grunting and groaning, was the hottest thing I had ever heard.

"Evie, I love you. I think you're… I'm going to…"

The most amazing flash of energy, light, and love filled my body, blinding me for a second and sucking every last drop of air from my lungs. Nate was hovering above me. His body was stiff and shuddering, pumping slowly into me, his face buried into my neck.

"Oh my God." He collapsed on top of me and gently sucked the flesh on my neck. "You're mine, Aoife. Tell me you're mine."

"I'm yours, Nate. Yours."

Chapter 32

Nate

I KISSED DOWN, WORSHIPED, AND PRAISED MY brave, stunning, fearless girl. I cleaned us up a little, then collapsed against her breasts, an exhausted, sated, spent wreck.

Listening to the clock on her bookshelf ticking in time with the pounding of her heart was when the panic set in. What should have been the perfect moment, meeting my dream girl in the afterglow, became a giant ball of, *Oh, fuck.*

Not because it wasn't amazing or because I held one single, solitary regret. No, it was quite the opposite. Being with Evie was everything I had hoped it would be and more. The best sex of my life with the first and only love of my life. But the only thing rattling around in my mind was Evie saying, *'I am not coming home with you.'* Confidence, and perhaps arrogance, in my ability to win her over and convince her to return to Byron with charm, wit, and a sizeable cock had been high. But after that, after being inside her, as close as two people could be, a sliver of doubt and fear crept in. *What if…?*

Evie's shaking voice snapped me back to the present. "Oh God, Nate. You have to get off me. Please, get off me." She began panicking, clawing, and punching me to move.

"Gidge, calm down. What's wrong? Are you in pain? Shit, did I hurt you?" I kissed her on the shoulder again and again, and as I rolled to my side, I saw the tears running down her face.

"Nothing, please, I just need to get out of here." She moved to slide from the bed, but I grabbed her wrist and pulled her back to me.

"Tell me, please." She looked between me and the door, clearly planning her escape. "Do you regret it? Did you not like it?"

"No!" She cupped my cheek in her hand and smiled softly. "No, it was wonderful, Nate. Really. I loved it. I didn't think I could ever feel like that. It's... I'm embarrassed. I'm a mess and... I think I'm bleeding."

I lifted the sheet and saw two or three tiny blood spots. "It's okay, Eves. Please don't be embarrassed. It's normal for a lot of women, and I'm pretty sure it's confirmation that I am, indeed, the pure god of sex that you suspected—and I knew—I was."

"You are such a dick," she giggled sheepishly.

"So, I'm a dick now? That's quite the upgrade from an idiot." I wiped the tears from her face, gave her a wink, and rolled from the bed. Standing before her naked as the day I was born, I held out my hand to her. "Let me help you get cleaned up." She made no reply. She was too busy checking me out. "Stop ogling me, and let's take a shower. If you're lucky, I'll allow you to praise, preen, and polish every inch of my body." I took her hand, pulled her to her feet, and slipped my hand around her waist, groaning to feel her soft, plump breasts pressing against my bare chest. "You blow my freaking mind, Evie Austen." I captured her mouth in a long, deep kiss. "You are so fucking amazing. And so bloody sexy. Look." Her eyes followed mine, and she bit her lip to see my cock once again hard and ready.

"Does it always just pop up like that straight away?"

"Definitely not. This is one hundred percent the Evie effect. The poor little guy's been waiting a long, *long* time to be buried inside you."

The sweetest blush rose to her cheeks. "You're not turned off? Don't you think it's gross? The blood and the...wetness?"

she whispered. "I'm pretty sure most of your conquests wouldn't require a hose down in the backyard once you've finished."

"Uhh, nothing about this is gross, Evie. It's sexy as fuck. You're wet because you got so horned up and then came like a fucking champion. You have a tiny drop of blood because it was your first time being impaled with my massive schlong, and you don't *need* a hose down, not even a shower. A tiny wipe with a cloth would set you right. I'm taking you to the shower because I want to lather you up, get your nipples all slippery and soapy, and then eat out that delicious, tight little pussy."

"Oh."

"Have you experienced that before? I mean, I know you were a virgin, but..."

"Have I been...*eaten* before?"

"Yes, Shirley. Have you had a man—or God help me, a woman—kneel before you, spread your legs open, and press their face inside you?"

Her jaw dropped, her eyes almost popped from their sockets, and her crazy-hot, dance-toned body jiggled with laughter. "No, I haven't, and why the hell are you calling me Shirley?"

It was hard to focus on a reply. The hypnotic bouncing of her bare breasts as she laughed required an awful lot of attention. "Uhhh, Shirley is your new nickname."

"Why?" She chuckled. "Why in hell would you call me Shirley? I sound like that cloned sheep on the news years ago."

"Nah, you're thinking of Dolly. *You* are Shirley, as in Shirley Temple. It's a non-alcoholic cocktail...a virgin cocktail....get it? See how funny, and observant, and good at listening I am?"

"Oh my God. You are such an idiot." She grabbed my hand and dragged me into the bathroom."

"Wait, I have to get my notepad. I need to record the idiot. I've done a shitty job of keeping track today. You and your luscious boobies have been too distracting." She dropped my hand and huffed.

"Touch that notepad, and you won't touch me again. Choice is yours."

Pretending to ponder my nonexistent conundrum earned me a slap on the arm. "Alright, then, Shirley. I guess the notepad can wait. Let's go eat."

Water streamed over us. Soapy bubbles dripped from her freshly and thoroughly cleaned nipples onto my head as I pressed kisses between her thighs. "I know you're going to call me a pig, but knowing you've never been touched by anyone else, that your pussy is mine…mine and no one else's…makes me feel invincible". I buried my face inside her, nosing apart her folds and slowly licking from front to back with a flat tongue.

"Oh my God, oh my God, oh my God." She fell forward, braced herself on the wall with one hand, and roughly ripped and tugged my wet hair with the other.

"You like that, Lil One? You like it when I taste you?"

"Uh-huh."

"Just wait. It only gets better."

I split her open with my fingers, assaulted her clit, and licked her entrance. "Holy shit! It's too much!" She pounded her fist into the tiles, shaking her head and trying to shift her hips away, but I gripped her ass cheeks and pulled her back onto me.

"You have no idea how many times I've dreamt of doing this, Gidge. Those silly, black bikinis with their fucking tiny triangles hiding your pussy have been teasing and tormenting me for years, begging me to slide that fabric over and eat it every damn time. So, now you need to be a good girl and take what Natey gives you, okay?"

She pulled her lips into her mouth, nodded, and hissed, "Yesssss."

Every moan, whisper, and purr not only told me where and what she liked but turned my dick to stone, making me more desperate to have and feel her break on my face. "Are you watching me, Gidge?" I gasped and swallowed a mouthful of water. "Can you see what you do to me? You have me on my knees and harder than I've ever been."

Evie growled and pushed me deeper into her glistening cunt. "Shush, I'm trying to concentrate." My laughter must have tickled in all the right places as I felt her legs weaken and her grip tighten till I feared she may soon hit bone. "There, there, there, there. Stay right there. Don't you dare move."

I wanted to argue, to withdraw my tongue, look up at her flushed face, and tell her that *she* was causing the majority of movement by rolling and grinding against my lips, but I was kind of scared she'd waterboard or snap me like a twig, which, for some reason, turned me on even more. It was a dilemma for the ages, wanting to please my woman, to give her this new, mind-blowing experience. To make her come again and again, but also enjoying the fuck out of her inflicting pain and bossing me around. I wanted to be her brat. To be reprimanded. To be scolded. When she had smacked my ass earlier, I nearly blew a gasket. Little Evie Austen and her hot, grumpy ass uncovered a new kink—one I looked forward to exploring.

But I had a job to do, and do it I did.

Zoning in on her swollen clit as ordered, I picked up speed and held as still as I could. Her nails dug into my scalp, and I felt her begin to tense. I was about to praise her, to urge her on with some of my favorite filth, but before I could, her knees buckled, and she collapsed over my shoulder. "What the hell!" she screamed—legitimately screamed—as she squirted all over my tongue.

I cradled her limp, slippery body in my arms and sat back on my heels with her perched on my knees. She nestled into my neck and gently sucked the skin into her mouth before flopping against me. "Shit, did I just wet myself?"

"No, baby. You came like a fucking queen. I knew you had it in you."

She giggled nervously and sighed. "God, I've wasted so much time."

"Don't worry, Shirley. We've got forever to make it up."

Chapter 33

Evie

NATE LAY BESIDE ME, KISSING AND COUNTING the freckles that laid just above my hip. Each time he made it to thirty, he got distracted, lost count, and started over.

"I'm glad you're doing a thorough job, but I keep telling you I don't have freckles on my boobs."

"Yeah, I see that now. But one can't be too careful." He propped himself on his elbow and smiled lazily. "I want to stay in bed with you forever, Gidge. Can we? Please? It would be so romantic. We can just order food and get a sexy maid to come in to give us a sponge bath and empty our chamber pots."

I screwed my face in disgust.

"I dunno what sick kind of fantasyland you're living in, but that does not sound romantic. It sounds smelly and gross. Besides, you have a farm to get back—"

Nate pressed his finger against my lip to shush me.

"Save it, Shirley. Today is all about revealing our deepest, darkest secrets, long-held desires, and guilty, filthy kinks. I have little to no tolerance for reality." He took my hand and slapped himself on the cheek with my open palm. "I'll go first. I have a new kink."

"Oh Lord." I rolled my eyes. Nate ignored me and kept talking.

"I liked—no, loved—it when you

spanked me. I nearly blew my load every time you did it, and I'm fairly confident that if
you ever wanted to bring a whip into the bedroom, I would *not* be opposed."

"A whip? What the hell, Nate? I lost my virginity thirty-five seconds ago. I don't think I'm ready to be a dominatrix. "

"Fuck, just hearing you say that has me gagging for it." He ran his finger over my lip and hissed when I bit down. "You may think you're not ready, but I saw the fire in your eyes when you brought your hand down on my cheeks and told me what to do. Being a violent, bossy bitch just comes naturally."

I slapped him across the head, proving his point.

"Why don't we just tuck that away for later? Besides, we can't get too comfortable with this whole intercourse thing. This is only temporary."

"Gidge, nothing between us has ever been, nor ever will be, temporary. And no reality, remember?"

Pulling away from Nate's naked body that I, despite refusing to admit the fact, never want to stop touching, I almost fell from the bed, taking the sheet with me and wrapping it around my equally bare body. "I'm going to take another shower...alone this time. Jocelyn and Iris will be back soon, and this room smells like a bloody brothel. I need to wash the sheets and get rid of the man-smell before the old girl catches a whiff."

Nate's horrified face tickled me to no end as I sashayed into the bathroom and locked the door.

It was only then, as I leaned my palms against the marble vanity and faced my reflection, that I allowed myself to swoon. "Oh my God. I lost my virginity... I fucked Nathaniel Myers, the hottest guy in Byron Bay," I whispered to myself as I performed a little happy dance on the cold tiles. "Eat shit, Luke Bailey."

After I showered, and while Nate did the same, I got a warning text from Jocie that they were a few minutes away, and I unsuccessfully tried calling Finn again as I stripped the bed.

"Stubborn shit," I muttered as I slipped my phone into my

pocket and attempted to slip from my room before Nate reappeared. With my big toe barely hitting the wood floor of the hall and my arms full of sheets and a quilt cover, two strong and sexy arms snaked around my waist. I smiled despite myself. "Hands off, bucko. You have to get dressed, and I have to get this laundry in the wash before Jocie gets back…which will be any minute."

Nate pressed his lips to the crook of my neck and let me go. When I returned, his new khaki chinos were on, and his white tee was slipping over his head. Damn, his body was insane. With his arms stretched like that, every muscle in his arms, chest, abs, and obliques were on display.

"I can sense you, Evie. Stop watching me." Gorgeous brown eyes met mine as his face appeared and tanned skin was covered by cotton. To hide my blush, I threw the fresh linen in his face and barked orders. "Stop being an idiot and help me." He kissed me hard and raw, and it took all my strength not to throw him on the bed.

"I'm not sure why we're bothering with this." He winked and tossed the sheet over the mattress with one annoyingly easy flick of the wrist. "We're only going to mess it back up later."

Deciding whether or not to argue back or ignore his cockiness was an easy decision. "Snort. You're confident, aren't you? How do you know I'm not done with you now that I've gotten what I wanted?" Nate dropped the pillow he was wrangling into a pillowcase, grabbed my wrists, and pulled me against him, kissing me fiercely.

"Because I heard your whimpers and cries as I fucked you." He kissed me again. "I saw your face as you fell apart on my mouth." Then he ran his nose down and devoured my neck. "Despite the lies that spout from those pretty lips I'll soon have wrapped around my cock, I know you want me as much as I want you. Your body always tells the truth." Goosebumps broke out all over me as Nate's lips continued to pepper my neck. "See, look what it does when I talk dirty. Your body betrays you. It loves my filthy mouth."

I crashed my lips into his, pushed him back on the bed, and

straddled him. "Fuck you, you arrogant sexy asshole," I snapped as I ripped my top over my head.

"No bra? God, you're fucking amazing." Nate sat up and latched onto my right nipple while rolling the left between his fingers. Cocky or not, he knew me. The sheets weren't even tucked in, and they were wrapping around us.

A car horn beeping at the rear of the house broke us apart. "Shit, it's Jocie!" I leapt from Nate in such a rush that I stepped smack dab on the middle of his stomach. "Get up, you fool." I threw my top back on and straightened out the bed around him while ignoring his wails of pain.

"I would if I wasn't in agony. Come back to bed and heal me."

"No, I can't," I laughed despite myself. "Please, just get up and act normal." After groaning and wailing a little more, Nate jumped from the bed, followed me out the door, and grabbed me again.

"Now, you listen to me," I snapped as he pressed me against the wall in the middle of the staircase, in full view of the door that rattled as Jocelyn fumbled with the lock, and kissed me for the four hundredth time in an hour. "Not a word about us to anyone. Finn thinks he's so clever. He thinks he knows it all, but he doesn't *really* know that what *he* thinks is happening *isn't* really happening. As per usual, the guy is clueless."

"He's not the only one." Nate rubbed the back of his neck. "I have no idea what you just said."

"Just keep your hands and lips to yourself. Jocie was sus this morning, but she has no evidence. It's all filthy speculation, and I want to keep it that way."

"Sure, keep telling yourself that, Gidge."

The door swung open, and I ran down the remaining stairs. "Hey, guys, how was—"

"Evie and I are a couple. We're dating!" Nate shouted at the top of his lungs. His words hung over my head, suspended in mid-air like a bucket of water that drenched me when Jocelyn squealed in delight.

"Nate!" I spun on my heel and found him striding toward me.

"Sorry, Eves, but I refuse to play games. I love you, and I want the world to know." Jocelyn gasped as Nate laced his hands through my hair and pulled me into a brain-frying kiss. The second he moved away, she latched onto Nate's face and squished his cheeks like he was a fat man-baby. She then tried it on me, but I stealthily dodged her affections.

"Evie," Iris said thoughtfully, "do you love Uncle Nate too?"

Nate was standing just out of my view behind me, but I knew his eyes were on me. I could feel the heat of his gaze. "Sure I do, bubs." My shadow inhaled sharply and squeezed my thigh. "*Like* I love my favorite pjs or roast potatoes."

"Geez, don't get all mushy on me, woman." Nate huffed, releasing his grip. I turned to face him, and though his words were playful, and he wore a smile, it was not his real smile—the one that lit his eyes and took my breath away, that had me surrendering and falling harder and faster than I'd imagined possible or planned to ever admit.

After blushing, squirming, and grouching my way through the fuss and excitement of the delighted duo, I hung Iris's coat and neatly placed her shoes in the rack by the door. We then followed her and Jocie in their matching rainbow socks toward the kitchen. Nate's hand rested on the small of my back, the gentle heat of him driving me crazy. "I thought I told you not to say anything," I whispered from the side of my mouth. "It was supposed to be a secret."

Suddenly, Nate pushed me into the laundry room, quietly closed the door behind us, and pressed me against the washing machine. "We don't have time for secrets, Gidge. Remember what you said in the shower after I made you come? '*I've wasted so much time.*'" He ran his thumb over his lip like he was holding back or deciding his next move. "Damn it, Evie." He surrendered and kissed me like it was against his will, and it was desperate, needy, and full of possessive tongue and lip sucking and biting. "You keep saying you're not coming home with me…well, fine. I'll let you be stubborn and pigheaded about that for now, but you can't say that what's between us isn't real or pretend that it's not happening, 'cause it's bullshit. Everybody can see it, Evie. Everyone. You want me. I want you. Let's just stop the charade, enjoy whatever this is, and not waste another minute, okay?"

Stunned, I heard a whispered, breathy, "Okay," leave my lips as he kissed me again. He then adjusted his cock, which had hardened deliciously as he pressed into me, opened the door, and confidently waltzed out. "So, Iris, did you buy your Uncle Natey a present?"

Sitting around the kitchen table, I half-heartedly listened to the conversations flowing around me. Nate and Jocie tried again to contact Finn and gave up, while Iris gave us a fashion parade featuring all the outfits she managed to swindle from her great-aunt.

Despite the happiness and laughter surrounding me, a darkness I fought valiantly to repress every day consumed my thoughts.

I was twenty when my mum and dad—whom I had always scoffed at when they declared their soulmate status—drove to Sydney to pick up a gift for Finn's birthday and to enjoy a rare night alone together in the city. They never came home.

The years of grieving that followed shaped me, and I'd always joked that their sudden, tragic death stunted me not only emotionally but physically. But it had done much more than that. My loss hardened my heart and reinforced the already steely belief I, for some reason, always had. I was cold, and I was going to end up alone.

I wondered if that was why I had clung so fiercely to Jocelyn and Finn, and why Iris had become my whole world. Frigid Evie could only rely on her family, and even they could be taken away in a heartbeat. But as memories of my sweet mum and her beloved flower garden below the kitchen window, and dad with his hideous jokes and constant, embarrassing public affections toward his treasured wife coursed through my veins, I was not alone. A warm hand was holding mine, and loving, soft eyes that seemed to read what I was thinking checked on me silently and constantly.

Was this my chance?

Was the boy who grew up down the road—the one who followed me around like a stinky, lost puppy while winking and flirting with every girl he saw—*my* soul mate?

It was a thought that would normally induce an ironic snort laugh, but looking down at his thumb sweeping back and forth over my knuckles, I was overwhelmed by a wave of feelings I was too scared to put a name to as it swept me away.

I stretched up, planted a kiss on Nate's cheek, and whispered in his ear, "I don't know how long this will last, or where it will end up, but I'm in."

That night, I lay in bed, regretting my decision to keep Nate at bay in his own room. As soon as Iris had gone to bed, he'd smugly waltzed into my room, kicked off his socks, and lay down, but I wasn't having it. Fooling around while no one was in the house was one thing, but doing what I wanted to do to him…what I wanted him to do to me while my niece slept down the hall was another.

"Damn my prudishness." I tossed to my side and his stinky socks, discarded on the floor, caught my attention. "I wish the rest of you was here."

BANG!

What the fuck is that?

BANG BANG SCREEAACCHH.

It was my window. Someone was banging on my window. *This is just fucking great! I just lost my virginity, and before I can practice some more, I'm going to be murdered in my bed. Bloody typical.*

Squeaky glass told me the damn thing was being slid open. My curtains parted.

I saw a foot.

Then a leg.

Paralyzed with fear, I held my breath and tried to scream, but nothing but a pathetic whimper Superman couldn't hear came out.

More scraping followed, more bangs, then grunting and laughing, and a large head covered in messed-up hair popped through. White teeth shone like a beacon through the dark, and familiar, dangerous eyes met mine.

"Nate! You fucking idiot. You scared me half to death." The rest of his body comically fell through, and he collapsed onto the ground with a thud, but I was too angry and kinda traumatized to laugh. "Shhhh, you idiot. You'll wake the entire house, and I don't want anyone to hear the sounds you make when I freaking kill you!"

Rising to his feet, he scoffed and stalked toward me, removing his shirt and pants as he went. With no underwear to rein him in, his cock sprang free, immediately standing tall and true, bobbing with each step.

"That's nothing compared to the noises I'm about to get out of you."

The noises he's gonna get out of… My vagina pulsed in time with my heart. *Wow, that's new.*

I ignored my treacherous, hungry body and a good portion of my brain. "How the hell did you even get in here? We're on the second floor."

"Not gonna lie, it wasn't easy, but nothing comes between me and my girl."

"Your girl," I whimpered, trembling with want as his finger swept over my bottom lip. "I'm not your girl."

"You are, Gidge. I know it. You know it. And now, you're going to take off that silly scrap of clothing you call a nighty. I'm going to lay you down. You're going to spread your legs like the good girl I know you are, and I'm going to eat your pretty little cunt till you come so hard and scream so loud that the whole world will know it too."

Chapter 34

Evie

ONE DAY ROLLED INTO ANOTHER, AND BEFORE we knew it, Thanksgiving had come and gone. It was the first time our collection of traveling freaks celebrated Turkey Day, and it most definitely showed. It was also my first time at Scarlett's house, and it was a gorgeous, colorful, chaotic mess when we arrived and remained that way the entire time. A nervous, what-the-hell-are-we-doing excitement buzzed through the air. A lot of that was due to my idiot brother who, after begrudgingly apologizing for his outburst, accepting, and saying he was semi-okay with my relationship with his best friend, still gave us filthy looks every time we touched, and also because his love for Scarlett was finally out in the open—and I mean open. The two of them spent the morning mauling each other in a manner he would have throttled me and Nate for.

Predictably, the kids were thrilled and squealing shrieks of delight as they watched the parade, ate, staged a mini food fight, and played till they fell asleep on the couch. The food was amazing—excluding Scarlett's disgusting Banoffee pie—and the company was even better. The only things that weren't top-notch were poor Teddy, pining for Asher after they broke up, and the other all started with a giant...W.

Will you be going back with Nate?
Will you be staying with Evie?

What will happen with the farm?

What would happen with your teaching?

What about Iris?

In the days following *the one* that changed everything—the one we came to refer to as my *awakening*—the subject of Nate and I parting ways in a matter of weeks hadn't been broached. In fact, it was actively avoided. Laughing and fucking each other stupid in a bubble of denial was simply too much fun. While we had an unspoken agreement to dodge all talk of the future, no one else seemed to get the memo. The inquisition may have hastened our retreat, but the lure of each other's bodies had a large, penis-shaped part to play.

Turned out I loved sex. Took to it like a duck to water I did. And with Nate as the master, and me, his more-than-willing apprentice, following along blindly, time passed in a blur of passionate kisses, intimate discoveries, and moments of increasing filth that were taken at every opportunity and in every possible location.

We'd fallen into a blissful routine of indulgent domesticity. Waking early to partake in lazy, sleepy sex, and enjoying naked breakfast in between the sheets before rousing the rest of the house was a goddamn delight. As was showering together, then falling back into bed in the evening.

It wasn't just in the bedroom—and laundry, and garage, and kitchen, and the bathroom at the Chinese place on 7th—where things were going well. Aided by Christian's continuing absence, I successfully navigated my return to teaching, doing so well that I picked up an extra two classes a week. While I was dancing my tush off, Nate discovered the hidden and not-so-hidden treasures of New York City, often dropping in to see me in a ridiculous Statue of Liberty hat or Staten Island tee for a picnic lunch we would eat on a rug spread out over the polished wooden floor. It was oddly romantic and sweet, and I took to the open affection and spoiling in a way I feared my icy heart and reunited departments of my brain would never have allowed. I found myself laughing so hard and so often that my abs hurt.

All around, Nate made me…happy. I was smiling more and being less grumpy me-ish than I had ever thought possible. I was writing like an absolute demon too. Who knew a sexy man by your side could be such an excellent muse?

While I was gone, Nate kept himself busy, assuring me not all of his days were spent bingeing Kardashians—which he still denied watching—or wandering the streets waiting to do me—though, I suspected it was on his brain a good portion of the time. Hours were devoted to remotely managing the farm's upcoming harvests and networking with boutique specialty stores to extend their organic macadamia exports in the States. Doing whatever it is men do during quality bro time with Finn and spending quality time with Iris were further perks, and watching the uncle-niece bond strengthen both warmed and broke my heart. Like our *relationship*, their togetherness was temporary, and every joyful minute collectively spent made the prospect of what lurked around the corner even more ominous.

How long would I have these arms wrapped around me?

"What are you pondering over there, Shirley?" Nate snapped me back to the present, pinching my hip and rolling to lay his beautiful face on my bare stomach.

"Can we lose Shirley, already?" I joked, blinking away the emotion lurking beneath the surface. "I think it's safe to say, after what you just did to me, I'm not a virgin anymore."

"True. You're a regular old hoochie now. But I think the name stays. It suits you, and I get a little dick-buzz from the filthy look you give me."

My giggles shook his face. "Did your delight in being bossed around start with me, or do you have some long-held and weird mummy issues?"

"Definitely not mummy issues…shit…I don't think so, anyway." He scrubbed his hair thoughtfully as he continued, "But I'm sorry to say you weren't the first woman of questionable morals and a stern hand to take my fancy."

"Oh, God, you don't mean Pol—"

"Ah, ah, ah. Don't even think about saying that name. It was someone from Byron, though. Do you, by chance, remember Mrs. Fraser?"

I bolted upright and sent Nate rolling onto the foot end of the mattress. "Mrs. Fraser, our English teacher? Mrs. *When You Get Stuck, Remember…Pen to Paper, Pretty it Up Later?*"

He closed his eyes, nodded, and sighed.

"She was so fucking hot, Eves. That accent with its rolling r's. The French twist thingy she did with her hair. The tight black pencil skirt, the white shirt inappropriately unbuttoned to her navel that she sometimes topped with a vest that pushed her unbelievable tits even higher." He sucked in a breath and rolled onto his hands and knees, growling as he crawled the length of my body. "And that ruler she wielded and smacked into her palm when we had a test. Fuck. That ruler wasn't the only long, hard piece of wood in the room."

"You're one sick puppy," I laughed.

Nate barked and whimpered, nuzzling into my neck. "What about you? Did you have any inappropriate teacher crushes?"

I screwed my lips to the side and winced as mental images of my uninspiring facility flashed before my eyes. "Nope. Not one. Though…" A tall, dark, handsome face, bulging biceps, and an amazing ass popped into my brain.

"Alright, who do I have to beat up? I can see your cheeks blushing, and I don't think it's because of me."

"It's not. It's Constable Mason."

"The cop? You got a thing for men in uniform, Lil One?"

"What woman doesn't? Mason was hot. Jocie lost her phone once, and someone turned it in to the police station. Mason, the cheeky bastard, used it and took a smiling selfie with his massive guns in the frame before he returned it. Jocie found it on her camera roll a few days later, and I can tell you now that the selfie was shared and viewed by every straight woman and queer man in town."

"Not just queer men. Mum showed Dad and me too. Barry was not impressed."

"Hmm, I can imagine. Bet it spiced up Janet in the bedroom that night, though." Nate gagged and dry-heaved as he climbed from atop me and slid off the bed.

"Could we please not talk about my parents and their bedroom? How would you like it if I talked about Jocie like that?"

"Please, I have heard more about Jocelyn's sex life than the world knows about Hugh Hefner's. She is an open and terrifying book."

Admiring Nate's naked glory, I rose to stand beside him. "You two should talk tomorrow when I'm at work. Maybe she could *teach* you a thing or two since you love teachers so much. Just don't fall in love with her." I smacked his ass and sauntered into the bathroom. "Speaking of grossness, I need a shower. My hands have been up a giant turkey's ass, and I can still feel its bits."

"The words every man wants to hear from his woman after sex." Nate rolled his eyes and pushed me back on the bed. "You stay here and hold off on that shower. I will run you a bath, and after you've soaked in the bubbles while touching yourself as you think of me, I have a surprise to give you."

⁂

My bath was Chandler Bing-level opulent—soft music, candles, an exorbitant amount of bubbles, and a giant rubber ducky. Unlike Chandler, I had Nate perched beside me because we were rapidly forming an unhealthy codependency. At first, his presence was just him hovering over me annoyingly in amazement at how my nipples always seemed to burst through the bubbles like an irrepressible ray of sunshine through the clouds, no matter how much bubble bath he added. After complaining about the hardness of the cold tiles on his knees, rather than just stop, he set off in search of a stool and returned with the stepstool from the kitchen in one hand while the other had something hidden behind his back.

"Is that my surprise?" I squeaked in an embarrassingly girly tone that the hulking farmer seemed to keep drawing out of me.

"Nah, it's the stepstool from the pantry."

"Not that, you idiot. Whatever it is you have behind your back."

"Oh, this?" he said flatly, flashing a dark, navy-blue book quickly in my face. "Yes, this is a surprise. It's a collection of amazing short stories I came across during my daily snooping, and I would like to read some to you as you bathe.

"Aww, that's really lovely, Natey. Thank you. What's it called, though?"

Never one to take anything too seriously, Nate ignored me and loudly cleared his throat while I ducked and weaved to try and see the cover of the book he stubbornly concealed. I couldn't see the title, but it was a beautiful deep blue with a twisting floral pattern and red, large bold font like you'd see on an old-fashioned fairy tale.

"I will begin on a random page, and you have to guess. Ready?"

"Yes, I'm bloody ready. The water will be cold if you don't hurry up."

"Okay, here we go…. She is all beauty and grace, flittering and fluttering like a delicate fairy, twirling on a shimmering, golden string. But her true and mighty heart beats with the ferocity of a medieval knight, and her blood runs red, burning with the fire of the dragons she will one day slay. She yearns for adventure, for independence. For stages and strangers with interesting faces. Of finding her own way. Of making mistakes and occasionally learning. Of finding and falling in love."

"Nate! That's one of my stories! The one you remembered!" I jumped to my feet and, of course, almost slipped on my ass. With hero-like reflexes, he dropped the book, caught me in his arms, and attempted to lift me from the water. "No!" I cried. "No!" With all my strength, I pulled him to my lips, then dropped back into the water, bringing him, fully clothed, with me. There, I continued to pepper him with kisses, undo his belt, and interrogate him. "What did you do? How did you do that?"

"I accidentally, well, not accidentally, deliberately searched for and found some of your writing. Then Teddy and I collated it, Finn did the cover and illustrations, we submitted it to a printer, and had it turned into a book."

"Oh my God! That is such a violation of privacy *and* the most beautiful thing anyone has ever done for me." With all my might, I pushed him off me and kept on pushing until he fell backward. "I'm so fucking mad at you. Thank you so much." Looking rightly bewildered, Nate's back cracked into the enamel, and as soon as he maneuvered his long, thick legs from beneath him, I was able to free his hard cock from his pants and slowly slide down his hard length. "Oh God, oh God, oh God."

"Evie, condom."

"I don't care! I'm on the pill now!" I screamed as I began to rock and grind and bounce. It was still a relatively new thing for me, being on top. I'd been thoroughly enjoying the weight and pressure of Nate's body crushing me, but I felt powerful, and angry, and loved, and even though I couldn't find the words to tell him, I could show him.

Grabbing his hands from my waist, I pressed them against my breasts and held them there, cupping and squeezing.

"You're so fucking hot, Evie." He sighed, biting his lip, and hypnotically watching the bounce of my breasts.

I ignored him, shot my right hand out, wrapped it around his throat, and lightly squeezed in time with the hand still held to my breast. "It was wrong of you to go through my things." I gripped tighter, feeling his pulse race beneath my fingers and his cock swell inside me. I pushed his head back against the bath wall, enjoying the sense of control. "You need to ask me for permission. Don't you?"

"Yes, Evie," he moaned, his voice hoarse and so fucking sexy.

"Good boy." *Where the fuck did that come from?* Nate growled and wildly bucked his hips up into me. His enthusiastic reaction to my aggressive domination was both frightening and turning me on. "Don't do it again, Nathaniel." With one last squeeze, I released his throat and his hand.

"Yes, Evie." He gasped for air, slid down farther, grabbed the flesh of my hips, and pulled me down against him. His grip was hard, his nails digging into my skin, the sharp pain exciting. Sending buttons flying, I ripped open his shirt and took his nipple into my mouth. One at a time I licked then bit them, each nip drawing a louder cry. "Fuck, I'm gonna come, Evie." Hearing those words after what I'd just done spurred on my own sudden rush of pleasure. I dropped my hand to my clit, stroking only three or four times before my whole body shook, and the most intense, air-stealing, time-warping orgasm splintered through me.

"Holy fucking hell," he groaned and shuddered beneath me as I felt the pulsing heat of him coming inside me.

My forehead fell to his. "You're part of me, Nate. I can feel you. I can feel you."

◆

Nate kissed my shoulder, wrapped, and dried my shivering body in a towel, and lovingly dried me off. His gesture and my force had rendered me, for once in my life, utterly speechless.

The book, *my* book, laid open on the floor before me. The title, now visible, was *Aoife*. Tears poured down my face as I studied the stars, flowers, and beautiful fairy ballerina. All I wanted to do was tell him how I felt. To beg him not to make me choose. And to ask for him to stay.

But my fierce bravery, the girl who slayed dragons, was gone. I couldn't, and I didn't.

Chapter 35

Evie

I'D JUST FINISHED MY CLASS, HAD SAID goodnight to all the kids, fielded all the parents' questions, and was looking forward to going home to Nate when I felt a light tap on my shoulder. Before I could see who it was, I could sense it, and Jody yelling over my head all but confirmed it. "What are you doing here? I was supposed to talk to Evie first."

"I'm sorry," a familiar voice said quietly, "I got the days wrong, I guess. She never used to work on Thursdays." Every hair on my body stood to attention.

I spun and came face to face with Christian. Disappointingly, he looked amazing. Half of me—well, maybe more than half—had hoped he would look like shit when I saw him again, just like he did before starting rehab, but he had always been a beautiful man, and a few weeks away from work hadn't altered that. Gone were the bags under his red eyes, and the gray, sallow skin was no more. His complexion, his general vibe was bright and happy like the day he had goofily asked me out and gave me the Tim Tams. Unlike that day, there were no butterflies in my belly or trembling in my loins. He was just a man—one that made me cautious and slightly uncomfortable—that I no longer liked or hated, but was mostly indifferent to, and I was thrilled that was the case.

"It's alright, Jody," I said, flashing her a reassuring smile. "He's right. I didn't work Thursdays last time he was here. It's okay, really." Standing proudly, I raised my chin and looked Christian right in the eye. "How are you, Christian? You look well."

"I am, Evie." He smiled. "I'm sober, eating well, dancing again, and loving it. I'll be teaching Iris's class tonight, actually. It'll be my first one back." I tried to grin and nod casually, but the longer I faced him, the closer he edged, and the faster my heart began to beat. But it wasn't attraction as it once was. It was the memory of his hand gripping and bruising mine. "Will you be there tonight?" he asked. "Maybe we can talk? I want to know how you've been doing since—"

I cut him off before he could finish his thought. "I'm…happy. I'm really happy. Finn is bringing Iris tonight, so we'll have to catch up another time. I'm done for the day." I grabbed my bag and headed out the door. "I'll see you tomorrow…maybe." *Hopefully not.*

Feeling like I wanted to vomit, I set off to Iris's school and quickly messaged Finn, asking if it was okay for him to take her to class alone tonight and why. We often went together on Thursdays and would take our starving little dancer out for dinner afterward. It was a fun little tradition that had helped us discover the best local food, including our favorite, Rubirosa.

Finn: No worries, Sis. I can't believe that mongrel is back already. What did Nate say? I'll be home asap.

What would Nate say?

Anxiety-induced ghosting took place as I ignored Finn's barrage of texts while I waited at the school gate and as we continued home. Fear over Christian hurting me again wasn't the problem. I was more worried about Nate. How would he take the news? How would I react to his taking of the news? Levelheaded responses weren't my strong suit…or his…and the timing sucked. I'd finally allowed myself to feel what I'd denied for years, even if only to myself. I was happy. *We* were happy. Would fuckface—as Nate called him—reappearing upset our newly discovered and untested balance?

The man in question—Nate, not Fuckface—was gloriously shirtless in the kitchen when we walked inside. His face was covered in flour, his jeans in cake batter. "You're home! Look, ladies, I made cupcakes. And don't look at me like that, Gidge. I FaceTimed mum, and she walked me through it, and they're bloody delicious. Here!" A vanilla cake with pink icing and sprinkles was gleefully shoved in my face by a beaming man who was so excited and proud that I decided to keep Christian's return to myself. *For a little while at least, just till I know how things will settle at work,* I told myself as I bit into the surprisingly light and fluffy treat.

After a quick cake and cuddle stop, Iris ran to her room to change for dance class, and I stood watching Nate ice the remaining cupcakes and lick canned frosting from his fingers. He was equally sweet and delicious, I needed his comfort, and I couldn't stay away. Moving to his side, I dipped my finger in the frosting and had a taste. Nate's eyes almost popped out of his head, so of course I did it again. This time, I spread the sugary creaminess over his lips and was in the process of licking it off when Finn walked in.

"Jesus, can't a guy walk into his own house without seeing this?"

"Yes, he can," I snapped. "Why don't you go buy one and try it out?"

Finn maturely replied by flipping me the bird and stealing a cupcake. "These are good, Eves. Make me a batch, and I'll take them with me to my new pad."

"I didn't make them. Natey made them for me," I crooned, kissing Nate again.

Finn's eyebrows raised in surprise. "So, did you do something stupid, Natey," he said, his voice dripping with eww, "or was this sweet gesture an attempt to cheer Grumpy Guts up after the Christian news?" Nate dropped the spatula, and I dropped my foot onto Finn's. "Ow! What was that for?" he whined.

"Christian news? What Christian news?" Nate asked, separating Finn and me from our slapping match. "Evie, what news do you have about that asshole?"

"He's back at work. He surprised me today, and we talked,

and everything was fine. He'll be at Iris's class tonight, so Finn is going to take her, and I'll talk to Jody tomorrow and make sure I see him as little as possible. There is nothing to worry about," I said in one breath, gasping when I was done.

"Bullshit! That asshole fuckface manhandled you in public." Nate puffed his chest, his fists clenching at his side. "I'm coming with you, Finn."

"No, you're not!" I said, pushing him back against the counter. "I have this under control. I don't need you two idiots barging in there, getting me fired." Said idiots scoffed and crossed their arms across their chests. "Christian has cleaned himself up and deserves a second chance."

"He doesn't deserve shit, Gidge. The bloke is an asshole, and *you're* kidding yourself. You have no control whatsoever over him… or me, for that matter. I'm going, and you can't stop me."

"No, you're not!" I said, pressing my index finger into his ribs.

"Uhhh, I'll be leaving now," Finn wisely whispered as he snuck from the room. "Iris, let's go!"

Nate and I stood face to face, eyes locked in silent battle, until the front door clicked shut, and we realized we were alone. "Where the hell do you get off talking to me like that?"

"Like what? Truthfully? You don't have any control in this situation, Gidge, and you know it. That's why you're pissed."

"I'm not pissed because of Christian. He was always coming back, and eventually, I was always going to have to deal with it. I'm angry at you for having so little confidence in me to handle it myself. You think I need you clowns storming in there, busting heads? What's that going to accomplish? It doesn't give me control over anything except whether or not I bail your dirty ass out of jail."

"But you would, though." He lowered his mouth to my ear, his whole demeanor switching on a knife's edge. "You'd bail my bad ass out, bring me home, and punish me till I was your good, obedient boy again."

We stood face to face, our cheeks flushed, our chests heaving.

"Fuck yes I would." I lunged at Nate, and he scooped me up

and into his arms, gripping my ass and kissing me hard as I wrapped my leg around his body and clung for dear life. "I'm so fucking angry at you," I growled as he licked my neck. "Take me to bed."

Halfway up the stairs, with my tongue halfway down Nate's throat, a muffled request was made. "I know I've been bad, but I want you to call me a good boy again, Evie. I need you to punish and forgive and praise me, and I'll do whatever it takes to earn it."

The throb of lust and power was dizzying. "Whatever it takes?"

He stopped in his tracks, and that same rumble flowed through him. "Yes, Evie."

The remaining distance was taken in strides the BFG would have been proud of. Once in my room, I was recklessly thrown on the bed. Nate had the door locked and was undressing before I'd even gotten my bearings. The sound of his belt unbuckling then sliding through each loop increased the pounding of my heart, and he pulled it free, then threw it on the bed beside me, and I feared cardiac arrest. "Tell me what you want, and I'll do it."

I looked at the leather strap laying against my thigh. My mouth watered, and I knew how to teach my brat to behave. Moving to the edge of the bed, I slowly spread my thighs and eyed his erection straining against his zipper. "Will you let me spank you?"

His eyelashes fluttered uncontrollably, and his head rolled backward. "Fuck yes, Evie. I want you to...I want you to hurt me."

Before I lost my nerve, I lunged at Nate and pulled him onto his knees between my thighs. "Get naked. I'll be back." He nodded obediently, smiled a smile I'd yet to see in all the years of knowing him, and began to remove his jeans. "Actually, leave your boxers on," I ordered. "I want to take them off you." He nodded again and began awkwardly removing his jeans while remaining on his knees in a way that would normally have me laughing. Then he stilled, his eyes closed, his body waiting. He looked amazing—shirtless, kneeling, his hair already a sweaty mess from anticipation alone. It was so tempting and would have been so easy to push him onto his back and ride him then and there on the floor, but having him do as I say, begging for punishment and praise, was so fucking sexy I had to follow through. I pet his hair, whispered, "Good boy," then left him and stepped into my walk-in closet.

Unbeknownst to Nate, after hearing his horny-ass teenage confessions about our old English teacher, Mrs. Fraser, I decided to dress as her for Halloween. Teddy had escorted me on a little shopping trip downtown and helped me choose the perfect outfit, but with Finn and Iris out trick-or-treating and Jocelyn out to dinner with friends, Nate and I decided to stay at home and enjoy a rare night just the two of us. I still could have worn the outfit, of course, but I chickened out at the last minute. Halloween may have come and gone, but the costume still hung in my closet, and I was not wimping out this time.

As fast as I could with trembling hands, I slipped out of my leggings and hoodie and into a scandalous, Carrie Bradshaw-worthy black bustier, white shirt, and black vest. Just as with Mrs. Fraser, the majority of buttons were accessories and lay undone, exposing the lacy bustier beneath. My tits looked fantastic, so good that when I tried it on at the store, Teddy claimed even he would fancy a motorboat ride.

Nerves built as I pinned my hair into a makeshift chignon, painted my lips with the darkest red lipstick I owned, then stepped into the tight leather pencil skirt. As I shimmed it over my hips, I felt the final haunting remnants of Frigid Evie leave my body. Nate may have wanted this, he may have gotten off on me bossing him around and enjoyed the stinging pain, but this was for me too. I couldn't tell him that I loved him. I couldn't tell him that he was mine. But like this, I could claim not only my sexuality, but my control. I could command, own, and praise him in such a way that even when he went home, when he let go of me and moved on, he would know he once belonged to me.

With the black stilettos I could hardly walk in crippling my feet, I strutted before my still kneeling man. Fisting his hair, I slowly raised his head, allowing him time to take in and hopefully appreciate my attire. "Holy mother of fuck, Evie." I was desperate to smile but held it in.

"You know I'm a rookie. I don't know what I'm doing, but I want to play a game with you." Nate nodded and wet his lips. "You've been bad Nathaniel, and it's time for me to give you your punishment. Oh, and you can call me Mistress Evie, young man." I took the meter ruler—or yardstick as the guy in the shop insisted on calling it—and tapped it into my palm. In an instant, the grin that spread across Nate's lips and the hungry look in his eyes was tattooed into my eyelids.

"Mistress Evie," he sighed. I ordered him to stand, and when he did, I took his place, dropping the ruler and dropping to my knees. In all the sexual exploration I had undertaken, I had yet to go down on Nate, and that was about to change. "You don't have to do this, Eves." I slapped his thigh. "Mistress Evie," he corrected.

"I know I don't have to. I want to. I want to taste you." His guttural moan spurred me on. Shaking, I took the waistband of his boxers in my teeth and slowly tugged them down. My eyes followed the direction of his incredibly cut V that was so fucking hot I had to pause and lick it, causing another, deeper groan, and twitch. *If I can make him react like that with that one tap of my tongue, what will he do when I take him in my mouth?* Again, I took the cotton between my teeth and pulled, eyeing his emerging cock that was so big and hard and, apparently, pinned down like a tightly coiled spring. That thing burst to life like a fucking jack in the box, smacking me right in the chin and knocking me onto my ass in a fit of laughter. "Eves! I'm so fucking sorry!" The poor guy looked trapped between mortification and wetting himself laughing.

I shook my head, regained my composure, and resumed my position. "Mistress Evie, remember?" Before he could reply, I cupped his balls in my hand and lightly tugged.

"Mistress Evie," he squeaked.

"Good boy."

Chapter 36

Nate

ON THE EVER-GROWING LIST OF THINGS EVIE and I never discussed—Polly, Fuckface Christian, how many women I'd slept with, that fucking asshole Luke Bailey, me leaving, her *not* leaving—Evie going semi-domme, and me loving it, was my favorite. I never pegged myself as the type. But it was Evie. My Evie. I'd let her tear out my heart and eat it if I thought it would make her happy.

Those playful yet forceful slaps on my ass the first time we were together should have given it away, but I was too overcome by the enormity of the choking situation to give it due thought. But with the benefit of hindsight, and the constant replaying of the moment in my head, the arrows lined up and pointed in one kinky direction.

It was easy to see how Little Evie Austen, a woman who'd reined in her sexuality and denied herself pleasure for so long, whose life had been controlled by her desire to please and care for those around her, had lost her sense of self. And why she would seek some kind of control when trying to find it. Luckily with me, she was comfortable to both let it all go and reclaim it…or at least begin to. And I was more than willing to be her tool of self-discovery.

The memory of that bath was always there, following everywhere, swirling around and between us like one of my many beer farts…but much more enjoyable. Whatever the scenario, wherever I was, each time the word *yes* left my lips, I heard my submissive, *Yes, Evie.* And her forceful, sexy-as-fuck, *Good boy.*

Each day began with me desperate to hear her praise. To feel her fingers slip around my throat, her nails dig into my flesh, and her pussy tighten around my cock as she squeezed. But my forceful little vixen had yet to produce an encore performance.

Until…

Our first make-up sex gifted me the opportunity I'd been waiting for. After asking to spank me and dressing as the sexy fucking teacher I told her I'd once fantasized about, she was kneeling before me, about to take me into her mouth. I wasn't quite sure how this was punishment, but I wasn't about to complain. Her tits were bursting from her black lingerie, her sexy ass was squeezed into a black leather skirt, and she wielded a meter ruler, just like Mrs. Fraser had done all those years ago, but a thousand times hotter.

"Can I please touch you?" I whispered.

"You may touch my hair. Only my hair."

Quick as a flash, I loosened the clip hiding her killer curls away and watched as they gracefully fell around her shoulders. Her eyes narrowed.

"I said you could touch my hair, not undo it. You're such a brat." The world and everyone but us stopped as she opened her mouth. "But you have such a beautiful cock." She took a deep breath, smiled, and licked the tip of my painfully hard length. "So smooth," she sighed before wrapping her lips around me.

Her palms rested on my thighs, pushing against me as she slid over me, once, twice, three times. Her right hand shifted, caressing my balls briefly before gripping me. While fisting my base, she took me deeper, moaning as her tongue swirled. "Are you sure you haven't done this before?" I grunted as she hollowed her cheeks.

"Does it feel good, Nate? I want to please you."

"Yes, Evie. Fuck, yes. It's amazing. You're gonna make me come so fast." She looked up at me and smiled, then doubled her speed, bobbing up and down, taking me deeper and deeper, gagging, eyes watering. I tried to pull away, not wanting her to be uncomfortable, but she gripped my ass with her left hand and pulled me even closer.

"I want this," she sighed, my dick still between her lips.

The sight before me was too much and no way near enough. The sexiest moment of my life. Evie was on her knees, my hand was tugging her hair, my hips thrusting. I was fucking Evie Austen's mouth and was on the brink of the most embarrassingly fast, mind-bending orgasm. Every muscle in my body tensed as I pulsed on her tongue. I closed my eyes, waiting for the rush of heat and relief. I could feel it coming... With a *pop* I felt in my bones, she pulled away, sprung to her feet, and slapped my cheek. Not to be dramatic, but it felt like she'd sucked my insides out, leaving a horny, hollow, empty shell of a man. "See how in control I am?"

She pressed her finger to my lips and winked, then sashayed her hot ass in that criminally tight skirt away, grabbing her robe off its hook as she entered the bathroom and locked the door. *What the fuck just happened?*

In one move, Evie had handed me a painful reminder *and* taught me a valuable lesson. I may have had more experience in the bedroom, but she was the boss, my teacher. I was merely the dumb kid lucky enough to be along for the ride. And as fun as it was, as strong as a role she played, Evie had exposed a side of herself that may have left her feeling vulnerable.

Again, I realized how lucky I was to be here with her and to experience any of what she shared. I moved to the door, rested my hand, and still flushed cheek on the cool and refreshing wood, and knocked.

"Are you okay, Eves? I'm sorry for how I reacted earlier. We're good, yeah?"

I heard her long, shaken exhale. "Not gonna lie, Nate. I'm still kind of pissed, but yeah, we are good. Or we will be once I calm down. I'm going to take a bath. Thank you for...for listening and accepting. No one's ever seen me like you do, and I think you might know how raw that can feel, 'cause I think I'm the first to see the real you too."

It's not easy to explain the impact those words had. Even while adorning her with the greatest esteem for years, I knew I had *grossly* underestimated that woman.

※

Skating on thin ice was not a new hobby of mine, but after apologizing and an hour or so of semi-silent treatment from Evie *with* a semi that wouldn't budge, dodging the cracks became a little too perilous. So, as many generations of Australian men had done before, I left the little lady at home and went to the pub. As I fled, an SOS was dispatched to Finn and my new mate, Teddy, begging them in the manliest way possible to join, commiserate, and get drunk with me. Twenty minutes later, Teddy burst through the door, looking as though he'd run the whole way from the office he shared with Scarlett and Finn, and the latter joined us as soon as he got home from Iris's dance class. Taking the stool beside me and ordering his favorite Aussie beer, a James Squire One Fifty Lashes Pale Ale, he sighed and shook his head. "What did you do? Evie is next-level shitty."

I shook my head and looked up to the giant TV replaying the Australian Football Grand Final—our version of the Super Bowl. "Trust me, mate. You don't want to know."

"Well, I do," complained Teddy. "And I've been trying to get it out of him since I got here, Finn. My usual trick of getting you so drunk you spill all your secrets isn't working. Nate holds his alcohol much better than you." Finn looked offended for a second before nodding in agreement and sipping from his beer. "Holy shit!" Teddy yelled suddenly. "Nate, your little spat with Evie doesn't have anything to do with a certain leather, lace, and rough loving, would it?"

Before I could answer, Finn climbed off his stool. "Fuck this, I'm out."

"Sit down, you clod." Teddy laughed, grabbing Finn by the

arm, and pulling him back down. "Your sister is a big girl with a healthy sexual appetite. She's not doing or receiving anything you're not giving or receiving from Scar."

"Oh, God," he groaned again and buried his face in his hands. "This is not happening."

"Shut it, Finn, or Nate will become my favorite and usurp the title of Captain Koala, and I know how much you love that shit." Teddy turned to me. "So, was it the outfit or not?"

"It *may* have been involved, but I can neither confirm nor deny. How do you know about it, anyway?"

Teddy gripped onto my bicep and squeezed. "I took her shopping. I tried to talk her into some whips and cuffs too, but she was too intimidated. So how did it go? Did she spank you? Fuck, she spanked you, and you freaked out, didn't you?"

"Really? I have to leave." A pale and clammy Finn guzzled his beer and fled before we could stop him. He didn't leave, though. He just moved to a table out of earshot behind us.

"There was no spanking. It was alluded to, but she blue-balled me before we got to that point, and I absolutely, one hundred percent, kind of, maybe didn't deserve it… but also kinda did."

"Look at you taking responsibility…kinda. And if it makes you feel any better, I'm going through something similar myself with Asher."

"He's into spanking too?"

He sighed and glumly sipped from his drink. "I wish. No, he dumped me and blocked my number."

I studied him for a moment, not sure if he was serious. "Sorry, mate, really. But how is that similar to Evie's and my situation?"

"It's not at all. I just needed to get it off my chest and wanted to make it about me." Our shoulders shook with silent laughter.

"Teddy, I find your frankness incredibly refreshing. It's a trait you share with Evie and one of the things I love most about her. She's normally the most brutally honest person I know. You always know how she feels, and she doesn't have to say a word. Her face will *always* tell the truth. That's how I know she loves me. I see it every time she looks at me." I finished my beer and signaled the cute bartender for another one. She winked at me as she took my empty glass, and I realized that, in a different time, I would have been on her like a rash. *I really have changed.* "The thing is, I thought doing everything I could to show her how I feel, being patient, and giving her time would help her open up, but I'm starting to have my doubts. I was so convinced she would come home with me, Teddy. I don't know what I'll do if she doesn't."

Slapping his hand on my shoulder way harder than needed, Finn resumed his seat next to me. "What I'm about to do makes me sick to my very core, so you better listen 'cause I am only gonna say it once." He took a deep breath and slapped his own thigh for encouragement. "Nate, she loves you, mate. I see it too, and believe me, I've tried bloody hard not to. You're her favorite person in the world. She thinks the sun shines out of your ass, and she always has, and I've seen her smile more in the time you've been here than I have since Mum and Dad died. The bigger the cow she is to you, the more she cares, and that's why she calls you an idiot so much. To her, that's a term of endearment and as good as a formal declaration of love. And finally, Evie needs to feel needed. Important. Useful. She loves bossing Jocie, Iris, and me around because it gives her a sense of purpose. She's only just found her job and is just getting to know people here. If she left us, she'd be back to no job and no family to take care of. Plus, as much as she has a go at me for the same thing, she would have no control. If you want her to come home with you, you need to find her a purpose and let her think she thought of it. That's the key."

"A purpose," I sighed, stroking my chin with my index finger and thumb in a manner befitting a Disney villain.

"You mean apart from lying half naked on an Aussie beach and bonking his brains out every five minutes?" Teddy added.

"Wha—Jesus, Teddy. Yes, apart from that." Finn couldn't help but laugh, but I could only manage a half grin. I was already too busy plotting.

Chapter 37

P EOPLE WHO HAD PIC AFTER PIC SAVED ON multiple Pinterest boards about bedroom layouts, paint schemes, decorations, and furniture always bugged me. They could spend thousands of dollars on bloody cushions, creating a mood, a peaceful haven, a respite from the outside world, but then complain endlessly about how expensive little Daisy's dance classes were and not pay their bill on time.

My bedroom, my bed, had never been thought of like that. Growing up with the attitude and mouth I had, my *haven* was associated with being in trouble. *Go to your room, young lady. Go do your homework, or bloody go to sleep!* And sleep itself was never something I savored. It was done out of necessity, as an unavoidable part of life. In the months and years following the loss of my parents, in the hours spent alone in the dark, I was often consumed with grief, worrying over the what-ifs and never-going-to-bes. I'm surprised the patch of paint on my ceiling didn't melt from the intensity and duration of my gaze.

Being with Nate changed all that. My room became our oasis. A place I longed to be. A place that I raced home from wherever I was to be and that I never wanted to leave. Even when we were slightly pissed off with each other or walking on eggshells, like we had been in the days following Nate's little lesson on control, we always managed to come together in that space and sort everything out. Even when our bodies weren't twisted around each other, we were as close as could be—bingeing *Sex and the City*, laughing till we cried over *The Office*, and setting unrealistic expectations with endless Austen adaptations.

It was where I felt my most powerful, the most in control. The most *me* I'd ever been. Where I was declared his queen, heralded, and treated as such, my body worshipped, my mind adored.

And that was how it happened. In my quest to nurture that, to create our own little world where our pasts and the future held no importance, I became a Pinterest person. Whenever I was able to separate her from Finn's hip, Scarlett—my enabler—and I would hit the shops, searching for, and spending ridiculous amounts of money on linens and lamps, artwork and pillows, knick-knacks, and indoor plants to further invigorate my—*our*—space.

The changes were significant—in the room and in me. The wee hours became treasured, occupied by the giving, receiving, making, and declaring of love in every way possible...bar none. Despite what was bubbling below the surface, threatening to spill from my lips each time he brought me to the peak of pleasure, I stubbornly refused to tell Nate what I'd finally acknowledged to myself...

That I was hopelessly, madly, frustratingly, lustfully in love with Nathaniel Myers.

That the thought of him leaving in a few weeks split my soul in two.

That I wanted to ask him to stay.

That I knew he wouldn't.

So, I couldn't.

"Exactly how many pillows does one need on a bed?" Nate asked as I correctly remade the bed he'd made while I was in the shower.

"When I hit the right amount, I'll let you know." I threw my latest buy at his head, then quickly ran to pick it from the floor when I missed, dusting it off and correcting the unaligned ruffles. "They look pretty, though. Don't you think they make the room seem cozier? More…intimate?"

"Intimate? You know, I do like intimacy, but I can honestly say I've never equated it with cushions."

"Me either. But here we are." The pile was perfect. Everything where it should be, the colors arranged in a beautiful boho ombre….until Nate dived into them like a four-year-old in a ball pit.

"Speaking of intimate…" He tapped the bed and gave me the wink-wink. "How about it?" Wink-wink.

Intimacy had occurred twice already this morning. I'd woken him with my lips wrapped around his morning wood, then tied him up, spanked his thighs, and lost my mind as I had my first go at reverse cowgirl…and still he wanted me.

I wanted him too. So much it hurt—as would my hoo-ha if I had sex again. "I'd love to, really, but I have a class today, remember? I'm filling in for Kim, the usual Sunday teacher, and I can't let Jody down. She'll be there by herself otherwise."

"This little job of yours is really eating into our sex time, Gidge. I'm glad that when you come home with me, you can be a lady of leisure, and I can have you at my beck and call.

"There are so many things wrong with what you just said that I'm not even bothering to argue."

"But I love it when you argue with me. That's why I said it." Stretching his long, sexy arms out, Nate slapped my ass and attempted to pull me back to bed. "I freaking love those leg warmers too. You look so hot. Come on, Shirley. Give me fifteen minutes with those fluffy legs wrapped around my neck. I promise I'll make it worth your while."

"As complimentary and enticing as having my legs referred to as fluffy is, it's a huge group today, and I can't be late, or they'll eat Jody alive." I blew him a quick kiss, and I and my fluffy legs hurried out the door before he could change any of our minds.

⸙

Greeting me from behind the desk, with bright eyes that shone even more so as I neared and that toothpaste-commercial-worthy smile, was a face I had not expected.

Fuck.

"Where's Jody?"

"Good morning, Evie. You look beautiful today. How are you? I brought you a coffee, cream and two sugars, just how you like it."

"Thanks," I grunted, accepting the coffee I was never in a million years going to drink. Today was not the day I felt like being roofied. "I'm fine. Never been better. Where is Jody?"

"You didn't know? Oh…um…please don't be upset, but she's sick, with the same virus as Kim I suspect. She messaged me an hour ago, asking me to take her class and promising that she would call you."

"Well, she didn't." Without taking my eyes off Christian, I sat the possible liquefied poison on the desk and pulled out my phone. "Oh…wait, she did. She called three times and sent two messages. My phone was on silent. Bloody Nate."

Christian stood and stalked around the desk. "You're still with him, then? With Nate, I mean?"

Staring at my feet, I tried to ignore Christian and head to the studio, but he placed himself in the middle of the hallway, blocking my escape. I sighed, swallowed the panic-chuck rising in my throat, and raised my head.

"My…*situation* with Nate isn't any of your business."

"I think it is my business, because this place"—he waved his hands around the air like a stupid fucking magician—"is my business and because I care about my employees. I'm worried, Evie. He seemed like an aggressive kind of guy. Are you boyfriend and girlfriend? Talking long-term? Are you in love?"

"I'm not sure where *you* get off calling anyone aggressive, but I can assure you he *is* not, and I *am* not in lo—" I paused. "—not answering questions you have no right to ask. A rehab stint, coffee, and a friendly, 'Good morning,' don't earn you anything."

With all the arrogance in the world, he turned and rested his back against the wall, his arms crossed over his chest. "So, it's not serious, then?"

"How did you deduce that from a polite, mind-your-own-bloody-business statement?"

"Well, you referred to him as a situation. And to me, if you were in love, you'd be screaming it from the rooftops. Especially when you know how jealous it would make me."

"Snort! Why the hell would you be jealous? I'm just a childish, dancing wannabe, remember? There are a million of us out there."

Shame colored Christian's face as he winced, pushed off the wall, and rubbed the back of his neck. "Look, Evie. I know my behavior was abhorrent, but I was in a dark place and lashing out at anyone close to me. It's not an excuse, but please don't doubt my affection toward you. I genuinely liked—still like you. You're a beautiful, special person. I want you to be happy."

"Well, then, you have nothing to worry about because I am happy and will remain so—with or without a man in my life." My words were for myself as much as for the man before me.

Chilly, autumn air brushed against the backs of my legs as the front door slid open, and our tiny dancers began to fill the foyer. As usual, I had more to say, so I pulled Christian closer by the arm, and I quickly whispered, "Look, I understand you've been going through a rough time lately, and I'm willing to forget the past and move on if you are. Everybody deserves a second chance. Let's just be professional, do our jobs, and get today over with." I stuck my hand out to shake on it. "Deal?"

Mr. Smooth held and pressed it to his lips instead. "Deal."

I can't believe I ever fancied this douche.

"Ooohhhh," Cole, Iris's little, loud friend, appeared at my

hip. "He kissed you! How romantic." Half a dozen kids and some immature parents joined in too. I was embarrassed as all hell. Christian seemed to relish the attention.

"If you liked that, guys, you'll love this. I'm going to make you all a deal. If you behave yourself and work really hard today, Miss Evie and I will do a dance for you at the end of class. And we all know dancing is more romantic than a silly kiss on the hand."

"Christian," I spat through gritted teeth, "I'm not dancing with you."

"Ahh, don't be a stick in the mud. You want to move on and work together, don't you? What displays a united team more than the Adagio from the Sugar Plum grand pas de deux?" Selecting what he and the kids knew was my favorite-ever piece, and saying it loud enough for all to hear, meant they were too bloody excited for me to say no.

"Fine, *one short section,* and that's it. And only if everyone remembers all their positions, and I don't have to repeat myself once." That should have all but guaranteed I wouldn't have to dance with former HotBoss…TepidBoss. Kim and Jody had often described their Sunday class, which consisted of juniors from ages six to twelve, as *Lord of the Flies* meets *The Hobbit.*

Thirty minutes into the fifty-minute class, I started to feel ill. Not only had bloody Christian shown frequent glimpses of the patient, kind, and gentle man I first met, which made staying pissed off at him almost impossible, but the cute little arseholes I was depending on had actually been listening to everything we said and hadn't set a foot wrong. Positions were perfect, held for a bizarrely long time, and general behavior was exemplary. Jody and Kim were either full of shit, or someone—AKA TepidBoss—shot them up with a magic potion when I wasn't looking. Even though my soon-to-be partner had been on his best behavior, having his meaty paws all over me was still undesirable, and by the forty-five-minute mark, I was panicking and seriously contemplating pushing my mini-Baryshnikov's over, so they'd lose balance.

Had I been bestowed with Finn's or Nate's disposition, the whole scenario could've been taken as a positive—as a demonstration of my superior instructor skills and how professional I could be when working with someone who only weeks ago had terrified me. But being the grumpy to their sunshine, I chose to take it as further evidence that the universe hated me and loved royally screwing me over. A fact that was confirmed when, minutes later, Christian appeared with a tutu and tiara and exclaiming, "If we're going to do this, we're going to do it right."

Chapter 38

Nate

THE MINUTE FLUFFY SEXY LEGS LEFT, I TOOK matters into my own hands…and for once, *matters* wasn't code for cock.

It was Sunday in New York, but Monday at home, and though still painfully early, I shot an email off to the estate agent I'd been dealing with for the last few days. He was a friend from school, and I'd been hounding him relentlessly.

> **To**: Brendan Salmon
>
> **Subject:** Come the fuck on.
>
> Hey, Brendan,
>
> Nate here again. Have you heard any news from Cheryl at the tennis club? It's been days, and you've given me nothing.
>
> I'm really keen to get a hold of the hall before Christmas, Brenno. I need this. Don't make me remind you that I am the one that got you and your lovely wife together.
>
> You owe me this.
> Nate.

Surprisingly, my phone pinged with a reply almost immediately.

> **To:** Fucking Nate
> **Subject:** Fuck Off
>
> Since you're emailing me at 4am on my

personal, not work address, I can safely tell you to fuck right off, you arrogant prick.

Also, I'm not sure how sleeping with, then ditching Dee on her 19th birthday is getting us together, but whatever. I have her now, lying naked next to me, and you have nothing but an apparently tiny dick and a six-month lease and option to purchase on a filthy old hall that smells like mouse shit.

Also, you're a fucking asshole, and Evie is right to fuck you off back home alone. She can do better.

Also, Dee isn't next to me. I just got home from the pub. I'm pissed as a fart and smell twice as bad. Dee is making me sleep on the couch. She was naked, though. I miss her.

Also, call me when you get home, and we'll go out for a beer. Hopefully, Evie will be with you.

Brendan.

A massive fist pump heralded my success. With this hall, I was handing Evie exactly what Finn said I needed to…a purpose. Her very own dance studio.

This was it. This was the golden ticket that would have Evie's ass in a plane seat before I could say *I told you so*.

I had it all planned. As soon as we arrived home, we would begin renovations. The bones of the building were good, but the floors were old, the colors dated, and the bathrooms hadn't been updated since the '50s. Brendan had warned me the tennis club wouldn't foot the bill, and if they agreed to only lease and not sell, any work done was my cost—and loss—when the lease expired. The money meant nothing to me. I had enough saved to cover it all, and there was nothing in the world I would rather spend it on than securing Evie's happiness and keeping her by my side. Mum squealed with delight when I first shared my idea and instantly promised the help of the CWA gals to organize a grand opening that everyone would be talking about. Even Dad was in on the act. Apparently, the minute I was off the phone, he was out in the shed, working on a hand-carved sign to hang above the door.

Miss Evie's.

It was going to be perfect. I just had to convince Evie of that, and I was fairly positive…almost certain…kinda…that this was going to work.

Maybe.

That was where the next step—or person—in my plan came in.

After a short search of the house, I found Jocelyn in her study, trawling over the latest Tarrytown house plans Scarlett had sent her. Suddenly nervous, I hovered by the door. Not many women flustered me. I trusted my abilities to charm my way into and out of most situations, and I'd known Jocie for years. But the woman was incredibly intimidating and was rightly protective of Evie.

"Are you just going to just stand there and watch me, Nathaniel, or is there something I can help you with?" she asked briskly without shifting her gaze from the laptop.

"Sorry, Jocie. I just… I need to ask you a favor."

"Does this favor involve my darling girl?"

"Very much so."

"Hmm. Figured as much. And a ring?" Her eyes shot to mine as she pushed her glasses to the tip of her nose where they dangled precariously. "Because I'll tell you now, she's not ready for that, Nate. You pop the question now, and you'll have her running for the hills."

Taking the brutal blow to my ego as well as I could, I approached her desk with caution.

"Don't stress. I'm not planning on proposing…not yet, anyway. I wanted to ask if Evie and I could stay at your place in Tarrytown for a few nights?"

Jocelyn closed her eyes and sighed while pinching the bridge of her nose. The woman thought I was an idiot. Just like Evie. However, Jocelyn's patronizing eyerolls were much less of a turn-on.

"Nate, there is no *place* in Tarrytown. There's an empty block of land and a half-completed image on a screen. Scarlett is designing my home, remember?"

"Yeah, I know, but I want to hire a car and take Evie away for a couple of days. She has no classes till Wednesday afternoon, and I was hoping it would be okay if we camped there. She works so hard and is always looking after everyone else. I wanted to do something nice for her."

"And you think making her sleep on dirt in a tent in late autumn is nice?"

"Well, yeah. She used to love camping when we were kids." *And I'll be there to keep her warm.*

Jocelyn's eyes narrowed in skepticism. "Maybe you're right. She does always tell me off for my excessive spending. If you think she would enjoy it, you're more than welcome. But I can see a worryingly increased glimmer of mischief in your eyes, so let me remind you again. Your *Gidget* is not one to be pushed. Don't be the hare to her tortoise. Slow and steady wins the race."

Disregarding Jocelyn's words to the nth degree, I raced to pack everything we needed, including the crappy and rough-as-fuck designs I'd made for the studio. I raided Finn's room and garage for camping supplies and loaded up his Jeep that Jocie insisted we take. I also called Rubirosa and ordered two large pizzas and mozzarella sticks to go, and Candice was boxing the first of the pizzas as I arrived.

"I was starting to think you must have gone home. Evie too. I haven't seen either of you for weeks. I take it by the goofy, love-drunk look on your face that things are going well with you two?"

"Things are unbelievably brilliant," I replied, unable to suppress my grin. "That's why I'm planning a surprise for her. After I leave here, I'm picking her up from work and then driving her to Tarrytown for a few days. Well, technically, Jocelyn is driving me to pick her up, and then Evie will have to drive us upstate. In my haste to get going, I forgot I don't have a license here in the States."

"I'm glad you remembered before attempting to drive thirty-odd miles on the wrong side of the road. Is this pizza to eat on the way?"

"Yup. Evie eats like a horse after class. She'll probably eat a whole large herself."

"I was surprised to see she was teaching today. My nephew Cole takes Kim and Jody's Sunday class, and I always drop him off for my sister."

"Oh, you saw her? Was she still wearing the legwarmers? Pretty hot, eh?"

Candice laughed and placed the two boxes before me. "Missed the legwarmers, I'm afraid. I just dropped Cole off in the front. I only know she was taking the class because Kim sent us a message to say they were sick, and it would be Evie and Christian instead. She's a better person than I am. There's no way I would have been prepared to work with that douchebag so soon."

"What?" I snapped. "Christian? She was teaching with Christian?"

Candice winced. "Why do I have the feeling I've fucked up?"

Abandoning the steaming boxes of deliciousness, I threw cash on the counter and took off, running the four blocks to VAAD, bursting through the doors and past the foyer.

I saw her straight away—sorry, *them*. I saw *them* straight away. Dancing. Together.

Christian stood behind my girl, holding her waist in a partnered pirouette. Evie looked angelic, wearing a white tutu and tights, her blush-pink pointes tied with ribbons up to her calves, and a shimmering tiara was pinned into her slicked-back hair. I hadn't seen her in full costume for years, and she was breathtaking. Hypnotized by her fluidity and strength, my anger was lost in her grace.

I'm not sure how long I stood there watching or how she didn't see me pressed up against the glass, but I bloody well knew Christian was aware of my presence. The smirk on his face when he held her body in a fish lift, carried her across the room, then caught and supported her by the thigh and waist into a perfect arabesque lift enraged me once more. He dropped her to her feet, and she flowed into another partnered pirouette, but I could see something was wrong. The sway of her body, wobbling on her feet, and sudden stiffening of her grip on his arm was telling. They were performing a section from *The Nutcracker*. Evie had made Finn, Shelby, and I watch it every Christmas, and that was never part of the dance. Fuckface stopped her early in the final rotation, so her back was to me. He didn't want her to know I was there.

Slowly, he lifted his eyes from hers, looked directly at me with a smug smile I wanted to slap from his face, then cupped her cheeks in his hands. I could see her body tense and begin to pull away, but he held her still.

That was it.

Disregarding the twenty-odd children I almost stepped on to get to her, I stormed into the room. "Get your hands off or I'll un-alive you so hard," I bellowed, ripping his arm free and pushing him in the chest so hard he fell on his ass and skidded across the floor.

Spinning to face me, Evie gasped. "Nate! What are you doing? You can't do that!" Then, in a move that tore my guts out, she rushed to Christian and helped him to his feet. "Christian, I am so sorry."

"It's okay, Evie. You don't need to apologize for him. You're not responsible for his stupidity or his actions. Threatening me like this, this aggression, is exactly what I was talking about earlier and why I am worried."

"You're calling *me* aggressive?" My response was halted by several rightly horrified-looking parents making their way into the classroom to collect their children. They, along with Evie and Fuckface, continued to stare at me like I was an absolute freak—a giant, classless savage let loose amongst the gentry.

"I am so sorry for this," Evie said as more parents bustled in. "Please forgive Nate. He's a good friend and also…well, an over-protective idiot."

"Friend? I'm your overprotective friend? Ahh, okay, that's soul-destroying, but putting that tidbit aside, can you blame me—your *friend*—after what this turd burger pulled? I can't believe you would put yourself in this situation."

"No. I can't believe you would put me in *this* situation. It's completely unacceptable, Nate. You need to leave."

"Uh-huh. No way. I'm not leaving you here with him. You need me—"

"I don't *need* or want you here or anywhere. You have absolutely humiliated me, Nate. I don't even want to look at you. Just go."

"Sorry. Not gonna happen." I point-blank refused to leave, so Christian and I stood face to face, eyeballing each other as Evie continued to apologize profusely to the kids and the last of the tutting family members. With the audience gone, I pulled Evie away to the side.

"Of all people, why did you have to shut me down like that in front of him? I fucking hate that guy. He hurt you, Gidge. He bruised you. I don't give a shit if he was high on elephant tranquillizers at the time, you don't lay your hands on a woman. Especially not my woman."

If I thought she looked pissed before, my words inspired her discovery of a whole new level of rage. Her face was beyond red, almost purple, as she took to the balls of her feet, straining to stand as tall and strong and proud as she could, her chin jutted in defiance.

She looked at me like she hated me. "I am not *your* woman."

I stepped back, blinking away the tears I could feel building as adrenaline coursed through me. Sweat beaded on my brow, and if I clenched my jaw any tighter, I wouldn't have a tooth left in my mouth. I waited for my brain to deliver a stinging comeback. To tell her she was wrong, that she was mine. For my hand to snake around her waist and claim her. For the fight to arrive.

But it never did.

Something else had replaced it.

Resignation.

"No. As always, Gidge, you're right. The Evie I've loved my whole life would never defend someone like him"—I stabbed the air in Christian's general direction—"over me. You're not mine, and you've told me a hundred times. I'm sorry it's taken me so long to get it, but it is now…*gotten*."

Chapter 39

Evie

ACCORDING TO ALMOST EVERY SITCOM I HAD ever watched, ice cream was the universal cure for all the problems of womankind. Whatever the crisis, be it work life, love life, or no life, we gals loved nothing more than shoveling down a pint or two of Ben and Jerry's. Since I was currently facing dilemmas in all of these areas, I decided to stop for a scoop on the way home.

If the fun and games of the afternoon hadn't been enough to end me, a text message from Polly as I swallowed my first mouthful of Peanut Butter Half Baked plunged me further into the abyss. That bird sure had some shitty timing.

Hearing from her had become a weekly occurrence, with each jagged little pill of a message planting another seed of self-loathing paranoia in my belly. It felt like she and Christian had formed an international support group, the sole purpose of which was to fuck up my life even more than I had done myself. The scene in *The Office* where Dwight proposed an alliance with Jim popped into my brain. *God, I love that show.*

But it wasn't the time to muse over my love for Kelly Kapur or hatred for Todd Packer. Everything with Nate was shit, I was in a certifiable stink, and had an unread message from a bitch staring at me from the table.

Hope you're well, my homely little friend.
I was just cleaning and found this pair of

boxers behind the bed. I think Nate threw them across the room in a fit of passion, haha.

Can you let him know I'll drop them off when he comes home. Oh, and tell him I can't wait to see him. Xxoo.

As she often did, Polly had attached a photo with the message. This one featured her artificially whitened smile, her giant rack, a tiny bikini, and the offending briefs held in her claw-like nails as she posed before her unmade bed. Sitting smack-dab in the middle of that bed was a multipack of the very same briefs she apparently "found" while cleaning.

I'd politely blown off her provocations for weeks, holding my tongue till the damn thing near bled, but the shit had to stop.

Hi Polly, I'm doing incredibly well, thanks for asking. Though, girlfriend to girlfriend, I can hardly walk. Nate absolutely railed me with three rounds of the most amazing sex before I left for work. Haha. And I'm so glad you finally cleaned—a little birdie with a massive cock had let it slip that your room was filthy and smelled weird and kinda funky.

Oh, and next time you send me a photo of something Nate left behind, make sure you hide the packaging before you take the photo. XXOO.

I then celebrated my pettiness with another scoop, this time Salted Caramel Blondie, the flavor of which lingered on my tastebuds till I finally got home.

The house appeared empty as I hung my jacket by the door, so I sulked to my oasis, my room, hoping to find Nate lying on the bed, ready and waiting to make up. But like the rest of the house, the room felt empty, like it had lost its newly acquired ambient serenity. The beachy, boho-princess sparkle was gone, as were Nate's things…and Nate.

My declaration of independence in front of Christian was

wanted me gone, I'd have to leave or it would start a war between him and the guys.

Or he'd have me killed. Would he ask the guys to do it? Would they if he did? No, they wouldn't. A war might be a walk in the park compared to how it might all go.

Leo looked back at me, his gaze unwavering. "You had no idea?"

"None." It was an effort not to flinch, but I managed.

"I didn't—" Mum started.

He cut her off. "I want to hear it from Kennedy." He gave her a glance that clearly said he'd deal with her later. It seemed the honeymoon was over.

I was sorry for that but I'd had no choice but to drop this grenade in the middle of everything. Besides, I wanted the answers myself. Even if they came with a lot more questions.

"I didn't have a clue until he told me," I said. "Even then, I didn't believe it until Mum confirmed it. I mean...he put me in that basement room. That's not exactly the thing a loving father does to his daughter."

I was struggling to get my mind around any of this. When had every aspect of my life become so complicated? Oh, right, before I was born. All of this nothing I hadn't said before in the heat of various moments, but doing it in Fuckface's presence seemed to have added some extra sting.

I should have sought Nate out, tried to make things right. After all, you should never go to sleep angry. But I was too freaking mad at him for going back to his room and too freaking proud to ask him to come back. I was also too scared.

So, I lay on my bed—our bed—worrying that I had pushed too far this time, and stared at that patch of paint on the ceiling. Just like old times.

Not that I was standing by the door listening or anything, but I heard Nate emerge and clomp down the stairs around seven am. Neither of us had left our rooms all night.

Trying to avoid the appearance of over-eagerness, I waited seven seconds before venturing out. Braiding my hair as I walked, I was forced to pause at the top of the stairs to ride out a wave of panic-chuck, but sorted myself out and carried on, only to be told by Jocie as I entered the kitchen that he was already gone.

She was sitting at the table, eating breakfast beside Finn and Iris, and all three kept their heads low as I stomped around and made myself a coffee and some toast. I think my overly aggressive Vegemite spreading triggered a fight-or-flight response in Finn as he quickly stood and grabbed Iris by the arm.

"Hey, Bub, why don't we go to the park before school?"

"But I haven't finished my toast!"

"Never mind your bloody toast. I'll stop and get you some pancakes."

Iris squealed with delight and ran to collect her things while I applied the same aggressive stance to eating my breakfast as I did to prepare it.

In a flash of color and movement, Finn and Iris bailed, leaving Jocie and me alone.

Compared to Finn, she was as cool as the gallon of ice cream

I'd eaten last night that was still causing digestion issues, appearing almost serene as she poured us some tea from her favorite Royal Daulton pot.

"He tried to book a flight home yesterday." I nearly choked on my crust. "I managed to convince him to stay, but he wouldn't tell me or Finn what happened. So, why don't you?"

An arctic wind swept over me. "He was going to go home?"

"Apparently so."

"I can't believe he would do that without even talking to me."

"And have you been talking to him? Have you told him that you're in love with him, for instance?"

"God, why is everyone so obsessed with that stupid, pointless word?" The frustrated slamming of my teacup against the saucer earned me a frown from Jocie. "I talk to Nate almost every minute of every day. We share everything—food, drinks, the shower, our bed!" I blushed, remembering who I was speaking to, but continued. "If Nate is so prepared to just up and leave, whether it be today, tomorrow, three weeks, or three years from now…if it's going to end, what's the point of a grand declaration? I'm going to be alone anyway."

"And tell me, Nostradamus. Why does it have to end? How do you know you won't remain glued at the hip for another seventy years?"

"Because forever is a fairy tale. How many times have you thought you'd found forever? Yet, here you sit, sharing breakfast with me, none of your forever's at your side." Cringing at the harshness of my words, I shot an apologetic look at the woman who had given me so much. "I'm sorry, you didn't deserve that. I'm just… I mean, look at Shelby and Finn or Mum and Dad, for fuck's sake. Nothing lasts forever, Jocie. Nothing. Why would I risk losing you and Finn and Evie just to end up alone thousands of miles away from everybody I love. I won't do it. I won't. I refuse to put myself through the pain of losing my heart and soul again."

A shocking amount of ugly crying commenced, and I was

swept into Jocelyn's arms and held as the fear and frustration and pain leaked from my traitorous eyeballs.

Remorse filled Jocelyn's voice as she whispered into my hair, "I warned him not to push you. I told him it would scare you off, and here I am, doing the exact same thing. I'm sorry, my darling."

"When?" I sniffed. "When did you tell him not to push me?"

"This morning, before he came to surprise you with the trip."

"A trip? Was he planning on taking me on a trip?"

"He didn't tell you?"

"No, he came to work, but he saw Christian and me dancing, freaked out, barged into the studio, and pushed Christian onto his ass in front of all the kids and their parents. It was mortifying, Jocie. And we had a big fight. I said he was my friend, and he told me I was his woman, and then I yelled that I wasn't his woman, and then he cried and left."

"Oh, my poor darling."

The flood continued until my tears made Jocelyn's favorite nightgown frighteningly transparent. She left to change and returned a few minutes later with the car keys and a determined glare. "He was going to take you camping at Tarrytown. He wanted to treat you because, and I quote, *'She works so hard and is always looking after everyone else. I wanted to do something nice for her.'"* Jocelyn threw me the keys and smiled. "Get in the car. Go away together for a couple of days. I've booked you the same enormous house we stayed at last time, so you can have separate wings if you like. But don't let it end like this because I promise you'll regret it.

At that very moment, the front door opened, quietly closed, then Nate appeared before me with a bunch of blue hyacinths. His pain was all too evident in his beautiful brown eyes, now red with dark shadows circling them completely. Pouting so cutely it broke me, he watched me sniffle and dry my eyes with my sleeve, then held the bouquet before me.

"The lady at the shop said blue hyacinths represent making peace. I'm sorry I was such a clown and a bully. And I'm super sorry that I made you cry, 'cause I never want to make you cry, Gidge."

"Nate," I sobbed, "I don't want to make you cry either, you big bully clown-boy, and I'm sorry too. I should never have spoken to you like that, especially in front of Christian." Until then, I hadn't noticed that Clown-Boy—which was absolutely going to stick—was holding his breath. But he was, and the epic exhale that chased my words would have knocked all three little pigs' houses over in one go. The hyacinths were laid on the table, and I cautiously wrapped my arms around Nate's waist, resting my head on his chest and listening to his pounding heart. "I heard you were going to take me away."

His silent chuckle shook me in his arms. "Gee, I wonder where you heard that from?"

Jocelyn, who remained in the room, watching and theatrically dabbing tears from her eyes, raised her hand and smiled. "No camping, though, Nathaniel. You're right about Evie deserving a break, and I have booked just the place. The car is still packed. Now get the hell out of here and go have some amazing upstate make-up sex."

Chapter 40

Nate

THE AIR MAY HAVE BEEN CLEARED WHEN WE left the house, but a chill reminiscent of the approaching winter lingered. Our hands were locked the entire drive, alternating thighs every few miles, and the little conversation we had was forced, almost disingenuous. Not talking about things we desperately needed to talk about had become our thing. It was a disturbing pattern that even my useless himbo man brain knew was trouble. As my mum always said, "*There's only so much you can sweep under the rug before it becomes a trip hazard.*"

I didn't want Evie and I to trip. But I also wanted to avoid more conflict.

Tarrytown was quintessential upstate New York… apart from the fact that it moonlit as *the* Sleepy Hollow.

Evie was keen to show me Jocelyn's land, so we drove straight to the house, emptied the car into the mansion that had been so generously gifted, and took a walk. As we trudged up the hill then back down to the block, I couldn't help but smile, thinking over how far we've come since Evie was here last. How hot she looked in braids and a beanie when we FaceTimed, and how embarrassed she was when she fell on her tight little ass.

Back then, she was barely willing to show her face on camera, and now…now I'd seen every inch of her naked body from every angle.

Was I pleased?

Is the Pope Catholic?

Standing at the very edge of the plot, my gorgeously rosy-cheeked girl described the house, proudly boasting the inclusions that had been her ideas, and pacing out the length of the porch Scarlett and Finn added that, when complete, would wrap around the entirety of the house, allowing the family to chase the sun and take in the stunning Hudson River views no matter where they chose to sit.

"It really is beautiful, Eves," I said, kissing the top of her head and holding her tight. "You suit this place, somehow. Like, I can just imagine you sitting outside on one of those porch swings you see on American telly, with a cuppa in your hand and balancing your laptop on your knees." *Shit. I can imagine her living here.* It was yet another horrifying moment of halfhearted resignation. The second in twenty-four hours. Was I losing hope?

"I know. I can't wait. I love the city, but it's like I can really breathe and be me here." We sat on a fallen log, again in silence, until Evie sighed and took my hand in hers. "What about you, Clown- Boy. Ever dream about…oh, doesn't matter."

"About? Come on, Gidge. You can't leave me hanging. Do I dream about what?"

With an expression that stopped my heart and possibly time itself, she studied me through her thick lashes, chewed her lip, then began kicking the wet, fallen leaves laying at our feet. "Do you ever imagine something different? Have you considered a life away from the farm?"

"Shit yeah! Only every forty-five seconds or so. But farming, the farm, is in my blood. I've never been anywhere but home, the Gold Coast, or here. And I wouldn't have a bloody clue of what else I could do for a living. A career as an international gigolo has crossed my mind on occasion, but I don't think I'm cut out for that anymore."

"And why is that? Nate the Great hasn't lost his mojo, has he?"

"Nah, the mojo is present and accounted for, but my heart

wouldn't be in it. I can't share with others what belongs to you." I traced the line of her neck with my finger, felt the shiver run through her body and into mine, then turned her face and kissed her.

"I'm so sorry, Nate." She pulled away and buried her face in her hands. "I should never have started this. I knew it was going to end like this. I knew I'd...I'd...feel things. I knew you'd break my heart."

That was the closest she had come to confessing the love for me that I knew she felt, but I couldn't dig any deeper, couldn't further open the wound that threatened to bleed out, so I changed tactics, brought it back to the one thing I felt secure in: our physical connection. "Why did you never kiss me before?"

She was silent for what felt like an eternity before a broad, cheeky cackle broke free. "I did once."

"What? When? You're fibbing. You have to be. I can't see how you could possibly have kissed me without me knowing." I ran my thumb over her bottom lip, my cock springing to life in a heartbeat. "These lips could wake a man from a coma."

"But I did," she whispered, her warm breath tickling my cheek as I nuzzled into her neck. "I swear. It was the last Christmas we spent together at home. Everyone was asleep. And you... Oh, that feels nice... You were passed out cold on the couch. I was sitting opposite you in Barry's armchair, just watching you breathe. Even with your mouth open and drool dripping from your lip, you looked so bloody gorgeous. You have such beautiful, thick eyelashes. Has anyone ever told you that?" she asked, pulling away to study my face and sweep the hair from my eyes. I shook my head and returned to my favorite, warm nuzzle spot. "So yeah, I knelt before you, clapped a couple of times to make sure you were out, and then..."

"And then?"

"Hmmm, you know, I can't remember."

I sighed, hating to leave the crook of her neck again, but it was a hundred percent worth it to find her playfully rolling her eyes and biting that plump, pouty little lip. "Please tell me, Gidge. Please. I'm begging."

"Well, okay, then. Since you asked like such a good boy."

We both froze, our chests rose and fell sharply, the memory of the last time she spoke those words weighed the air, making it hard to breathe.

"So, yes, I made sure you were out of it, then I ran my finger down your face, under your chin, and across your bottom lip. Then, I kissed you."

A low and breathy voice I hardly recognized rumbled from my chest as I stood, lifted her from the stump, and laid her on the ground. "Evie, I feel so violated."

"Why are you kneeling between my legs, then?"

"Because…" Holding the small of her back, I rolled onto my own and positioned her over my hardness. "I want you to violate me some more."

Shaking with want, her hand went straight to my throat, and it hit me. Her tightening grip was not only a paralyzing act of passion and lust and kink for control. She needed me to ground her. I was her anchor. Just as she'd always been mine.

"Harder," I groaned as she pulled me onto her lips, biting and sucking them almost violently as her free hand fiddled to free me from my jeans.

"Fucking fuck it," she spat, ripping at the zipper. I could have helped, but I was too busy trying to get to her tits. "You really need to start wearing sweats more often. It's much easier to get them off… Fuck it. I'll do me, you do you. Break."

After her quarterback-like coaching, she pushed me off her and began rolling side to side, laughing at our ridiculousness, discarding her pants and knickers in one tug, then ripping her top over her head.

"Fuck, your tits are perfect," I growled, bent down, teased her pebbled nipples with my tongue, then took one into my mouth as I pushed my jeans over my thighs and lined myself at her entrance.

Again, her hand came to my throat, but this time, it slipped upward till she grasped my jaw, her thumb digging into my cheek. She held me steady, her eyes locked into mine. "Tell me you're mine. Please, please, tell me. I need it so bad."

"I've always been yours, Evie. Always."

Burying myself inside her, feeling her warmth wrap around me as she writhed, and moaned, and called my name was a re-birthing. The anger, stress, and fear was banished to a past life. Forgotten. Here, I was safe. Hopeful. The future, the unknown, loomed ominously on the horizon, but it didn't matter. When I was inside her, everything felt new, the possibilities endless, and the now was all that mattered.

✿

Fucking Evie till she couldn't walk in the space that would one day be her aunt's kitchen was fun. Piggybacking her sexy but limp and spent body home? Not so much. Though, I did enjoy the feel of her boobs pressing into me.

My broad, muscular, manly back must have acted as some kind of charging station as she made a miraculous recovery by the time we made it upstairs to the bedroom.

Promising me her fatigue guaranteed she'd behave, I was promptly dragged into the shower. I was hard as soon as I saw her naked, and she dropped to her knees and politely asked per-mission to go down on me.

"Umm, if this is you behaving, I'd hate—no, love—to see you be naughty."

I don't think I'll ever forget the look on her face as she looked up at me from the tile floor, pouting and blinking rapidly as the hot water stung her eyes and trickled down over her lip, then dripped onto her hard nipples. She gripped me at the base, kissed and licked my tip, then whispered against it like she was talking into a phone. "Please, Nate. I want to suck this beautiful cock and swal-low everything it gives me." I feigned resistance for maybe one-tenth of a second, then gave in, twisting her hair around my wrist, holding her to me and fucking her pretty little mouth till it was me that needed support to stand.

We eventually made it back to bed and had a leisurely cuddle before she left me to sleep while she went into town to pick up some food and supplies dressed as the sexiest snow bunny this side of Boner-ville—her golden hair in braids, a red beanie, a cute skirt over tights, leg warmers, and boots. It was hard to let her go, but as she'd proven in the shower, nothing stopped my Gidge when she was hungry.

After dozing on and off for an hour or so, still absolutely wrecked, and freaking starving, I took my position at the kitchen table to wait for the food.

That was where I was when the message that altered my world came through, slumped over the ebony wood table that probably cost as much as my truck and wouldn't fit into my cabin.

Gidget: Stay.

That was all it said. One word with the potential to change everything.

Gidget: Stay.

I must have read it a hundred times, searching for any meaning other than the one I instantly knew in my heart.

Gidget: Stay.

Evie, the one and only love of my life, was asking me to choose her. To stay.

I'd never even considered it. I was a farmer. It was all I knew, all my family knew. What the hell was I going to do in New York?

Chapter 41

Evie

MY JOURNEY TO TOWN BEGAN AS AN exercise to pick up essentials. Chocolate, toilet paper, alcohol—you know, essentials. After forty-five minutes of shopping, none of the above had been purchased, *but* I did find the coolest vintage store in existence. I bagged some cute pink heart sunglasses; a white, fluffy, bally '80s sweater; some funky roller skates; and a retro typewriter that didn't work but would look great in my room. Food was still on the list, but since I was on a roll, I hit a gift-slash-bookshop Finn had recommended for a new read and the tackiest Sleepy Hollow crap I could find for Nate. It was a mistake.

A friendly but overly attentive Scottish sales assistant incessantly rambling about Austen and Brontë had me trapped. While silently cursing how much I hated people and attempting to escape, I felt a light tapping on my shoulder. "Evie? It's me, Shannon. Remember? From the airport? I insulted you. You made me cry, then we ate doughnuts and waited for our boys?" My eyes widened in recognition. "Shit! Oh my God. Yay! You're not pregnant anymore!"

"Nope! I popped that kid right out. Practically flew out, she did. Only took seventeen hours and a third-degree tear!"

With that lovely image bleeding into my eyes, Shannon took the headless horseman coffee mug from my hand and locked me into a tight embrace. "I'm so happy to see you. I've thought of you from time to time and wondered how you were doing."

Struggling to breathe, I glanced over her shoulder and saw and waved to her husband, Sgt Ryan, holding the fattest, cutest baby—excluding Iris, of course—I'd ever seen. "Me too. You look amazing! And congratulations. She's beautiful."

After several cuddles with baby Ellie, we moved to a table in the attached cafe and talked all things New York, diapers, and Army life, but like a dog after a juicy bone, Shannon kept steering the conversation back to Nate. "How are things with you two?" she asked, wiping little Ellie's vomit off Ryan's shoulder.

I completely ignored her question and attempted a flawless change of subject. "So, you're here on vacation? Isn't Tarrytown freaking gorgeous? I could so easily see myself living here. Nate too."

Shit. I ruined my own diversion.

Her eyes dilated at a rate I was sure she wished her uterus would have when popping out Ellie. "He's here with you?"

"Umm, yes. He is. We're staying in a rental just outside of town. It's the first time we've had any real time away together. Will probably be the last time too."

"IImmm," Shannon hummed, frowning. "So, you're together, but he's still going back home? Are you going with him or doing the long-long-long-distance thing?"

I sipped from my tea, searching my brain for another diversion but came up short. "None of the above. He's leaving. I'm staying. And that will be the end of…that." I could barely finish my sentence before my tears began dripping into my half-empty cup.

Ryan was on his feet, ripping his baby from her mother's arms in seconds. "Uhh, why don't I take Ellie for a walk?"

With her hands free, Shannon drank the last of her enormous coffee, then leaned across the table and took hold of my hands. "You love him, don't you?"

I scream-cried rather than spoke my reply. "Yes. Yes, I do.

I love Nate. I love him so much I'm going to chuck right now 'cause I haven't allowed myself to say that out loud. How pathetic is that? I can tell you I am in love with him, but God forbid I confess it to him."

Slow circular motions were rubbed into my back as I freaked the fuck out. "It's not pathetic, Evie. You're just afraid of being hurt. Let me tell you a little story about Ryan and me. We'd only been dating for three months when he went on his first tour. I knew I loved his dick for sure, and I suspected I felt the same about the rest of him. I was quietly confident he felt the same, too. Neither of us had the courage to confess anything, though. I was very much like you, keeping my heart guarded, too afraid to commit to something I feared couldn't last. And he was too scared to ask me to wait for him. So, he didn't, and I didn't."

"So, what happened? How did you end up together?"

"Well, we said our goodbyes. He left for Afghanistan, and I thought that might have been it. Then, on his second day there, his unit came under fire. He lost a lot of friends in the blink of an eye and was lucky to escape with some survivable injuries. But it changed him, made him see how short life could be. As soon as he could, he called me on Skype and told me he'd never met anyone like me and that the first time we kissed, he knew I was the one. He almost cried because it was so perfect, and he loved me from that moment on. I couldn't speak because I was crying, and when he asked me to be his and begged me to wait for him, all I could do was sniffle and nod. Then we had phone sex. It was hot." Caught in the void between laughing and crying, I glanced to my left. Ryan stood in front of the cafe, holding his little girl in the air, blowing raspberries on her tummy. It was so easy to picture Nate playing in the same way with our own little girl or boy. As I glanced away, I noticed two fingers missing on Ryan's left hand. In all the excitement and confusion at the airport, I'd missed it. "Don't let fear ruin what you have with Nate. You never know what can happen. What twists and turns your lives will take. But Evie, if you think he may be *your* one, don't wait. Tell him."

"He is my one. I know it. And I want to tell him every time he touches me. I do, but I just can't bear the thought of leaving my family behind."

Shannon shrugged and took a giant bite of the Oreo doughnut sitting before her. "Also, just saying, why do you have to be the one to give everything up? Have you thought about asking him to stay?"

"A few times…a minute."

"So, ask him."

"What, right now?"

"Why not? This way, you have me here for moral support, and you don't have to look into those big beautiful brown eyes or be distracted by those arms or that broad, hard, firm chest as you ask."

"Geez, Shan. Sounds like you want him to stay more than I do. Since you're so keen, imagine you're me, picture yourself with him, and tell me what you would say."

"Duh. Picturing myself with Nate isn't hard, but telling you what to say is. Hmm…" She tapped her chin and stared at the roof in consideration. "I guess I would drag my eyes off his body, look into my heart of hearts, and tell him what I saw there…what *I* wanted. What is it that you want, Evie? Do you even know?"

With zero hesitation, I replied, "I want him to stay."

"There you go. That's what you ask."

Before I could wimp out, I picked up my phone and sent one word that had the power to change everything.

Me: Stay.

When I was in the supermarket, a lady at the register called her husband an idiot, and I nearly lost it. Inner grit helped me hold it together till I faced the cashier. But when that bitch had the gall to ask how my day was politely, I fell to pieces. I'm talking the ugliest of ugly cries—so much that my sweater was soaked.

All this because he still hadn't replied.

Me: Stay.

The words sat on my phone. Just staring. Hounding me. Unanswered like an invite to an all-you-can-eat buffet at Hannibal Lector's. I couldn't even pretend he hadn't received it because of the seemingly giant READ sitting beneath it.

Why hadn't the asshole answered? Surely some kind of acknowledgment was warranted. Even a, 'Let's talk when you get home.'

Then the panic-chucks commenced as I drove back to the house. I was pulled over on the side of the highway, saying hello again to the blueberry muffin I ate while talking to Shannon, when he replied.

Nate: Yes.

Crap on a cracker!

Making a miracle recovery, I changed into my new sweater before Nate saw-smelled me and hit the road.

Snow began falling as I pulled into the drive. Nate was waiting, pacing back and forth in shorts, his beloved Wallabies rugby hoodie, and flip-flops, his feet pretty much purple.

Before I could chastise him or even turn off the ignition, he opened the door, pulling me to my feet and onto his still-warm lips. "Evie, baby, I love you so much."

His body pressed against mine, the warmth welcoming as he ground into me against the car door. I stepped back, breaking the kiss, and tried to focus on the matter at hand and not the bulge in his shorts visible from space. "Nate, I…" *Just say it. Say I love you too!* "I…I…" With every stutter, hope inflated Nate's chest. His smile spread. He was waiting, wanting to hear those three little words. "I…need to know what you said yes to. Does yes mean you're staying in New York? For good?"

I swear I heard that bubble of hope pop. His lips quivered, but the smile remained, though the light that shone so brightly in his eyes had noticeably dulled.

"Yes, Evie. That's exactly what I meant. I love you, and I know you have reservations about coming home, maybe even some over my trustworthiness. So, if this is what it takes to show you that I'm serious, that Nate the Slut is dead and buried and that I'm dedicated to you, then I'm willing to do it. Home isn't home if you're not there."

I was lost for words and feared my goofy laugh and doofus expression bore an uncanny resemblance to Cletus, the slack-jawed yokel, one of my favorite characters on *The Simpsons*. "Jesus Christ, Nate, are you for real? That's a really beautiful thing to say. I'm kind of…I dunno what to do. I feel utterly unequipped to respond appropriately."

Nate dropped his head to my neck and nuzzled. "Just tell me what you feel, Gidge."

What do I feel? The ceasefire in my brain seemed over. The head honchos, the lonely, cranky, moody, virgin spinster full of fear department—the LCMVSFF—was under attack by the lustful *Sex and the City* crew. The latter demanded I climb Nate like a pole and slip on down, while the bitter bunch deemed Nate's affections worthy of an overly cautious response. I chose somewhere in the middle.

"I don't know how to express myself with words, a cruel irony since I claim to be a writer. But I *can* show you. Take me inside."

The speed at which Nate had his hands skimming the lines of my thighs, gripping my ass, and wrapping my legs around his waist was nothing short of freakish but welcomed. My body ached for relief. How could I keep craving this man more and more? Now that he was staying, could this last? Would it fade?

"Back to me, Gidge," he demanded as he buried his chilly face in my neck, nipping at my neck. "I can hear you thinking. Everything is good. *We* are good." I clung even tighter as his lips trailed toward my ear, then back down to my lips. That was where he froze. "Gidge, are those roller skates in the car? Oh my God, can I please do you while you wear them?"

"Yes! But not now. No time!" He carried me inside, and more

belly laughs were expelled as I worked on untying the knot on his shorts' drawstring. "Why is this knot so tight?"

"My ass kept hanging out of my shorts when I made the bed. I think I've dropped a couple of pounds with all the pleasure I've been delivering. Nate the Great is fading to a shadow."

"Okay, if I need to stop thinking, you must stop talking."

We'd only made it through the expansive entryway when Nate paused. "Love these sunglasses, by the way." He laid me on the soft, silk rug. "The sweater too. You're so sexy, Eves." Said sweater was yanked over my head, my skirt hitched to my waist, while my tights were torn from my body with a grunt that had me begging.

An annoyingly simple flick of his wrist undid the knot I struggled with, and he dropped his shorts and crawled between my legs. "No bra. I likey. Let's get rid of these silly knickers too."

Nate leaned down, kissed the lace of my briefs, and captured them between his teeth. His hair tickled my skin as he slid them down, revealing my wet and ready sex.

Soft, sensual silk caressed my bare back as Nate latched onto my breast and licked my nipple. "God, it's like bonking on a cloud," I sighed. Then I remembered why. "Shit, shit, shit. Nate, get off me. This rug is an Alexander McQueen. Jocie was obsessed with it and Googled where to get one. It costs, like, fourteen thousand dollars. We cannot fuck on this rug!" I wriggled to free myself, but Nate grabbed my wrists and pinned them above my head.

"Like hell we can't. You're not McQueen, but you are *my* queen." He winked as I rolled my eyes and tried not to laugh. "You deserve the best, and I'm the guy to give it to you…while in rented accommodation I could never afford."

With a growl, I was impaled. "So damn wet." Soft, sandy hair tickled my nose, and he collapsed to the crook of my neck and paused. "Just gimme a minute. This pussy is so perfect. If I move, I'll blow."

After defiling me *and* the rug, Nate carried me to bed and

served me yet another orgasm or three with his tongue before we collapsed into a light coma.

⁑

Unseasonably early snow thumping against the window woke only me. As he slept, I studied, memorizing the light flaring of his nostrils on exhale, their pinch together on inhale. His eyelashes fluttered and his lip twitched when I would teasingly blow into his face, and he cutely scratched his belly and mumbled as he rolled to his side to escape it.

Nate was so beautiful, and I was so in love it hurt to breathe. I treasured many things about him and wanted to convey them but couldn't voice it. "Maybe I can write them," I whispered. I watched his surf-tanned back expand in and out, kissed his shoulder, and crept from bed, slipping on his green-and-gold hoodie, and snuggling beside the fire.

Should it be a letter? A poem? I looked to my left. *A PowerPoint presentation? I do have my laptop.*

"Just start with a list, idiot. Think of Mrs. Fraser: *Pen to paper. Pretty it up later.*"

Nate,

♥ I love your hair. How it flops into your eyes when you lie down, when you tie up your shoelaces, or when you read, and I really love when you blow it away from the side of your mouth.

♥ I love that we went surfing. You spent more time watching me than the waves but still managed to catch every one you wanted.

♥ I love your abs, your arms, your cockiness, your pride, your work ethic. I love that you notice your mum has different cake tins for different flavors and that you work so hard to maintain and build on the traditions your dad established.

♥ I love that you cherish our childhood so much that you have my hanky and our photo in your pocket.

♥ I love how you take care of everybody, how you always say sorry when you fart, how you play with Iris and talk to her like the little mini adult she is instead of an idiot like a lot of people do.

♥ I love how you can say the most romantic, sexy things a woman could dream of, then come out with the dumbest shit I've ever heard a second later.

♥ I really love your bum.

♥ I love your daisy tattoo. And I love that it's over your beautiful heart.

♥I love that you make me cupcakes and clean the kitchen afterward. That you clean the shower and make the bed, even putting the pretty pillows you apparently hate back into perfect order while I'm at work.

♥ I love that you're willing to give up your life to come here for me, even when I was too scared to do the same for you.

♥ I love that you tell me you love me every day, even when I can't.

♥ I love how much you love me.

♥ I love you.

"Hey, get back here, Gidge. My fingers are feeling mighty feely."

Smiling, I quickly folded the paper and tucked it in his suitcase on the way back to bed.

Chapter 42

Nate

"NATHANIEL. I'M SURE I AM overreacting, but something's wrong with Finn. He barricaded himself in his room last night and won't come out. Scarlett is constantly calling. The poor thing is beside herself, as is Iris—oh, hello, darling." Voices dulled, like Jocelyn dropped the phone against her neck or into her palm. Even so, I could hear Iris's little voice and footsteps in the background. "Why don't you get yourself some breakfast? There might even be a little bit of that yummy cake left over."

I heard Iris's little, "Yummmssss," and then the clatter of plates and scraping chairs on the floor. Jocelyn stayed silent for a second or two once all fell silent, then returned to the phone, her voice dropping to a whisper. "Nate… It's bad, Nate. I could hear him crying, sobbing all night…and not Olaf-melting-in-*Frozen-Two* sobs. I'm talking *Inside-Out*-Bing-Bong-fading-level distress."

She may have been making light, but the unmistakable tremble of fear in her voice was jolting. Hopefully, it wasn't justified.

When my twin sister, Shelby, died at seventeen, so dark was the depression Finn fell into that we all feared we had lost him too. What Jocelyn described as Finn locking himself away, hiding from the world, was how he coped with Shelby's loss. It took years for him to find his way back to the light. Seeing him finally content with Scarlett meant so much to us all. The guy deserved a break—just not the kind that involved his heart.

Rolling away from the still-snoozing Evie, I slipped from the bed and hid in the bathroom, my toes curling as they hit the cold tiles. "Shit, Jocie. What the hell happened? He's been so happy."

"I don't know, darling. He won't say a word. I've tried to manage it without ruining your time away, but Iris and I need Evie back here. Now."

A selfish part of me considered saying no. That Evie wouldn't be coming back early. That Jocie had to wrangle Finn out of his spiral by herself. That Evie...that Evie and I deserved some time alone. That this damn call was proving Evie right.

They needed her.

But I did too.

A shudder of shame rolled through me, and I replied the only way I could. "Of course. I'll wake Gidge, we'll pack up the car and be home as soon as we can."

Jocelyn released a tired, heavy sigh. "Thank you, Nate."

Then she was gone, taking with her a fraction of the hope I'd been clinging to.

❦

We'd been back in the city for a few hours, and things weren't going well...for anybody. Particularly the innocent timber of Finn's bedroom door that had almost been ripped, kicked, and torn off its hinges as we hit stage four of Evie's let-me-help-you-dammit rage cycle.

The rage was as predictable as the sun rising in the east and setting in the west and loosely followed the path set by the traditional five stages of grief.

1. Denial - "I can't believe this might be happening again. It can't."

2. Depression - "We are just not meant to be happy. Love is useless. Life is shit."

3. Bargaining - "Please, Finny. If you just come out and talk, then afterward, I will take you to get pizza…or chocolate. I saw they had some Caramello Koalas at the Down Under deli. What about it?"

4. Anger - "Finn Austen, you massive ass. Open this door now, or I will smash it and your face."

5. Acceptance.

For my own safety, I'd left Evie to pace the halls when she hit stage four, so I couldn't exactly say what acceptance looked like. But from past experience, it would have been something like, "Well, I guess there's not much I can do. We just have to wait whatever the hell it is out."

While that was happening upstairs, I faced an inquisition from Jocelyn, who had swapped her concerns for Finn to doubts over my decision to stay in New York.

"What are you planning to tell your father?"

"Dunno."

"Your poor mum? Janet's going to have an absolute cow."

"Dunno."

"Well, what are you going to do for a job?"

"Dunno."

"What are you—"

I braced Jocelyn by the shoulders and dropped my head. "Take the hint, Jocie. I haven't thought this through." She rolled her eyes—a family tradition—and muttered something derogatory-sounding about men under her breath. "Give me a break, Jocie. Not everyone is like Finn-I've-scheduled-Iris's-school-lunches-until-2030-Austen. I don't walk around with a three-year plan in my back pocket."

"No, just a decade-old handkerchief and a stolen photo of the girl that lived next door."

I'd never been easily embarrassed. But that got me.

"What? How did—"

"Nothing happens in this house without me knowing about it, Nathaniel—except for whatever is happening with Finn, obviously. And *trust me,* there is no longer a plan in that boy's pocket. Scarlett's heated gaze incinerated it the first time she fluttered past him in a little skirt."

I scanned the room for Evie and leaned across the table. "Look. I may have acted a little impulsively by saying yes straight away. But it was the first time Evie had given me anything, Jocie. I had to take the chance. If I said no, I might have lost her."

Jocelyn's bottom lip dropped into the same cute pout her niece often sported as she sighed sympathetically and patted my head like a dog. "Oh, Nathaniel, you sweet, sweet boy. You won't lose her."

"You can't say that for sure, and I'm not willing to risk it. She's it for me, Jocie—"

"Yes! Yes, she is yours!" Before I could blink, she was pulling me into a fierce hug. I let my body go limp as she squashed my face between her breasts, giving her time to swoon, collect herself, and then release me.

"I tried to call the oldies first thing this morning, but they had just come home from the tennis club social, and Mum was a bit tipsy on Fluffy Ducks. With her dancing around the kitchen in her knickers, I couldn't tell Dad, so I told him to call me back when they wake up."

"She still drinks those things. Does she still call them Duffy Flucks after a few?"

"Of course. She's famous for it."

The head patting suddenly stopped. Jocelyn ran her hand down to my shoulder and pinched. "Boy, I love you like one of my own. But I tell you this now…you better talk to them and sort this out today. I will not have you dicking around my girl. Capisce?"

Had that dicking-around comment not been made by her aunt, I would have been all over it. But it was, so I shut my mouth. "Don't make me regret being cool with this, Nathaniel. You should never have agreed to stay before you talked to Barry. Both you and your mum have told me he's not up to running the farm by himself."

"He may not be, but he won't have to. I'm going to hire a manager like you used to."

"Nate, I ran multimillion dollar market gardens and cattle stations. Not a small-time family sheep, daisy, and macadamia farm."

"Why does everyone call them daisies? They're not daisies."

"Fine, chamomile. Like it makes a difference. You're dreaming if you think you have enough income to support a manager. And would Barry even allow it? I know he had a stroke, but—"

"Who had a stroke?" Returning with arms full of the wine from the cellar, Evie sexily marched to the table, dropped the bottles, and inspected us with hands on hips. Even with tired and puffy eyes from crying, she looked so hot. "Who had a stroke?" she repeated, her voice laced with suspicion.

Jocelyn leapt to her feet, "Oh! Is that the time? I have to go get things from…places." Then she pretty much ran from the room.

"My dad," I mumbled, swallowing my warranted fear, and nonchalantly picking up a bottle of red. "Ooh. This is a good vintage."

The wine was snatched from my hand. "Barry? Barry had a stroke. When did Barry have a stroke? Why didn't I know Barry had a stroke? Shit, I said Barry a lot. Am I having a stroke?"

In much the same manner as I had done with her aunt, but with an added boob graze, I braced Evie by the shoulders. "Come and sit, Gidge." I took the wine from her, placed it on the table, and sat in the chair. Before she could argue, I pulled her into my lap and rejoiced that, for once in her life, she didn't argue. She just tucked her head beneath my chin and sighed.

"The day after you arrived in New York, Dad and I were mucking around with the new sweeper harvester. He was so excited, like fat little Finn when he got some chocolate. Anyway, mid-sentence, he stopped talking and went all pale and limp. We were squatting next to the tractor, and he tried to stand and couldn't. He kind of rolled over and started to vomit. I remembered the signs of a stroke from when we did our bronze medallions with the lifeguards at school, so I called an ambulance straight away. We were really lucky. One was almost passing our place on the way back to town, so they arrived in minutes."

Soft kisses were placed on my neck, and Evie wrapped her arms around me. Emotions I didn't even know I'd buried within me bubbled to the surface. I struggled to stem the tears. "I'm so sorry, Nate. God, that must have been terrifying. Obviously, Barry is okay. I mean, I've spoken to him on the phone. He seems fine."

"He is now." I sniffed, wiping away what felt like acid rain forming in my eyes. "It was considered a minor stroke, but he was off his feet for a few weeks. Every day, he had these terrible headaches and would be sick if he moved too quickly. Couldn't ride in the car for long. And sleep…fuck. He could sleep twelve hours a night, be up for a few, then go back and sleep another five or six. Poor Mum was at her wit's end, but thankfully, he got better bit by bit."

"Why didn't you tell us, Nate? I would have come home straight away."

"That's exactly why I didn't tell you. I knew you would want to come home, and I worried about how you'd cope. Finn was worried too. He knew how homesick you were, and we agreed that coming back so soon would make it even harder to leave again."

A rapid chill hit the room.

"Wait. Back up."

Oh, shit.

Ominously, Evie slid her arms away and folded them in her lap. "Finn. Did you tell Finn about your dad and not me? And then you two knuckleheads pooled your pitiful mental resources and decided poor little Evie couldn't cope?"

"You're blowing this way out of proportion. Finn is my best mate and—"

"You told me I was your best mate, too. Did you tell me that just to woo me? To sleep with me?"

"Shit, no, Evie. No, of course not."

"I don't know why I'm surprised. Old dogs don't learn new tricks, after all."

The spite in her tone stole the air from my lungs.

"That's really unfair, Gidge. When Dad had the stroke, I really struggled. You and I hadn't been talking as much. I had no idea we could become even closer than we already were—closer than Finn and I were. He was the only one I had to talk to, and all we did was try and look after his little sister—"

That had her up on her feet and firing. "I am not his little sister! I am older than him, numb nuts. Yes, I am twenty feet shorter, but I am equal in strength, if not stronger, than Finn. I would have been just fine."

"But I fucking wasn't!" I roared. My fist slammed into the table and then shot back into my hair. "Jesus, Evie. I'm sorry that you, for once in my life, were not my first thought."

You'd have thought I had slapped her by the look on her face. "The worst thing is, if I think about it now, that's not even true. Everything was on me. I had to look after Mum and Dad, and the farm, and my fucking self. But as I held his hand in that ambulance, praying he would be alive when I got out of it, can you guess what I was thinking? I thought of nothing but you…you and your lips, and how they quivered and shook, and were red and puffy for weeks after your parents died. I remembered how sad you were. How physically ill you were. You said grief was the worst thing ever, and you never wanted to feel that wretched again."

"Nate," she sobbed.

"No, don't cry. 'Cause I can't handle it when you're sad. It breaks me, Eves. And then I'll cry, and I am a dude, and I am not fucking crying in front of you. I never, *ever* wanted to see you that miserable, to hurt again like you did with them and like I did when we lost Shelby. I knew your coming home would bring it all up, and I would do anything to protect you from it. The reality of your family leaving was already killing me, and I couldn't bear to make you sad again. Even if that meant I had to go through the scariest thing that had happened to me alone."

Just like I'd pictured in that ambulance, Evie's lip dropped and began to tremble. "You sweet, sweet, man. I am so bloody sorry for everything. For your dad and… Please forgive me for being so selfish."

My anger lasted as long as it took her tiny fingers to caress my cheek. "Of course I forgive you."

"How?" she laughed almost bitterly. "How can you say that so quickly?"

I pulled her against my body and clung for my life. "Don't you get it, Gidge? I am a complete blithering fool for you. You are it for me. I love you with every part of me. There is nothing you can do to make me not love you. You say you're cold and don't feel, but it's crap. Everything you do is love. You eat, breathe, and sleep it. You love your family, friends, writing and dancing, and work."

"Nate, I…I—"

I couldn't bear to hear her struggle to admit what I knew was true, so I silenced her with a kiss. "And I know you love me. And like I said, one day, you'll say it, and whenever that day is, I'll be ready."

Chapter 43

Evie

THE PENDULUM OF LIFE SWUNG SO QUICKLY IT could be hard to keep your bearings.

The home that had been so full of love and light just twenty-four hours ago was unrecognizable. Finn remained locked in his room, playing the saddest music Australia had produced on repeat and refusing to divulge the source of his doldrums. After thousands of calls, emails, and texts from Scarlett, I was none the wiser. Because other than implying he'd somehow made a fool of himself, Scarlett refused to say more. "That's Finn's story to tell. Just tell him to call me. Please."

Between fretting over Finn and overanalyzing everything with Nate, I had the shittiest of shit sleeps. When the haze-tinted sun finally rose the next morning, the realization that no part of me deserved the man that lay beside me came with it. Nate was forgiving, wonderful, and caring even when I had been an Elsa-level ice queen. My shitty attitude was going to ruin everything, and I had no idea how to change it. I felt lost. Useless. Undeserving and absolutely overwhelmed.

With my eyes hanging from my head, I left Nate and Jocelyn to take care of the big, giant man-baby, took Iris to school, and headed to work. I should have had more sympathy for him, but I was tired. It was just easier to switch my concern into snark. "Finn is a massive drama queen," I told myself.

And he was. Honestly, he could have been sulking over anything—from Scarlett using the last of his expensive curly hair conditioner to them breaking up. I hoped to God it wasn't the latter. That man had suffered so much loss. I dreaded thinking how he'd cope if he lost Scarlett too.

Iris was full of questions about her sad daddy on the walk, but I managed to answer most tactfully, and those I couldn't were silenced by buying her a smoothie half her size.

As soon as Iris was safely in the school gates, the heavens opened. I was drenched and mega pissed off by the time I arrived at the studio. Seeing Christian pacing the entry didn't improve matters.

"Good morning, Evie. Jody and I need a word with you in her office." Yep, the day's fate was sealed. It was a shit one...or was it? "We recognize your contributions to VAAD in the short time you've been here. Loyalty and perseverance, your unbelievable work ethic, and most of all, the compassion and strength you have demonstrated. Not many people were willing to do what you've done for me, Evie. Especially after I teased Nate like that. Your forgiveness has helped me stay sober, and your talent and empathy deserve recognition and reward. We want to make you an equal partner in VAAD. Will you consider it?"

My mood swing gave me whiplash. "I don't need to consider anything. Yes. I say yes!"

Both seemed surprised by my eagerness. "Are you sure? There is a lot involved, and not just work-wise. Financially too. It's a big commitment, and I know Nate still wants you to return to Australia. Before we do anything, you need to make sure—"

"I am sure, Jody. Nate and I have already talked, and he is staying with me in New York. I'm ready to do this. Whatever it takes. I didn't know I wanted this as badly as I do, but I really want it."

I jumped on poor Jody, wrapping her into a fearsome hug, then released her and shifted into an awkward handshake with Christian. I'd rather have chewed my hand off than touch him, but considering the opportunity he'd handed me, it was the least

I could do. "We're really happy that you're so happy. It will take a few weeks to get the paperwork sorted, especially with Christmas looming. Things may not be sorted till the New Year. But, unofficially, welcome aboard. Partner."

Walking—no, running—home down Sixth Avenue, I had the feeling that, for once, things were looking up for me. And maybe the good vibes would infiltrate Finn. I had a job I loved. I was going to be a business owner. Nate chose me, was staying in New York for me, and when I got home, I was going to tell him I loved him. My life was back to being a dream.

Within seconds of entering the safety and sanctity of our room, I remembered why I wore crotchety as a badge of honor and positivity could go get fucked: dreams *always* came to an end because no matter how hard you tried, there was always a rude awakening.

⁂

"Please don't cry, Mum. We'll be home as soon as we can. I promise…yep, the first flight I can get….yep. I'll make sure I wait for a Qantas flight… Yes, I know they have the best safety record of all airlines."

Nate's sweet and reassuring conversation with his mum went on and on. That wasn't the real issue. The issue was that while Nate was talking, he was packing, not just his things, but also mine, into the two matching suitcases on the bed.

"What are you doing? What's with the suitcases?" I whispered, waving to get his attention.

Proving he'd spent too much time around me, Nate shook his head and rolled his eyes. "Mum, Evie is home. I've gotta go… yep…yep, I'll get her to talk to you as soon as we're done… No, Mum, I don't mean sex. As soon as we are done talking and packing…yep, I'll give you the flight number as soon as I get it. And don't worry. Everything will be fine. It's just a bump in the road." He hung up, walked to me with his head down, and buried his face into my shoulder. "I'm so glad you're home."

"Me too. And I'll be even happier if you answer my question. What are you doing?"

He didn't move. He stayed buried. "I'm packing. We need to be at the airport in six hours. Unless you want to try and get a later flight."

"Why are you talking to me like I know what the hell is happening? What flight to where?"

"Where do you think? Home, Gidge. We're going home."

Wriggling free of his clutches, I put a few paces between us. "I'm already home, Nathaniel. I thought you were too."

"Yeah, well, things changed. Mum and Dad have pulled the pin on Fiji. Dad's sick. He started hurling and hasn't kept any fluids down. It's not another stroke or anything, probably just the stomach flu or mild food poisoning, but he's not as strong as he was, and Mum is freaking out. She thinks he can't run the place on his own after all and wants us home asap. She's bloody loopy, though. Even with Dad sick, she's so excited to have you there, Gidge. She's even discussing renovating your Mum and Dad's place for a homecoming present."

"Homecoming…Nate." I sighed and covered my face to hide the tears welling.

"Eeevieee," he mocked, disguising his fear and tears with sarcasm as he moved onto emptying my drawers. It was a tactic I knew well and had perfected. "We need to hustle, and I chose to start with your underwear." I dropped onto the bed and watched him select his favorite bras and knickers. "Ooh, these are new… and deliciously pointless. I could see everything in them, Gidge. They are definitely coming home."

"Stop and listen. I can't come back with you." Nate began to whistle. "Don't ignore me. We need to sit down and talk about this. We never really talk about anything. We fight then fuck, but we can't do that now. I'm not sure how often I have to say this, but if you need to hear it again, here it is one last time. Nate, I'm not—"

"Enough!" his bitter voice boomed through the room as he kicked the suitcases closed. "You don't have to say it again. Christ,

I thought once push came to shove… Evie, when I told you about the stroke, you told me you would have come home if you knew Dad was sick. Well, now he's sick, and now you know. You also know Mum's worried he can't do everything alone. Do that math, Evie. One plus one equals two bums on a plane to Sydney."

"Oh, and you just decided I'd be fine with this and started packing?"

"As you see."

I jumped to my feet, ripped the case open, and began removing its contents. "Don't do this. I'm sorry Barry is sick, but I told you from the start—"

Nate grabbed my wrist to stop me. "Give me a reason, and don't you dare—"

"I don't love you."

What was that old song, by the lady with the big hair and G-string…that line, *'words are like weapons.'* My stinging rebuke wounded Nate. I physically felt his heart tearing, watched his whole-body shudder, resembling the carnage of flesh with a bullet's fatal entry. But he remained upright, withstanding my barbed lies.

He shook his head in defiance…or denial. "Bullshit. I know you love me."

I stood my ground, staring into his eyes while wiping the liquid weakness from my cheeks with the sleeve of my pajamas, and jutting my chin. "I *never* told you that, and even if I did, it doesn't matter. My life is here."

A scoff of indifference inserted the dagger. "What, teaching toddlers to dance and being a surrogate mother to your niece is more important than me and your own happiness?" And those words pressed the rusted and blunt blade into my heart.

"I'm going to ignore the cruelty of your words because I know you are scared and hurting, but I need you to listen. I cannot and will not leave Iris and Finn behind."

Nate laughed and pinched his nose between his thumb and index finger. "Fuck. You do know Finn is a big boy who should be able to sort his own shit. And Iris is *his* kid, not yours."

"Fuck, yes, I know the big idiot will be fine, but Iris *is* mine, you asshole."

"No, Evie," he spat, stepping into my face. "No, she is not. She's your niece, just like she is mine."

I tried to step back, but he held me to him. "Why are you being such a cruel prick? I may not have carried and birthed her, but I have been with her since the day she was born, Nate. She *is* mine in every other sense of the word. I raised her. I stayed up, fed her, bathed her, and held and rocked her upright because she was puking all night with reflux. I was there when she learned to walk and talk. She is my heart, and walking away from her would be like losing a piece of me. Why don't you understand that?"

"Because one day soon, Finn will make up with Scarlett and leave to make his own home…a home that will most likely include Iris, *his daughter*. You need to make a life for yourself, and that could be done so easily at home with me. I'll marry you. Is that what you want? Because if that's what it takes, I'm willing."

"You're *willing?*"

He nodded as though nothing was wrong with the words that had just left his lips.

"You're willing?" I repeated.

"Uhh, yeah. That's what I said. And it's not the only thing. I leased the old town hall near the farm so you can run your little dance school. That way, I have what I want—you—and you have me, and a purpose, and you don't have to work with Fuckface anymore."

Never in my life had I *seriously* contemplated murder. Sure, with my level of people-hatred, there were always some low-level violent fantasies, but Nate looking at me like he looked at Finn when he tried to speak Mandarin was as close as I ever wanted to actually, for real, commit a homicide.

"I'm not sure how you think insulting, patronizing, and degrading me would be an enticement to leave the family and job you suddenly hold such little regard for. Nor am I sure on what planet you think it's okay to bribe someone with a business doing the same thing you just verbally shit all over. Or…or…where *that* is an acceptable way to propose marriage. But I assure you, it is most definitely *not* the one we inhabit. I promise you this, Nathaniel Myers. I will never, *ever* come back to Byron, and I sure as fuck will never, *ever* marry you." With that, I pulled the metaphorical dagger from my heart and plunged it into Nate's.

"You wanna go home, fine. Go home. It doesn't affect me one way or the other because whatever we had is done."

Chapter 44

Nate

"**F**INN! I KNOW YOU'RE IN THERE. I COULD smell you from the backyard. Open the bloody door."

A dull thud I presumed was Finn's forehead, whacked against the door, then his equally gloomy voice replied, "Leave me alone. I want to fade to nothing in peace."

"Jesus Christ, dude. I need to find Evie. She's taken off and blocked my number. I messaged the two people I knew, and they were clueless. I'm pretty sure Teddy knows and was trying to drop hints or tell me what I should do in some snobby, philosophical way, but I didn't get it. I shouldn't even care, but I can't leave without saying goodbye."

Grunts echoed through timber, along with giant clown footsteps moving away from then back to the door. The intensifying stench of heartbreak reached knock-a-man-off-his-feet levels as Finn swung open the door. "What do you mean you're leaving?"

"Bro. You look and smell like shit."

"Thanks, asshole. You don't look so great yourself. Cut the pleasantries and tell me where you're going."

I pinched my nose to reinforce the fact that he stank. "Dad's sick. I'm going home. I've got an hour and forty-five minutes to get to the airport, and only a man on the edge will be willing to drive fast enough to get me there on time." I patted his shoulder and watched the dust take flight. "I believe you are that man, stinky."

"Sorry. I know I've been busy wallowing in my own filth, but I feel like I'm missing something."

"You are. I'll explain in the car. Now, for shit's sake, take a freaking shower and make it quick."

Finn scratched his head and looked up and down the hall. "But what about Evie?"

I kept walking. It was time to be stoic or fall apart. "No time for questions. Tick-tock, mutha-fucka!"

Stoic Nate lasted seven minutes and twenty-two seconds into the drive. "I can't believe this is happening, Finn. She's really not coming with me." My hands trembled as I sipped from my fortieth coffee of the day. "Not only that, but after everything that's happened between us, she still refuses to admit she loves me. Now I can't even say goodbye."

With his own voice breaking, Finn delivered a stinging slap on my left shoulder. One so hard my head smashed into the side window. "Mate, I've got two things to say. One, being a complete cunt a few hours before your flight probably didn't help you on either of those things."

"Gee, thanks for the reassurance, *mate*." I tutted, rubbing my temple. "How do you know I was a cunt, anyway? Before, you made out like you didn't know what was happening. It sounds like you had your big ears pressed against the door."

"Uhhh, Nate. I heard the yelling. Shit, the Russians could have heard you yelling from their space station. That doesn't mean I knew that Evie took off or where she went."

"Okay, then, smartass. What's the second thing?"

"Nate, you, and me. Me and you. We're better off baching it like we did in the old days. Women are trouble…love is trouble. If you look at it one way, Evie refusing to say she loves you is a good thing. Trust me, it's better to make the break now, because every day you spend together will only tighten the vise-like grip she has on your heart till you walk in on her making life plans with her ex, and she refuses to marry you, and then it all explodes in a shower of vibrant, sticky, bloody confetti." His depressing tone was matched by the radio station Finn selected. Actually, Kurt Cobain was probably cheerier.

"Wow...that is terrifyingly graphic."

Unlike me, Finn had never been afraid to cry, and the waterworks ominously lingered. "Going home is the right thing to do... maybe not just for you."

"Please don't tell me you're thinking about joining me."

"There's nothing here for me, for us, anymore, Natey. Scarlett turned me down, just like Evie did to you. Us boys need to look after ourselves. Bros before h—I can't call my sister a ho. Or Scarlett, for that matter, because she is the most beautiful woman alive... Christ, I miss her." More sobbing. "So, yeah. Yeah, I am thinking about going home."

The irony was blinding. "So, we're both fucknuts that stupidly proposed. Evie has taken this giant, refusing-to-be-parted-from-her-precious-Finny, noble stance, and you'll ditch her the first time something goes wrong?"

"I'm not ditching her. Not for sure. Anyway, I don't know why you're pissed about it. Imagine if she comes with me. You'll be getting exactly what you wanted."

"What I wanted? Finn. Evie chose you and your daughter over me. Even if she did come home, it doesn't mean she's ready to let go of you and make a life with me. And no offense, but living the rest of my life following your stinky ass around town doesn't do it for me."

Arguing and Finn crying, intertwined with bursts of rage, continued all the way to the airport. An angry-sad Finn was nothing new to me. The guy was a control freak, even more than Evie, and Finn not in command was not pretty. In the end, all I could do was sit and listen. He was also shattered. As was I. The difference was Finn wore his heart on his sleeve. I could hide my emotions behind a facade of bad jokes and return to ho-life references.

The facade began to drop when we pulled into the parking lot, and Finn began hauling his massive body from the car.

"Wait! I don't want you to come in. If you're there, I don't know if I can do it."

"Couldn't you have said that before I paid seventy-five dollars for parking?" He was smiling, but tears still rolled down his cheeks. I had a lot to say to the guy, correcting his bullshit about the parking being one, but the words wouldn't come out. I still gave him some cheek.

"How are you not dehydrated by now? I swear you cry more than a Kardashian."

"I know. It's terrible, but Scarlett said she loves a man who isn't afraid to show emotion. Fuck I miss her. Did I say that already?" A massive and extended man hug took palace where a little precipitation may have been present on my cheeks too. "I'm so sorry things ended up like this, Natey. It's just shit. I guess us Byron Boys ain't living it up in NYC no more."

"Understatement of the millennium, Finny." I started to get out of the car but stopped. "I'm sorry, too, dude. I swear, I never wanted to hurt her. And I don't want you to be hurting either. We've all had enough loss in our lives."

"I know, dude."

It was awkwardly silent for a few heartbeats, so I made it even more so. "You're an amazing brother and dad, Finn, and I know things will work out with Scarlett. You just need to let yourself be happy. Shelby would want that. She'd be really proud of you." For some reason, I kissed said dude's forehead and quickly removed myself from the emotional aftermath by grabbing my bags and saying goodbye to another Austen.

Chapter 45

WEIGHED DOWN BY UNSHED TEARS, RAGE, a bottle of wine, and a bag of Maltesers so large I could call it home, I arrived at Teddy's front door. The wear and tear of the last few days were evident immediately. He was struggling, possibly more than I, and it was little wonder why. His darling Scarlett was a mess, and now I'd turned up looking like the undead. Plus, he was still dealing with an Asher breakup hangover. In the blink of a bloodshot eye, my own worries were forgotten. But Teddy refused my offered shoulder to lean on and seemed determined to ward me off with playful insults and sarcasm. Maybe that was why we got along so well. Two peas in a pod.

"We need Kylie and wine, Little One."

His face carried the regret of using Nate's nickname for me the second it left his lips, and he quickly displayed his high-level deflection skills. The demonstrably underrated *Impossible Princess* was set on his record player, and the questions began. "So, now that you're a co-owner at the studio, will you be in charge of hiring staff? If so, I hereby volunteer my services as your assistant. I can take photos—some of which I may permit you to see. I'm punctual and will try to curb the swearing should any minors be present. I need to find a new man, and what better way to do it than exploiting my power over someone's employment? I can just imagine all the hotties in their tights. God. I feel better already."

"I hate to break it to you, but not all male dancers are gay, and almost none would wear tights in an interview or class. That's performance attire."

"The gay ones might, though. That's how I'd weed them out." The straight face he was trying to hold broke, and we both burst into giggles. "And you're right. I shouldn't stereotype. Wanna watch some *Golden Girls*? I can't get enough of those old ladies calling each other sluts."

"Sure. But before we do, I need you to promise to talk to Ash. I know you really care about him, and I can see you're hurting."

"If I have to talk to Ash, why don't you have to talk to Nate?"

"Because Asher is kind, sensitive, hot as hell, and just a confused pup. He also lives in your city, which is a major advantage. There's hope for a future. Nate lives on the other side of the world. We have no future. He's also a prick."

"No, he's not."

"No, no, he's not," I cried, rolling onto my back, and shoveling a handful of chocolate in my face. "He's lovely and hot and made me a book, Teddy. Did I tell you he made me a book?"

"Yes, darling, you did. Several times. And I also told you I helped him make that book. Credit where credit is due, please." He grabbed me by the arms and pulled me into an upright position. "You'll be okay, Eves. We both will."

"Promise?"

"Ehh, sure."

"That's not very convincing, Teddy."

"Sorry, babes. It's about all the 'vincing I have left in me now. Come on, let's go laugh at some old sluts."

Once I had eaten enough Maltesers to feed a small nation, and laughed all I could at Blanche and Rose, I staggered home and joined Finn slumped on the floor of his room. It stank. But it was better than sitting in the cauldron of eye-stabbing memories that was my room. He was reading *Pride and Prejudice*. I was writing a suitably unharmonious ending for Stevie and Nathan, the erotic novel I had started working on what felt like a hundred years ago to try and unleash my inner hoochie. A new chapter had been added almost every day since Nate's arrival—never had the words flowed so freely. But it was time to toss this baby with the bath water.

What I believed was a diamond was merely glass. Beautiful but weak and fragile, it shattered under self-imposed pressure.

Fucking was one thing. Love was another. One that was not meant for me.

Time had lost all meaning. I had no notion of how long we sat there, spiraling in silent misery, until Jocelyn stormed in, pulling the cork with her teeth, and then slurping straight from a bottle of red.

"Alright, I've had enough of this! I've just taken Iris to Cole's house, where she will remain for the next few days. *We"*—she drew a circle around Finn and me with her finger—"need to get away from the city and chill the fuck out!" She screamed this, super chill-like, then drank again. "I have not worked my ass off to rebuild this family and interfere in your love lives, only to watch your fragile, idiotic hearts burn it to the ground. We will go away, we will drink, and shit *will* be sorted."

"Excuse me?" snapped Finn. "Who said you could take Iris to Cole's? Does everyone in this house think they can take my parental duties into their own hands whenever they see fit?"

"Yes!" Jocie and I chorused, but she continued, "You bloody well know that's how this family works. When one is down, the others pick up, carry on, and do what needs to be done. Finley. You're brokenhearted, but you've locked yourself in the room with no explanation and left us to puzzle out what happened from poor Scarlett's umpteen calls a minute. You're hardly functional, and you smell ghastly. And you, my darling Evie, are not much better. So yes, I made the executive decision. Get over it. Tough titties. Stiff shit." She disappeared around the corner and popped back seconds later with three wheelie suitcases. "The car will be here in fifteen minutes. My aim is to be so drunk by the time it arrives that I can't walk to the curb unaided. I've packed your bloody things already, so let's drink." She skulled again and retreated into the shadows.

❁

We'd been on the road to Tarrytown for maybe half an hour when Finn dropped a bomb. Just as Nate had done to me, he'd sprung a moronic proposal on Scarlett—one she had rightly refused. He'd then ignored her for days. I was sure if he and Nate shared a brain cell, they'd be dangerous. Just when I couldn't think less of my brother's emotional intelligence, he came out with, "I'm considering going back to Australia with Iris. I can't be here anymore. There's nothing for me."

Well, I was furious. First, I still couldn't believe Finn hadn't told me about Barry. And with these words, Nate's ridiculing my decision to stay with Finn felt fully justified. I wanted to rage, but Finn was struggling as much as I was. So, I tried to be reasonable and measured.

That lasted maybe three seconds before I slapped him on the back of the head and launched into a tirade. "You're a freaking idiot, Finn. Honestly, you're lucky she didn't knock you out. I would have. I'm tempted right now."

"Well if you're such a romantic genius who knows all the rules in love, why are you sitting here with us while your boyfriend is waiting for a flight to get away from you? Come on, let's hear it, Evie."

Finn winced, rightly expecting further violence. I didn't think either of us expected what I did, though.

I fell apart, sobbing.

After arriving at our luxury accommodation, the woebegone mood lingered, and the drinking commenced. My bags lingered by the door, abandoned after I lost my shit over the McQueen rug Nate, and I had made love on. I could hardly tell my aunt and brother that I was crying because that was one of the last places I shagged Nate, especially when they were both on their hands and knees, trying to remove me from it.

Eventually, I left the rug, and my grief and lovesick hysteria was soon replaced by rage. In a desperate attempt at diversion, I brought up Finn's earlier car truth-bomb and began throwing shoes. "I can't believe I sacrificed my life with Nate for you, only to have you throw a hissy fit and toss me to the side."

"For starters," he said as he ducked and weaved, "I'm not tossing you anywhere. I presumed you'd come back with me. And please, don't use me as an excuse for being a coward."

That was when the wrestling commenced.

"Maybe the alcohol was a bad idea." Jocie snatched our beers from the coffee table where they sat waiting.

"No one said you shouldn't or couldn't go, Evie," Finn growled as he placed me in a headlock and commenced noogies. "You may recall that *I*, your big brother, gave you *my* blessing despite the fact that *I* wanted to barf whenever I saw *you* two together. It's not my fault you didn't love him."

"God, you stink! When was the last time you showered? And who said I didn't love him?"

Finn released me from his vise-like grip.

"Do you?" he and Jocelyn chorused.

"Did you two rehearse that?" I snorted.

"Answer the damn question, Evie!" they argued, again, in unison.

Yes, I love him. I love every idiotic part of him.

Smoothing my frizz-ball hair brought me valuable seconds to come up with a more…me reply. "Well, I don't *not* love him."

Words can't quite describe the sound Finn emitted, but Jocie said, "Jesus Christ. I really did fail you two, didn't I?"

"Me? What did I do?" whined Finn as his phone grunted in his pocket. Iris had a habit of changing his tone to Daddy Pig, Peppa's dad. Finn hated it. I encouraged it.

Tearing at it with such aggression he almost ripped a hole in his jeans, he took one look at the screen and scoffed. "Speak of the devil. Nate says his flight has been delayed, and Eves, he's asked me to ask you if you found the things on your bed."

"What things?" I snatched the phone from his hands.

"How the hell am I supposed to know?" He swiped it back. "I'm here, dodging your junk punches and weapons."

My head spun to Jocelyn, and the braiding of my still poofy hair and pacing in circles began. "Did you see anything when you packed my bag?"

"Other than your hundreds of pillows? No. Sorry, darling, I didn't notice anything."

"Huh. Well. Whatever it is, it's of little consequence to me. Unless he's gone mafia style and left a severed horse head on my pillow."

"No, I saw the pillows, remember. There were definitely no animal heads of any kind. I wonder what it could be?"

"Like I said, I don't care. Not a bit. Nope. Couldn't care less… Jocie, can I take the—"

"The car is on its way."

※

A late-night snow flurry, mid-city traffic jam, and a nervous breakdown or two later, I was stumbling up the stairs and kicking in the door of my room. I saw it immediately.

In the center of my bed, and tied with an orange ribbon, was a brown paper package.

Pacing back and forth, I studied it. Considering. Pondering my next move.

I'd raced home from the city to ensure my room was animal-head free, and it was. I'd answered that important question and could go back to my family. Or to sleep.

Nothing was going to change my mind. There could be a freaking fairy waiting to cast a love spell inside that bundle, but my icy heart would remain unmoved. Stubbornness was my forte, and I was almost positive I was fairy-magic resistant.

It was decided. Nate and his stupid present could go take a flying leap. He told me he'd stay, and not even a week later, he was gone. It was over…if it had ever begun.

I sat on the bed, and the dipping of the mattress sent the parcel rolling toward me till it bumped my thigh. It was almost like it was teasing me, taunting me. Daring me. *Open me, Evie. Open me!*

Stupid present.

It wouldn't hurt to give it a light squeeze, I thought. The type of innocent feel-up I'd performed on the presents I'd found in Jocelyn's closet every Christmas.

For some reason, even with my mind made up, with my eyes closed so tightly it kind of hurt, I accidentally picked it up. Then, not at all on purpose, I opened it.

"Oh, Nate."

Inside was my handkerchief, the one Nate had carried in his pocket for years; the photo he stole from his mum, the one of us from Christmas; the stupid little notebook he had written the idiot count in right up to the day he left, the one I had no idea he was still doing; and a handwritten note.

Aoife,

I'm not going to pretend I possess your ability to convey emotion with written words. I guess I'm more Christian (not FuckFace Christian) than Cyrano, but here we go...

When it comes to women, I have made many, many, many mistakes in my life, and I have equally as many regrets. Traveling to New York on a whim to tell you I love you is not one of them.

Returning a broken, alone, shadow of myself is not the triumphant homecoming I'd envisaged, but I wouldn't change a thing about the last few months. For a moment in time, I finally got to call you mine, and for that, I would give anything. Without a shadow of a doubt, you are the most amazing woman I've ever known and the only woman I have ever and will ever love.

I have faith in you. In us.

If you change your mind, you know where I am. You're the boss here, Gidge. You're in control.

Forever your idiot,
Nate the Great.

The letter fell to my feet.

What have I done?

In my blind rush to get back to Nate, I'd left my phone in Tarrytown, but thankfully, Jocelyn was one of the few remaining people in New York to insist on keeping a landline. Having not remembered a phone number for more than half my life, it took three goes to get the right one, and even then, there was very little help coming from the other end. The two of them were drunk as skunks, and I knew I wasn't getting anywhere the minute Finn started quoting Shakespeare.

"For fuck's sake, Finn. Shut up. Did Nate tell you what time his flight was or not?"

"I'm not telling you. You're gonna do something stupid like try and stop him. And I only just finished reading the end of your story. Your beautiful heart *is* glass, Evie. If you go to stop him, it's only gonna get more shattered."

Jocelyn took command of the phone. "Don't listen to Finn. You've got an hour and a half, Evie. Go get him, darling."

❦

Regret bubbled in my veins as I sat in the middle lane of I-495. There would be no movie-style, grand gesture at the airport. The snow had taken care of that. I'd left too late.

The lady from the car behind me, Karen, had just escaped. The poor thing had tapped on my window, wished me a Happy Hanukkah, then handed me a hot chocolate she poured from a steaming thermos.

In payment for her kindness, she received a cry-fest of such magnitude that she was willing to sit in the car of a complete stranger for forty-five minutes and offer them comfort. Karen was possibly the kindest and most understanding person I'd ever met. She also gave her name a much-needed boost.

As the traffic finally started to flow an hour later, very little of Karen's love hypothesis remained in my brain. But one part did.

"They always say things happen for a reason. Maybe you just

need to wait a little longer to find out if Nate is your *beshert*. That's Yiddish for soulmate."

I didn't think I took it as Karen meant—who knew—but what if my negative-leaning was right? What if the reason was as simple as Nate and I weren't meant to be? Perhaps Mother Nature herself had intervened because, as ridiculous as it sounded, Nate was not my fate.

If I was truly meant to be with him, the snow would have cleared, and a Moses-style parting of traffic should have occurred. It was almost Christmas, after all. Wasn't that the time for a miracle? 'Tis the season and all that crap.

The entire concept was well and truly played out by the time I made it home. I was exhausted, over it, and already rebuilding the walls of ice around my heart.

Chapter 46

Nate
Eight weeks later

SUMMER IN AUSTRALIA WAS AMAZING, especially when you lived where I did. Daylight Savings provided oodles of hours to hit the beach, the pool, the shops, or whatever took your fancy.

Dank is what had taken my fancy in the painful few weeks of self-indulgent wallowing I'd partaken in. The absolute bare minimum had been done around the farm, most of which was completed half-heartedly in the early morning before anyone else was awake. It seemed my lifetime of extroversion was over.

I sought no one's company, and given my mood, no one sought mine. No one except Mum. After two weeks of near-constant cake deliveries, badgering, and reminders that I was home and it was time for my heart to join my body, I was finally unpacking the suitcase that had sat by the door. It was a stinging reminder of my time in New York with Evie, but I couldn't bring myself to empty it. I knew once I did that, it was really done.

But done it was, and I had to accept it. Evie didn't want me. I got it.

Just as I struck the dreaded pile of worn, unwashed boxers at the bottom, I found a letter from Evie.

Nate,

♥ I love your hair. How it flops into your eyes when you lie down, when you tie up your shoelaces, or when you read, and I really love when you blow it away from the side of your mouth.

♥ I love that we went surfing. You spent more time watching me than the waves but still managed to catch every one you wanted to.

♥ I love your abs, your arms, your cockiness, your pride, your work ethic. I love that you notice your mum has different cake tins for different flavors, and that you work so hard to maintain and build on the traditions your dad established.

♥ I love that you cherish our childhood so much that you have my hanky and our photo in your pocket.

♥ I love how you take care of everybody, how you always say sorry when you fart, how you play with Iris and talk to her like the little mini adult she is instead of an idiot like a lot of people do.

♥ I love how you can say the most romantic, sexy things a woman could dream of, then come out with the dumbest shit I've ever heard a second later.

♥ I really love your bum.

♥I love that you make me cupcakes and clean the kitchen afterward. That you clean the shower and make the bed, even putting the pretty pillows you apparently hate back into perfect order while I'm at work.

♥ I love that you're willing to give up your life to come here for me, even when I was too scared to do the same for you.

♥ I love that you tell me you love me every day, even when I can't.

♥ I love how much you love me.

♥ I love you.

I didn't know if she had meant to put it in there, or if it was an accident, but either way, it ended up in my hands as I lay crying on the floor of my bathroom. I read it over and over again in the two or three days I lay in the same position and only let it go when mum threatened to open the window and turn the hose on me.

She snatched it from my hand as I got up and was soon as busted and broken apart as I was. "You really do have beautiful hair, Nate," she said as she smothered me in mum kisses.

That note became both a lifeline and nail in my coffin. It gave me hope. I resumed my attempts to contact Evie, but the way she refused to speak to me or reply to any form of communication brutally dashed it the second it bore any weight.

Christmas and New Year's came, and with the passing of time, I increased my amount of time out of my solo pity party and got out of the house, mainly doing meaningless farm duties to keep myself as busy as I could. I caught up with friends a few times, but my heart wasn't in it. How could it be when, like mum said, it was still in New York?

Not caring if I ever surfed another wave again, I sold my surf-board and instead started spending my spare time at the Austen's' old place, working on their gardens. Mum had been looking after it since they'd been gone, but between Dad and the farm, her old neighbors' yard had slid down her list of priorities.

It would have broken Finn's and Evie's hearts to see it the way it was. And their dad, Russ, too. He loved watching his wife toil away as much as I loved watching Evie dance or write.

I spent a fortune on fresh topsoil and new, mature plants. Had an arborist deal with the overgrown trees, re-sowed the lawns, and redid all the garden edging, but my first point of order had been Saoirse Austen's flower bed.

Remembering Saoirse with such warmth and admiration had somehow infused into my blood, making me love her kids more. That woman was joyous and wise. Caring and smart. Pure sunshine. Evie always joked that she was her antithesis, but she couldn't be further from the truth. Those beautiful qualities were as strong in my Evie as they were in her mum. Evie just chose to hide them.

"Don't you think it's time to stop going there, Natey," Mum said one morning, her worried face leaning in the car window to give me a kiss. "I don't want you to spend all that time there only to be broken all over again when she doesn't come home."

"That's not why I'm doing it, Mum," I lied to myself and her. "I know Evie's not coming back. I'm doing this for Saoirse and Russ."

She'd smiled and nodded, then rustled my hair and sent me off with another piece of bloody cake. "You're a good boy. But you're getting too thin."

Every minute spent with the Austen ghosts was glorious torture. I was intoxicated by memories, high as a kite until it was time to leave, then low as they came when forced to deal with the emotional hangover when back at my empty home. Going back every day was the hair of the dog.

After yet another day of self-inflicted wounds, I needed a distraction.

This time, I chose actual alcohol. I was all out, so I braved heading into town.

As it always was that time of year, Byron was pumping. There were only two pubs that locals from my side of town would hit up in the summer. The first I tried was wall to wall ex-flings and school friends. I was in no mood for small talk, so I decided to go to the second, but that, too, came with a problem—a curvy problem named Polly.

I had no idea if she would be working. Her large family usually escaped town over the holidays, but I had a vague memory of her telling Evie that Holly, her sister, was heading home from Sydney.

Thankfully, I had successfully dodged Polly since I'd been home, and even if she was working, at this time of year, she'd be run off her feet. I could probably escape with a wave or a short and polite, 'How was your Christmas? Happy New Year.' It was a conundrum.

Beer vs Polly. Was my need for beer worth the risk? An image of Evie's love letter smacked me in the chops.

❤ I love how much you love me.
❤ I love you.

Yes. Yes, it was.

I'd successfully snagged a table in the darkest corner of the bar, and my dedication to refreshment went well for the first hour. I bumped into my friend Brendan in the restroom and managed to string together an excuse as to why I hadn't paid him a visit, but I bolted back to the darkness when he asked me about the lease on the hall. There, I continued to drink and was well on my way to oblivion when I saw—or rather, felt—her.

"Look what the cat dragged in." Her soft, amazing-smelling hair tickled my face after *she* dragged her boobs across my back, then whispered into my ear, "I heard you were back in town. And solo, too, I believe."

I stood and waved. "Hi, Polly. Bye, Polly." But she grabbed the waistband of my shorts and yanked me back into my seat.

"Don't be like that, Natey. We have always been good buds. I bear you no ill will. Even though you broke up with me when I was naked and covered in food." The guy sitting behind us almost choked on what looked like his white wine spritzer. "I only have ten minutes of my break left. Let me buy you a drink, then we can talk, and I'll fuck off and leave you alone for the rest of the night. I'm worried about you, Nate. I promise I mean no harm, but it's up to you."

"I'll have a beer."

Polly kept her promise. We sat and talked—well, she mostly talked—for the rest of her break, and then she was gone. The only time I saw her for the rest of the night was when I got yet another drink.

As I drank, I stared at my phone and the pain it carried inside it. Photos, hundreds of them, ninety-nine percent of which were of Evie, beamed into my eyeballs.

I stared at her for hours. She was so beautiful and looked so happy. She was damn sexy too, even when—especially when— she didn't look so happy. Those damn pouty lips and big blue eyes had my cock jumping with every shot. If only I still couldn't smell her, taste her, feel her skin beneath my fingers.

That hope I had when I read the letter was starting to fade. My birthday was coming up in days, but I held little expectation that I would hear from her then.

Finn offered little in the way of gossip. He was likely too scared of Evie's revenge if he told me too much. What he did tell me, though, was that she was struggling. That she was always sad and often cried herself to sleep. But he also told her she seemed happy at work, and that she was officially a partner in VAAD.

My heart was as full of pride as it was pain.

Around the time I could barely lift my pitiful head from the table, my friend returned. "Hello, Polly Waffle. Have you come to cheer me up?"

"Someone's had a few too many. Obviously, you haven't been coming to my side of the bar. I would have cut you off a keg or two ago."

"Don't be like that, Pol. I know I'm a few sheets to the wind, but like you said, we're mates." I hiccupped in her face. "Mates that have seen each other in the nude, and I'm sad. Hey, do you remember that time I asked you to fix me?"

Polly sighed and sat beside me. "Yes, Nate. I do remember. I remember it very well."

"Oh, that's nice. I think I remember it too. Maybe I need you to get me to ask if you'd fix me again because I don't feel too good. It hurts, here, Pol." I took Polly's hand and, to the best of my ability, held it over my chest, albeit the wrong side. "Can I tell you a secret, Polly Waffle? Evie broke my heart. She let me fall even more in love with her and let me think she loved me too, but then she wouldn't come home with me. That's why my heart is hurt. 'Cause Evie didn't love me enough."

I think I cried then, and I do believe Polly was almost crying too.

"You need to go home, Nate. I'm calling you a cab." Polly then leaned in and kissed my cheek. That was the last thing I remembered.

❧

A distant voice roused my sweaty, smelly body from slumber. "Nate! I'm here! You're not still in bed, are you?"

"Evie?"

"Nate?" it repeated.

It's a dream. It must be a dream. Evie's in New York, and I'm home alone and drunk.

"Nate, how could you?"

My eyes shot open. A blinding pain pierced my brain as a halo of blonde curls, blue eyes, and a white dress came into focus. "Gidge, you're here?" She looked like an angel, but she was crying. *Why is she crying?*

"Good morning, Evie." A second voice hit me harder, flooring me like a fucking sledgehammer to the head. It, too, was familiar, but shrill and unwelcome. It was also closer, much closer.

Shivers and an Arctic chill followed the hand I felt running down my chest. I turned in slow motion and found Polly, with my sheets wrapped around her body and twisted in her fingers beneath her chin, lying beside me.

"What the fuck, Polly?" My stunned face turned back to Evie, who seemed frozen. Her mouth was wide open, her fists clenched at her sides, and she didn't appear to be breathing. The only movement was one tear sliding down her flushed cheek. "I didn't know she was here, Eves. You have to believe me. Nothing happened... I think... I mean, I'm sure—"

Evie suddenly stumbled back. "Oh God!"

I thought my words had snapped her trance, but it was the graceful movement of my bedmate, who, naked as the day she was born, slipped from the bed, and stepped toward Evie. Polly stopped when they stood toe to toe, bit her lip, and slowly ran her finger along Evie's quivering bottom lip.

"Why don't you join us in bed, Evie? Maybe the three of us could have a little fun. I'll even let you be in charge, *Mistress* Austen."

The horrified gasp Evie released was a sound I never wanted to hear again, as was the expression of pain and betrayal possessing her face. "You told her?"

Like Evie had been seconds ago, I seemed incapable of movement, remaining fixed in the same position even when every muscle in my body called me to action. "No. No, I swear I didn't. I don't even know why she's here. I was drunk at the pub last night, and I remember leaving and walking home. I must have passed out as soon as my head hit the pillow. That's all I remember, but I'm sure nothing happened. Tell her, Polly. Please tell her nothing happened."

Polly ignored my pleas and continued baiting her victim.

"Come on, Evie. I know you're not a virgin anymore. What's wrong? Don't tell me it wasn't just Luke Bailey who couldn't get you wet. If you don't like Nate fucking you either, maybe you'd like it better with just me."

She leaned down and chastely kissed Evie's lips. "Unless, of course, you're still just a cold, frigid, little bitch."

Her cruel laughter was drowned out by the sharp slap of Evie's hand across her cheek, then hurried footsteps as she fled my room.

"Evie! No, no, no!"

Years of nameless faces—girls I could've been nicer to that I maybe hurt, girls I should've stayed away from and that should have stayed away from me, girls that I owed heartfelt apologies to—flashed before my eyes. The accumulated shame burned to my core, but right then and there, only one apology, one perfect, precious face mattered.

Only then, once it was too late, was I capable of movement. Though my frozen state may have been a blessing in disguise, as it was only when I fell from the bed that I realized that I, too, was stark naked. Dressing as quickly as I could, I watched Polly proudly pop herself back into my bed and snuggle between the sheets as if nothing had happened. I was so angry at her I could have screamed, but this was on me…well, maybe a little was on her too, but this fuck-up was my cross to bear. It was my accumulated disgrace, arrogance, and ineptitude as a man that led me, and Polly, to this point.

If only I'd been brave enough to tell Evie how I felt years ago, none of this would've happened. We could be married, living by the beach, surfing every morning, making love in the sand, whispering promises we'd keep forever. Fuck, we could be in the heart of New York or the fiery pits of hell—I wouldn't care. I'd go wherever she wanted. I would endure anything and more for her.

"Come back to bed, Nate."

Anger and a sprinkling of sickly-sweet nausea surged through me as I snapped my head back to Polly. "What the fuck is wrong with you? Do you have any idea what you've done? For months, I've told her I'm not the person everyone has said I am. The slut. The fuckboy. The cheap whore she couldn't trust. She was finally starting to believe in me, and now she must think… Christ, what she must be thinking of me." I slipped my shirt over my head and searched for my keys. "Fuck, Polly. I love her so fucking much. Why?"

My guest sat up straight, looking genuinely surprised but not the least bit remorseful. "So, you really do love her, then?"

"Yes, I really love her. What the fuck do you think I flew to America for? A fucking 'I heart NYC' mug? She's the first and only woman I have ever loved, and she is going to fucking hate me because of whatever sick little game you're playing. I may have been off my face last night, but I know I didn't fall asleep with you here, and I'm sure as hell that my cock was in no state to fuck you, even if I had wanted to…which I didn't." Keys in hand, I slid on my boots and clomped my way to the door. "You need to leave."

"Natey, please. Where are you going?"

"Where the fuck do you think, Polly? I'm going to find Evie."

I didn't have to search far.

Chapter 47

Evie

JANET MYERS HAD DONE A WONDERFUL JOB looking after Mum's garden. It was immaculate. Dad would have been proud but equally jealous of the lawns. I didn't think he'd ever had them so neat. There was no way he'd have let us play soccer out back if he did.

I was surprised to find the flower bed looking just as it did the day Mum died. Not that I could see a lot. My vision was completely blurred by tears as I knelt on the ground, picking daisies, snapdragons, and sweet peas.

Finn talked about this damn garden all the time, but he was lucky like that. He had the ability to look back at Mum and Dad and see the good things, the happy times. Reciting stories of weekends away, of Dad losing his shorts and mooning the entire beach while surfing, of Mum cursing a blue streak when I cut my own bangs as well as Bluey's, Finn's horse's, mane, and tail, was one of his favorite things to do. For him it kept them alive as well as filled the heart of the granddaughter they never knew with love.

My heart and I were stuck on the day they died. On the pain and sorrow. I remembered the bad things. The frustration my smart, teenage mouth caused Mum, and the headaches my silly drive to be independent caused Dad. Wallowing in the depths of negativity came so naturally I deliberately avoided thinking of them too often. Maybe that was why I clung to Finn so much. His memories nurtured my soul like Janet and her compost had done for Mum's flowers: all the goodness without the shit.

The dress I bought last night in Sydney was, like my life, ruined—covered in dirt, grass stains, and whatever else it collected while stuck in the car door and dragged along the ground on the drive back to my childhood home.

It was supposed to be part of the surprise.

I flew into Sydney last week with Finn, Scar, Iris, and Ben. It was Scar's and Ben's first time in Australia, so I'd been tagging along as they did the usual touristy things. We drove down the coast, stopping at every bakery until we reached Wattamolla. Finn was more vanilla slice and chocolate Big M than man by the time we set up camp and slept for a solid two hours before the kids dragged him out of his sleeping bag. We swam at the beautiful waterfalls and trekked through the national park before winding our way back to town the next morning. Yesterday, Scarlett and I did partake in a little shopping, and that was when I found it—or rather, Scarlett did. Hidden in Forever Vintage, my favorite store in Woollahra, was the dress my dreams were made of.

I knew what was coming the minute she held it up before me. She did too.

My ass was on the next flight to Byron. Despite my desperation to see Nate, it was after one am when I arrived in town. I was exhausted and looked and felt like shit after picking up some kind of bug or food poisoning on the flight, so I spent the night at Mum and Dad's, surrounded by memories and mementos.

It also gave me time to girly myself up. Turning up in a white dress after weeks apart was a play on a white flag of surrender, the white dove of peace, and I hoped it would send a subtle sign to Nate that if he still wanted me, I would be his bride someday.

I looked like a fool, and Polly made sure I knew it.

Waves of tears continued. I couldn't clear the image from my mind—her naked and taunting me as Nate, white as the sheets, doing a shithouse job of hiding his morning wood, lay behind her.

I could easily understand why he, or anyone, would sleep with her. She was stunning. Her dark hair laid over her breasts as she floated toward me. Her body was incredible, so curvy, tall, and feminine. She was every man's desire. Unlike me.

"You're still just a cold, frigid, little bitch."

"Mistress Austen."

"Stupid, gullible fool," I repeated, chastising no one but myself. I'd allowed this to happen. Almost made it happen. I manifested it, worried it into existence. It was equally my mistake. Any idiot could see what he was, what he'd been his whole life, but I needed to believe he'd changed.

Part of me, a really thick, moronic, and probably horny part, believed his declaration of innocence. He looked more shocked and enraged with every word that fell from Polly's mouth. But even if he was telling the truth and didn't have sex with her, revealing our intimate secrets, giving her that knowledge, that power, was an equal injustice and almost the bitterest of pills to swallow.

He knew how insecure I was, how I compared myself to her. How she herself had betrayed me with Luke and how she had rubbed in her relationship with Nate.

He also knew how hard it was for me to trust, to be vulnerable, to open myself up to him. The thing was, I never really did. A part of me remained closed off. I had never been anyone's favorite anything, but I was *his* everything, and it terrified me so much that I couldn't face how he had become mine too.

I never told him I loved him. I used my family as an excuse to run rather than face a future I knew we both wanted, because I lacked the courage he had always claimed I had.

I took the easy way out.

I wasn't brave enough.

I let him down because I feared how much I felt, and the fear of loss, of grief—of what it would do to me to give myself fully, to taste true and real and honest love and hold it in my hand only to one day feel it slip away—was unbearable.

Perhaps that was the cruelest of all our betrayals.

As though summoned by the devil himself, a message from Polly lit up my phone. Then another and another. There was nothing that bitch had to say that I wanted to hear. That was why I waited almost two seconds before I read them.

> **Polly: Evie Austen. You have beaten me in everything. School grades, athletics, swim meets, selling the most cakes at bake sales. You name it, you beat me. I really liked Luke Bailey, and when you stole him from me, it crossed a line. The joy I felt when he finally listened to me and dumped your ass was the ultimate high. As was bagging Nate once I realized how much he missed you. He told me a few times that he loved you, but I never believed he was capable of true love and fidelity. Not until today.**

> **Polly: I saw you drive through town last night. I'd just finished work and was on my way home. I'd called a cab for Nate before I left but then saw him walking along the side of the road. The cabbie had thrown him out when he puked in the car. It was a sign. I knew why you were back, and God was handing me a platter to serve the sweetest of revenge.**

> **Polly: Nate was in the car when I saw you, but he was so drunk he didn't notice. I had to drag him inside when we got home, and he was asleep before his head hit the pillow. That's when I went through his phone and that's how I knew about the sex stuff.**

> **Polly: We didn't have sex. I tried but he refused and was so drunk he couldn't have even if he wanted to. He loves you, Evie. More than I knew his ho-heart was capable of. I would say I'm sorry for putting you through this, but I'm not. I still hate you for Luke, but maybe we are even now.**

I didn't hear the car pull up behind me.

But I felt *him*.

"Gidge, you're here."

"Yes. And you've got some giant cojones showing up here after the shit you pulled. I shouldn't be talking to you right now."

"I didn't mean to pull anything. Polly was doing all the pulling…but not of me or my…you know. Shit. God that was a really dumb thing to say. I really am an idiot, but I swear I didn't sleep with her. You have to believe me."

"I do believe you."

"Don't be so stubborn. Please, just list—Wait. What? You do? Why did you run off, then?"

"Well, I didn't come to that conclusion immediately on seeing you naked in bed with Slutface, Nate. I was hurt and embarrassed. I made a fool of myself in front of Polly and thought you made a fool of me too. And because I hadn't read this then."

Chancing my ability not to kill him, I peeked at Nate over my shoulder, tossed him my phone, and watched the emotions ripple across his face. Even terrified and broken he was so damn beautiful.

"Bloody hell, Gidge. She's crazy…like, I'm talking bunny-boiling territory."

"That she is." I stood and dusted myself off. "You look like shit, Nathaniel Myers. But you're still the most gorgeous boy in the world." He also looked like he might faint.

"And you look fucking beautiful, just like you always have." He edged closer and rubbed the once pristine fabric of my dress between his thumb and index finger. "I love your dress. It almost looks like a wedd—"

"It was supposed to."

"Oh." The trembling of his hands intensified as his eyes filled with hope, and he uselessly tried to suppress his smirk. "I can't believe you're here. Why *are* you here?"

"I came back to weed the garden, but your mum beat me to it. What kind of fertilizer does she—"

"Please…don't play with me, Aoife. I've had enough games. Why are you here?"

"For you, Nate. I came back to say Happy Birthday, and to tell you I love you and—"

He swooped, capturing my face in his hands, and resting his forehead on mine. "Please, shut up and say that again."

"What, the bit about the flowers, or the I love you?"

"The I-love-you bit. Tell me again, Gidge. Please, I need to hear it."

I fisted his shirt and pulled him onto my dusty lips. "Nathaniel Myers. I love you with all my heart. I think I always have. And I know I always will."

He broke away, came for another quick peck, then pulled away again. "Sooo, just checking. We're *us* again. We're together? 'Cause you love me?"

"Yes. I think so." I nodded. "But I want to make sure of it, so I think I need to talk to someone about my anxiety, and I guess I'll have plenty of time for it 'cause we'll be separated for the next twenty years or so."

His face dropped like I hoped Polly's silicone tits would some-day soon. "Because you're going home? You won't stay?"

"No, not because I won't want to stay, but because I'll be in jail for even considering what I'm going to do to Polly fucking Hart."

Nate laughed and kissed me again—so hard he knocked me backward. He was there to catch me, though, placing his hand on the small of my back and dipping me toward the ground. It was so romantic, so sweet, and I knew he'd never let me go again.

"Evie."

"Yes, Nate."

"I've dreamed of this forever. Please, I really wanna do you in your room. Let me fuck you in your little white bed." Mr. Romance himself.

I shrugged nonchalantly. "Eh, okay."

Nate picked me up, threw me over his shoulder, and was carrying me inside when I saw his parents' car approaching. I was upside down, patting his ass and laughing but figured Barry and Janet would be okay with it.

The latter leapt from the car and sprinted toward us, waving like her head was on fire. "Sorry to interrupt, but we had to come and make sure everything was okay. That trollop Polly Hart told me you and her were back together and that you told Evie to piss off! I'd come to beat the shit out of you, but by the looks of it, Polly's lying through her ass again."

Sighing, Nate gave my bum one last squeeze, then gently placed me on my feet. "Don't worry, Mrs. Myers," I said, smiling and kissing Nate on the cheek. "Polly is…well, it doesn't matter what she is. Her psychiatric well-being is of no consequence to us. I came to tell Nate I love him. He loves me too."

"Well, of course he does, honey. Barry is the biggest fool in town, but even he knew you too were crazy about each other for years. Does this mean you're staying?"

Nate cut my reply off with a kiss, then answered for me. "We don't know, Mum. We haven't figured that out yet. All we do know is, wherever we are, we'll be together."

Chapter 48

Evie
A few weeks later.

"I CANNOT BELIEVE WE ARE ACTUALLY HERE. Like, pinch me please. This place is real."

"Hate to say I told ya so…but I told ya so. Google and I never lie, Gidge. Also, I'd love to pinch you, but I think my f- f-fingers are f- f-frozen."

"Oh my God, Nate. Look, there he is,—Captain Dildo himself!"

"Is it weird that I'm turned on?"

"Please, I would think it weird if you weren't. The old captain is hot as fuck. Let's go back to the hotel."

It was hard to believe we were actually here, but here we were. We had fucked our way around Canada for what was the coldest but happiest month of my life. We of course made it to Blow Me Down and various other oddly named places through-out the country—Spread Eagle, Saint-Louis-du-Ha! Ha!, Sexsmith, Finger, and my personal favorite, Climax.

Nate was relaxed and carefree, and I was too. It was hard not to be with that level of sex-induced endorphins swimming through our veins.

And it wasn't just that. As much as we were enjoying having fun together, like so many other backpacking couples we met on our trip, we felt safe and secure in the knowledge that we were going home together. We even talked about marriage, and for once, I didn't break out in hives, panic-chuck, or run. I'd simply said that yes, that's what I wanted too.

Dildo was the last place on our tour, and Nate had promised I wouldn't be able to walk out of the place.

As Nate kissed me and kicked the door of our room open, his phone started ringing in his pocket. "Ignore it. Ignore it. I need to be railed, and I need it now."

"God, you're awesome." The meddlesome ringing stopped but started again just as Nate's pants hit the floor and my legs wrapped around his waist. "I better check it, Gidge. Just in case something's wrong at the farm."

"If that's Finn, and he's not half dead, I'm gonna kill him."

Nate lunged for the phone on the floor. "Your threats of violence make me so fucking hard."

A loud groan echoed through the room. "Wow, guys. I really didn't need to hear that."

Tears poured down Nate's cheeks. "Shit. Finny. Sorry, mate. I must have put it on speaker."

"You don't sound sorry. Also, don't ever call me mate again. Now tell me where the spare key to the back shed is. The guy's here to fix the quad bike, and I can't find it. And before Evie asks, yes, I called Barry, and he couldn't remember."

"It should be on the same keyring as the shearing shed. It's a really old, brass-looking one, looks almost rusty." Key-jangling sounds could be heard and then a triumphant, "Ah-ha!"

"Got it?" Nate asked, dropping the phone on the bed, and pulling his shirt over his head from the back the way all hot guys seemed to do.

"Got it. Thank you, and let's never speak of this aga—"

"Yep, gotta go do your sister now, dude. Later."

I could hear Finn whining before the phone became muffled by my ass. "God, I thought he was never going to shut up." I pulled Nate on top of me, then flipped him onto his back. I straddled his chest, then leaned back and gave his thigh a good smack.

"I'm going to ride your face now, and you're going to eat me out till I scream this place down."

"Yes, yes, Miss Evie."

"Good boy."

Before sliding into position, I slipped the straps of my bralette over my shoulders. It was Nate's favorite by an Aussie designer, Viktoria & Woods. It was soft, subtly orange, which I loved, but frilly and so sheer Nate could see my nipples from the other side of the room. Luckily for both of us, he was beneath me, and distance wasn't an issue. I left it, preferring that he pull it down over my breasts with his teeth.

"Ooh, that's a bit rough, Natey," I said with another slap to his thigh. "You don't want to rip our favorite. Slow down. We have all day."

"You might have all day, but if I don't get that wet little pussy on my tongue in twenty seconds, I'm gonna blow myself down prematurely."

My eyes rolled to the back of my head. The way this boy made me melt with his filthy mouth would never get old. I slid forward, leaving a trail of moisture on Nate's chest, rejoicing in the feel of his stubble caressing my tender flesh before finally setting myself down on his parted, waiting lips.

One stroke of his tongue had me crying his name and laughing breathlessly at how easily this man could bring me undone. I stroked my fingers up Nate's cheek, feeling the thin layer of sweat already building, before grabbing hold on either side of his ears and rocking, riding his face. Nate teased my clit, side to side, back and forth, then dragged his tongue lower to my pussy and fucking inside me. I lifted up a little to give him greater access, almost collapsing back down when he hit *that* spot. I rose, grinding away, relishing the feel of his grip on my ass, of his fingers digging into my flesh.

His speed increased, and it felt incredible, but I needed him back on my slit, so I dropped my ass and rolled my hips back. His tongue swept forward, and bam!

"Oh, Nate. I'm gonna come."

"Evie, my God. Yes, baby. You taste so sweet. Come like my fucking queen."

He tickled with the tip of his tongue fast then slow, bringing me to the edge, then pulling me back till I could take no more. Nate continued to moan beneath me. I let go of his hair, ran my hands over my breasts, up my neck, and into my hair, tugging and pulling, and I rocked and rocked. I was a complete wreck, my thighs shaking, gripping tighter and tighter as my pussy did the same. One hand drifted back down to my breast, squeezed, and pulled at my nipple, then traveled to his throat. I could feel his pulse pounding away, increasing as I squeezed tighter and tighter. I looked down, and my eyes met Nate's as he shook his head frantically from side to side, tormenting my clit, and I throttled him.

"I love you, Nate. You're mine. I love you. I'm coming!" I screamed so loud the entire population of Dildo would have heard me, but I was sure it was nothing new. Nate kept licking, and I kept coming in waves that rolled through my whole body. I slowly began to come down, and before I could think, Nate had his hands on my waist and was lifting me off, flipping me onto my elbows and knees, and pulling my ass up into the air.

"Please tell me you don't need more time, because I have to fuck you right now."

I looked over my shoulder and nodded. "Please."

Nate smiled. Licking his lips, he inserted two fingers deep inside me and tickled my tight, puckered hole with his thumb. My arms gave way, and my face hit the mattress. I remained looking over my shoulder as Nate withdrew his fingers, displaying my wetness, then licking it off.

"Had to have one last taste." He impaled me then, driving me forward till my head hit the headboard. "Lord, nothing feels like you do, Evie. Nothing makes me feel more alive, more like a man, than fucking this tight, little, perfect, pretty cunt."

"Nate!" I screamed again, and another climax tore through me.

"Can't stop," Nate growled.

"Don't stop. Fill me up, baby."

"Jesus, Evie." He pumped hard, four times. Each time wilder, each more animal. On the last push, he gripped my hips and pulled me tightly against him, holding me still as he did just as I asked, rocking into me, filling me with everything he had till he collapsed on top of me. "Dildo for the win!"

⁂

Nate was gone when I woke the next morning. I hated waking up without him.

After our reunion in Byron, I'd stayed for two weeks, then returned home to organize things with Jody and Christian, set myself up with a therapist I could do video appointments with while on the road, then flew on to meet Nate in Vancouver. It was our third reunion, and we promised each other—as we classily fucked in the airport bathroom—that we would not spend more than a few days apart ever again.

The timing of our impromptu backpacking vacation had been perfect. Finn and Scar were desperate to stay in Australia longer, and we were busting to leave it. They remained on the farm, using it as the base for their travels and helping Barry and Janet whenever they needed and supplying them with quality time with their beautiful granddaughter.

"Nate. Babe, are you here?" When no answer came, I rolled from bed and walked naked to the bathroom. We were staying at the most beautiful property called the Doctor's House. It was like something from a movie. The rest of our stays had mostly been youth hostels and cheap Airbnb's, but Nate had insisted for our last few nights, we would be in luxury. We had our own guest house, that was designed for families, all to ourselves. It overlooked the beautiful Trinity Bay that Dildo was positioned on—snort—had two beautiful bedrooms upstairs, the main with a sweeping balcony, huge bath, and the comfiest bed ever. Two more bedrooms were tucked away downstairs and yet another balcony with a massive hot tub we had sex in the minute the sun went down.

I stuck my head in the bathroom, hoping to find him naked and slippery in the shower. But no. After a quick pit sniff, I decided it was probably best to take one myself.

Taylor serenaded me as I scrubbed myself raw, and I sang along, thinking about my own king of my heart and how far we'd come.

"Nate, are you back yet? I hope you brought some food," I bellowed as I left the bathroom wearing the ridiculously soft robe gifted to us by the hotel when Nate fibbed and told them we were on our honeymoon.

I knew something was up the minute I stepped back into our room. Rose petals had appeared where there were no rose petals before. I turned to my left, to the bed, and there laid a clear garment bag. Inside it was the most beautiful, vintage, lace gown I'd ever seen. Beside it was a pair of heels, a floral headband, and a note.

Wear me. Please.

"Evie, are you decent?"

I know that voice. I know that posh little accent.

"Scarlett?"

A mop of crazy red curls flashed before my eyes, and my heart seized. "Hi, Eves. Surprise!"

"What the hell are you doing here? How are you here? Is Finn here? Am I here? She stepped into the room, falling over a chair after three paces. "You can look up, Scar." I laughed, helping her to her feet. "I'm wearing a robe."

"Surprise!" she shouted again.

"Yes, we have established it's a surprise. To quote Clarke W. Griswold, '*If I woke up tomorrow with my head sewn to the carpet, I wouldn't be more surprised than I am now.*' We talked to Finn yesterday, and he was at the farm."

"No, he wasn't. He was ten minutes away at our hotel. Sorry for fibbing."

Disbelief stole my words before I could form them. I just stood there, my eyes switching between the dress and Scarlett, while she seemed caught between wanting to hug me and being scared for her life. Laughter eerily similar to my aunt's wafted into the room from downstairs "Well, are we just going to stand here like idiots and pretend Jocie isn't outside, or are you going to tell me why you're here and why there is a wedding-looking dress on my bed."

"Because it's your wedding day—please don't hurt me," she spat out.

"What? My what?"

Teddy and the still-laughing Jocelyn burst in. "Surprise!" Within seconds, the room was a flurry of tears and hair dryers and boob tape. My heart was racing, possibly not as much as Scarlett's, who still looked terrified that I would rip her eyes out. Six months prior, I might have, but for some reason, I didn't choose violence. I chose affection.

"Please hug me and tell me what he's done." Three bodies clung to mine, holding me up and infusing me with more love than I thought my heart was capable of feeling.

"Our Nathaniel has organized your wedding day. You should see downstairs, darling. It's incredible. He's really gone all out," whispered a crying Jocelyn into my hair. "I know you like to be in control, darling. But he's worked so hard and loves you so much. He wanted to surprise you. Please tell me you're happy."

My reply came without a second's delay. "Of course I'm happy. Today I'm going to marry my best friend."

As I walked down the stairs of our suite, my heart—time itself—stopped.

Never had I seen such a gorgeous man, and never had I felt more gorgeous.

He was wearing a tux, looked as though he'd somehow snuck in a fresh haircut, and was beaming. My hair was pinned up, but a few loose curls, a mixture of design and tempestuousness, sprung free, framing my face.

The gown Scarlett and Teddy helped Nate pick, via what was apparently the most chaotic video call ever, was so me and fit like a glove, showing off every curve that Nate loved, and had kissed, so much. My makeup was light, natural. Me.

With the sheer terror I felt in my veins lightened when I finally took the last step, Nate broke out into a dazzling smile, yet again ceasing the pounding in my chest.

Then my view morphed from Nate's face to his mum's as she kissed me repeatedly. "You look stunning, dear. I'm so bloody happy and proud, Evie. And I want you to know, whatever happens after this, wherever you and Nate decide to settle, Barry and I will be fine. We just want the two of you to be happy." She kissed my cheek, then tutted as she rubbed it. "Now I've gotten my lipstick on you. Gah, I can't believe we're here. All those weeks Nate struggled, working himself to the bone at our place and at yours too. I never dreamed it would—"

"What? Did you and he work at our place?" I interrupted.

"Saoirse's garden. Didn't he tell you? He was looking after it when he came home. Spent hours there, cleaning it all up, re-sowing the lawns, and reviving the flower beds. I kept telling him to stop and rest, but he wouldn't. He wanted it to be perfect for you. Just like he did today."

"He…did?" Nate had replanted my mum's garden. Had spent hours toiling at my old home after working all day on his own, and he let me believe it was Janet.

Even when he didn't know if I'd ever see it. Even though I'd broken his heart. He still did it.

Nate cleared his throat. "Mum, could you let go of Evie now? I've kind of got something to ask her."

"Oh, yes, yes. I'm sorry. It's just…I'm just so happy." After a final hug and kiss, I was released and sent onward.

"I can't believe you did this. It's perfect," I whispered when I stood at his feet.

"You're perfect. You look like an angel." He looked around

the room, leaned into my ear, then whispered, "One I can't wait to defile later."

"Christ," muttered Finn, who was already a puddle of tears. "You need to work on your whispering, Nathaniel."

I accepted Nate's outstretched, trembling hand and was immediately pulled into a deep kiss I would never have wanted to end…if I wasn't about to become his wife.

He then dropped to one knee.

"It's taken me twenty years, a million silent prayers, and countless mistakes. I know I am doing this the wrong way round, but somehow that makes it even more us."

"Nate."

"Aoife Mary Austen. I have loved you my whole life. You're my best friend, my everything, and I can't wait to share every damn second of my life with you. Will you marry me?"

"Yes, Nate. A thousand times, yes."

Epilogue

Two years later

ON THE LAST DAY OF SUMMER, AND WITH A smile I'd worn with more regularity in the past two years than any other time during my life, I stood and stretched. My weary bones cracked after hours of writing in the study that afforded me a million-dollar view over the Pacific Ocean—and of the loves of my life.

Daddy's little shadow, Brittney, wriggled on the ground, awkwardly slipping into her tiny wet suit, then grabbing her board and running to the water. Her adoring audience—Nate, her daddy; her cousins, Iris, Ben, and their baby sister, Shelby; and finally, Brittany's own sister, her twin sister, Emily—applauded as she paddled her boogie board out to the shallows, then nailed the first wave back to shore.

Our fraternal twins each took after one of their parents more than each other. One blonde, one brunette, one considerably smaller, and at almost two, it was clear their personalities were equally opposed. Britty was an outdoorsy extrovert who loved mud and dirt and adventure, while Em was more inclined to creative pursuits—dance, drawing, writing. Like her sister, Emily also loved the water but was too busy coloring to join in. The lower half of her body was also buried in sand.

"You home, Eves?" a raspy, tired voice traveled up the stairs.

"I'm in the study, Finn. Don't bother coming up. I'm on my way down."

I found my hungover, sunburnt brother in the kitchen, reaching for an ice-cold hair of the dog from the fridge. He and Nate had a two-man farewell slash early birthday party last night, and to say he was looking a little worn out would be an understatement.

"Don't let Scarlett catch you with that." I smirked, nodding to the beer. "Let me quote you from last night. 'I promise, Red. No more booze, Red. I'm doing a dry July, Red.'"

"Did I? When? I don't remember that."

"Since you didn't remember it was January, not July, that doesn't shock me." I hit Finn in the back of his head and rejoiced in the shudder of pain and forehead grasp it provoked. "It was around two am, when she was trying to get you out of the bathtub you had decided to sleep in."

"I'm surprised I could fit in your bathtub. It's smaller than ours."

"It was more surprising that Nate fit in there with you."

"Hey, if a guy can't share a tight bathtub with his best bro to celebrate their joint almost-thirtieth birthday, when can he?" Finn's and Nate's birthdays were only days apart, so he dove into his leftover cake sitting on the counter and looked around the room. "Where is my birthday bath time pal, anyway? Bet the party-pooper is still in bed."

"I'd hate to burst your bubble, father, and idiot of the year, but you're only twenty-seven. As for Nate, he's on the beach, watching over his two and *your* three children."

"Shit. The kids are here?" Finn wandered to the chalkboard Nate had hung in our kitchen and added to the idiot tally he and Nate thought was a hilarious addition to the new house we built. It was our dream home, still on Myers land but on the crest of a hill and closer to the water. It was also farther away from his parents and, despite what Finn said, had a ginormous bathtub—two, actually.

"Yes, we are, Dad. Nice to know you care." Iris wandered in, blowing her gorgeous mop of strawberry curls from her eyes, and carrying baby Shelby. "Mum dropped us off two hours ago. You were asleep on the couch when we left. She tried to wake you up, but you just rolled over and flashed us all your butt. Almost ten-year-old kids shouldn't have to see their dad's bare butt."

"Sorry, kiddo." Finn winced as he put his beer down, took Shelby into his arms, and kissed Iris's head. "Uhh, where's your mum now?"

"Don't worry, Dad. She's gone into town to get some lunch. She'll be back soon, though, so you better finish your beer."

Much to Finn's displeasure, the room exploded in sound as the remaining mini members of the Austen/Myers clan arrived. Like a honey to a bee, Nate headed straight to me, wrapping his arms around my waist, and planting a kiss on my lips. "You taste all salty," I whispered, kissing him right back.

"Let's go wait on the porch, kids," Finn sighed. "I'm already having enough trouble keeping my guts where they belong without seeing this."

With the house clear of minors, Nate hoisted me onto the kitchen island and stepped between my spread legs. "I feel like shit, Gidge. Since we're alone, why don't you sneak into the shower with me and make me feel better."

"Alone? Nate, there are six legitimate children and one giant man-child in the house. What part of alone don't you understand?"

Nate's eyes rolled around his head as he did the math. "Six kids? Iris, Ben, Shelby, Em, and Britty. Who's the sixth?"

I bit my lip and patted my belly. "This one."

The fifteen or so beers Nate had consumed over the past twenty-four hours had slowed his thinking considerably, and it was fun to watch the last puzzle piece slip into place. "Evie?" he said disbelievingly. "Are you…? Are we…?"

"Yep. I'm pregnant, Nate."

"EVIE, I LOVE YOU SO MUCH, AND MY SUPERMAN SPERM HAS KNOCKED YOU UP AGAIN! YESSSSSSSS!"

Alone or not, being kissed to within an inch of sanity had my legs wrapping around Nate's waist of their own accord. My hips seemed to have a mind of their own too, and they began to grind against his rapidly increasing hardness as he carried me upstairs. "We need to celebrate, Gidge. And you know fucking is my favorite way to celebrate."

"I know. I'm pretty sure what we're celebrating was conceived over Christmas."

Kicking the bedroom door open, I was gently laid, not thrown as per usual, on the bed. I watched on as Nate ran back to the door, locked it, then sprinted to the windows and drew all the blinds. He was stark naked and practically drooling by the time he made it back to bed. Unsurprisingly, so was I. "Is it weird that I am so turned on by you being pregnant? I know it's super Neanderthal-caveman-like, but fuck. Knowing I have the power to put a life inside you is the ultimate aphrodisiac."

"Snort. You sure do think a lot of yourself, don't you?"

"Yep, you do too. That's why I knocked you up like a fucking champ." We kissed in between trading insults. A good verbal tussle was always a fun build-up to the between-the-sheets kind. The jibes ended, though, when Nate stopped fucking around with what he called, "the world's most beautiful tits," and started fucking the quote,

"tightest, wettest, knocked-up pussy ever."

My legs were whipped over Nate's shoulders, and he rose to his knees and started pounding away. At this angle, his cock and hair teased my clit with every thrust. "God, Nate. I will never tire of you and your filthy mouth. Or how you rail me with absolutely no regard to my well-being."

"Gidge, we have two-year-old twins. We have no time for health and safety precautions. Only bonking."

Nate leaned down and took a hard and tender nipple into his mouth, I winced and writhed beneath him, my body becoming even wetter. "I love pregnant boobs. God, they're so big. How did I not notice? I want to bury myself between them for the next nine months. Ohh, can I fuck them? Please let me fuck them."

"Nine? Nate, I'm almost two months in. You have seven months tops with these puppies before they belong to the baby. Enjoy them while you can. And yes, you can fuck them, but later." Nate's lips moved to my neck and bit down, stinging and reddening my flesh. He continued to push inside me, each time deeper, harder. Even after all this time together, his prowess never failed to amaze me. I was so close already.

A door slammed downstairs, and we both froze.

"It's all good. It's all good. There are no footsteps," I whispered. I pulled my legs from Nate's shoulders and flipped, resting on my hands and knees, and wagging my ass in his face. Do me from the back."

"Damn, I love you, Mrs. Myers." My hair was wrapped around his wrist, my hips pulled higher up into the air, and my ass slapped. "Just let me do this real quick." I couldn't see what he was doing, but I certainly felt his tongue lick me back to front, tickle and pull and suck on my clit.

Another bang echoed downstairs, then a voice—or two, or three.

"Nate, hurry, please."

Desperate to ease the ache, find my release, and feel the power of Nate's, I collapsed forward, slid one hand beneath me, and began rubbing my soaked flesh. "Please, Nate. Please. I want to come. Make me come."

"Fuuuuccckk." Nate pulled my hair tighter and slammed inside me, his thrusts almost violent. "You look incredible. So freaking hot when you rub that pussy."

"Nate!"

The world turned upside down. Still inside me, Nate rolled to his back. He knew how I loved control, the power of being on top. Pushing my boobs out for his pleasure, I pinched my nipples, then ran my hands through my hair, and I ground down. Nate rubbed my clit and pushed up into me, and I rode him hard. Every muscle in my body was liquid and tense simultaneously. Nate pinched, then pressed that perfect little button and groaned, "Come for me, baby. Let that sweet cunt come all over my cock."

That was it. That filthy mouth and those devilish fingers did it again. "Nate!" I screamed as quietly as I could. Nate bucked wildly beneath me.

"Coming," is all he could manage. I ground down once more, pinched my nipple, and exploded. Squirting all over Nate, I soaked his abdomen and legs and ruined the new sheets I'd only just put on the bed.

"Holy shit, Gidge!" I felt his hot streams filling me. My whole body trembled above him as we rode out the wave.

◆

They say fortune favors the bold, and in the case of my family, *they* were spot on.

After our surprise wedding in Canada, my new husband and I had another decision to make, one that was harder than my instant acceptance of Nate's proposal. One we'd avoided for weeks.

It was time to go home. But where was *home?*

New York or Byron Bay?

As the little girl in the taco commercials used to say, *why not both?* Or, as Nate so Nate-ly put it… "Let's follow the sun, babe."

Excluding the last few months of my pregnancy, Nate and I had spent the entirety of our marriage doing just that, avoiding the winters while chasing the sun, sand, surf and seemingly endless orgasms and avoiding the winters. It was something made possible by a decision by Finn and Scarlett. They'd had enough of the States and big-city life and came home.

Scarlett took a shine to farm life while farm-sitting and, in its absence, her love and yearning for it continued to grow. She and Finn established their own architectural firm, specializing in redesigning and restoring old farm homes, and popped out baby Shelby almost two months ago.

Nate ran the family farm with his dad. We scaled back the sheep and expanded the organic macadamia and chamomile crops, doubling our exports. My man had become quite a successful businessman. Each summer, once the harvests were done and the two families were getting sick of the sight of each other, Finn would step in to take care of the farm, and we would take off to NYC. Jocelyn had moved into her dream home in Tarrytown but kept the house in the city, which we lived in when in town.

As for me, I wasn't doing too bad myself. Nate and his *purpose*, the dance hall he leased for me, turned out to be perfect. From there, I ran Miss Evie's, my very own and best-in-town dance studio, and a sister studio to the one where I remained a silent partner, VAAD.

Oh, and I published my first book too. My collection of stories, the very same one Nate had gifted to me, went on to become a bestseller.

It may not be possible when the kids were older, but for half the year, our children would now grow up side by side like we had. The only difference was that I lived on the Myers side of the fence, and there was a new Austen woman running the show on the other.

After years of pain and loss, we had been gifted an incredible amount of love and happiness. If there was one downside to our nomadic wandering, it was the goodbyes… and the jetlag. Be it a whispered New York, 'Au revoir,' with Jocelyn; a danced, drunk, and hugged out, 'Catch ya later,' with Teddy; or with a teary, hugfest farewell at the airport with the Aussie Austen's in Sydney… each time hurt. But they were also a celebration and exciting time too because we always knew that whatever side of the world we were on, we were at home when we were together.

Life was good…great…extraordinary.

Having said that, I tended to lean toward crotchety, some may dare to say grumpy—very few to my face—but I was okay with me for the first time in my life. I had a family that I would do anything for, a career I could never have dreamed of, and I had Nate, my best friend, lover, chief knocker-upper, and still the only person to call me Aoife.

BEFORE YOU GO!
For all you Teddy fans out there, be on the lookout for book three—the tale of Teddy and Asher- early in 2024.

And stay tuned for an extra special announcement… Did someone say book four????

Acknowledgments

Thank you for reading my second novel! I hope you enjoyed reading Evie and Nate's story as much as I loved writing it.

The publishing journey for Secrets was so different from Rules. For starters, it didn't feel like I was trying to rip my brain out through my nose. I was more relaxed-slightly-the process was mostly fun, and I felt more confident in my writing. For that to happen, there were many amazing people involved.

I am starting with my Markie, my girls, Molly, and Emma, and paw babies Charlie and Penny. I love you so much. You make me so happy, and I'm so proud of you all. Thank you for putting up with me.

To my sisters and my in-laws, thank you for all your support. Love you guys.

To my editor, Jen Lockwood. Your patience and understanding towards the challenges I face with my dyslexia is so, so appreciated. I know you have a big job, but you always come through.

Thank you to Stacey at Champagne Book Design for the beautiful formatting. The team at Wordsmith PR, especially Autumn and Roxie, you're amazing. Thank you. And Haya, from Haya in Designs for another beautiful cover.

To Alissa and Amanda, my beta readers. Thank you for wading through the mud with me. I can't express how much your help and happy squeals mean to me.

Thank you the clever and inspiring bookstagrammers who have

helped me along the way, especially @thesmuttybookworm, @getbookedwith_ae, @romcombookreader @kiwinikkilovesreading @rowe.reads and @reading_romanceee.

My beautiful circle of friends, Annette, Tori, Carolyn, Kelly. I love you guys and hope you know how much you mean to me.

To my OL and fanfic family, especially Renee M, I said this last time, but it remains the same. I would not have been able to do this without you. Thank you for the laughs, the tears, the fangirling, and the unbelievable support.

To the incredible Author and my dear friend, Maisie Myers. Thank you again for holding my hand. You still inspire me daily, as a writer and a person.

To Ryia, Jen, Lissa, Britty, AE, Dani, Ellie, Melody, Anna Rae, Avie, Jacki, Hailey, and Robyn. You guys are my rocks. Love you bb's. Thank you from the bottom of my heart for your friendship, and support, your crazy, filthy minds, and potty mouths.

Finally, Brittiany, Shan, Era, Jen, Anne Elizabeth, Alissa, and Emily. You have given me so much. This last year has been one of the most challenging on a personal level and you've stuck by me. Thank you for it all. I love you.

As with book one, my final words go to anyone living with mental health issues, including me. You are so much more than your anxiety, your ED, your depression, your OCD, PTSD, ADHD, and Bipolar.

You can accomplish so much. Do not believe the prick that stalks your thoughts. You are not a burden. You are someone's light. You are safe. You are whole. You are loved. You are enough.

XO,
Bindi.K.

About the Author

#1-selling, funniest, and sexiest author in her house… possibly her whole street.

Bindi Kennedy is an up-and-coming romance author from Melbourne, Australia. A devoted wife to her husband of 20 years, she is mum to two eternally embarrassed daughters and, most importantly, two fur babies. In her spare time, you can find Bindi writing and reading, keeping fit, or focusing on her unhealthy obsession with Scottish Highlanders in kilts… and Hockey romance. Fun, flirty and spicy romcoms are her jam- as is avoiding eye contact with family members after reading said spice. Adding a twist of angst and a pinch of mental health and disability representation and awareness to all her work is something Bindi takes pride in.

Her debut novel, Rules in Love, was released in May 2023 and is part of the West Village series. Book three coming soon.

Contacts.
Stay up to date with Bindi's work.
Instagram @bindikennedyauthor
TikTok @bindikauthor
Facebook @bindikauthor

www.ingramcontent.com/pod-product-compliance
Lightning Source LLC
Chambersburg PA
CBHW050115120726
47904CB00004B/1361